The Preacher of Cedar Mountain

A Tale of the Open Country

Ernest Thompson Seton

Alpha Editions

This edition published in 2024

ISBN 9789361474323

Design and Setting By

Alpha Editions
www.alphaedis.com

Email - info@alphaedis.com

Contents

"'You must choose between us. Is it Belle or Blazing Star?'"

PREFACE

Most of the characters in this tale are from life, and some of the main events are historical, although the actual scenes and names are not given. Many men now living will remember Fighting Bill Kenna and the Horse Preacher, as well as the Fort Ryan races. These horse races are especially well known and have been described in print many times. I did not witness any of them myself, but listened on numerous occasions when they were described to me by eye-witnesses. My first knowledge of the secret try-out in Yellowbank Canyon was given to me years ago by Homer Davenport, the cartoonist, with permission to use the same.

But all of these more or less historic events are secondary to the intent of illustrating the growth of a character, whose many rare gifts were mere destructive force until curbed and harmonized into the big, strong machine that did such noble work in the West during my early days on the Plains.

ERNEST THOMPSON SETON.

BOOK ONE

THE CHILD OF THE STABLE YARD

CHAPTER I

THE HOME LAND OF LITTLE JIM HARTIGAN

A burnt, bare, seared, and wounded spot in the great pine forest of Ontario, some sixty miles northeast of Toronto, was the little town of Links. It lay among the pine ridges, the rich, level bottomlands, and the newborn townships, in a region of blue lakes and black loam that was destined to be a thriving community of prosperous farmer folk. The broad, unrotted stumps of the trees that not so long ago possessed the ground, were thickly interstrewn among the houses of the town and in the little fields that began to show as angular invasions of the woodland, one by every settler's house of logs. Through the woods and through the town there ran the deep, brown flood of the little bog-born river, and streaking its current for the whole length were the huge, fragrant logs of the new-cut pines, in disorderly array, awaiting their turn to be shot through the mill and come forth as piles of lumber, broad waste slabs, and heaps of useless sawdust.

Two or three low sawmills were there, each booming, humming, busied all the day. And the purr of their saws, or the scream when they struck some harder place in the wood, was the dominant note, the day-long labour-song of Links. At first it seemed that these great, wasteful fragrant, tree-destroying mills were the only industries of the town; and one had to look again before discovering, on the other side of the river, the grist mill, sullenly claiming its share of the water power, and proclaiming itself just as good as any other mill; while radiating from the bridge below the dam, were the streets—or, rather, the rough roads, straight and ugly—along which wooden houses, half hidden by tall sunflowers, had been built for a quarter of a mile, very close together near the bridge, but ever with less of house and sunflower and more of pumpkin field as one travelled on, till the last house with the last pumpkin field was shut in by straggling, much-culled woods, alternating with swamps that were densely grown with odorous cedar and fragrant tamarac, as yet untouched by the inexorable axe of the changing day.

Seen from the road, the country was forest, with about one quarter of the land exposed by clearings, in each of which were a log cabin and the barn of a settler. Seen from the top of the tallest building, the sky line was, as yet, an array of plumy pines, which still stood thick among the hardwood trees and, head and shoulders, overtopped them.

Links was a town of smells. There were two hotels with their complex, unclean livery barns and yards, beside, behind, and around them; and on every side and in every yard there were pigs—and still more pigs—an evidence of thrift rather than of sanitation; but over all, and in the end overpowering all, were the sweet, pervading odour of the new-sawn boards and the exquisite aroma of the different fragrant gums—of pine, cedar, or fir—which memory will acknowledge as the incense to conjure up again in vivid actuality these early days of Links.

It was on a sunny afternoon late in the summer of 1866 that a little knot of loafers and hangers-on of the hotels gathered in the yard of the town's larger hostelry and watched Bill Kenna show an admiring world how to ride a wild, unbroken three-year-old horse. It was not a very bad horse, and Bill was too big to be a wonderful rider, but still he stayed on, and presently subdued the wild thing to his will, amid the brief, rough, but complimentary remarks of the crowd.

One of the most rapt of the onlookers was a rosy-cheeked, tow-topped boy of attractive appearance—Jim; who though only eight years old, was blessed with all the assurance of twenty-eight. Noisy and forward, offering suggestions and opinions at the pitch of his piping voice, he shrieked orders to every one with all the authority of a young lord; as in some sense he was, for he was the only son of "Widdy" Hartigan, the young and comely owner and manager of the hotel.

"There, now, Jim. Could ye do that?" said one of the bystanders, banteringly.

"I couldn't ride that 'un, cause me legs ain't long enough to lap round; but I bet I could ride *that* 'un," and he pointed to a little foal gazing at them from beside its dam.

"All right, let him try," said several.

"And have his brains kicked out," said a more temperate onlooker.

"Divil a bit," said big Bill, the owner of the colt. "That's the kindest little thing that ever was born to look through a collar," and he demonstrated the fact by going over and putting his arms around the young thing's gentle neck.

"Here, you; give me a leg up," shouted Jimmy, and in a moment he was astride the four-month colt.

In a yard, under normal kindly conditions, a colt may be the gentlest thing in the world, but when suddenly there descends upon its back a wild animal that clings with exasperating pertinacity, there is usually but one result. The colt plunged wildly, shaking its head and instinctively putting in practice all the ancient tricks that its kind had learned in fighting the leopard or the wolf of the ancestral wild horse ranges.

But Jim stuck on. His legs, it was true, were not long enough to "lap round," but he was a born horseman. He had practised since he was able to talk, never losing a chance to bestride a steed; and now he was in his glory. Round and round went the colt, amid the laughter of the onlookers. They apprehended no danger, for they knew that the youngster could ride like a jackanapes; in any case the yard was soft with litter, and no harm could happen to the boy.

The colt, nearly ridden down, had reached the limit of its young strength, and had just about surrendered. Jim was waving one hand in triumph, while the other clutched the fuzzy mane before him, when a new and striking element was added to the scene. A rustle of petticoats, a white cap over yellow hair, a clear, commanding voice that sent the men all back abashed, and the Widdy Hartigan burst through the little circle.

"What do ye mean letting me bhoy do that fool thing to risk his life and limb? Have ye no sense, the lot of ye? Jimmy, ye brat, do ye want to break yer mother's heart? Come off of that colt this holy minute; or I'll—"

Up till now, Jim had been absolute dominator of the scene; but the powerful personality of his mother shattered his control, dethroned him.

As she swept angrily toward him, his nerve for the time was shaken. The colt gave a last wild plunge; Jim lost his balance and his hold, and went down on the soft litter.

As it sprang free from its tormenter, the frightened beast gave vent to its best instinctive measure of defense and launched out a final kick. The youngster gave a howl of pain, and in a minute more he was sobbing in his mother's arms, while one of the crowd was speeding for the doctor.

Yes, the arm was broken above the elbow, a simple fracture, a matter of a month to mend. The bone was quickly set, and when his wailing had in a measure subsided, Jim showed his horseman soul by jerking out: "I could have rode him, Mother. I'll ride him yet. I'll tame him to a finish, the little divil."

CHAPTER II

THE STRAINS THAT WERE MINGLED IN JIM

Clearly one cannot begin the history of the French Revolution with the outbreak of 1789. Most phenomena, physical and spiritual, have their roots, their seeds, their causes—whatever you will—far behind them in point of time. To understand them one must go back to the beginning or they will present no logic or *raison d'être*. The phenomenon of James Hartigan, the Preacher of Cedar Mountain, which is both a physical and a spiritual fact, is nowise different, and the reader must go back with me to some very significant events which explain him and account for him.

Little Jim's father was James O'Hartigan in Donegal. The change in the patronymic was made, not by himself, but by the Government Emigration Agent at Cork. When James, Sr. came forward to be listed for passage, the official said: "Oh, hang your O's. I have more of them now than the column will hold. I'll have to put you in the H's, where there's lots of room." And so the weight of all the Empire was behind the change.

James Hartigan, Sr. was a typical Irish "bhoy," which is high praise. He was broad and hearty, with a broad and hearty grin. He was loved and lovable, blessed with a comely countenance and the joy of a humorous outlook on life and its vicissitudes. You could not down Jimmy so low that he might not see some bright and funny aspect in the situation. This was not only a happy temperamental trait, but it also had a distinct advantage, for in the moments of deepest self-invited degradation he never forgot that somewhere ahead, his trail would surely lead to the uplands once again.

He was what the doctors called "normal human," muscled far above the average, heart action strong and regular. This combination often produces two well-marked types—a high-class athlete and a low-class drunkard. Often these are united in the same individual; or, rather, the individual appears in the first rôle, until the second comes to overmaster it. Such was Jimmy Hartigan, Sr., whose relation to the Preacher may be labelled Cause Number One.

Those who knew her people said that the forbears of Katherine Muckevay had seen better days; that the ancient royal blood of Ireland ran in her veins; that the family name was really Mach-ne-veagh; and that, if every one had his own, Kitty would be wearing a diamond tiara in the highest walks of London importance. In ancient days, the Kings of Ulster used to steal a bride at times from the fair-haired folk across the sea; maybe that was where Kitty got her shining hair of dusty yellow-red, as well as the calm control in times of stress, something the psychologists call coördination, which is not a Celtic characteristic.

Of book learning Kitty had almost none, but she had native gifts. She had wits, good looks, and a wealth of splendid hair, as well as a certain presence which was her perpetual hedge of safety, even when she took the perilous place of maid in the crude hotel with its bar-room annex, whither the hand of Fate had brought her, an Irish immigrant, to find a new life in the little town of Links. Kitty was Cause Number Two.

Jimmy did not chance to cross on the same ship. But the time had come; and by chance, which is not chance at all, he drifted into the same corner of Canada, and had not half a day to wait before he was snapped up by a local farmer seeking for just such a build of man to swing the axe and scythe upon his farm.

Farm life is dreary enough, at least it was in those days. It was hard work from dawn to dusk, and even then the feeble, friendly glimmer of a caged candle was invoked to win an extra hour or two of labour from the idleness of gloom—hours for the most part devoted to the chores. The custom of the day gave all the hired ones freedom Saturday night and all day Sunday. Wages were high, and with one broad epidemic impulse all these thriving hirelings walked, drove, or rode on Saturday night to the little town of Links. Man is above all a social animal; only the diseased ones seek solitude. Where, then, could they meet their kind?

The instinct which has led to the building of a million clubs, could find no local focus but the bar-room. John Downey's "hotel" was the social centre of the great majority of the men who lived and moved around the town of Links. Not the drink itself, but the desire of men to meet with men, to talk and swap the news or bandy mannish jokes, was the attracting force. But the drink was there on tap and all the ill-adjusted machinery of our modern ways operated to lead men on, to make abstainers drink, to make the moderate, drunken.

If the life in Downey's stable, house, and bar were expanded in many chapters, the reader would find a pile of worthless rubbish, mixed with filth, but also here and there a thread of gold, a rod of the finest steel, and even precious jewels. But this is not a history of the public house. Downey's enters our list merely as Cause Number Three.

Those who study psychological causation say that one must find four causes, accounting for place, matter, force, and time. The three already given are well known, and I can only guess at the fourth, that referring to the time. If we suppose that a sea pirate of a thousand years ago, was permitted to return to earth, to prove that he had learned the lessons of gentleness so foreign to his rapacious modes of thought, and that, after a thousand years of cogitation in some disembodied state, he was allowed to reassume the flesh, to fight a different fight, to raise himself by battle with himself, we shall, perhaps, account for some of the strangely divergent qualities that met in the subject of this story. At least, let us name the ancient Sea-king as Cause Number Four.... And conjunction of these four was affected in the '50s at Downey's Hotel, when Jim Hartigan met Kitty Muckevay.

These were the strains that were mingled in little Jim; and during his early life from the first glimpse we catch of him upon the back of the unbroken colt, he was torn by the struggle between the wild, romantic, erratic, visionary, fighting Celt, with moods of love and hate, and the calmer, steady, tireless, lowland Scottish Saxon from the North who, far less gifted, had far more power and in the end had mastery; and having won control, built of his mingled heritages a rare, strong soul, so steadfast that he was a tower of strength for all who needed help.

CHAPTER III

The immediate and physical environment of Links was the far backwoods of Canada, but the spirit and thought of it were Irish. The inhabitants were nearly all of Irish origin, most of them of Irish birth, and the fates had ruled it so that they came from all parts of the green isle. The North was as well represented as the South, and the feuds of the old land were most unprofitably transferred to the new.

Two days on the calendar had long been set aside by custom for the celebration of these unhappy feuds; the seventeenth of March, which is St. Patrick's Day, and the twelfth of July, on which, two hundred years before, King William had crossed the river to win the famous Battle of the Boyne. Under the evil spell of these two memorable occasions, neighbours who were good and helpful friends, felt in honour bound to lay all their kindness aside twice every year, and hate and harass each other with a senseless vindictiveness.

At the time with which this chronicle has to do, Orange Day had dawned on Links. No rising treble issued from the sawmills; the air was almost free of their dust, and there were hints of holiday on all the town. Farmers' wagons were arriving early, and ribbons of orange and blue were fastened in the horses' headgear. From the backyard of Downey's Hotel the thumping of a big drum was heard, and the great square piles of yellow lumber near Ford's Mill gave back the shrilling of fifes that were tuning up for the event. As the sun rose high, the Orangemen of the Lodge appeared, each wearing regalia—cuffs and a collarette of sky-blue with a fringe of blazing orange, or else of gold, inscribed with letters and symbols.

The gathering place was in the street before the Lodge Hall, and their number was steadily increased by men from the surrounding farms. The brethren of the opposite faith, the Catholics—more often called "Dogans" or "Papists"—were wisely inconspicuous. Had it been their day, their friends, assembled from far places, would have given them numbers enough for safety and confidence; but now the boys in green were, for the most part, staying at home and seeking to avoid offence.

In the stable yard of Downey's Hotel, where Jim Hartigan—the father of our hero—and several others of his Church were disconsolately looking forward to a dreary and humiliating day, the cheery uproar of the Orangemen in the bar-room could plainly be heard. James himself was surprised at his restraint in not being there too, for he was a typical Irish "bhoy" from the west coast, with a religion of Donegal colour and intensity. Big, hearty, uproarious in liquor, and full of fun at all times, he was universally beloved. Nothing could or did depress Jim for long; his spirits had a generous rebound. A boisterous, blue-eyed boy of heroic stature, he was the joy of Downey's, brim-full of the fun of life and the hero of unnumbered drinking bouts in the not so very distant past. But— two months before—Jim had startled Links and horrified his priest by marrying Kitty Muckevay of the gold-red hair. Kitty had a rare measure of good sense but was a Protestant of Ulster inflexibility. She had taken Jim in hand to reform him, and for sixty days he had not touched a drop! Moreover he had promised Kitty to keep out of mischief on this day of days. All that morning he had worked among the horses in Downey's livery stable where he was head man. It was a public holiday, and he had been trying desperately to supply a safety valve for his bursting energy. His excitible Irish soul was stirred by the murmur of the little town, now preparing for the great parade, as it had been stirred twice every year since he could remember, but now to the farthest depths.

He had swallowed successfully one or two small affronts from the passing Orangemen, because he was promise-bound and sober; but when one of the enemy, a boon companion on any other day, sought him out in the stable yard and, with the light of devilment in his eyes, walked up holding out a flask of whiskey and said: "Hartigan! Ye white-livered, weak-need papist, ye're not man enough to take a pull at that, an' tip the hat aff of me head!" Hartigan's resolutions melted like wax before the flare of his anger. Seizing the flask, he took a mouthful of the liquor and spurted it into the face of the tormentor. The inevitable fight did not amount to much as far as the casualties went, but what loomed large was the fact that Hartigan had filled his mouth with the old liquid insanity. Immediately he was surrounded by those who were riotously possessed of it, and in fifteen minutes Jimmy Hartigan was launched on the first drunken carouse he had known since he was a married man in public disgrace with the priest for mating with a Protestant.

The day wore on and the pace grew faster. There were fun and fighting galore, and Jimmy was in his element again. Occasional qualms there were, no doubt, when he had a moment to remember how Kitty would feel about it all. But this was his day of joy—mad, rollicking, bacchanalian joy—and all the pent-up, unhallowed hilarity of the bygone months found vent in deeds more wild than had ever been his before.

The Orangemen's procession started from their lodge, with three drums and one fife trilling a wheezing, rattling manglement of "Croppies Lie Down," whose only justification lay in the fact that it was maintaining a tradition of the time; and Jimmy Hartigan, besieged in the livery yard with half a dozen of his coreligionists, felt called upon to avenge the honour of the South of Ireland at these soul-polluting sounds. Someone suggested a charge into the ranks of the approaching procession, with its sizzling band and its abhorrent orange-and-blue flags, following in the wake of Bill Kenna, whose proud post was at the head of the procession, carrying a cushion on which was an open Bible. The fact that Bill was a notorious ruffian—incapable of reading, and reeling drunk—had no bearing on his being chosen as Bible carrier. The Bible fell in the dust many times and was accidentally trampled on by its bearer, which was unfortunate but not important. Bill bore the emblem of his organization and, being a good man with his fists, he was amply qualified for his job.

But the sight of all this truculence and the ostentatious way in which the little green flags were trampled on and insulted, was too much for Jimmy and his inspired companions.

"Let's charge the hull rabble," was the suggestion.

"What! Six charge one hundred and twenty!"

"Why not?"

The spirit of Gideon's army was on them, and Jimmy shouted: "Sure, bhoys, let's hitch to that and give it to 'em. Lord knows their black souls need it." He pointed to a great barrel half full of whitewash standing in a wagon ready for delivery next day at the little steamer dock, where a coat of whitewash on the wharf and shed was the usual expedient to take the place of lights for night work.

Thus it came about. The biggest, strongest team in the stable was harnessed in a minute. The men were not too drunk to pick the best in horses and harness. The barrel was filled brim-full with water and well stirred up, so that ammunition would be abundant. Jimmy was to be the driver; the other five were each armed with a bucket, except one who found a force pump through which the whitewash could be squirted with delightful precision. They were to stand around the barrel and dash its contents right and left as Jimmy drove the horses at full speed down the middle of the procession. Glorious in every part was the plan; wild enthusiasm carried all the six away and set the horses on their mettle.

Armed with a long, black snake whip, Jimmy mounted the wagon seat. The gate was flung wide, and, with a whoop, away went that bumping chariot of splashing white. Bill Kenna had just dropped his Bible for the eleventh time and, condemning to eternal perdition all those ill-begotten miscreants who dared to push him on or help his search, he held the ranks behind him for a moment halted. At this instant with a wild shout, in charged Jim Hartigan, with his excited crew. There was not a man in the procession who had not loved Hartigan the day before, and who did not love him the day after; but there was none that did not hate him with a bitter hate on this twelfth day of July, as he charged and split the procession wide open.

The five helpers dashed their bewildering, blinding slush fast and far, on every face and badge that they could hit; and the pump stream hit Kenna square in the face as he yelled in wrath. The paraders were not armed for such a fight. Men that could face bullets, knives, and death, were dismayed, defeated, and routed by these baffling bucketfuls and the amazing precision of the squirting pump.

Strong hands clutched at the bridle reins, but the team was plunging and going fast. The driver was just drunk enough for recklessness; he kept the horses jumping all down that Orangemen's parade. Oh, what a rout it made! And the final bucketfuls were hurled in through the window of the Orange Lodge, just where they were needed most, as Jimmy and his five made their escape.

The bottle now went round once more. Shrieking with laughter at their sweeping, bloodless victory, the six Papists saw the procession rearrayed. Kenna had recovered and wiped his face with one coat sleeve, his Bible with the other. The six dispensers of purity could not resist it; they must charge again. Hartigan wheeled the horses to make the turn at a run. But with every circumstance against him—speed and reckless driving, a rough and narrow roadway beset with stumps—the wagon lurched, crashed, upset, and the six went sprawling in the ditch. The horses ran away to be afterward rounded up at a farm stable three miles off, with the fragments of a wagon trailing behind them.

The anger of the Orangemen left them as they gathered around. Five of the raiders were badly shaken and sobered, one lay still on the stones, a deep and bloody dent in his head. The newly arrived, newly fledged doctor came, and when after a brief examination, he said: "He's dead—all right," there was a low, hollow sound of sympathy among the men who ten minutes before would gladly have killed him. One voice spoke for all the rest.

"Poor lad! He was a broth of a bhoy! Poor little Widdy Hartigan."

CHAPTER IV

THE ATMOSPHERE OF HIS EARLY DAYS

There were many surprises and sharp contrasting colour spots on the map of the "Widdy's" trail for the next nine years. With herself and the expected child to make a home for after that mad Orange Day, she had sought employment and had been welcomed back to the hotel where she had ever been a favourite.

The little room above the kitchen which projected over the yard was her only resting place. The cheapest, simplest of wooden furniture was all it held. On a tiny stand, made of a packing case, was her Bible and, hanging over it a daguerreotype of her husband—his frank, straight gaze and happy face looking forth with startling reality. Outside and very near, for the building was low, the one window looked upon the yard of the hotel, with its horses, its loafers, its hens and its swine; while just above the shutter's edge a row of swallows had their nests, where the brooding owners twittered in the early summer morning, as she rose with the sunrise and went about her work. A relief at first, the duties Kitty had undertaken grew heavier with the months, till at last the kindly heart of the owner's wife was touched, and a new *régime* of rest ensued.

Eight months after that fatal Orange Day, James Hartigan, Jr., was born in the little room over the yard; and baby wailings were added to the swallows' chirps and the squeals of pigs. Mother Downey, rough and rawboned to the eye, now appeared in guardian-angel guise, and the widow's heart was deeply touched by the big, free kindness that events had discovered in the folk about her. Kitty was of vigorous stock; in a week she was up, in a fortnight seemed well; and in a month was at her work, with little Jim— named for his father and grandfather—in hearing, if not in sight.

Then, quite suddenly, Mrs. Downey died. A big, gaunt woman, she had the look of strength; but the strength was not there; and a simple malady that most would have shaken off was more than she could fight. With her husband and Kitty by the bed, she passed away; and her last words were: "Be good—to—Kitty, John—and—Little Jim."

It was an easy promise for John Downey to give and a pleasant undertaking to live up to. Before his wife had been dead three months, John Downey had assured Kitty that she might become Mrs. Downey Number Two as early as she pleased. It was not by any means the first offer since her loss.

Indeed, there were few free men in Links who would not have been glad to marry the winsome, young, energetic widow.

But all her heart was on her boy, and until she could see that it was best for him she would take no second partner. Downey's proposal was a puzzle to her; he was a big, strong, dull, moderately successful, unattractive man. But he had a good business, no bad habits, and was deeply in love with her.

It was the thought of little Jim that settled it. Downey showed genuine affection for the child. To give him a father, to have him well educated—these were large things to Kitty and she consented. As soon as the late Mrs. Downey should have been laid away for six months, the wedding was to be and Kitty moved to other lodgings meanwhile. But Fate's plans again disagreed with Kitty's. A few weeks after her consent, the town was startled by the news that John Downey was dead. A cold—neglect (for he did not know how to be sick), and pneumonia. The folk of the town had much to talk of for a day, and the dead man's will gave still higher speed to their tongues, for he had left the hotel and all its appurtenances to Widdy Hartigan, as a life interest; after her death it was to go to a kinsman. Thus, out of John Downey's grave there grew a tree with much-needed and wholesome fruit.

Now Kitty was in a quandary. She was an abstainer from choice rather than principle; but she was deeply imbued with the uncompromising religion of her Ulster forbears. How could she run a bar-room? How could she, who had seen the horror of the drink madness, have a hand in setting it in the way of weak ones? Worst dilemma of all, how could she whose religious spirit was dreaming of a great preacher son, bring him up in these surroundings—yet how refuse, since this was his only chance?

She consulted with her pastor; and this was the conclusion reached: She would accept the providential bequest. Downey's would be an inn, a hotel; not a bar-room. The place where the liquor was sold should be absolutely apart, walled off; and these new rules were framed: No minor should ever be served there, no habitual drunkard, no man who already had had enough. Such rules in Canada during the middle of last century were considered revolutionary; but they were established then, and, so far as Kitty could apply them, they were enforced; and they worked a steady betterment.

With this new responsibility upon her, the inborn powers of Kitty Hartigan bloomed forth. Hers was the gift of sovereignty, and here was the chance to rule. The changes came but slowly at first, till she knew the ground. A broken pane, a weak spot in the roof, a leaky horse trough, and a score of little things were repaired. Account books of a crude type were established, and soon a big leak in the treasury was discovered and stopped; and many little leaks and unpaid bills were unearthed. An aspiring barkeeper of puzzling methods was, much to his indignation, hedged about by daily accountings and, last of all, a thick and double door of demarcation was made between the bar-room and the house. One was to be a man's department, a purely business matter; the other a place apart—another world of woollen carpets and feminine gentleness, a place removed ten miles in thought. The dwellers in these two were not supposed to mix or even to meet, except in the dining room three times a day; and even there some hint of social lines was apparent.

In former times the hotel had been a mere annex of the bar-room. Now the case was reversed; the bar-room became the annex. The hotel grew as Kitty's power developed. Good food temptingly served brought many to the house who had no interest in the annex. Her pies made the table famous and were among the many things that rendered it easy to displace the brown marbled oilcloth with white linen, and the one roller towel for all, with individual service in each room.

In this hotel world the alert young widow made her court and ruled as a queen. Here little Jim slept away his babyhood and grew to consciousness with sounds of coming horses, going wheels; of chicken calls and twittering swallows in their nests; shouts of men and the clatter of tin pails; the distant song of saw mills and their noontide whistles; smells of stables mixed with the sweet breathings of oxen and the pungent odour of pine gum from new-sawn boards.

And ever as he grew, he loved the more to steal from his mother's view and be with the stable hands—loving the stable, loving the horses, loving the men that were horsemen in any sort, and indulged and spoiled by them in turn. The widow was a winner of hearts whom not even the wife of Tom Ford, the rich millman and mayor of the town, could rival in social power, so Jim, as the heir apparent, grew up in an atmosphere of importance that did him little good.

CHAPTER V

LITTLE JIM'S TUTORS

"Whiskey" Mason had been for more than three years with Downey. He was an adroit barkeep. He knew every favourite "mix" and how to use the thickest glasses that would ever put the house a little more ahead of the game. But the Widow soon convinced herself that certain rumours already hinted at were well-founded, and that Mason's salary did not justify his Sunday magnificence. Mason had long been quite convinced that he was the backbone of the business and absolutely indispensable. Therefore he was not a little surprised when the queen, in the beginning of her reign, invited him to resign his portfolio and seek his fortune elsewhere, the farther off the better to her liking.

Mason went not far, but scornfully. He took lodgings in the town to wait and see the inevitable wreck that the widow was inviting for her house. For two months he waited, but was disappointed. The hotel continued in business; the widow had not come to beg for his return; his credit was being injured with excessive use; and as he had found no other work, he took the stage to the larger town of Petersburg some thirty miles away. Here he sought a job, in his special craft of "joy mixer" but, failing to find that, he turned his attention to another near akin. In those days the liquor laws of Canada provided a heavy fine for any breach of regulation; and of this the informant got half. Here was an easy and honourable calling for which he was well equipped.

It has ever been law in the man's code that he must protect the place he drinks in, so that the keepers of these evil joints are often careless over little lapses. Thus Whiskey Mason easily found a victim, and within three days was rich once more with half of the thousand-dollar fine that the magistrate imposed.

He felt that all the country suddenly was his lawful prey. He could not long remain in Petersburg, where he was soon well known and shunned. He had some trouble, too, for threats against his life began to reach him more and more. It was the magistrate himself who suggested contemptuously, "You had better take out a pistol license, my friend; and you would be safer in a town where no one knows you."

In those early days before his dismissal by Kitty, Mason's life and Little Jim's had no point of meeting. Six years later, when he returned to Links,

Jimmy was discovering great possibilities in the stables of the Inn. Mason often called at the bar-room where he had once been the ruling figure, and was received with cold aloofness. But he was used to that; his calling had hardened him to any amount of human scorn. He still found a kindred spirit, however, in the stable man, Watsie Hall, and these two would often "visit" in the feed room, which was a favourite playground of the bright-haired boy.

It is always funny if one can inspire terror without actual danger to the victim. Mason and Hall taught Jim to throw stones at sparrows, cats, and dogs, when his mother was not looking. He hardly ever hit them, and his hardest throw was harmless, but he learned to love the sport. A stray dog that persisted in stealing scraps which were by right the heritage of hens, was listed as an enemy, and together they showed Jim how to tie a tin can on the dog's tail in a manner that produced amazingly funny results and the final disappearance of the cur in a chorus of frantic yelps.

These laboratory experiments on animals developed under the able tutors, and Jim was instructed in the cat's war dance, an ingenious mode of inspiring puss to outdo her own matchless activity in a series of wild gyrations, by glueing to each foot a shoe of walnut shell, half filled with melted cobbler's wax to hold it on. Flattered by their attentions at first, the cat purred blandly as they fitted on the shoes. Jim's eyes were big and bright with tensest interest. The cat was turned loose in the grain room. To hear her own soft pads drop on the floor, each with a sharp, hard crack, must have been a curious, jarring experience. To find at every step a novel sense of being locked in, must have conjured up deep apprehensions in her soul. And when she fled, and sought to scale the partition, to find that her claws were gone—that she was now a thing with hoofs—must have been a horrid nightmare. Fear entered into her soul, took full control; then followed the wild erratic circling around the room, with various ridiculous attempts to run up the walls, which were so insanely silly that little James shrieked for joy, and joining in with the broom, urged the cat to still more amazing evidences of muscular activity not excelled by any other creature.

It was rare sport with just a sense of sin to give it tang, for he had been forbidden to torment the cat, and Jim saw nothing but the funny side; he was only seven.

It was a week later that they tried the walnut trick again, and Jim was eager to see the "circus." But the cat remembered; she drove her teeth deep into Hall's hand and fought with a feline fury that is always terrifying. Jim was gazing in big-eyed silence, when Hall, enraged, thrust the cat into the leg of a boot and growled, "I'll fix yer biting," and held her teeth to the grindstone till the body in the boot was limp.

At the first screech of the cat, Jim's whole attitude had changed. Amusement and wild-eyed wonder had given way to a shocking realization of the wicked cruelty. He sprang at Hall and struck him with all the best vigour of his baby fists. "Let my kitty go, you!" and he kicked the hostler in the shins until he himself was driven away. He fled indoors to his mother, flung himself into her arms and sobbed in newly awakened horror. To his dying day he never forgot that cry of pain. He had been in the way of cruel training with these men, but the climax woke him up. It was said that he never after was cruel to any creature, but this is sure—that he never after cared to be with cats of any sort.

This was the end of Hall, so far as his life had bearing on that of James Hartigan Second; for Kitty dismissed him promptly as soon as she heard the story of his brutality.

Of all the specimens of fine, physical manhood who owned allegiance to Downey's Hotel, Fightin' Bill Kenna was the outstanding figure. He was not so big as Mulcahy, or such a wrestler as Dougherty, or as skilled a boxer as McGraw; he knew little of the singlestick and nothing of knife- or gun-play; and yet his combination of strength, endurance and bullet-headed pluck made him by general voice "the best man in Links."

Bill's temper was fiery; he loved a fight. He never was worsted, the nearest thing to it being a draw between himself and Terry Barr. After that Terry went to the States and became a professional pugilist of note. Bill's social record was not without blemish. He was known to have appropriated a rope, to the far end of which was attached another man's horse. He certainly had been in jail once and should have been there a dozen times, for worse crimes than fighting. And yet Bill was firmly established as Bible bearer in the annual Orangemen's parade and would have smashed the face of any man who tried to rob him of his holy office.

Kenna was supposed to be a farmer, but he loved neither crops nor land. The dream of his exuberant life was to be a horse breeder, for which profession he had neither the capital nor the brains. His social and convivial instincts ever haled him townward, and a well-worn chair in Downey's bar-room was by prescriptive right the town seat of William Kenna, Esq., of the Township of Opulenta. Bill had three other good qualities besides his mighty fists. He was true to his friends, he was kind to the poor and he had great respect for his "wurd as a mahn." If he gave his "wurd as a mahn" to do thus and so, he ever made a strenuous effort to keep it.

Bill was madly in love with Kitty Hartigan. She was not unmoved by the huge manliness of the warlike William, but she had too much sense to overlook his failings, and she held him off as she did a dozen more—her devoted lovers all—who hung around ever hoping for special favour. But though Kitty would not marry him, she smiled on Kenna indulgently and thus it was that this man of brawn had far too much to say in shaping the life of little Jim Hartigan. High wisdom or deep sagacity was scarcely to be named among Kenna's attributes, and yet instinctively he noted that the surest way to the widow's heart was through her boy. This explained the beginning of their friendship, but other things soon entered in. Kenna, with all his faults, was a respecter of women, and—they commonly go together—a clumsy, awkward, blundering lover of children. Little Jim was bright enough to interest any one; and, with the certain instinct of a child, he drifted toward the man whose heart was open to him. Many a day, as Kenna split some blocks of wood that were over big and knotty for the official axeman, Jim would come to watch and marvel at the mighty blows. His comments told of the imaginative power born in his Celtic blood:

"Bill, let's play you are the Red Dermid smiting the bullhide bearing Lachlin," he would shout, and at once the brightness of his mental picture and his familiarity with the nursery tales of Erin that were current even in the woods created a wonder-world about him. Then his Ulster mind would speak. He would laugh a little shamefaced chuckle at himself and say:

"It's only Big Bill Kenna splitting wood."

Bill was one of the few men who talked to Jim about his father; and, with singular delicacy, he ever avoided mentioning the nauseating fact that the father was a papist. No one who has not lived in the time and place of these feuds can understand the unspeakable abomination implied by that word; it was the barrier that kept his other friends from mention of the dead man's name; and yet, Bill spoke with kindly reverence of him as, "a broth of a bhoy, a good mahn, afraid of no wan, and as straight as a string."

Among the occasional visitors at the stable yard was young Tom Ford, whose father owned the mill and half the town. Like his father, Tom was a masterful person, hungry for power and ready to rule by force. On the occasion of his first visit he had quarrelled with Jim, and being older and stronger, had won their boyish fight. It was in the hour of his humiliation that Kenna had taken Jim on his knee and said:

"Now Jim, I'm the lepricaun that can tache you magic to lick that fellow aisy, if ye'll do what I tell you." And at the word "lepricaun," the Celt in Jim rose mightier than the fighting, bullet-headed Saxon. His eager word and look were enough.

"Now, listen, bhoy. I'll put the boxing gloves on you every day, an' I'll put up a sack of oats, an' we'll call it Tom Ford; an' ye must hit that sack wi' yer fist every day wan hundred times, twenty-five on the top side and siventy-five on the bottom side for the undercut is worth more than the uppercut anny day; an' when ye've done that, ye're making magic, and at the end of the moon ye'll be able to lick Tom Ford."

Jim began with all his ten-year-old vigour to make the necessary magic, and had received Bill's unqualified approval until one day he appeared chewing something given him by one of the men as a joke. Jim paused before Bill and spat out a brown fluid.

"Fwhat are ye doing?" said Bill; then to his disgust, he found that Jim, inspired probably by his own example, was chewing tobacco.

"Spit it out, ye little divil, an' never agin do that. If ye do that three times before ye're twenty-one, ye'll make a spell that will break you, an' ye'll never lick Tom Ford."

Thus, with no high motive, Kenna was in many ways, the guardian of the child. Coarse, brutish, and fierce among men, he was ever good to the boy and respectful to his mother; and he rounded out his teaching by the doctrine: "If ye give yer word as a mahn, ye must not let all hell prevent ye holding to it." And he whispered in a dreadful tone that sent a chill through the youngster's blood: "It'll bring the bone-rot on ye if ye fail; it always does."

It is unfortunate that we cannot number the town school principal as a large maker of Jim's mind. Jim went to school and the teacher did the best he could. He learned to read, to write and to figure, but books irked him and held no lure. His joy was in the stable yard and the barn where dwelt those men of muscle and of animal mind; where the boxing gloves were in nightly use, the horses in daily sight, and the world of sport in ring or on turf was the only world worth any man's devotion.

There were a dozen other persons who had influence in the shaping of the life and mind of Little Jim Hartigan; but there was one that overpowered, that far outweighed, that almost negatived the rest; that was his mother. She could scarcely read, and all the reading she ever tried to do was in her Bible. Filled with the vision of what she wished her boy to be—a minister of Christ—Kitty sent him to the public school, but the colour of his mind was given at home. She told him the stories of the Man of Galilee, and on Sundays, hand in hand, they went to the Presbyterian Church, to listen to tedious details that illustrated the practical impossibility of any one really winning out in the fight with sin.

She sang the nursery songs of the old land and told the tales of magic that made his eyes stare wide with loving, childish wonder. She told him what a brave, kind man his father had been, and ever came back to the world's great Messenger of Love. Not openly, but a thousand times—in a thousand deeply felt, deeply meant, unspoken ways—she made him know that the noblest calling man might ever claim was this, to be a herald of the Kingdom. Alone, on her knees, she would pray that her boy might be elected to that great estate and that she might live to see him going forth a messenger of the Prince of Peace.

Kitty was alive to the danger of the inherited taste for drink in her son. The stern, uncompromising Presbyterian minister of the town, in whose church the widow had a pew, was temperate, but not an abstainer; in fact, it was his custom to close the day with a short prayer and a tall glass of whiskey and water. While, with his advice, she had entirely buried her doctrinal scruples on the selling of drink to the moderate, her mother-heart was not so easily put to sleep. Her boy belonged to the house side of the hotel. He was not supposed to enter the saloon; and when, one day, she found an unscrupulous barkeeper actually amusing himself by giving the child a taste of the liquid fire, she acted with her usual promptitude and vigour. The man was given just enough time to get his hat and coat, and the boy was absolutely forbidden the left wing of the house. Later, in the little room where he was born, she told Jim sadly and gently what it would mean, what suffering the drinking habit had brought upon herself, and thus, for the first time, he learned that this had been the cause of his father's death. The boy was deeply moved and voluntarily offered to pledge himself never to touch a drop again so long as he lived. But his mother wisely said:

"No, Jim; don't say it that way. Leaning backward will not make you safer from a fall; only promise me you'll never touch it till you are eighteen; then I know you will be safe."

And he promised her that he never would; he gave his word—no more; for already the rough and vigorous teaching of Bill Kenna had gripped him in some sort. He felt that there was no more binding seal; that any more was more than man should give.

When Jim was twelve he was very tall and strong for his age, and almost too beautiful for a boy. His mother, of course, was idolatrous in her love. His ready tongue, his gift of reciting funny or heroic verse, and his happy moods had made him a general favourite, the king of the stable yard. Abetted, inspired and trained by Kenna, he figured in many a boyish fight, and usually won so that he was not a little pleased with himself in almost every way. Had he not carried out his promise of two years before and thrashed the mayor's son, who was a year older than himself, and thereby taught a lesson to that stuck-up, purse-proud youngster? Could he not ride with any man? Yes, and one might add, match tongues with any woman. For his native glibness was doubly helped by the vast, unprintable vocabularies of his chosen world, as well as by choice phrases from heroic verse that were a more exact reflex of his mind.

Then, on a day, came Whiskey Mason drifting into Links once more. He was making an ever scantier living out of his wretched calling, and had sunk as low as he could sink. But he had learned a dozen clever tricks to make new victims.

At exactly eleven o'clock, P.M., the bar-room had been closed, as was by law required. At exactly eleven five, P.M. a traveller, sick and weak, supported by a friend, came slowly along the dusty road to the door, and, sinking down in agony of cramps, protested he could go no farther and begged for a little brandy, as his friend knocked on the door, imploring kindly aid for the love of heaven. The barkeeper was obdurate, but the man was in such a desperate plight that the Widow Hartigan was summoned. Ever ready at the call of trouble her kindly heart responded. The sick man revived with a little brandy; his friend, too, seemed in need of similar help and, uttering voluble expressions of gratitude, the travellers went on to lodgings on the other side of the town, carrying with them a flask in which was enough of the medicine to meet a new attack if one should come before they reached their destination.

At exactly eleven ten, P.M., these two helpless, harmless strangers received the flask from Widow Hartigan. At exactly eight A.M., the next day, at the opening of the Magistrate's office, they laid their information before him, that the Widow Hartigan was selling liquor out of hours. Here was the witness and here was the flask. They had not paid for this, they admitted, but said it had been "charged." All the town was in a talk. The papers were served, and on the following day, in court, before Tom Ford, the Mayor, the charge was made and sworn to by Mason, who received, and Hall, who witnessed and also received, the unlawful drink.

It was so evidently a trumped-up case that some judges would have dismissed it. But the Mayor was human; this woman had flouted his wife; her boy had licked his boy. The fine might be anything from one hundred up to one thousand dollars. The Mayor was magnanimous; he imposed the minimum fine. So the widow was mulcted a hundred dollars for playing the rôle of good Samaritan. Mason and Hall got fifty dollars to divide, and five minutes later were speeding out of town. They left no address. In this precautionary mood their instincts were right, though later events proved them to be without avail.

Just one hour after the disappearance of Mason, Kenna came to town and heard how the Widow's open-hearted kindness had led her into a snare. His first question was: "Where is he?" No one knew, but every one agreed that he had gone in a hurry. Now it is well known that experienced men seeking to elude discovery make either for the absolute wilderness or else the nearest big city. There is no hiding place between. Kenna did not consult Kitty. He rode, as fast as horse could bear his robust bulk to Petersburg where Mason had in some sort his headquarters.

It was noon the next day before Bill found him, sitting in the far end of the hardware shop. Mason never sat in the saloons, for the barkeepers would not have him there. He did not loom large, for he always tried to be as inconspicuous as possible, and his glance was shifty.

Bill nodded to the iron dealer and passed back to the stove end of the store. Yes, there sat Mason. They recognized each other. The whiskey sneak rose in trepidation. But William said calmly, "Sit down."

"Well," he continued with a laugh, "I hear you got ahead of the Widdy."

"Yeh."

"Well, she can afford it," said Bill. "She's getting rich."

Mason breathed more freely.

"I should think ye'd carry a revolver in such a business," said William, inquiringly.

"Bet I do," said Mason.

"Let's have a look at it," said Kenna. Mason hesitated.

"Ye better let me see it, or——" There was a note of threat for the first time. Mason drew his revolver, somewhat bewildered. Before the informer knew what move was best, Kenna reached out and took the weapon.

"I hear ye got twenty-five dollars from the Widdy."

"Yeh." And Mason began to move nervously under the cold glitter in Kenna's eyes.

"I want ye to donate that to the orphan asylum. Here, Jack!" Kenna called to the clerk, "Write on a big envelope 'Donation for the orphan asylum. Conscience money.'"

"What does it say?" inquired Bill, for he could not read. The clerk held out the envelope and read the inscription.

"All right," said Bill, "now, Mason, jest so I won't lose patience with you and act rough like, hand over that twenty-five."

"I ain't got it, I tell you. It's all gone."

"Turn out your pockets, or I will."

The whiskey sneak unwillingly turned out his pockets. He had fifteen dollars and odd.

"Put it in that there envelope," said Bill, with growing ferocity. "Now gum it up. Here, Jack, will ye kindly drop this in the contribution box for the orphans while we watch you?" The clerk entered into the humour of it all. He ran across the street to the gate of the orphan asylum and dropped the envelope into the box. Mason tried to escape but Bill's mighty hand was laid on his collar. And now the storm of animal rage pent up in him for so long broke forth. He used no weapon but his fists, and when the doctor came, he thought the whiskey man was dead. But they brought him round, and in the hospital he lingered long.

It was clearly a case of grave assault; the magistrate was ready to issue a warrant for Kenna's arrest. But such was Bill's reputation that they could get no constable to serve it. Meanwhile, Mason hung between life and death. He did not die. Within six weeks, he was able to sit up and take a feeble interest in things about him, while Bill at Links pursued his normal life.

Gossip about the affair had almost died when the Mayor at Petersburg received a document that made him start. The Attorney General of the Province wrote: "Why have you not arrested the man who committed that assault? Why has no effort been made to administer justice?"

The Mayor was an independent business man, seeking no political favours, and he sent a very curt reply. "You had better come and arrest him yourself, if you are so set on it."

That was why two broad, square men, with steadfast eyes, came one day into Links. They sought out Bill Kenna and found him in the bar-room, lifting the billiard table with one hand, as another man slipped wedges under it to correct the level. Little Jim, though he had no business there at all, stood on the table itself and gave an abundance of orders.

"Are you William Kenna?" said the first of the strangers.

"I am that," said he.

"Then I arrest you in the Queen's name"; and the officer held up a paper while the other produced a pair of handcuffs.

"Oi'd like to see ye put them on me." And the flood of fight in him surged up.

He was covered by two big revolvers now, which argument had no whit of power to modify his mood; but another factor had. The Widow who had entered in search of Jim and knew the tragedy that hung by a hair, sped to his side: "Now, Bill, don't ye do it! I forbid ye to do it!"

"If they try to put them on me, I'll kill or be killed. If they jist act dacent, I'll go quiet."

"Will ye give yer word, Bill?"

"I will, Kitty; I'll give me word as a mahn. I'll go peaceable if they don't try to handcuff me."

"There," said Kitty to the officers. "He's give his word; and if you're wise, ye'll take him at that."

"All right," said the chief constable, and between them William moved to the door.

"Say, Bill, ye ain't going to be took?" piped little Jim. He had watched the scene dumbfounded from his place on the table. This was too much.

"Yes," said Bill, "I've give me word as a mahn," and he marched away, while the Widow fled sobbing to her room.

That was the end of Kenna, so far as Jim was concerned. And, somehow, that last sentence, "I've give me word as a mahn," kept ringing in Jim's ears; it helped to offset the brutalizing effect of many other episodes—that Fighting Bill should scoff at bonds and force, but be bound and helpless by the little sound that issued from his own lips.

Bill's after life was brief. He was condemned to a year in jail for deadly assault and served the term and came again to Petersburg. There in a bar-room he encountered Hall, the pal of Whisky Mason. A savage word from Bill provoked the sneer, "You jail bird." Kenna sprang to avenge the insult. Hall escaped behind the bar. Bill still pursued. Then Hall drew a pistol and shot him dead; and, as the Courts held later, shot justly, for a man may defend his life.

It was a large funeral that buried Bill, and it was openly and widely said that nine out of ten were there merely to make sure that he was dead and buried. The Widow Hartigan was chief mourner in the first carriage. She and Jim led the line, and when he was laid away, she had a stone erected with the words, "A true friend and a man without fear." So passed Kenna; but Jim bore the traces of his influence long and deeply—yes, all his life. Masterful, physical, prone to fight and to consider might as right, yet Jim's judgment of him was ever tempered by the one thought, the binding force of his "wurd as a mahn."

CHAPTER VI

JIM LOSES EVERYTHING

The Widow never forgot that her tenure of the hotel might end at any time; and, thinking ever of Jim and his future, she saved what she could from the weekly proceeds. She was a good manager, and each month saw something added to her bank account. When it had grown to a considerable size her friends advised her to invest it. There were Government bonds paying five per cent., local banks paying six and seven, and, last of all, the Consolidated Trading Stores paying eight and sometimes more—an enterprise of which Tom Ford was head.

The high interest was tempting, and pride was not without some power. Kitty was pleased to think that now she could go to the pompous Mayor as a capitalist. So, creating with an inward sense of triumph the impression of huge deposits elsewhere, she announced that she would take a small block of stock in the C. T. S. as a nest-egg for her boy. Thus the accumulations of ten years went into the company of which the Mayor was head and guide. For a time, the interest was duly paid each half year. Then came a crash. After the reorganization the Mayor continued in his big brick house and his wife still wore her diamonds; but the widow's hard-earned savings were gone. Kitty was stunned but game; falling back on the strength that was inside, she bravely determined to begin all over and build on a rock of safety. But fortune had another blow in store for Jim. And it fell within a month, just as he turned thirteen.

It was the end of the Canadian winter. Fierce frost and sudden thaw were alternated as the north wind and the south struggled for the woods, and the heat of work in the warm sun left many ill prepared for the onset of bitter cold at dusk. Bustling everywhere, seeing that pigs were fed, pies made, and clothes mended; now in the hot kitchen, a moment later in the stable yard to manage some new situation; the Widow fell a victim to pneumonia much as John Downey had done.

For three days she lay in fever and pain. Jim was scarcely allowed to see her. They did not understand pneumonia in those days, and as it was the general belief that all diseases were "catching," the boy was kept away. The doctor was doing his best with old-fashioned remedies, blisters, mustard baths, hot herb teas and fomentations. He told her she would soon be well, but Kitty knew better. On the third day, she asked in a whisper for Jim, but told them first to wash his face and hands with salt water. So the long-legged, bright-eyed boy came and sat by his mother's bed and held her hot hands. As he gazed on her over-bright eyes, she said softly:

"My darling, you'll soon be alone, without friend or kith or kin. This place will no longer be your home. God only knows where you'll go. But He will take care of you as He took care of me."

For the first time Jim realized the meaning of the scene—his mother was dying. She quieted his sobs with a touch of her hand and began again, slowly and painfully:

"I tried to leave you well fixed, but it was not to be. The hotel will go to another. This is all I have for you."

She drew a little cedar box from under the covers, and opening it, showed him her Bible, the daguerreotype of his father and a later photograph of herself.

"Jim, promise me again that you will never touch tobacco or liquor till you are eighteen."

"Oh, mother, mother!" he wept. "I'll do anything you say. I'll promise. I give you my word I never will touch them."

She rested in silence, her hand was on his head. When her strength in a little measure came again, she said in a low tone:

"My wish was to see you educated, a minister for Christ. I hope it may yet be so."

She was still a long time; then, gently patting his head, she said to those around:

"Take him away. Wash him with salt and water."

Thus it came about that the hotel which had been Jim's only home and which he thought belonged to his mother, passed into the hands of John Downey, Jr., nephew of the original owner. It was Mrs. John Downey who offered the first ray of comfort in Jim's very bleak world. When she saw the tall handsome boy she put her arms around him and said:

"Never mind, Jim, don't go away. This will always be home for you."

So the lad found a new home in the old house, but under greatly changed conditions. The new mistress had notions of her own as to the amount of education necessary and the measure of service to be returned for one's keep. Jim was able to read, write, and cipher; this much was ample in the opinion of Mrs. Downey, and Jim's school days ended. The understanding that he must make himself useful quickly resulted in his transference to the stable. A garret in the barn was furnished with a bed for him, and Jim's life was soon down to its lowest level. He had his friends, for he was full of fun and good to look upon: but they were not of the helpful kind, being recruited chiefly from the hostlers, the pugilists, and the horsemen. He had time for amusements, too; but they were nearly always of the boxing glove and the saddle. Books had little charm for him, though he still found pleasure in reciting the heroic ballads of Lachlin, the Raid of Dermid, the Battle of the Boyne, and in singing "My Pretty, Pretty Maid," or woodmen's "Come all ye's." His voice was unusually good, except at the breaking time; and any one who knew the part the minstrel played in Viking days would have thought the bygone times come back to see him among the roystering crowd at Downey's.

The next three years that passed were useless except for this, they gifted Jim with a tall and stalwart form and shoulders like a grown man. But they added little to the good things he had gathered from his mother and from Fightin' Bill. At sixteen he was six feet high, slim and boyish yet, but sketched for a frame of power. All this time his meagre keep and his shabby clothes were his only pay. But Jim had often talked things over with his friends and they pointed out that he was now doing man's work and getting less than boy's pay. The scene that followed his application for regular wages was a very unpleasant one; and John Downey made the curious mistake of trying to throw young Jimmy out. The boy never lost his temper for a moment but laughingly laid his two strong hands on the landlord's fat little shoulders and shook him till his collar popped and his eyes turned red. Then Jim grinned and said:

"I told ye I wasn't a kid anny more."

It was the landlady's good sense that made a truce, and after a brief, stormy time the long-legged boy was reinstated at wages in the yard.

At seventeen Jim was mentioned among the men as a likely "bhoy." Women in the street would turn to look in admiration at his square shoulders, lithe swing, and handsome head. But the life he led was flat, or worse than flat. The best that can be said of it is that in all this sordid round of bar and barn he learned nothing that in any sort had power to harm his rare physique. His language at times was the worst of its lurid kind. His associates were coarse and drunken. Yet Jim lived with them in all their ways and neither chewed, smoked, nor drank. How or why, none understood. He said simply that he "didn't feel like he wanted to." With the liquor it was a different matter. Here it was a question of principle and his word to his mother helped him where by nature he was weak. So he grew up, hedged about with a dignity that was in some sense a foreshadowing of his destiny. But there was much dross to be burned away and the two great passions that stood between Jim Hartigan and full spiritual manhood had their roots in these early years at Downey's. Later he matched his strength against theirs and with that struggle, in which no quarter was asked or given, these pages are ultimately concerned.

CHAPTER VII

HE GETS A MUCH-NEEDED LESSON

Many a man has been ruined by a high, unbroken level of success. Intellectually it makes for despotism and a conviction of infallibility. In the world of muscle, it creates a bully.

Young Jim was far from losing his interest in the ring, and he was growing so big and strong that there were few in town who cared to put on the gloves with him. All that Bill Kenna had taught him, and more, was stored as valued learning. Kenna used to say, in his Irish vein: "There is twelve rules for to conduct yourself right in a shindy; the first is, get your blow in first; and, if ye live up to this, ye needn't worry about the other iliven rules." Jim accepted this as fundamental truth and thereby became the aggressor in nearly every brawl.

His boiling, boisterous, animal nature grew with his body and he revelled in the things of brawn. He responded joyfully when he was called on to eject some rowdy from the bar-room, and begetting confidence with each new victory, he began to have a vast opinion of himself. About this time a powerful rival of Downey's, known as the Dummer House, claimed attention at the other end of town. One was located to catch the inbound from the west; the other, those from the east. And when the owners were not at war, they kept at best an armed neutrality.

John Downey had delivered himself of some unhallowed hopes concerning the rival house, and Jim, as he passed the opposition Inn on a certain evening, had the picturesque devastations vividly in mind. It so happened that a masting team of oxen was standing patiently outside awaiting the driver who was refreshing himself at the bar. A masting team consists of six to twelve strong, selected oxen, yoked two and two to a mighty chain with which they can drag forth the largest pines that are saved for masts. Jim's too-agile mind noted the several components of a new and delightful exploit: a crowd of noisy teamsters in a log house bar-room, a team of twelve huge, well-trained oxen on a chain, the long, loose end of which lay near him on the ground. It was the work of a minute to hook the chain around a projecting log of the house. A moment more and he had the oxen on the go. Beginning with the foremost pair, he rushed down the line, and the great, heaving, hulking shoulders, two and two, bent and heaved their bulk against the strain. The chain had scarcely time to tighten; no house could stand against that power. The huge pine log was switched out at one end as a man might jerk a corn cob from its crib. The other end, still wedged in its place, held for a moment; but the oxen moved slowly on like a landslide. The log was wrenched entirely away and the upper part of the building dropped with a sullen "chock" to rest a little lower. There was a wild uproar inside, a shouting of men, a clatter of glass, and out rushed the flushed-faced rabble, astonished, frightened, furious to see the twelve great oxen solemnly marching down the street, trailing the missing log, the fragment of their house, while beside them, running, laughing, hooting, was a long-legged boy.

Jim's intention had been to clear out, but the trick proved so screamingly funny that he stood for a minute to enjoy the scene. Shelves had fallen and glasses had broken, but no person had been hurt. There was a moment's uncertainty; then with an angry shout the enraged patrons of the Dummer House swept forward. Jim discreetly fled. In the centre of the town friends appeared and in the street he turned to face his pursuers. Jim had already proved himself one of "the best men in Links" and it was with a new burst of hilarity that he wheeled about among his backers to give them "all they wanted." Instead of the expected general onslaught, a method new to Jim was adopted. The teamsters of the Dummer House held back and from their ranks there issued a square-jawed, bow-legged man, whose eye was cold, whose step was long and quick. With the utmost deliberation he measured Jim with his eye. Then he growled:

"Come on, ye ill-born pup. Now ye'll get what ye desarve."

The sporting instinct was strong in the crowd and the two were left alone to fight it out. It took very little time. Jim had made a mistake—a serious one. This was no simple teamster, guileless of training, who faced him, but a man whose life was in the outer circle of the prize ring. The thrashing was complete, and effective for several weeks. Jim was carried home and ever after he bore upon his chin a scar that was the record of the final knockout from the teamster's iron fist.

The catastrophe had several important compensations. The owner of the Dummer House decided that the boy was punished enough, and took no legal proceeding against him. On his part, Jim began to think much more seriously before giving reckless rein to his sense of humour. On the whole, his respect for the rights of others was decidedly increased. His self-esteem shrunk to more normal proportions and if he thought of the incident at all it was to wish very earnestly that some day, somewhere, he might meet the teamster again on more even terms.

Unfortunately these salutory results were negatived some six months later by an event that took place in Downey's bar. It was Jim's birthday; he was eighteen and he announced it with pride.

"And here's where ye join us," said several.

"No, I don't care about it," said Jim.

"Ye ain't promise bound now, are ye?"

"No," replied Jim, "but——"

"Make him a sweet one with syrup and just a spoonful of the crather to take the curse off."

Refusing, protesting, half ashamed of his hesitation, Jim downed at a gulp a fruity concoction, much to the delight of the assemblage. It was not so bad as he had expected it to be and the crowd roared at the expression on his face.

"Ye're a man for yourself now, lad," said a woodsman clapping him on the shoulder. "Come boys, another round to Hartigan's health."

It could not be said of Jim that he was normal in anything. In a rare and multiplied degree he had inherited the full muscling and robust heart of his folk in both lines of forbears. It was a great inheritance, but it carried its own penalty. The big animal physique holds a craving for strong drink. Physical strength and buoyancy are bound up with the love of bacchanalian riot. Jim had given his word to abstain from liquor until he was of age; he had kept it scrupulously. Now he had tasted of it the pendulum swung full to the other side. That was his nature. His world might be a high world or a low world; whichever sphere he moved in he practised no half-way measures.

From that eighteenth birthday Jim Hartigan waged ceaseless warfare within himself. During the early days he was an easy victim. Then came a shock that changed the whole aspect of his life, and later one stood beside him who taught him how to fight. But until those events took place, the town of Links knew him for what he was, a reckless, dare-devil youth, without viciousness or malice, but ripe for any extravagance or adventure. His pranks were always begun in fun though it was inevitable that they should lead to serious consequences. It was admitted by his severest critics that he had never done a cruel or a cowardly thing, yet the constant escapades and drinking bouts in which he was ever the leader earned him the name of Wild Jim Hartigan.

After each fresh exploit his abject remorse was pitiful. And so, little by little, a great nature was purged; his spirit was humbled by successive and crushing defeats. At first the animal rebound was sufficient to set him on his feet unashamed. But during the fourth year after his coming of age, an unrest, a sickness of soul took possession of Jim and no wildness sufficed to lift this gloom. And it was in frantic rebellion against this depression that he entered upon his memorable visit to the Methodist revival.

BOOK II

THE CONVERSION

CHAPTER VIII

THE CONVERSION OF JIM

There was much excitement in Methodist circles that autumn. A preacher of power had come from the east. The church was filled to overflowing on Sunday, and a prayer meeting of equal interest was promised for Wednesday night.

The people came from miles around and there were no vacant seats. Even the aisles were filled with chairs when the Rev. Obadiah Champ rose and bawled aloud in rolling paragraphs about "Hopeless, helpless, hell-damned sinners all. Come, come to-day. Come now and be saved." A wave of religious hysteria spread over the packed-in human beings. A wave that to those untouched was grotesque and incomprehensible.

"Sure, they ain't right waked up yet," said one of Jim's half-dozen unregenerate friends who had come to sit with him on the fence outside, and scoff at the worshippers. Jim was silent, but a devil of wild deeds stirred irritatingly within him. He looked about him for some supreme inspiration—some master stroke. The crowd was all in the church now, and the doors were closed tight. But muffled sounds of shouting, of murmurings, of halleluiahs were heard.

"They're goin' it pretty good now, Jim," said another. "But I think you could arouse 'em," he added, with a grin.

Standing by the church was a tall elm tree; near by was a woodshed with axe, saw, and wood pile. Jim's eye measured the distance from trunk to roof and then, acting on a wild impulse, with visions of folk in terror for their bodies when they professed concern for nothing but their souls, he got the axe, and amid the suppressed giggles and guffaws of his chums, commenced to fell the tree. In twenty minutes the great trunk tottered, crackled, and swung down fair on the roof of the crowded building.

The congregation had reached a degree of great mental ferment with the revival, and a long, loud murmuring of prayers and groans, with the voice of the exhorter, harsh and ringing, filled the edifice, when with a crash overhead the great arms of the tree met the roof. At first, it seemed like a heavenly response to the emotion of the congregation, but the crackling of small timber, the showering down of broken glass and plaster gave evidence of a very earthly interposition.

Then there was a moment of silence, then another crack from the roof, and the whole congregation arose and rushed for the door. All in vain the exhorter tried to hold them back. He shrieked even scriptural texts to prove they should stay to see the glory of the Lord. Another flake of plaster fell, on the pulpit this time; then he himself turned and fled through the vestry and out by the back way.

Jim's following had deserted him, but he himself was there to see the fun; and when the congregation rushed into the moonlight it was like a wasp's nest poked with a stick, or a wheat shock full of mice turned over with a fork. The crowd soon understood the situation and men gathered around the sinner. There was menace in every pose and speech. They would have him up to court; they would thrash him now. But the joyful way in which Jim accepted the last suggestion and offered to meet any or all "this holy minute" had a marked effect on the programme, especially as there were present those who knew him.

Then the exhorter said:

"Brethren, let me talk to this heinous sinner. Young man, do you realize that this is the House of God, which you have so criminally destroyed?"

"The divil an' all it is," said Jim. "Sure, ye ain't got the cheek to call a Methody shindy hall the House of God. I think ye ought to be ashamed of yourself to give a lot of dacent farmers the hysterics like yer doin'."

"Young man, the spirit of the Lord is mighty, and cometh like a strong wind on the four corners of the house."

"Then why in the divil did ye blame me for it?" was the answer.

"Oh, son of Belial! Hell fire and eternal damnation, a portion in the pit that burneth with fire, is the lot of those that desecrate the sanctuary of the Most High. I tell you it were better for you that you had never been born——"

"But sure, I am born; and it's mesilf that's aloive yet an' going strong."

"Oh, unregenerate blasphemer——"

But a sudden cry and commotion interrupted the preacher.

"Here, lay her down, get some water."

A little girl had been hurt in the crush and now she had fainted. The threats of the men had roused Jim to his joyful, battle enthusiasm. The onslaught of the preacher had stirred his sense of humour; but the poor, limp, and seemingly dead form of the little girl, a child whom he knew and had often petted, was an attack he was ill-prepared to meet.

"There, see what you have done. It were better that a millstone were hanged about your neck and that you were cast into the depths of the sea than that you should have harmed this little one. Her blood be on your head."

The mother was kneeling by the child, unwisely holding up its head. She was praying intently; the air was full of religious fervour. "Oh, God, spare my baby. Oh, God, be merciful."

Jim heard the words and they entered his soul like a two-edged sword. All the fun of the incident was gone, and all the cruelty, the unkindness, the wickedness, loomed large and larger. With his intense nature, subject to the most violent reactions, the effect was profound. It seemed to him, as he stood there, that a veil dissolved before his eyes and that he saw himself and his life for the first time. There had ever been two natures struggling in his soul, the calm and wise one of his Ulster blood of placid Saxon stock, and that of the wild and fiery Celt from Donegal, ready to fight, ready to sing, ever ready for fun, but ever the easy prey of deep remorse in even measure with the mood of passion that foreran and begot it.

Smitten from within and without, utter humiliation, self-accusation, and abasement filled his soul. Jim sank to the ground by the little girl, and wept in an agony of remorse.

"Young man," said the exhorter, "if God in His mercy has sent me here to save your soul from eternal damnation by this hellish deed of yours, then shall I rejoice and praise the Lord, that out of fire and brimstone He can create a golden pathway."

The little girl now opened her eyes and with a cry of relief the mother sought to lift her up, but had not the strength. Jim's mighty arms were eager for service, and with that soft, limp little body against his broad chest, her head on his shoulder, his heart was filled with inexpressible emotion.

"Bring her in here," and the remnant of the congregation reassembled in the church. In the very front was Jim, sitting by the mother with the little girl between them. His head was bowed on his hands, his elbows on his knees.

Then the exhorter began again. Full of scriptural texts charged with holy fire, abounding in lurid thoughts of burning lakes, of endless torment; gifted with the fluency that sometimes passes for logic and makes for convincement, he dwelt on the horrors and the might-have-beens. He shouted out his creeds of holiness, he rumbled in his chest and made graphic mouthings. He played on all the emotions until he found the most responsive, and then hammered hard on these. The big broad shoulders before him shook, tears fell from the half-hidden face. Then the preacher chanced to strike on the note, "your mother," and Jim Hartigan's breakdown was complete. He sobbed, "Oh, God, be merciful to me, a sinner," and rising, staggered to a place on the upraised bench—the seat of those who dared to hope for salvation—and wept.

Carried away by his own vehemence, the exhorter wept, too. There was no human being in the hall who could stand the overwhelming surge of emotion. The congregation wept. Then Jim arose and in broken voice said: "My mother's dying prayer was that I might join the Church and be a witness for God. As sure as she is looking down on me now I promise that I will join His people and niver rest till I have been made fit to stand among those who bear His message. I give my word as a man."

CHAPTER IX

JIM HARTIGAN GOES TO COLLEGE

Hartigan never walked in the middle of the road. He was either in the ditch or on the high place. Having "got religion" it was inevitable, with his nature, that he should become a leader in the fold. That vision of himself as a preacher, fully ordained, which had burst upon him at the revival, filled his mind. His mother's last wish resounded in his ears with all the imperative force of a voice from the grave and he was emotionally ripe for such inner urgings.

The difficulties in the way of such a course would have daunted most men; but Jim was going strong for the moment, and to him impossibilities were mere trivialities. The Rev. Obadiah Champ, with others who were proud of the new convert, took him before the Board of Deacons and there Jim made his ambitions known. He was illiterate, friendless, penniless, and already twenty-three. He had no taste for study or a life of self-control; meekness and spirituality were as much to his liking now as travelling on a bog is to a blooded horse.

But his magnificent presence, his glib Irish tongue, his ready wit, his evident warmth and sincerity, were too much for the reverend bearded ones of the Board. They were carried away, as most humans were, by his personal charm. They listened with beaming faces. They cast significant glances at one another. They sent Jim into another room while they discussed his fate. In twenty minutes he was brought back to hear their decision. "Yes, they would accept him as a chosen vessel to bear the grace of God abroad among the people. They would educate him without expense to himself. He might begin his college career at once."

In the ordinary course, Jim would have set to work with a tutor in Links to prepare himself to enter Coulter College at the next term. But life seemed to order itself in unusual ways when it was a question concerning Jim. He had no home in Links; he had no money to pay a tutor; he was as eager as a child to begin the serious work; and his ardour burnt all the barriers away. He became at once an inmate of Coulter, a special protégé of the president's, admitted really as a member of the latter's family, and bound by many rules and promises. In preparation for his formal entry he was required to devote six hours a day to study, and those who knew him of old had given the president a hint to exact from Jim his "wurd as a mahn" that he would do his daily task.

In looking back on those days Jim used to revile them for their uselessness and waste. What he did not understand until life had put him through the fire was that the months at Coulter broke him to harness. It was beyond the wildest imagining that a youth brought up as Jim had been should step from a life of boisterous carousing in a backwoods settlement into a seminary and find congenial or helpful occupation among books. And yet the shock, the change of environment, the substitution of discipline for license and, above all, the heroic struggle of the man to meet this new order of existence—these were the things, the fine metals of a great soul, which life was hammering, hammering into shape.

What this period meant to Jim no one but himself knew. The agony of spirit and of body was intense. He had given his word to go through with it and he did. But every instinct, every association of his old life led his mind abroad. Every bird that flew to the roof or hopped on the lawn was a strong attraction; every sound of a horse's hoof aroused his wayward interest; and the sight of a horse sent him rushing incontinently to the window. At the beginning, the football captain had pounced on him as the very stuff he needed, and Jim responded as the warhorse does to the bugle. He loved the game and he was an invaluable addition to the team. And yet, helpful as such an outlet was for his pent-up energy, his participation merely created new tortures, so that the sight of a sweater crossing the lawn became maddening to him in the hours of study. He had never liked books, and now as the weeks went by he learned to loathe them.

It is greatly to be feared that in a fair, written examination with an impartial jury, Jim Hartigan would have been badly plucked on his college entrance. But great is the power of personality. The president's wife behaved most uncollegiately. She interested herself in Jim; she had interviews with the examiners; she discovered in advance questions to be asked; she urged upon the authorities the absolute necessity of accepting this promising student. The president himself was biased. He hinted that the function of examiners was not so much to make absolute measurement of scholastic attainments as to manifest a discretionary view of possibilities, and to remember that examination papers were often incapable of gauging the most important natural endowments of the candidate; that sometimes when it was necessary to put a blood horse over a five-barred gate, the wisest horseman laid the gate down flat.

The admonitions were heeded, the gate laid flat, and the thoroughbred entered the pasture. But to Jim, caught up in the wearisome classroom grind, the days held no glimmer of light. Of what possible value, he asked himself again and again, could it be to know the history of Nippur? Why should the cuneiforms have any bearing on the morals of a backwoods Canadian? Would the grace of God be less effective if the purveyor of it was unaware of what Sprool's Commentaries said about the Alexandrian heresy? Was not he, Jim Hartigan, a more eloquent speaker now, by far, than Silas McSilo, who read his Greek testament every morning? And he wrote to the Rev. Obadiah Champ: "It's no use. I don't know how to study. I'm sorry to get up in the morning and glad to go to bed and forget it. I'd rather be in jail than in college. I hate it more every day." But Jim had given his "wurd as a mahn" and he hammered away sadly and sorrowfully as one who has no hope, as one who is defeated but continues to fight merely because he knows not how to surrender.

CHAPTER X

ESCAPE TO CEDAR MOUNTAIN

It is generally admitted that a college offers two main things, book learning and atmosphere. Of these the latter is larger and more vital, if it be good. If the college lose ground in either essential, the loss is usually attributable to a leading set of students. Coulter was losing ground, and the growth of a spirit of wildness in its halls was no small worry to the president. He knew whence it sprang, and his anxiety was the greater as he thought of it. Then a happy inspiration came. Jim's dislike of books had intensified. He had promised to study for one year. According to the rules, a student, after completing his first year, might be sent into the field as an assistant pastor, to be in actual service under an experienced leader for one year, during which he was not obliged to study.

To Jim this way out was an escape from a cavern to the light of day, and every officer of Coulter College breathed a sigh of relief as he packed his bag and started for the West.

It was in truth a wending of the Spirit Trail when Jim set out; as if the Angel of Destiny had said to the lesser Angel of Travel: "Behold, now for a time he is yours. You can serve him best." Jim's blood was more than red; it was intense scarlet. He hankered for the sparkling cups of life, being alive in every part—to ride and fight and burn in the sun, to revel in strife, to suffer, struggle, and quickly strike and win, or as quickly get the knockout blow! Valhalla and its ancient fighting creed were the hunger in his blood, and how to translate that age-old living feeling into terms of Christianity was a problem to which Jim's reason found no adequate answer. He talked of a better world, of peace and harps and denial and submission, because that was his job. He had had it drilled into him at Coulter; but his flashing eye, his mighty sweeping hand, gave the lie to every word of meekness that fell from his school-bound tongue. He longed for life in its fullest, best, most human form. He was fiery as a pirate among the wild rowdies he had lived with yet he had that other side—a child or a little girl could bully him into absolute, abject submission.

Whoever knows the West of the late '70s can have no doubt as to where the whirlpool of red-blooded life surged deepest, most irresistibly; where the strong alone could live and where the strongest only could win. In the Black Hills the strongest of the savages met the strongest of the whites, and there every human lust and crime ran riot. It was not accident but a far-sighted wisdom on the part of his directors that sent Jim to Cedar Mountain.

This town of the Black Hills was then in the transition stage. The cut-throat border element was gone. The law and order society had done its work. The ordinary machinery of justice was established and doing fairly well. The big strikes of gold were things of the past; now plodding Chinese and careful Germans were making profitable daily wages; and farmers were taking the places of the ranchmen. But there was still a rowdy element in the one end of the town, where cowboy and miner left their horses waiting for half the night, by the doors of noisy life and riot. This was the future field of pastoral work selected for the Rev. James Hartigan by elders wise in the testing of the human spirit.

All alone, Jim set forth on his three days' journey from Coulter, by way of Toronto, Detroit, and Chicago, to the West, and seldom has a grown man had so little knowledge of the world to rely upon. On the train he met with a painted woman, whose smirks and overtures he did not understand; and some farmer folk of simple kindness. In the coach, where all slept on their seats at night, he was like another brother to the little folks, and when a lumberjack, taking advantage of his size, sought to monopolize two seats, whereby the old farmer was left standing, Jim's mild and humorous "Sure, I wouldn't do that; it doesn't seem neighbourly," as he tapped the ruffian's shoulder, put a new light on the matter; and the lumberjack, after noting the shoulders of the speaker, decided that it *wasn't* neighbourly, and removed his feet.

Most of the passengers said "good-bye" at Chicago, and the rest at Sidney Junction, where Jim changed cars for the last leg of the journey.

He had no sooner transferred himself and his bag to the waiting train than there entered his coach five new passengers who at once attracted his full attention—a Jesuit missionary and four Sioux Indians. The latter were in the clothes of white men, the Jesuit in his clerical garb. They settled into the few available places and Jim found himself sharing his seat with the black-robed missionary.

All his early training had aimed to inspire him with hatred of the papist, and the climax of popery, he believed, was a Jesuit. He had never met one before, yet he knew the insignia and he was not at all disposed to be friendly. But the black-robe was a man of the world, blessed with culture, experience, and power; and before half an hour, in spite of himself, Jim found himself chatting amicably with this arch enemy. The missionary was full of information about the country and the Indians; and Jim, with the avidity of the boy that he was, listened eagerly, and learned at every sentence. The experience held a succession of wholesome shocks for him;

for, next to the detested papist, he had been taught to look down on the "poor, miserable bastes of haythens," that knew nothing of God or Church. And here, to his surprise, was a priest who was not only a kindly, wise, and lovable soul, but who looked on the heathen not as utterly despicable, but as a human being who lacked but one essential of true religion, the one that he was there to offer.

"Yes," continued the missionary, "when I came out here as a young man twenty-five years ago, I thought about the Indians much as you do. But I have been learning. I know now that in their home lives they are a kind and hospitable people. The white race might take them as models in some particulars, for the widow, the orphan, the old, and the sick are ever first cared for among them. We are told that the love of money is the root of all evil; and yet this love of money, in spite of all the white man can do to inculcate it, has no place at all in the Indian heart."

Jim listened in astonishment, first to hear the dreadful savages set so high by one who knew them and had a right to speak, but chiefly to find such fair-mindedness and goodness in one who, according to all he had ever heard, must be, of course, a very demon in disguise, at war with all who were not of his faith. Then the thought came, "Maybe this is all put on to fool me." But at this point two of the Indians came over to speak to the missionary. Their respectful but cordial manner could not well have been put on and was an answer to his unspoken question.

"Are these men Catholics?" he asked.

"I'm afraid not yet," said the priest, "although I believe they are influenced strongly. They observe some of the practices of the Church and cling to others of their own."

"Their own what?"

"Well, I may say their own Church," said the father.

"Church? You call theirs a Church?" exclaimed Jim.

"Why not? Their best teachers inculcate cleanness, courage, kindness, sobriety, and truth; they tell of one Great Spirit who is the creator and ruler of all things and to whom they pray. Surely, these things are truth and all light comes from God; and, even though they have not learned the great story of the redemption, we must respect their faith so far as it goes."

"And these are the 'beasts of heathen' I have always heard about."

"Oh, yes," said the missionary, "they have many habits that I hope to see stamped out; but I have learned that my Church was wise when it sent me, not to antagonize and destroy, but to seek for the good in these people and fortify that as a foundation on which to build the true faith."

"Well, this is all a great surprise to me," said Hartigan; and again his deepest astonishment lay in the new knowledge of the papist, rather than of the Indian.

They were several hours together. The missionary and his Indian friends finally left the train at a station nearest their home in Pine Ridge and Jim was left alone with some very new ideas and some old-time prejudices very badly shaken.

The rest of the journey he sat alone, thinking—thinking hard.

There was no one to meet him at the Cedar Mountain station when he stepped out of the car—the last passenger from the last car, in the last station—for at that time this was the north end of the track. All his earthly belongings, besides the things he wore, were in a valise that he carried in his hand; in his pocket he had less than five dollars in money, and his letter of introduction to the Rev. Dr. Jebb of Cedar Mountain.

In all his life, Jim had never seen a mountain, nor even a high hill; and he stood gazing at the rugged pile behind the town with a sense of fascination. It seemed so unreal, a sort of pretty thing with pretty little trees on it. Was it near and little, or far and big? He could not surely tell. After gazing a while, he turned to the railway agent and said:

"How far off is that mountain top?"

"A matter of two miles," was the answer.

Two miles! It did not seem two hundred rods; and yet it did, for the man on horseback half way there looked toy-like; and the distance grew as he gazed. A rugged, rocky pile with white snow-ravines still showing in the springtime sun, some scattering pines among the ledges and, lower, a breadth of cedars, they were like a robe that hid the shoulders and flanks of the mountain, then spread out on the plain, broken at a place where water glinted, and later blended with the purple sage that lent its colour to the view.

It was all so new and fairylike; "the glamour and dhrei that the banshee works on the eyes of men," was the thought that came, and the Irish tales his mother used to tell of fays and lepricauns seemed realized before his eyes. Then, acting on a sudden impulse, he dropped his bag and started off, intent on going up the mountain.

Swinging a stick that he had picked up, he went away with long, athletic strides, and the motor engines of his frame responding sent his blood a-rushing and his spirit bounding, till his joy broke forth in song, the song of the singing prophet of Judea's hills, a song he had learned in Coulter for the sweetness of the music rather than for its message:

How beautiful upon the mountainsAre the feet of him that bringeth good tidings,That publisheth peace,That bringeth good tidings of good,That publisheth salvation,That saith unto Zion,"Thy God reigneth."

And when he reached the cedar belt he knew that the railway man had spoken the truth, but he held on up the ever-steepening trail, ceasing his song only when he needed the breath to climb. A cottontail waved its beacon for a minute before him, then darted into the underbrush; the mountain jays called out a wailing cry; and the flicker clucked above. Sharp turns were in the trail, else it had faced an upright cliff or overshot a precipice; but it was easily followed and, at length, he was above the cedars. Here the horse trail ended, but a moccasin path went on. It turned abruptly from a sheer descent, then followed a narrow knife edge to rise again among the rocks to the last, the final height, a little rocky upland with a lonely standing rock. Here Jim turned to see the plain, to face about and gasp in sudden wonder; for the spell of the mountain seen afar is but a little echo of the mountain power when it has raised you up.

He recalled the familiar words, not understood till now:

"Thy mercies are like mountains great,Thy judgments are like floods."

He gazed and his breath came fast as he took in the thought, old thoughts, yet new thoughts, strong and elusive, and wondered what he had found.

Crossing the little upland, he approached its farther end and stood by the pinnacle of rock that, like a lonely watchman, forever looked down on the blue and golden plains. A mountain chipmunk stared at him, flicked its tail, and dived under a flat ledge; a bird whose real home was a thousand miles off in the north faced the upland breeze and sang in its unknown tongue. Jim drew still nearer the rocky spire, rounded a ledge, and faced an unexpected sight. In a little open lodge of willows, bent and roofed with a canvas cover, sat an Indian youth, alone, motionless, beside him was a pot of water, and between him and the tall rock, a little fire, from which a tiny thread of smoke arose.

Hartigan started, for that very morning he had learned from the old Jesuit enough about the Red-men to know that this was something unusual. On the rock beyond the fire he saw, painted in red, two symbols that are used in the Red-man's prayers: "the blessed vision" leading up to the "spirit heart of all things." A measure of comprehension came to him, and Father Cyprian's words returned in new force.

The lad in the little lodge raised a hand in the sign of "Stop," then gently waved in a way that, in all lands and languages, means: "Please go away." There was a soft, dreamy look in his face, and Jim, realizing that he had entered another man's holy place, held back and, slowly turning, sought the downward trail.

It came to him clearly now this was one of the interesting things told him that morning by the Jesuit. This Indian boy was taking his *hambeday*, his manhood fast and vigil; seeking for the vision that should be his guide, he was burning his altar fire beside the Spirit Rock.

As he retraced his steps the wonder of this new world enveloped Jim. At the edge of the cedars he paused and, looking out over the great expanse of green plumage, he said aloud: "All my life have I lived in the bottom of a little narrow well, with barely a glimpse of the sky, and never a view of the world. Now I am suddenly brought forth to see the world and the bigness of the heavens, and the things I dimly got from books are here about me, big, living, actual."

He was himself so much, could he be also a part of this wonder-world? It seemed impossible, so wholly new was everything it held.

CHAPTER XI

A New Force Enters His Life

Back at the railway station, Hartigan looked for his bag where he had dropped it, but it was gone. The agent, glancing across and divining his quandary, said stolidly:

"I guess Dr. Jebb took it. Ain't you the party he's looking for? He said 'J. H.' was the initials. You'll find him at that white house with the flowers just where the boardwalk ends."

Jim went down the road with alert and curious eyes and presented himself at the white cottage. He found a grave and kindly welcome from Mrs. Jebb—a stout, middle-aged, motherly person—and from the Rev. Josiah Jebb, D.D., M.A., etc., pastor of the Methodist Church and his principal to be for the coming year.

A gentle, kindly man and a deep scholar, Dr. Jebb had no more knowledge of the world than a novice in a convent. His wife was his shield and buckler in all things that concerned the battle with men and affairs; all his thoughts and energies were for his pulpit and his books.

Failing health rather than personal fitness had to do with Dr. Jebb's being sent to the hills. But the vast extent of territory in his charge, the occasional meetings in places separated by long hard rides, together with the crude, blunt ranch and farmer folk who were his flock—all called for a minister with the fullest strength of youth and mental power. It was to meet this need that the trustees of the church had sent James Hartigan to supplement the labours of the Rev. Dr. Jebb. Thus these two, diverse in every particular of bodily and mental equipment, were chosen to meet the same religious problem.

The evening meal was spread by Mrs. Jebb herself, for their meagre stipend did not admit of a helper; and Jim, with his hearty, rollicking ways, soon won his accustomed place, a high place in their hearts. That night he was invited to stay with them; but it was understood that next day he would find permanent lodgings in the town. Not a complex task, since, to quote Mrs. Jebb, "his hat covered his family, and three hundred a year simplified the number of rooms."

Jim rose at six in the morning, lighted a fire in the kitchen stove—for this is etiquette in the simple regions where servants are not and the guest is as a son—and put on a full kettle of water. This also is etiquette; it assumes that the family will not be up for some time. Had it been near the breakfast hour, but half a kettle would have been correct. Then he left the house, stick in hand, for a long walk. This time he struck out in the direction of the open plains. The flimsy little town was soon behind him, and the winding trail among the sagebrush, went reaching out to the east. The pine woods of his native country were not well stocked with life; the feathered folk were inconspicuous there; but here it seemed that every bush and branch was alive with singing birds. The vesper sparrows ran before his feet, flashed their white tail feathers in a little flight ahead, or from the top of a stone or a buffalo skull they rippled out their story of the spring. The buffalo birds in black and white hung poised in the air to tell their tale, their brown mates in the grass applauding with a rapt attention. The flickers paused in harrying prairie anthills and chuckling fled to the nearest sheltering trees. Prairie dogs barked from their tiny craters; gophers chirruped or turned themselves into peg-like watchtowers to observe the striding stranger.

But over all, the loud sweet prairie lark sang his warbling yodel-song of the sun with a power and melody that no bird anywhere, in any land, can equal. It seemed to Jim the very spirit of these level lands, the embodiment of the awakening plains and wind, the moving voice of all the West. And all about, as though responsive, the flowers of spring came forth: purple avens in straggling patches; golden yellow bloom, with blots and streaks of fluffy white; while here and there, as far as eye could reach, was the blue-white tinge of the crocus flower, the queen of the springtime flowers, the child of the sky and the snow.

The passionate youth in him responded to the beauty of it; he felt it lay hold on him and he would have sung, but he found no words in all his college-born songs to tell of this new joy. "I didn't know it *could* be so beautiful. I didn't know," he said again and again.

At the seven o'clock whistle of a mill he wheeled about toward the town, and saw there, almost overhanging it, the mountain, bright in the morning, streaked with white, lifting a rugged head through the gray-green poncho of its cedar robe, a wondrous pile capped by the one lone tower that watched, forever watched, above the vast expanse of plains.

Jim was nearly back to the town when a horse and rig appeared coming rapidly toward him. He heard a shout and saw a man run from a house to look. The horse was going very fast and shaking his head; something was wrong. As it came toward him he saw that the driver was a young girl. She was holding with all her strength to the reins, but the horse, a tall, rawboned creature, was past control. Horses Jim surely understood. He stepped well aside, then wheeling as the runaway went past, he ran his best.

For a little while a swift man can run with a horse, and in that little while Jim was alongside, had seized the back of the seat, and, with a spurt and a mighty leap, had tumbled into the rig beside the driver. Instantly she held the reins toward him and gasped:

"I can't hold him; he's running away." Then, as Jim did not at once seize the reins, she hurriedly said: "Here, take them."

"No," he said with amazing calmness, "you *can* control him. Don't be afraid. You hurt yourself pulling; ease up. Keep him straight, that's all."

The sense of power in his presence and matter-of-fact tone restored her nerve. She slackened a little on the reins. The horse had believed he was running away; now he began to doubt it. She had been telegraphing terror along the lines, and now she began to telegraph control.

"Speak to him, just as you would if he were all right," said Jim in a low voice.

The girl had been pale and scared-looking, but she responded to the suggestion and talked to the horse.

"Good boy, good boy, Stockings; keep it up," just as though she had been putting him to his utmost.

There was open fareway straight ahead and little to fear so long as the horse kept in the road and met no other rig. In a quarter of a mile he began to slacken his pace.

"Will you take the lines now?" the girl asked shyly.

"No, it isn't necessary, and the horse would feel the change and think he had beaten you."

"My arms are tired out," she said rather querulously.

"Then ease up for a while. Don't pull so hard."

She did so and was surprised that the horse did not speed away. In a quarter of a mile more the victory was won. She gave the usual signal to stop and Stockings came gently to a pause.

"Now," said Jim, "if you like, I'll take the lines. The battle is over. You have won. From now on you will be able to drive that horse; but if I had taken the lines he would have felt the change; he would have felt that he could boss you, and ever after he would have been a dangerous horse for you to drive."

In the struggle, the horse had got one leg over the trace. Jim got out, spoke to the big, strong brute, and did the firm-handed, compelling things that a horseman knows. The tall creature stood a little trembly, but submissive now, as the man unhooked the trace, adjusted all the leathers, and then, with a word or two, adjusted the horse's mood.

"Shall I leave you now?" he asked.

"No," she said, "my arms are aching. I wish you would drive me home."

As he mounted the seat again and headed for the village, Jim had his first chance to look at the girl beside him. If fear had paled her face at all it was wholly overcome, for the richest glow of health was in her cheeks and on her brow. She was beautiful he knew, with her brown hair flying and brilliant colour, but these things did not entirely account for a charm of which he was delightfully conscious. Her hands were a little shaky from the struggle with the horse, but otherwise she was fully recovered and self-possessed and talked in an animated if somewhat nervous way about the adventure. In a land where rasping voices were the rule, it was instantly to be noted that her voice was soft and low.

"Stockings is not a bad horse," she said, "except in one way; the lines get under his tail. That always makes him back up and kick; then he got his leg over the trace, was frightened, and ran away. He's the only one of our horses that we have any trouble with. I was bound I'd drive him, in spite of Pa; but I'm thinking now that Pa was right." Then, abruptly: "I'm Miss Boyd; aren't you the new preacher?"

"Yes."

"I saw you at the station when you came yesterday."

"Sure, I didn't suppose a human being took notice of it," he laughed.

"Here's where I live. Will you come in?"

"No, thank you," he said; "I'm late now for breakfast at Dr. Jebb's." So he tied the horse to the post, helped her from the rig, and with a flourish of his stick and cap left her.

"The Rev. James Hartigan," she mused; "so that is Dr. Jebb's assistant." Then in Stockings's ear: "I think I like him—don't you, old runaway?"

CHAPTER XII

BELLE BOYD

Belle had been in the express office signing some receipts for goods consigned to her father when Jim stepped from the train. He appeared framed in the open doorway; six feet four, broad and straight, supple and easy, with the head of a Greek god in a crown of golden curls, and a dash of wild hilarity in his bright blue eyes that suggested a Viking, a royal pirate. He was the handsomest man she had ever seen and when he spoke it was with a slight and winsome Irish brogue that lent new charm to a personality already too dangerously gifted.

It seemed to her that Nature had given him all the gifts there were for man; and he was even better furnished than she perceived, for he had youth, health, happy moods, magnetic power in face and voice, courage, and the gift of speech. And yet, with all these unmeasured blessings was conjoined a bane. To be possessed of the wild, erratic spirit of the roving, singing Celt, to be driven to all ill-judged extremities, to be lashed by passion, anger, and remorse, to be the battle ground of this wild spirit and its strong rival, the calm and steadfast spirit of the North—that was a spiritual destiny not to be discerned in a first meeting; but Belle, keen and understanding, was to discover it very soon.

Belle Boyd was an only child. Her father was a well-to-do trader; he had had just enough schooling to give him a high notion of its value, and he resolved to equip his child with the best there was in reach. This meant an Illinois college. She entered at seventeen. Here many vague aspirations of schoolgirl life took definite shape, and resulted in some radical changes in her course of studies. Her mother had but one thought—to prepare Belle for being a good wife to some one. Her views on many subjects were to be left blank, so that she might at once adopt those of her prospective husband. Her tentacles alone were well considered in the maternal method, so that she could cling ivy-like to her oak, stay up with him or go down with him; but help him to stand up—no, never and not at all!

But Illinois was seething with a different thought in the late '70's. There were women who boldly proclaimed that sex and mind had little bearing on each other; that woman should train herself to be herself, and to stand on her own feet; that when woman had the business training of men, the widow and the unmarried woman—half of all women—would no longer be the easy prey of every kind of sharper. These new teachers were, of course, made social martyrs, but they sowed the seed and the crop was coming on. That every woman should prepare herself to stand alone in the world was the first article in their creed. This crystallized an old and shapeless thought that had often come to Belle, and the pointed application that she made was to focus her college studies on a business training. Bookkeeping, shorthand, and exact methods were selected for specialization; and when at the age of twenty Belle was graduated and went home to Cedar Mountain, she had, in addition to her native common sense, a disciplined attention that made her at once a power in the circle of the church. It was her own idea to take a business position at once. Her mother was absolutely opposed to it. "Why should her child be sent to work? Were they not able to keep her at home? What was the good of parents giving years to toil if not to keep their children at home with them?" Mr. Boyd was more inclined to see things Belle's way, and at length a compromise was reached by which Belle became her father's bookkeeper and secretary, and for a time all went well.

Then a new factor entered the case, one for which the reformer has not yet found a good answer. The daily routine of the desk was assumed as a matter of course; and Belle quickly got used to that and found abundant mental diversion in other things and in hours of freedom. But her body had less strength than her mind, and the close confinement of the office began to tell. Her hands got thin, her cheeks lost their colour, her eyes grew brighter. Mrs. Boyd began to worry, and sent secretly to Illinois for bottles of various elixirs of life, guaranteed to put health, strength, youth, and brains into anything. She also made foolish and elaborate efforts to trick the daughter into eating more at meals, or between meals, without avail. At this juncture a very capable person took matters in hand. Dr. Peter Carson, family physician and devoted friend, was consulted; his views were clear and convincing: Belle must give up the office for a year at least; she needed fresh air and sun; the more the better. Every girl in the Black Hills rides as a matter of course, and Belle was at home on a broncho; but now it must be, not an occasional run, but a daily ride in the hills—off for miles, till the vital forces had renewed their strength.

For a month or more Belle rode and browned in the sun. The colour came again to her cheeks, and zest to her life; and there also came a strong desire to be in a business of her own. But it must be something out of doors; it must be something of little capital; and something a woman could do. Belle studied her problem with great care and presently there began to arrive at the post office sundry catalogues of extraordinary hens with unbelievable records as producers of eggs and of rapid-raising broilers. The result was that the acre of ground behind the store was cut up into poultry runs for the various strains of stock that Belle decided on and that spring Belle launched out on her career as a poultry farmer. There were Leghorns and

Houdans for eggs, and Brahmas in another yard for mothers. Four things conspired to make her venture a success. She was the only one in Cedar Mountain with thoroughbred poultry, so there was a large demand for high-class eggs for setting. The eggs that for table use brought fifty cents a dozen were worth two dollars and a half a dozen for hatching. Her store training had taught her to watch the market reports in the papers, which arrived twice a week, and her college training taught her to study hen hygiene. Last but not least, she got their food for nothing.

On closing her books that autumn Belle found that on her investment of $250 capital borrowed from her father, she had cleared $250, and had all the capital to render back intact. She realized that while it was possible to make 100 per cent, on small capital, the rate decreased rapidly as the capital increased. She estimated that ten times as much capital would only produce about 25 per cent, because the possibility of personal management of every hen and every detail would grow proportionately smaller, and it was this personal touch which counted. Next, the sovereign advantages of grass range and table scraps must diminish with each additional hen; and if she had paid herself an adequate salary the profit would have been wiped out. Last, and perhaps the most important to her, she was absolutely tied to the farm. She could not be away one week without suffering loss. It was with ill-concealed admiration that her father listened to a summary of these conclusions; later, with the remarkable common sense that characterized most of her ways, Belle seized a chance to sell out and lodge her money in the local bank. But the venture had been a success in two respects. It had helped her to health and it had given her business experience and confidence.

The winter was now on, and Belle's outdoor activities were somewhat circumscribed, for there is a real winter in the Black Hills. But she was in robust health again and she turned her energies more and more to church work. She was depended on to get up the "sociables," to plan the entertainments, to invent new and happy games that would take them as near as they dared go in the direction of dance and stage without actually outraging the old-fashioned Methodist conscience by getting there. It was Belle who entirely refurnished the parsonage in one harmonious style by copying a mission chair and table from a picture, and then inviting each of the boys to make a like piece, and each of the girls to make a "drape" to match it. It was a sort of Noah's Ark trick, this gathering in of things in pairs, but it succeeded originally—the ark was full—and it succeeded now, for the parsonage was full; and it will always succeed, for it is built on the old fundamental pairing instinct.

Belle also imported and put in practical working the idea of a daily school 'bus, which gathered up the twenty-odd children for ten miles along the winter road and brought them on a huge hay rack to the Cedar Mountain School in the morning, and took them back at night to their homes. But in all these multiplied activities there was a secret dissatisfaction. She felt that she was a mere hanger-on of the church, a sort of pet cat to the parson's wife. She was not developing herself independently, and she began secretly to outline a scheme which meant nothing less than leaving home to take some sort of position on the west coast. She had no fear for her success, but she was restrained by two things: the question of health in case she could not find an outdoor enterprise, and the sorrow her parents would feel over her—to their thinking, unnecessary—departure.

For some time both in her school and church work Belle had been much associated with John Lowe, the schoolteacher. He was considered a well-meaning person, a dozen years older than herself, and had certain pleasing qualities, a suave manner—almost too suave—and a readiness of speech. He was fairly well educated, a good worker, a member of the church, and had no obvious bad habits. His history was not known; in fact, no one's history was known in those days of beginnings. Every one had to be taken as he was found and often on his own statement.

Lowe soon became a devoted admirer of Belle; and Mrs. Boyd, seeing a chance to beguile her daughter into settling down, did all she could to bring them together, never losing a chance of praising Jack. He was just what Belle needed as an executive help to realize much that she had planned. As a public reciter he had some little prominence; as a schoolteacher he was just a step nearer the world of brains than were the other possible men in town, and by that much more acceptable; and the inevitable result of propinquity was reached. The engagement of Belle Boyd and Jack Lowe was announced.

There was no ardent love-making on either side, and sometimes Belle, when left alone, would wonder why she was not more elated each time she heard him coming; rather, she seemed to feel weighted by the attachment. She reproached herself for this and as she strove to reach a more satisfactory state of mind she found herself thinking with a sigh of that free career she had planned in the business world. Mrs. Boyd's maternal hopes were too nearly realized to leave her with any discernment and Belle's father was too much wrapped up in business and small politics, to see even the mountains that were beyond his back yard; but another frequent visitor at the house was gifted with better eyes and more knowledge of the world.

Dr. Carson had never felt attracted toward Lowe. Instinctively he disliked him. He knew at the beginning that the teacher was much older than he admitted. The facts that the Boyds were well-to-do and that Belle was their only child offered, in his frame of mind, a suggestive sidelight. There were two other things that to Carson seemed important: one, that Lowe had rather obviously avoided any reference to his previous place of residence; the other that at one of the sociables he had amused them all by some exceedingly clever sleight-of-hand tricks with cards—not playing-cards, of course—they were unmentionable—but with a few business cards marked in a special way. Carson was sure he knew in what school such manual dexterity had been acquired.

The doubts in Belle's mind had not yet taken definite form when a new and unpleasant circumstance obtruded. More than once lately Lowe had come to the house carrying the unmistakable odour of drink about him. It was smothered with cloves and peppermint, but still discoverable. Belle's ideas were not narrow, but this thing shocked and disgusted her, chiefly because Lowe had repeatedly and voluntarily avowed himself as flatly opposed to it. She was thus drifting along in perplexity, taking the trail that her instincts said was not her trail, ever prompted to cut across to the other fork which meant developing herself, and always restrained by the fear of breaking with her people, when in the spring of that year the local press announced the coming to Cedar Mountain of the Rev. James Hartigan. And on the day after her meeting with him and their unexpected adventure with the runaway, the parson's wife gave a tea to introduce the young man to the congregation.

Jim's eyes met hers the moment she entered Jebb's parlour. His greeting was a joyous one and Belle felt the colour mount in her cheeks as Hartigan drew her aside to talk. There was something very stimulating about him, she found—a thrill in his voice, his eyes, and his presence that she had never experienced with Lowe.

A little later, Lowe himself arrived. Belle, as she turned to greet him, got an unpleasant shock to note the contrast between the frank, boyish face of the curly-haired giant and the thin features and restless eyes of the man she had promised to marry. Her conscience smote her for disloyalty; but in her heart she was not satisfied. Vague, unspoken, half-realized criticisms of past months rose to fill her with disquiet. A cumulative unhappiness in her association with Lowe took possession of her. And, as she watched with a little thrill the meeting between Jack and the Preacher, she read plainly on the face of her fiancé the disapproval that even his practised art could not conceal. For her, the meeting was portentous; it marked a turning-point; and as she thought of it later she took a slightly guilty pleasure in the fact that without a clash of words there was at once a clash of personalities, and that the Preacher had dominated the scene.

CHAPTER XIII

PREACHER JIM'S FIRST SERMON

The Sunday on which Jim first appeared in the pulpit will long be remembered in Cedar Mountain. The "grapevine telegraph" had been working hard so that all the world of that region had heard of the new preacher, and curiosity to see him was responsible, more than anything else, for a church filled with critical folk.

The sight of all the riot and wickedness about the Black Hills, the mad striving after sudden gold, and the total lack of real joy in its use after getting it, suggested to Jim a sermon founded on the proverb: "Better is a dinner of herbs and contentment therewith, etc...." But, for once in his life, Hartigan was a little abashed by the situation and, reciting the verses from memory, he managed to get them mixed and rendered them thus: "Better is a stalled ox and contentment therewith than a dinner of herbs with a brawling woman." It made an unexpected hit. Realizing his blunder, he smiled broadly and added:

"Well, if you have any doubts about Solomon's statement, you can have none whatever about mine."

He then went on to preach a most extraordinary discourse in which fun, wit, and humour were occasionally interspersed with allusions to the subject matter. No arguments, no logic, were discoverable; but there were plenty of amusing illustrations, a good deal that might better have been left out, and the audience was highly amused though wholly unedified.

"And how did ye like my sermon?" was the hearty greeting Hartigan gave Belle Boyd next day, as they met on the boardwalk of Main Street. She glanced up with a faint flush, looked down, then meeting his eyes squarely she said:

"Some parts I liked, but much of it I did not."

This was an unexpected reply; Jim had quite looked for a burst of admiration. In answer to his questions, Belle gave an analysis of the sermon, as they walked along, pointing out the clay and the gold, and the total lack of form.

His attitude, at first, had been superior and his tone frivolous. For, strange to say, the gallantry so strong in his Irish blood is ever mixed with, or maybe it is a mere mark of belief in, the superiority of the male. But, before Belle had finished two things had happened—he was much less sure of his sermon and was a little in awe of her. There could be no doubt that she was right. Yes, those two stories would have been better left out; an early paragraph should have been at the end, for it was the summing up; and the illogical conclusion, which had no promise in anything he said before, was weak, to say the least. Hartigan felt much as he used to feel when his mother had called him into a detailed account of some doubtful conduct.

"What are you going to give us next time?" inquired Belle.

"I thought of beginning a series of sermons on the bad habits of the congregation—swearing, drinking, gambling, horse-racing, smoking, and spitting. Last Sunday, right by the door in church, two men were smoking their pipes and spitting on the floor. It seems to me that Revelations XI:2 is about the right medicine for such conduct. This is the text: 'And he opened the bottomless pit and there arose a smoke out of the pit,' Or Psalms XXXVII:20: 'The wicked shall perish ... into smoke shall they consume away,' Then there is a passage in Jeremiah VII:30: 'They have set their abominations in the house which is called by my name to pollute it,' With these I think we have a good scaffolding to build on."

Belle looked puzzled and said nothing. Hartigan was waiting for her approval. He wanted it.

"What do you think?" he asked, a decided note of anxiety creeping into his question.

"I would not do it," was the answer.

"Why not?" said Jim instantly on the defensive. "Don't they need it, and aren't they awfully weak on these things?"

"Yes, they are," said Belle, "but———"

"But what?"

"Mr. Hartigan," she replied as she stopped at her gate, "if you wanted a rich man to help a poor widow, and went to him saying: 'You miserable old skinflint, I know you are as greedy as the pit, but I demand it as a human right that you help this poor woman out of your ill-gotten abundance,' how much are you going to get? Nothing at all; and the truer it is the less your chance. On the other hand, if you go to him and say: 'Mr. Dives, you are one of the few men in town who have the power to help this woman. I know she is well worthy of help, for she's having a hard struggle. Now, you had a struggle once and know what that means. It made a keen, successful business man of you; but I know you are kind-hearted and generous and that all you want is to be sure that the case is genuine. Well, I can assure you it is. Will you not help her with the rent till strawberry time, when she expects to get a little money?' That way you will get something. He *has* to become generous when you *say* he is; and I think that you will get more out of these people if you assume that they are something good. Later, when they know you better, you can put them right on their faults."

Hartigan stared at her with frankly admiring eyes.

"Well," he said, "you surely have the level head. You are right and I will do as you say. But I wonder why you take all this trouble with me?"

Flushed and happy over her victory and very deeply moved by the look she had seen on Jim's face, Belle realized the full meaning of her success and took a woman's pride in the fact that this great, powerful, self-confident, gifted man should in two short encounters completely change about and defer to her judgment. There was a moment's silence in which she sought to get her voice under control. Then she added:

"Will you let me know what you decide to preach on?"

"I will," said Jim, his eyes still on her face.

They had been standing at the door of the Boyd home. In that instant of his dependence upon her Belle had been conscious of a very sweet and precious bond between them. Without turning toward him, she touched his arm lightly with her hand and went into the house.

Jim's first effort had not encouraged Dr. Jebb to transfer much of the pulpit service to the young man. Subsequently, he had a long talk with him and pointed out some of the defects as Belle had done; also a number of lapses which, though purely academic, he considered of prime importance. Thus, more than a month elapsed before Jim was again called to fill the pulpit.

Meanwhile, he had had many experiences of value in his widespread congregation, among them the raising of a charitable fund for an unfortunate neighbour, and he had become well acquainted with Jack Shives, the blacksmith, a singular mixture of brusqueness and kindness. Shives was a good citizen who did good work at the forge, but he was utterly opposed to all creeds and churches. He made it a point to set all the weight of his solid character against these, as well as the power of his biting tongue.

As soon as Dr. Jebb asked him to take the pulpit, Jim called on Belle.

"Well, I'm to have another chance," he said, as with one hand he lifted an armchair that Dr. Jebb could not have moved at all.

"Good," said she. "What is the subject to be?"

"I have three subjects I wish to treat," he began; "one, foreign missions; the next is the revised version of the New Testament; and the last is the secularizing influence of church clubs. Which do you say?"

Belle looked serious. At length she said:

"Maybe you can make something constructive out of these ideas. It depends on how you handle them; but they seem to me far-off and doubtful."

He looked the disappointment he felt and waited for her to go on.

"What was the *good* thing that struck you most when you came among us?"

Hartigan gazed through the window at the round top of Cedar Mountain, then at the frank face of the slim girl, and with a little outburst of his real nature he cried:

"Bejabers, it was the kind way you all received me."

"All right, then; why not make *that* your subject for the next sermon? Let these people know that you think they are kind, and that they make you feel it, and they will become kinder. Then, when you are established in their hearts, you can talk about their faults. That will come later. Since we must find a scripture text to hang your talk on, let's take Ephesians IV:32: 'Be ye kind one to another, tender hearted, forgiving one another even as God for Christ's sake hath forgiven you.'"

The sermon was duly outlined. The outline was brought for Belle to hear. She was keenly interested because in some sense she was on trial; and under the stimulating influence of her attention, Jim expanded the outline to a whole sermon and preached it all to Belle then and there. It was full of eloquent passages and wholesome lessons, but it was far too long, as Belle insisted; and again there was a readjustment with the result that on the following Sunday Hartigan delivered a brilliant sermon on Kindness, the kindness he had received, the kindness that is the heart of all true religion. The quaint humour, the vivid presentation, and the every-day applications were new and true notes to that congregation. It shocked some of the old-fashioned type, but the reality it gave to religion was not lost, and the human interest and sincerity of it held every mind. It cannot be given in full, but the opening passages will illustrate Jim's theme and his method. After reading the parable of the Good Samaritan, he said:

"Now, friends, I have selected the story of the Good Samaritan for a starting point; and it's a good one, even if I never get back to it through the whole length of the sermon.

"I want you to understand that here was a man who was a kind of outcast; he didn't go to church and he didn't know or care a cent about doctrines or creeds; his people were notorious for wine drinking so that it's more than likely he was often drunk, and it's ten to one he swore every time he got mad. But he was ready to lend a helping hand to *anybody* that had need of him.

"And I want you to note that the men who would not do a finger's tap to help were a holy priest with a big salary and a highly respectable church member in training for the ministry. So you see, the Lord selected these three to illustrate this point then, now, and for all time, that he had nothing but contempt for the coldblooded holy-rollers and that the ignorant outcast infidel was his sort because he had a kind heart.

"Now, friends, we've all three kinds right with us all the time. Though I don't go much on mincing words, I won't specify the priest nor the Levite right here in Cedar Mountain; but I will make mention of the Good Samaritan.

"Ye see, it wasn't exactly a case of being held up by robbers; but we had to raise enough to get the Hanky family out of their troubles when Jack Hanky broke his arm, his leg, his buggy, and his bank account all on one and the same unlucky day; and it was my job to raise the wind to help him weather the storm. Well, I went about as you all know, and got a little here and a little there; then squeezed out a little more from some of the dry sponges, and still was short. So I went to Jack Shives and he contributed more than any one else; and then, on top of that, he put Hanky's buggy in good shape without a cent of pay, and went down night after night to sit at his bedside and help him pass the long hours away.

"Now the fact is, Jack Shives and I have had many a fight on religious questions. He swears and drinks all he wants to, which I'm bound to say isn't much. He jokes about the church and the preacher and every one that goes to church. He pokes fun at the hymn book and laughs at the Bible and every one that tries to follow it word for word. Jack thinks he's all kinds of an infidel; but he isn't. I have a notion of my own that he's a better Christian than he allows, better than a good many church members I could name. In fact, I believe if the Lord Jesus were to get off at Cedar Mountain from to-morrow's noon train, the first thing he would do would be to go to the post office and say: 'Can you tell me where Jack Shives, the blacksmith, lives? He's a particular friend of mine, he's done a lot of little odd jobs for me and I guess I'll put up at his house while I'm in Cedar Mountain.'"

And so he talked for the allotted time, translating the age-old truth into terms of to-day and personal application. A few of the older folk thought he treated some very serious subjects too lightly; they preferred the sing-song tone so long associated with scripture texts. Others had their doubts as to Jim's theology. His eulogy of the blacksmith was a little too impulsive, but none had any question of the thrilling human interest of his words and the completeness of his hold on every one's attention. It was wholesome, if not orthodox; it drove home with conviction; it made them laugh and cry; and it was a masterpiece of the simple eloquence that was so much his gift and of the humour that was the birthright of his race.

From that day forth the doubtful impressions created by Hartigan's first appearance in the pulpit were wiped out and he was reckoned as a new and very potent force in the community.

CHAPTER XIV

THE LURE OF THE SADDLE

One of the needs that Hartigan very soon became aware of in his far-flung pastoral work was that of a good saddle horse. An income of three hundred dollars a year will not maintain very much in the way of a stable, but a horse had to be got, and the idea of looking for one was exceedingly pleasant to him. It needed but the sight and smell of the horse leathers to rouse the old passion bred and fostered in Downey's stable. He loved the saddle, he knew horses as few men did, and had he been ninety pounds lighter he would have made a famous jockey.

For many days he was able to put his mind on nothing else. He eagerly took every chance to visit likely stock; he was never so happy as when he was astride of some mettlesome animal, interpreting its moods as only the born horseman can do, and drawing on the reserves of strength which are closed to all but the expert rider. He responded in every fibre of his great physique to the zest of this renewed experience of a loved and lost stable life, and yet the very passion of his enjoyment appalled him at times for it seemed to be in some sense a disloyalty to the new life he had taken up and to draw him away from it.

In those days there were motley bands of immigrants crossing the plains from the East, making for the Black Hills as an island of promise in the great open sea, and one of these wanderers from far-off Illinois arrived one evening with the usual outfit of prairie schooner, oxen, milch cow, saddle horses, dogs, and children. Calamity had overtaken the caravan. The mother had died; the father was disgusted with the country and everything in it; and his one idea was to sell his outfit and get the children back East, back to school and granny. At the auction, the cattle brought good prices, but no one wanted the horses. They were gaunt and weary, saddle-and-spur-galled; one young and the other past middle life. It was the young horse that caught Hartigan's eye. It was rising three, a well-built skeleton, but with a readiness to look alert, a full mane and tail, and a glint of gold on the coat that had a meaning and a message for the horse-wise. The auctioneer was struggling to raise a bid.

"Will any one bid on this fine young colt? All he needs is oats, and a few other things."

A laugh went up, which was just what the auctioneer wanted, for merriment is essential to a successful sale.

"Here now, boys, who will start him at five dollars? And him worth a hundred."

It was too much for Hartigan. He raised his finger to the auctioneer.

"There, now, there's a preacher that knows a horse," he prattled away, but no second offer came, and the colt was knocked down to Hartigan for five greasy dollars.

"A good clean-down is worth a bushel of oats to a horse," is old stable wisdom, "and a deal cheaper," as Hartigan added. Within the hour Blazing Star, as the new owner named him from the star blaze in his forehead, was rubbed and curry-combed as probably he never had been in his life before. He was fed with a little grain and an abundance of prairie hay, his wounds were painted with iodine and his mane was plaited. He was handled from forelock to fetlock and rubbed and massaged like a prizefighter who is out for mighty stakes.

"They are just like humans," Hartigan remarked to the "perchers" at Shives's blacksmith shop. "All they need is kindness and common sense."

Before a month had gone, Hartigan was offered fifty dollars for the colt; and this in a land where twenty-five dollars is the usual price for a saddle horse. In truth, no one would have recognized this fine, spirited young horse as the sorry jade that landed in the town a short four weeks before. But Hartigan, who had a trainer's eye, said to Shives and the "perchers":

"Wait for two months and then you will see something."

And they did. They saw the young Achilles riding down the street on the wonderful chosen steed of all the herd. There were perfectly balanced life and power in every move of both, the eagerness to up and do, the grace of consummate animalism. They had seen many a fine man on a noble horse, but never before had they beheld a picture so satisfying to both eye and heart as that of the Preacher on his five-dollar steed.

Five miles from Cedar Mountain is Fort Ryan and to the south of it a plain, where every year in the first week of July the Indians gather in their tepees and the whites in tents and prairie schooners for a sort of fair, in which are many kinds of sin on the largest scale. Herds of horses are there, and racing is a favourite sport. It was here on the Fourth of July that an Indian on a rough-looking buckskin pony had won, over all the field that year, a purse containing five hundred dollars. The whites, who had their racers set at naught, were ready for almost any scheme that promised them revenge, and they made an ill-favoured and sulky lot as they sat on the shady side of the movable saloon that lingered still on the racing plain. Their eyes were pinched at the corners with gazing at the sunlight, and their ragged beards were like autumn grass. A horseman appeared in the distance, and ambled toward them. This was a common enough sight, but the easy pace was pleasing to the eye, and when he drew near these men of the saddle found a horseman's pleasure in the clean-limbed steed so easily ridden.

"Guess it's the new preacher," said one with a laugh. "He's come down from Cedar Mountain to save us from Hell, as if Hell could be any worse than this."

Hartigan drew up to inquire the direction to a certain cabin and when he learned the way he rode on.

"Looks to me like he would have made a cowboy, if they had ketched him young."

"Do you see that horse? Ain't there some blood there?"

"Yes, there is," said Long Bill, "and it strikes me it is worth following up. Let's have another look."

The group sauntered to where the Preacher was making a call and one of them began:

"Say, mister, that's quite a horse you've got there; want to sell him?"

"No."

"Looks like a speeder."

"Yes, there's nothing in Cedar Mountain to touch him."

"Say, mister," said cattleman Kyle, "if he's a winner, here's your chance to roll up a wad."

Hartigan stared and waited. The cult of the horse is very ancient, but its ways are ever modern.

"You say he's a great speeder; will you try him against Kyle's horse?" said Long Bill.

Jim looked a rebuff and shook his head.

"Oh, just a friendly race," the man went on; "Kyle thinks he has the best American horse in town." And as various members of the party looked more critically at Blazing Star and felt his limbs they became more insistent.

When Jim had joined the Church, horse-racing was one of the deadly sins he had abjured. So while he refused to enter a race, he was easily persuaded to ride his horse against Kyle's for a friendly mile. Whether begun as a race or not, it was in deadly earnest after the first fifty yards and it proved just what they needed to know: that Kyle's horse, which had been a good second best with the Indian, was a poor second in the race with Blazing Star. With this essential information, Kyle asked if he could hire Hartigan's horse for a brush with the Indian.

Hartigan went through a most painful struggle with his conscience. But clearly "this was not a regular race." It was "just a sort of speed test with an Indian pony like the one he had had with Kyle." He was not going to ride in it. He would only rent his horse for wages. "Sure, every one hires out his horse when he has a good one." So Blazing Star was hired out to Kyle, and a new though unimportant race was arranged, for a stake, otherwise the Indian would not have taken the trouble to ride. The Red-men's black eyes looked keenly on as he measured the new horse. Then the unexpected happened. Blazing Star was not accustomed to the new jockey, the gentle ways that had fostered his speed were lacking. The rider's idea was whip and spur and go from the start. The horse got "rattled" and the Indian pony won. The defeat stirred Hartigan to a rage such as he had not experienced in months. The unrest of his conscience over the affair, coupled with his contempt and fury at the bad horsemanship of the rider, set loose from his tongue a lurid torrent blended of Links, Scripture, and Black Hills.

"Here, you jelly-backed cowpuncher, let me show you how to ride. Will you ride again?" he shouted to the Indian, as the latter put the roll of bills in his tobacco pouch.

The Indian shook his head.

"I will put that up twenty-five dollars to nothing," and Hartigan held up the twenty-five dollars he had received as hire for his horse. Again the Indian shook his head. "I'll give you that if you'll ride." Jim held up a ten, "and double it if you win."

With a gesture, the Indian consented, received the bill, and put it with the rest. They rode to the starting post, were unceremoniously started, and Hartigan showed how much a man could do for a horse. In spite of his rider's great weight that splendid beast responded to every word, and when on the home run Hartigan used the quirt, Blazing Star seemed to know it was merely a signal, not an insulting urge, and let himself go. The Indian pony, too, was doing his utmost, but Blazing Star swept past his opponent and led at the finish by more than a length; the race was won; and Hartigan wakened up as a man out of a dream to face the awful fact that he, a minister of the gospel, had not only ridden in a horse race, but had gambled on the same.

CHAPTER XV

PAT BYLOW'S SPREE

At the time of the incidents at Fort Ryan, Belle was away on a visit to Deadwood. Otherwise, Hartigan would surely have consulted her and profited by her calmer judgment in the matter of the race. As it was, his torturing sense of moral iniquity led him to preach a sermon in which he poured forth all the intensity of his nature. Quietly to drop the subject was not his way; he knew that every one was talking about it, so nothing would do but a public denunciation of himself, and all that followed the race track.

The text he chose was: "My wounds stink, and are corrupt, because of my foolishness" (Psalms XXXVIII:5). Jim's thought was that once the sinner is saved, all his sins become peculiarly and especially repugnant to him. They acquire nothing less than a stench in his nostrils, and henceforth are as repellent as once they were attractive, no matter what they may be; and he enumerated drunkenness, swearing, gambling, and horse-racing. At mention of the last a smile spread over the faces of the congregation. He noted it at once, and said:

"Yes, I know what you are thinking. You are wondering how I came to ride my horse in a race at Fort Ryan. Well, it was the devil laid a snare for me, and I fell in. But this I will say: I promise you I will never do the like again, and if each of you will stand up now and give me the same promise about your own particular besetting sin, then I'll feel that we have made a great gain, and I will be glad I rode that race after all."

In this land of the horse no one was long inclined to take the matter seriously. A nature so buoyant as his could not long be downcast, and Hartigan's sense of sin for his part in the race was soon put behind him. Then happened an incident that gave him a chance to score a triumph.

In a remote part of the valley some five miles back of Cedar Mountain was Bylow's Corner, a group of three or four houses near the road, the log cabins of homesteaders. These men had, indeed, few pleasures in life. Their highest notion of joy was a spree; and every month or two they would import a keg of liquor, generally of a quality unfit for human consumption. The word had been passed around that Pat Bylow had got a keg of the "real stuff," and the rest of the Corner assembled on a certain Saturday night for an orgy, which it was expected would last about two days. Word of it reached Hartigan, too, and he decided that here was a glorious opportunity to save bodies and souls at once. Without consulting any one he mounted

Blazing Star, and in half an hour was at the Corner. Tying his horse to a tree, he went to the house that was the known meeting place. There were lights in the window and boisterous noises issuing forth. At the door he stopped and listened; rough voices were grumbling; there was an occasional curse, a laugh, then a woman speaking shrilly; a minute's silence, during which the sweet song of a night bird was heard in the dark bushes by the stream, whereupon a hoarse, brutalized voice shouted:

"Oh, hurry up and start that bung, you act like a schoolgirl."

The Preacher knocked. There was no answer. He knocked again and much louder. There was a moment's silence. Then a heavy voice:

"Who's there?"

"It's me," was the unhelpful reply.

A man moved to the door again demanding:

"Who's there?"

"It's a friend who wants to join you."

There was some discussion, then the door was cautiously opened. The man inside got a glimpse of the tall form of the Preacher, let off a savage snarl and oath, and attempted to slam the door. But he was not quick enough; the Preacher got his foot in and pushed irresistibly. There were curses from within and others came to help. But the Preacher was too much for them; the door went back with a clatter and he stood in the middle of the room. The rude log cabin held five men, three women, and a table on which was a small keg of whiskey and some glasses. The keg had not yet been opened, and the glasses were empty.

"What do you want here?" growled the biggest of the men, advancing threateningly.

"Sure, I am here to spill that accursed stuff on the ground and hold a prayer meeting in the hopes of saving your souls," was the answer.

"Get to h—l out of this and mind your own business," he said, fingering an ugly knife he had snatched from the table.

Hartigan did not move. As the big brute edged in, not at all quickly, for the fight was scarcely yet on, Hartigan landed a swift football drop kick under the hand that held the knife. The weapon was dashed up to the ceiling and stuck shivering in the logs, while its owner stumbled and fell with a growl of pain, one hand hanging helpless. Two other men rushed to the attack. They had no weapons, and the Preacher man[oe]uvred to take them singly.

With two chops and an undercut he laid them on their backs, and the remaining men refrained from declaring war.

"Sure now," said the Preacher, as he looked calmly around, "I regret to have the meeting open so unrestful, when it was my intention to start it with a prayer, followed by a hymn with all of you joining in. But you seemed to want it this way and, of course, I had to humour you. Now I will begin by pouring out a drink offering on the altar of God."

He stepped toward the keg. It was unopened. He raised it in his hands and dashed it down on the floor. It bounded up unhurt. Realizing his purpose for the first time, the men gave vent to savage oaths backed by an assertion of property rights. Then, seeing that he was undeterred, they set upon him with a rush.

Jim, it must be confessed, found a new joy in that new attack. It gave him a chance to work off his superabundant energy. The confined space of the cabin was in his favour. He blocked all attempts to encompass him, while his mighty arms did terrific execution, and when the finish came it showed the would-be revellers lying around in various positions eloquent of defeat.

"Sure, it's mighty sorry I am, but I have to tend to my job."

Going to the fireplace, and picking up one of the bricks used to support the logs, he smashed in the head of the keg and spilled the odorous contents on the floor. The final splash he threw toward the fire, expecting to see it blaze into a blue flame, but it acted as water and the room was filled with an evil stench. The Preacher knew what it meant; his contemptuous "Humph!" expressed it all.

"Where are you going?" he demanded, as the tallest of the ruffians moved to the door.

"You mind your own business. I am going home," was the answer.

"Come back and join us, we're going to have a prayer meeting," and Jim stepped over to the door.

"Now get down on your knees, all of ye," and he himself kneeled. The little man and two of the women followed his example.

"Get down on your knees!" the Preacher thundered to those standing. The big fellow had got a stick of firewood for a weapon and, despite his crippled right hand, was disposed to fight.

"Oh, ho! shillelah play," chuckled Hartigan, "that's an ould, ould game with me."

He rose and picked up a leg of the table broken off during the struggle. It was not a heavy club, but it was in skilful hands. There is one move of the shillelah that the best experts have trouble to parry, that is the direct thrust. The slash right and the slash left, the overhead or the undercut have a simple answer; but the end-on straight thrust is baffling. Jim knew this of old, and a moment later the big woodsman was on the floor with a bloody nose, a sense of shock, and a disposition to surrender.

"Now come, every one of ye, and join in our prayer meeting. Come on," he beckoned to the other two, "or it will be me duty to knock sense into ye."

And so he gathered that graceless group around him. Kneeling in their midst, he prayed for help to make them see that he wanted to be their friend, that he was acting for their interests, that he knew as well as they did the hankering for drink.

"O Lord, you know. And I know that anyway that stuff was not whiskey at all, at all; that it would not burn in the fire, and I'll bet it would freeze if it were put out of doors"; and having contributed these expert remarks, he closed with, "Amen."

"And now we will sing a hymn," and he led them in "Come to Jesus." But it was not a success, so he fell back on the praying, which was his specialty, and more than once his congregation joined in with an "amen." Sulky Big Pat had to be threatened again, for he was of fighting stock; but the prayer meeting closed without further hostilities and the orgy had been made physically impossible. As he rose, Hartigan said in his inimitable way:

"Now, friends, I want to apologize to you all for seeming uncivil, but there are times when a man has to be a little abrupt, and if I have hurt your feelings or annoyed you in any way I am very sorry for it, because I'd rather be friends. Let's shake hands before I leave, and I will be glad to see any of you in church."

Then a strange thing happened. The little man had shaken hands effusively, the big one sulkily, but there was one there who took the Preacher's hand warmly and in a husky voice said:

"Mr. Hartigan, I want you to know you have made me think different. I am coming to church. I know you are right." Then turning to a woman by his side: "This is my wife—she feels as I do."

"Thank you for coming to-night," said the woman. "You *will* pray for us, won't you? We will try; only it is terribly hard, once you have taken on the habit."

"Sure, it's myself that knows it," said Hartigan. "I've been through it all, I tell you."

There was a brotherly warmth in the Preacher's handclasp and in his words as he turned to go out in the calm and beautiful blue night. The Black Hills' coyotes howled and Blazing Star whinnied a mild remonstrance at the long desertion. The Preacher mounted and as he swung lightly down the wagon trail, he had a sense of joy, of triumph, of uplift that had seldom been his. Here for the first time he had put his great physical strength to the service of the new life. It was a consecration, so to speak, of his bodily powers. And overtopping this was another happiness, which, he was just beginning to realize, completely filled his thoughts these days: the prospect of crowning each day's adventures by telling them all to Belle.

CHAPTER XVI

THE NEW INSURANCE AGENTS

Woman's suffrage was a disturbing question in the West of the '80's and it had not by any means passed Cedar Mountain by. There was more than one fiery dispute among the "perchers" of Shives's shop, where Jim was very fond of dropping in. Indeed the smithy was the public forum of the town.

Hartigan had very strong views, of the oldest and most conservative type, on the sphere of woman—notwithstanding the fact that his mother had been the capable leader of men. He did not say much about this; but he assumed that the absence of his father was the sole cause of his mother's dominance. He was fond of quoting St. Paul: "Let your women keep silence in the churches ... it is a shame for women to speak in the church" (I Cor. XIV:34-35), and from this he argued that silence was woman's only duty in all public matters of administration, because it accorded with her limitations.

Shives, being twice as old, was much less certain. He could cite Cleopatra, Catherine of Russia, Catherine de' Medici, and other familiar names to prove the woman's power; to which Hartigan replied:

"And a fine moral lot they were! Was ever power put to more devilish use?"

This was a jibe and not an answer. But it caused a laugh, and that always counts in debate. Then, with singular blindness to the fact that he himself was at the time being guided by a certain young woman, Jim issued his challenge:

"If you can show me a couple that started fair and square together on equal footing and didn't end with the man as head and leader in everything to do with fighting the battle of life, I'll give in—I'm licked."

Two mornings later, Dr. Carson was standing outside his office door, when he heard a quick stride on the boardwalk and the gay voice of the Preacher singing "Roy's Wife of Aldivallock."

"The top of the morning to ye, Doc," was his cheery greeting; and the doctor answered:

"Say, Jim, come here. I've got a good one for you. This is a brand-new one." They walked down the boardwalk to the place where most of the offices were and there read on a newly placed signboard the legend:

"John and Hannah Higginbotham, Insurance Agents."

"How is that?" said Carson, as he lit a cigar.

"Well, I'll be—surprised," was the answer.

As Jim looked in astonishment the door was opened and a dapper little man with a fuzzy red beard appeared.

"Good morning, gentlemen, good morning!" he said, in a perfectly good Yankee twang. "Can I do anything for you to-day in my line? Step in, gentlemen; I'm John Higginbotham." They entered and, behind the desk, sighted a stout woman of medium size, middle age, and moderately good appearance.

"Hannah, these are two of our fellow townsfolk, calling. Excuse me, gentlemen, I didn't get your names." He was enlightened and prattled on: "Oh, Reverend Hartigan and Dr. Carson. Good! Healing for the body and healing for the soul, and my healing is for the estate—happy trinity, isn't it? Sit down, gentlemen."

"Can we do anything for you in our line?" said the buxom lady behind the desk, in a strong, deep voice; and now Jim noticed for the first time her square jaw and her keen eye that brightened as she spoke.

"Not at present, thank you," said Jim. "We are merely making a neighbourly call."

"The fact is," said Dr. Carson, "the thing that stopped us this morning was your new signboard."

"There! There! I told you so; I told you it was good business," said the little man. "The first thing in commerce is to have a good article and the next is to win the attention of the public. I felt sure it was a good move."

"You've got the attention of the whole town at one stroke," said Carson. "If you have the wares to follow it up——"

"Wares! My company is The Merchants' Mutual. It is the——"

Realizing that he had injudiciously turned on a hydrant, Carson said heartily:

"Oh, yes, yes; of course; I should have known. Why, every one knows that The Merchants' Mutual is one of *the* companies. How did you come in, by rail or by the trail?"

At this point, Hannah rose and, passing out of the door, gave a momentary glimpse of a kitchen stove with pots and kettles boiling.

John smiled blandly, raised a flat hand with an oratorical gesture:

"Ah, that is an important question, and bears directly on the signboard. You see, we came from Bootlebury, Massachusetts. Hannah's father was quite a man in that town, and I worked my way up till I had a little insurance office of my own and married Hannah. Well" (he didn't say "well" and he didn't say "wall," but there isn't any in-between way to spell it aright), "if I'd got all the insurance business in Bootlebury, it would not have been horses and cushions, but I didn't get half of it, and Hannah says, 'John, I think we'd getter go out West,' for, somehow, she didn't want to stay in a place where folks said she'd had a 'come down.'

"We'd had about ten years of it, and I had just about come to her way of thinking when her dad died and left her quite well fixed. An' Hannah she had quite an eye to biz; she worked at my office desk as much as she did at the cook stove; an' now she says to me, 'Here is where we get out.'

"Every one was talking about the Black Hills then, and that was why we headed this way. Well, we figured out that the railway fares from St. Louis 'round to Sidney and north to the Hills were so much higher than the steamboat fare from St. Louis to Pierre, that we could save enough to buy a team of ponies and a buckboard at Pierre, and then cross the Plains with the settlers going in and be ahead by the value of the team, which would be needed in our country business anyhow."

"Time didn't count?" interrupted Carson.

"Not much; and we wanted to see the country."

"By George! I wish I'd been with ye," said Jim. "If only it had been a saddle trip it would have been perfect."

"Perfect!" exclaimed the little man; "I wish you could have seen us. The farther we went up that endless river of mud the worse it seemed; and when we landed at Pierre it did seem the last of all creation.

"I didn't have much heart to buy the ponies, but Hannah kept with me and never once seemed to feel discouraged. But when we crossed the river with our outfit and really set out on the blank, bleak plains, I tell ye, we felt heart-sick, sore, and lonesome—at least, I did."

At this moment Hannah came in from the kitchen and took the lead in conversation.

"Has John been giving you an outline of our policy in the matter of lapsing premiums and residuary annuities?"

"Now, Hannah," replied John, "I think that is a little too much like business for friendly callers."

"Business is always in order in the office," was Hannah's retort.

"I understand," said John, "that the Methodists are very strong in Cedar Mountain."

"Well, we think so," answered Hartigan.

"Good," said Higginbotham. "I have always felt that it was wisest to associate myself with the church that was spiritually strongest. I am not in sympathy with narrow views." He did not mention the fact that in Bootlebury he had associated himself with the Unitarians for the same reason.

A loud sizzling in the next room caused Hannah to spring up heavily and return to the kitchen.

Jim was more interested in their venturesome trip across the Plains than in reasons for doctrinal affiliation, and he steered the conversation by saying:

"How did you come out on the Plains trip?"

And John bubbled on with a mixture of fun, pathos, and frank admiration for his wife that appealed strongly to both hearers. His gift of language was copious without being varied or clever, but his homely phrases carried the thought.

"I'll not forget the morning of our journey. It was raining by the bucketfuls. 'Well,' says I, 'for a semi-arid country this is going some'; and I felt so homesick and sore, I said, 'Hannah, let's not go any farther'; and Hannah she just looked at me and said, 'See here, John, I've come out so far to go to the Black Hills and I'm going.' Then, when the weather let up a little, we started out; and, after a couple of hours we stuck in a muddy creek and were all day getting across. Next day a couple more gullies just as bad, and the rain came down till ever hole in the prairie was a pond; and I tell you I wished I'd bought a boat instead of the buckboard. And the mosquitoes, oh, my! Well, we floundered around about three days and got all our stuff wet and half spoiled. Then we found we'd missed the way and had to flounder three days back again. I tell you, I felt pretty much discouraged. Then we saw something a-coming. It turned out to be a settler going back. He said there was nothing but pond holes and bogs, the mosquitoes were awful, the boom was bust, and the Sioux on the war path. I felt pretty sick. That was a finisher; and when that man says, 'You better come back with us,' I was for going. But Hannah, she just boiled up and she says, 'John Higginbotham, if you want to go back with that bunch of chicken-hearts, you can go. I'm going to the Black Hills, if I have to go alone.' I tried to make her see it my way, but she got into the buckboard, gathered up the reins, and headed for the West. I had to get in behind as best I could. We didn't talk much. We weren't on speaking terms that day; and, at night, as we sat eating supper, it started to raining worse'n ever, and I says, 'I wish we'd gone back.'

"'I don't,' she snapped, an' we never spoke till the morning.

"Then she called me to breakfast. I tell you, I never saw such a change. The sun was up and the sky was clear. In a little while, we were out of the sloughs and had no mosquitoes. Then we got a bad shake. A band of horsemen came riding right at us. But they turned out to be U. S. cavalrymen. They put us right on the road, and told us the Indian scare was just fool talk, and had nothing back of it. After that, all went fine and in two days we were in the Hills.

"I tell you, I felt different as we stood there at our last campfire, and I says, 'Hannah, you're a wonder. You are the best of the outfit. It was your money we started on. It was your grit kept me going on when I was for quitting, and you are in every deal I make. You bet I'll let the world know we are partners.' So that's why that signboard went up. Not a bad ad I reckon, for no one sees it without taking notice; so, if there's anything in our line you need, let me know."

As Carson and Hartigan walked down the street, the doctor said: "Well, what do you think of Woman Suffrage now?"

Hartigan shrugged his big shoulders, gave a comical glance back at the signboard, and replied:

"You've got me!"

It was indeed a poser for Jim; a shock to a deep-set prejudice. Notwithstanding the fact that his mother had been a woman of power, the unquestioned and able head in a community of men, he had unconsciously clung to the old idea of woman's mental inferiority. In college he had had that notion bolstered up with Scripture texts and alleged Christian doctrine.

This was not the time or place, he felt, to discuss the principle of it, and his natural delicacy would, in any case, have kept him from a free expression; but later, in the blacksmith shop, that neutral territory of free speech, they had it out. Higginbotham was there and was ready and able to fight with Scriptural weapons. He pointed out that all the texts quoted, such as: "Wives be in subjection to your own husbands in everything, etc.," were from St. Paul, who was believed to have had a painful history in such matters; whereas, St. Peter, admittedly a far better authority, said: "Likewise, ye husbands, dwell with them, giving honour to the wife."

"Which may or may not be sound doctrine," said John, "but I know my wife brought me out here, it was her capital that set me up, she has a hand in all business, so why not say so on the signboard?"

Cedar Mountain had its fill of fun and there were many venerable jokes about "wearing the pants" and others about a spelling of "hen-pecked." "Wasn't it 'Hannah-pecked' now?" And some there were, even women, who condemned the innovation as godless; but all of these hostile comments died away when folk came to know the pair and realize how justly they were represented on the signboard: "John and Hannah Higginbotham, Insurance Agents."

CHAPTER XVII

BELLE MAKES A DECISION AND JIM EVADES ONE

It was late on Wednesday afternoon. Belle was working at the sewing machine in the back room of the Boyd home when there was a familiar knock at the front door. She was not unprepared for it and yet she dreaded this inevitable interview. Lowe had been pointedly cold for some time. He had been to the house only once in the past month and he had made it quite plain that Hartigan was the objectionable figure in the horizon. Belle realized that their relations had come to a crisis. She had not admitted frankly to herself what she would do when this talk took place, but in her heart there was not the slightest doubt.

At the sound of his step and knock she went into the parlour, closing the door into the rear room to insure some measure of privacy, and then admitted Jack. His greeting had the obvious air of a man who has been wronged. For a while, with characteristic obliquity, he talked of his school work. Belle sewed meanwhile, asking occasional questions. After a quarter of an hour of this the conversation languished. Belle was determined that he should open the subject himself, and in the awkward pause that ensued she busied herself basting up a lining for her frock. At last, clearing his throat, Lowe began:

"Belle, I've got something else to say to you."

She looked at him squarely, the direct gaze of her clear, dark eyes in striking contrast with his close-lidded, shifting glance. He went on:

"I think that you and the new preacher are going too far and it had better stop now."

"Just what do you mean, Jack? What do you accuse me of, exactly?"

From the very beginning of their friendship he had always writhed under the directness of her mental processes. He was ever for evasion, indirection; she for frank, open dealing in all things. He tried to retreat.

"I'm not accusing you of anything."

"No, but of *something*," she replied with a faint smile. "What is it?"

"There's a lot of talk about town—about you and Hartigan. It makes me a laughing stock. If we weren't engaged——"

Belle interrupted:

"That's just what I want to speak about. I've been wanting to have a frank talk with you for some time, Jack, and we may as well have it now.

"I have always liked you and you have been awfully attentive and helpful to me. I thought I was in love with you, but you know that when we had our talk a year ago, I begged you not to make an announcement and when you insisted on telling a few friends it was agreed that I was to have a year to decide finally. That was why I never wore your ring." She drew a box from her breast and held it out to him.

"We have both made a mistake, Jack. I made the worst one when I allowed you to over-persuade me a year ago; but we are not going to spoil two lives by going on with it."

Lowe's mind was not of particularly fine calibre. For some months, whenever he faced the truth, he had realized that he would never marry Belle. He was fond of her to the extent possible in a nature such as his and he was keenly alive to the financial advantage of becoming Boyd's son-in-law. His past history would not bear close inspection and latterly some of his youthful vices had come to light and to life. He knew only too well what a marriage into the Boyd family would do for his fortunes, financially and socially, and a dull rage of several weeks' nursing burned in him against Hartigan. As he took his hat to depart he was foolish enough to speak what was in his mind. He uttered a silly attack on the Preacher. It moved Belle and brought the colour to her face. His bitter comments on their own relations had not called forth any response from her, but this shaft went home, as he meant it should. She controlled herself and merely remarked:

"I would not say that; it might get to his ears."

And so he departed.

It was on that same afternoon that Hartigan had a new and, to him, terrifying experience in the dangerous world of the emotions.

He had ridden forth to make a pastoral call at the Hoomer homestead, out on the plain five miles northeast of Cedar Mountain. When first he glimpsed the house among the low log stables, there were two women in sight; when he came to the door and entered, there was but one, the mother. Half an hour later, the daughter, Lou-Jane, appeared arrayed for conquest. She was undeniably handsome, in spite of a certain coarseness that made Hartigan subtly uneasy, though he could not have told why. She was of the rare vigorous type that is said to have appeared in Ireland after many survivors of the great Armada were washed ashore on the rugged western coast. The mingling of the Irish and Spanish blood in her had resulted in black eyes, black eyebrows, and red, or golden-red hair, combined with a clear, brilliant Irish complexion. She was lively, energetic, rather clever, and tremendously taken with the new preacher.

Jim was naturally shy with women, as most big men seem to be, and the masterful Lou-Jane smote him with utter confusion. She prattled on about the tea, about the church, the Rev. Dr. Jebb, the local people, the farm, national politics, dry-farming, horses, cows and alfalfa, with the definite purpose of finding out his interests. Getting the best response on the topic of horses, she followed it up.

"You must come and see my pony. He's a beauty. I got first prize on him as girl rider at the fair last year. I'm so glad you like horses."

She laid her hand on his arm a dozen times to guide him here or there; she took his hand at last and held on, to his utter embarrassment, long after he had helped her over a fence, and looked disappointed when she got no flirtatious response. She led out her saddle pony and laughingly said:

"Here, give me a hand."

Grasping her raised foot, he lifted her with a sweep to the pony's bare back.

"My, you're strong," was her flattering comment, and she swung the hackima and loped the pony round the field and back to the stable, delighted to see in his eye a frank glow of admiration for her skill.

"Will you lift me down?" she said merrily; not that she had the least need of help, but she liked to feel those strong arms about her; and as he did so, she made herself quite unnecessarily limp and clinging.

Jim did not usually lack words, but Lou-Jane was so voluble that he was completely silenced. At the stable, where Ma Hoomer was milking, Lou-Jane delayed for a moment to whisper: "Stay here till I come for you."

Then she tripped on with Jim at her heels. As they entered the house Hartigan looked at his watch.

"Now please don't hurry," said Lou-Jane. "Ma'll be back in a few minutes, then we'll have a cup of tea. Sit here; you'll find it more comfortable," and she motioned to a sofa.

Sitting down beside him so that they were very close together and giving the archest of smiles, she said:

"I wonder if I might ask you a question."

"Why, sure," said Jim, just a little uneasy at the warmth of the tone. He had instincts, if not experience.

"Were you ever in love?" she said softly. Her arm, resting on the back of the sofa, moved accidentally and lay across his shoulder.

"Why, no—I—no—I guess not," and Hartigan turned red and uncomfortable.

"I wish you would let me be your friend," she continued. "I do like you very much, you know. I want to be your friend and I can help you in so many ways."

She leaned toward him, and Jim, being more terrified than he had ever been, murmured something inarticulate about "not being a lady's man." What he would have done to effect his escape he was never afterward able to decide. A spell of helplessness was upon him, when suddenly a heavy step was heard outside and Pa Hoomer's voice calling:

"Ma, Ma! Who's left that corral gate open?"

Lou-Jane sprang up, shook her bright hair from her flushed face, and with a hasty apology went to meet her father. The Preacher also rose with inexpressible relief, and, after a hurried farewell, he mounted and rode away.

CHAPTER XVIII

THE SECOND BYLOW SPREE

Woman to-day reverences physical prowess just as much as did her cave forebears, and she glories in the fact that her man is a strong, fighting animal, even though she recognizes the value of other gifts.

Belle was no exception to this human rule; and her eyes sparkled as she listened to Jim's story of that unusual prayer meeting held in the Bylow cabin. It was Hartigan's nature always to see the humorous side of things, and his racy description of the big man with the knife, down on his knees with one eye on the door and the other on the Preacher, was irresistible, much funnier than the real thing. It gave her a genuine thrill, a woman's pleasure in his splendid physical strength.

"Sure," he said with his faint delicious brogue, "it was distasteful to have to annoy them, but there are times when one has to do what he doesn't like."

Then he proceeded to a graphic account of the second ruffian smelling the palms of his hands and squinting through his fingers, praying for grace with his lips and for a club with his heart.

"I don't know what Dr. Jebb will say," she remarked at last, "but it seems to me we must judge by results in this case."

Hypocrite that she was! Had she not that very week denounced the opportunist doctrine that the end justifies the means? But in her delighted eyes and glowing interest Jim found a vast reward.

Dr. Jebb was human and discreet. He smiled and said little about the energetic methods of his assistant; and when next Sunday Charlie Bylow and his wife appeared in church and later joined the group on the anxious seat, he felt that the matter was happily ended as it had oddly begun.

Exactly four weeks after the strenuous prayer meeting word reached the Preacher in a rather pointed way that a keg of the "pizen juice" had arrived on the evening train and was to be carried at once to Pat Bylow's. Hartigan mounted his racer and sped thitherward at nightfall. A half mile from Pat's house was Charlie's, and at the door was the owner, apparently expecting to see him—though this circumstance did not impress Hartigan.

"Can I do anything to help?" he asked.

Hartigan shook his head, laughed lightly, and rode on. At Pat's shanty he tied his horse to the fence, stepped to the door, knocked, and, without waiting, went in. A woman's voice shrilled:

"Pat, here's that —— preacher again."

There were other voices, male and female, in the lean-to kitchen. Pat came in and glared at the intruder. There was a rising fury in his manner, but no evidence of drink.

"What do you want?" he asked.

"Well, to be frank with you," said Hartigan, "I have reason for suspecting an unhelpful indulgence is planned here for to-night, and I was hoping that I might persuade you to reconsider it beforehand. And sure we don't want to get agitated, and I don't want to use language that might sound like disapproval."

He glanced around. There was no sight of any spree in prospect. A glimpse of the kitchen showed only the preparations for an ordinary meal, and Hartigan wondered whether or not there had been a mistake. Could it be that he was the butt of a practical joke?

Pat was sulkily waiting, not knowing just what to say, when voices were heard outside and heavy steps; then the door opened and in came three men, the first carrying under his arm a barrel-shaped bundle. The presence of the Preacher was obviously disconcerting to the new-comers.

"Gimme that," growled Pat. He seized the keg and was marching off with it when Hartigan strode over in front of him.

"Hold on, Pat, let me see that."

Bylow exploded into a torrent of abusive profanity. Some of those present had been witnesses of the previous affair, and realizing what the pastoral visit might mean, they added their voices to the uproar. The language was emphatic rather than concise. The women, too, gave free rein to their tongues, but their observations reflected on their male escorts more harshly than they did on any one or anything else.

However puzzled Hartigan might be by the complexities of the female mind, the mental processes of the unlettered male were quite familiar to him and he showed his comprehension by a simple challenge.

"Now, boys, I don't want to seem thoughtless or indelicate, but I want you to know that I can lick the whole bunch of you with one hand tied behind my back and the other in a sling. Not that I have any intention of doing it, and I apologize to the ladies for mention of the subject, but it may help us to an understanding. If you have not yet gathered my meaning, I will put it simpler. I am here to stop this spree before it begins."

At this moment there was a light shuffling step outside and the door swung back revealing the small, familiar figure of Jack Lowe. A quick, meaning look and some sort of indistinguishable signal passed between Lowe and Pat, whereupon the latter at once placed the keg on the table.

"How do you do, Mr. Hartigan?" said Lowe. "I think we are here for the same purpose."

"Maybe so," said Jim dryly, "I don't know. I'm here to remove temptation from our friends, and before I leave I mean to spill that cursed stuff on the floor."

"You are right," said Lowe, "absolutely right. Pat, let me have that keg," and the schoolteacher proceeded to hammer around the bung, in the way of the orthodox bung-starter. There were murmurs and strong words, but he went on while Hartigan stood guard. The bung came loose, he lifted it out, and put his nostrils to the hole.

"That's the real stuff, just as it dropped from the quill. Smell that, Mr. Hartigan. Ain't that the real magollyon? But all the same here she goes." He tipped the keg a little and some liquor spilled out.

"See that? You get the gold? I tell you, Mr. Hartigan, that green rot-gut is poison, but you can tell when it's real by the shine. If it is whiskey it shines yellow like corn, if it is vitriol it shines green." He took a glass and filled it. "See the gold, and it smells like corn tossel." He put it to his lips. "That's what puts heart in a man, and makes him forgive his worst enemy.

"But here she goes." He spilled a little more on the ground. Then:

"You know, Mr. Hartigan, I am wholly in sympathy with this visit of yours, but I don't go as far as you do. I've been talking to Pat and he's a good sport. He realizes that you put up a fine fight that other time and that you cleaned them up single-handed. He doesn't want any further unpleasantness, but he doesn't see what right you have to keep him and his friends from using a moderate amount of this keg. Is that your idea, Pat?"

"An' what's the matter with it," growled Pat. "Why shouldn't I have one or two drinks? No man gets drunk on that."

"There you are," said Lowe, turning to Hartigan, "that's in reason. Why not have a drink all round and then talk it over?"

Hartigan was frankly puzzled by the turn of affairs. It seemed to be an offer of peace, after a fashion, but he could not fit Lowe into the scheme of things. He tried to read what was going on behind the schoolteacher's shifty eyes, but the face was a mask. At last he said:

"If these men and women," and Hartigan let his eyes travel over the faces about him, "could have stopped with one or two drinks I wouldn't be here now. Ye take one or two, but that is only the beginning. I know what drink is; I've been through it all, I tell ye, and there's no stopping if it gets the hold on ye."

"Leave it to the d—d preachers and there wouldn't be nothin' left to do in life," said Pat with a contemptuous sneer.

"Come now," said Lowe, eager to prevent hostilities. "You wouldn't object to liquor if nobody took too much, would you, Mr. Hartigan?"

"No," said Jim with a grim smile, "but I'm not to be taken in by the plausibilities of the Devil. That keg is going to be emptied."

"I'm with you to the finish there," said Lowe, "but what harm is there in filling these small glasses so"; he emptied a moderate draught into a row of tumblers set out upon the table.

"If Pat is willing to meet you half way and see this keg emptied on the floor, you wouldn't refuse a small drink with him in his own house, would you?"

Hartigan hesitated. He could not convince himself that the offer was genuine. And yet if he actually saw, with his own eyes, the keg emptied of its contents, what trick could there be? It seemed churlish to refuse. Suppose the offer were made in good faith, by not refusing that which in the male code is the sign of brotherhood and equality, he might secure an influence for good with the elder Bylow. And Lowe seemed to sense the thought, for he said, "If you take just a taste with these men now, all will come to hear you preach next Sunday. Won't you, boys?" And there was a grunt of assent. "All right; it's a bargain."

Jim was actually weighing the proposition—his old craving for drink was not by any means eradicated. The sight of the liquor and the smell roused an appetite that only an iron will had subdued. As he stood uncertain, debating, Lowe said, "Hold on; we're a glass short. Never mind, I'll find one"; and he hastened back into the lean-to kitchen and returned with a glass, which was partly concealed by his hand till it was filled with whiskey. Then he said, "If it was 'pizen juice' I wouldn't let any one touch it; but this is the simple clear whiskey, as you can prove for yourself. I wish we could send this to the hospital."

He offered it to Hartigan, who smelled it. Then Lowe said, "Well, here's to the empty keg."

The seductive liquor was potent in his nostrils, even there it had stimulation; and Hartigan, acting on a sudden impulse, drained the glass, as the others drank in silence.

There said Lowe, "You see it is the mildest of the mild; it wouldn't hurt a child." And he prattled away of truth and soberness, so that the potion should have ample freedom for its work; till the planned and subtle mixture should have time to dethrone Hartigan's reason, blind his spirit, and unhinge his will. The ancient fury in his hot young blood was all too ready to be aroused. Without a word, Lowe filled the glass again and Jim, no longer his best self, but dazed and reckless, drank with all the rest; then soon threw all restraint aside; and in the bacchanalian orgy that followed fast and filled the night, he was the stable-yard rowdy once again—loud and leading—but here let the curtain fall—draw down the thickest, blackest veil.

CHAPTER XIX

THE DAY OF RECKONING

The sun was high next day when the door of Pat Bylow's abode was opened, and a man entered. The scene that met his eyes is better undescribed, but to him it gave no shock. He came expecting to see it. In his hand he carried a tin pail. There were men and women lying about the floor. He stepped over them toward a tall form in soiled black clothes and knelt beside it. Pouring some water on a cloth he laid it on the pale forehead. The prostrate man opened his eyes and groaned.

"Mr. Hartigan," said the other. "It's me. It's Charlie Bylow. Won't you be after having a drink of water?"

Hartigan raised himself on his elbow, peered out of his bloodshot eyes, and drank eagerly. The cup was three times emptied.

"You better come over to my shanty and go to bed," said Charlie seriously. The Preacher groaned:

"Oh! God what have I done? What have I done?" He clutched his throbbing brow with both hands, as he rose and shakily followed Charlie.

"Oh! fool that I am. Oh, God! Ruined. All is ruined. I wish I were dead!" he exclaimed. "Oh! God forgive me."

As they passed the fence where Blazing Star had been hitched, Hartigan stopped and stared. Charlie said:

"It's all right, Mr. Hartigan, I took care of him. He is in the stable."

Coming to Bylow's house, Jim passed the entrance and went on to the stable. With trembling hands he opened the door and hesitated. He half expected Blazing Star to spurn and disown him. He was prepared for any and every humiliation, but the long, joyous neigh that greeted him was a shock, and a help.

"Oh! Blazing Star, if you only knew, you would not even look at me."

Charlie took the Preacher by the arm and led him to the house.

"Here, Mr. Hartigan, take off your clothes and go to bed. I will give you a wet towel for your head and, by and by, I will bring you some coffee."

"Oh! God be merciful, or strike me dead," and Jim broke down in an agony of remorse. "This is the end. All I hoped for gone. I don't want to live now."

"Mr. Hartigan, sure now I know how you feel. Ain't I been through it? But don't be after making plans that are rash when you ain't just yourself. Now go to bed and rest awhile," and his kind Irish heart was wrung as he looked on the utter degradation of the manly form before him, and the shocking disfigurement of the one-time handsome face. Charlie and his wife left Hartigan alone. They shut the door and Charlie went back to his brother's shanty to help the other victims of the orgy.

Jim tossed around uneasily, winning snatches of sleep, groaning, talking, abasing himself.

"Oh, Belle!" he moaned aloud. "Will you ever look at me again? Oh, God! And me a preacher."

Cedar Mountain was not so big but that every one knew everybody else's business; and Mary Bylow understood when she heard the name "Belle." But she didn't know just what to do. After an hour she again heard him.

"Oh! Belle, Belle, what will you say?"

Taking the hot coffee from the stove, Mrs. Bylow knocked at the door and went in.

"Take this, it will make you feel better."

She hoped he would talk, but he didn't. He only thanked her feebly. Then Charlie came back from his brother's shanty. He had remembered that, it being Sunday, the Preacher would be missed and he saddled his horse to set out for Cedar Mountain. As he left, his wife came out and said:

"While you are there, drop a hint to Belle Boyd," and Charlie nodded.

Arriving at Dr. Jebb's, Charlie explained the case to the pastor without detail:

"Sure, Mr. Hartigan had a little accident at our corner last night and sprained his ankle. My wife is nursing him, but he won't be able to preach to-day."

"Oh, dear! Oh, dear! Well, it is all right, I will take both services," and the blind and gentle old man turned to his books.

Then Bylow rode to the Boyd home. Here, he realized, was a much more difficult job. But he was determined to go into no details. It was Belle who answered his knock. Charlie began:

"My wife told me to tell you that Mr. Hartigan got hurt last night. He is at our house. He won't be in town to-day."

"What? Did he interfere in a spree?"

"Yes."

"Is he shot?"

"No."

"Is he wounded?"

"No, not exactly."

"What is the matter?"

"Only a general shakeup, he had a bad fall," and Bylow moved uneasily.

It was a simple matter to bluff a simple old clergyman, but it was another thing altogether to mislead an alert young woman. Belle knew there was something wrong—something more and different from what she had been told.

"Is the doctor with him?"

"No."

"I will get the doctor and come at once."

"No, I wouldn't; at least, not till morning."

Bylow's manner roused Belle all the more to prompt action. Seeing that all his explanations made things worse, Charlie abruptly left, mounted his broncho, and went "rockity rockity" as the pony's heels went "puff, puff" on the dusty trail around the hill and away.

The doctor was not to be found that morning and Belle found it hard to await his return. In the meantime, some strange rumour must have reached the town for in Sunday-school Belle met Eliza Lowe, the recently arrived sister of the schoolteacher. The look on her face, the gleam in her eye, were unmistakable. She had not yet learned of her brother's part in the affair. Belle found herself avoiding the sister's gaze.

As the hours passed the conviction deepened in Belle that there was something seriously wrong; she could feel it in the air. It was something more than an accident to Hartigan. There was the indefinable shadow of shame about it. The oppression became unbearable and on leaving Sunday-school, she went down to the doctor's house. He had just got in from a case near Fort Ryan and was eating a belated meal. Belle went straight to the point:

"Dr. Carson, I want you to take me at once to Bylow's Corner."

"Why?"

"There's something wrong. Mr. Hartigan is in serious trouble. I don't believe that he has fallen from his horse as they say. I want to know the truth."

Her face was pale, her mouth was set. The doctor looked keenly at her a moment and then, comprehending, said:

"All right, I will"; and in ten minutes the mudstained buckboard with a fresh horse in it was speeding over the foot of Cedar Mountain on the trail to Bylow's.

While Belle was fretting under the delay and marshalling her forces for the trip to the Corner, Hartigan lay in the quiet Bylow cabin and under the influence of cold water, coffee, and a more collected mind, gradually acquired some degree of composure. He had risen and dressed and was sadly musing on the wreck of all his life which that one fiery sip had brought about, when the thought of Blazing Star came to him. He went eagerly to the stable and as he rubbed the animal down he found help in the physical action. He hammered the currycomb on a log to clean it before putting it in the box, then gazing to the eastward along the trail that climbed around the shoulder of Cedar Mountain, he saw a buckboard approaching. In the Black Hills one identifies his visitor by his horse, and Jim recognized the Carson outfit. Sitting beside the doctor was a woman in a light-coloured dress with a red parasol raised above her. It smote him as no man's fist had ever done. He turned into the stable, put saddle and bridle on Blazing Star, swung to the seat, gave rein to the willing beast and, heading away from Cedar Mountain on the Deadwood Trail, went bounding, riding, stricken, too hard hit and shamed to meet the eyes of the woman whose praise he had come to value as the best approval he might hope to win.

The doctor's buckboard came to the door, tied up, and the two occupants went in.

"Where is your patient, Mrs. Bylow?"

The woman pointed to the bedroom door, went to it, knocked, opened it, and finding the room empty said:

"He was here a few minutes ago. I expect he is out to the stable."

Belle sat down. The nervous strain of the past hours was telling on her. She felt unstrung and vaguely depressed.

The doctor and Mary Bylow went to the stable. The empty stall, with no sign of saddle, bridle, or preacher, were enough. They returned to the house.

In answer to Belle's look the doctor made a gesture, and said simply:

"Gone."

"Where?"

The doctor shook his head and pointed northward.

"Please tell me all about it, Mrs. Bylow," said Belle.

"There is times to tell lies," said Mary naively, "but this ain't. I'll tell you the whole truth," and she did in a quivering voice, while tears ran from her eyes.

"Trapped, trapped," was Belle's only comment. "Where do you suppose he went?"

"Not to Cedar Mountain," said Carson, "that's sure. No one passed us."

Charlie Bylow, coming into the cabin, heard the doctor's last comment.

"He was heading due north and going hard when last we saw him," was his contribution.

"Dr. Carson, he's headed for Deadwood, and I'm going after him to bring him back." Belle stood up with sudden decision. The need for action once more present, all her strength responded.

The doctor shook his head. "I don't think you should go. You know what all the town would say."

"You are going with me," was the answer.

"When?"

"Right now."

"Better go home first."

"And have a fight with my folks? No, no! We go now. I have an aunt in Deadwood, you know!"

"It's forty-five miles, and we can't get there till midnight, even if my horse holds out."

"We may overtake him before that," said Belle, though she knew quite well they would not, for Hartigan would ride like a madman.

It had not been difficult to enlist Carson's sympathies. A sincere friendship had sprung up between the boyish preacher and himself and their total dissimilarity had made them congenial. Carson was amused in his quiet way to note how exactly Belle was moving as he thought best and surest, so now he merely added:

"Deadwood it is," and with a farewell word to the Bylows they were off.

CHAPTER XX

THE MEMORABLE TRIP TO DEADWOOD

It was a long, hard journey, and it was one o'clock in the morning before they reached Deadwood. Every public house that could get a license to sell liquor announced itself as a "hotel." Those few that could not, made a virtue of their failure and flaunted a sign, "Temperance House." The "wet houses" were on the main gulch, the "dry" ones in off nooks, or perched on breezy hills. To the best of these latter the doctor drove, had the luck to find the owner still on duty, and secured a room for himself. Then they drove to the home of Belle's aunt, Mrs. Collins. One has to take a hotel on its rules; but a relative may be called up and inconvenienced at any time.

"Well, Auntie, it's Belle Boyd. I want you to take care of me till the morning. I will tell you all about it later," this to the inquiring head that emerged from an upper window. So Belle was left and the doctor went to his hotel.

Up very early next morning, Belle went at once to the stable of the Temperance House. Yes, there he was, Blazing Star, in all his beauty. Then she went into the hotel and mounted guard in the little parlour. Dr. Carson came down and was sent to sit out of doors. At length the sound of the foot she awaited came from the stairs and she heard the landlady say:

"There's some one in the parlour waiting for you." For a moment there was no sound; then the footsteps approached.

Belle was at the window looking out, partly hidden by the cheap lace curtains. As the Preacher entered, she turned fully toward him. Her back was to the light and he did not immediately perceive her. Then with a gasp:

"Belle!" and, sinking into a chair, he covered his face with his hands.

She went to him, laid her hand on his shoulder, and stood there in silence. The great broad shoulders began to shake under that soft touch. There was no sound uttered for long, then, brokenly, his one refrain: "Oh, Belle!"

She sat down beside him, and took his hand—the first time she had ever done so—and waited in silence.

He wanted to tell her all, but found no words.

She said, "Never mind that now. Tell me what you are here for."

He tried again but in a wild, incoherent way. The sum of it all was that he was "ruined, degraded, and lost. He would go down to the Big Cheyenne and get a job as a cowboy."

"Now listen, Jim," she said. "You have made a bad mistake; but a man may make one big, bad mistake and still be all right. It is the man that goes on making a little mistake every day that is hopeless."

There was a long pause. Then she continued: "What is it you of all people admire most in a man? Is it not courage to see things through, no matter how black they look?"

In his then frame of mind Hartigan had expected drunkenness to be singled out as the worst of all sins; there was a ray of comfort in this other thought; he nodded and grunted an inarticulate assent.

"Jim, I don't doubt your courage. I know you too well, believe in you too much. I want you to drop the idea of the Big Cheyenne. Turn right around and go back to Cedar Mountain at once; and the sooner you get there the easier it will be."

He shook his head, and sat as before, his face buried in his hands. "I— cannot—do—it." He forced out the words.

"Jim Hartigan cannot—isn't brave enough?" she asked, her voice a little tremulous with sudden emotion.

In all his life, he had never been charged with cowardice. It stung. Of all things he most despised cowardice, and here it was, brought squarely home to him. He writhed under the thought. There was a dead silence in the little parlour.

Then Belle spoke: "Is this the only answer I am to have—after coming so far?" she asked in a low voice.

Oh, blind, stupid, cowardly fool that he was! He had not thought of that. How much was she braving for him! He was rated a man of courage among his friends, yet now he was yielding to miserable cowardice.

Then his impulsive nature responded. He blurted out: "Belle, I will do anything for you; I will do anything you tell me to." It was an unconditional surrender, and the wise victor gave the honours of war to the vanquished by changing the subject.

"Then come to breakfast," she said in a lighter tone and led him to Aunt Collins's house, whither the doctor had already gone.

A day's rest, a forty-mile ride in the wind, a change of scene, good friends, a buoyant disposition, a flush of youth, and Belle, absorbed in all he did and said—who would not respond to such a concentration of uplifting forces?

Hartigan's exuberance returned. His colour was back in his cheeks. His eyes sparkled and his wit sparkled, too. He won the heart of Mrs. Collins. She said he was "the beautifullest man she had ever seen." Even John Collins, a plough- and wagon-dealer by trade, was impressed with the mental gifts and manly appearance of the young preacher, and Belle knew that the thing she had set out for was won.

Instead of discussing plans she announced them as if they were settled. The doctor wished to stay a day or two in Deadwood, but that did not suit Belle at all. She was quite clear about it. Her aunt must drive back with her at once. The doctor and the Preacher must come, too, but arrive a little later in Cedar Mountain. So they boarded their buckboards, waved good-bye, and set their faces to the south.

The sun shone as it knows how in Dakota. The great pine-clad hills were purple in the lovely morning haze as the little party left Deadwood that day on the buffalo trail for Cedar Mountain. The doctor drove first in his buckboard, not without misgivings, for the good horse had had little rest since that forty-five mile drive. Next came the horseman on the gold-red horse that men turned to look after. Last, the prairie buckboard of the house of Collins with Aunt Anna driving and Belle at her side.

The prairie larks sang from low perches or soared a little way in the air to tell the world how glad they were on that bright summer morning. The splendour of the hills was on all things, and Jim on Blazing Star was filled with the glad tonic. For five miles they ambled along, and when the doctor stopped at a watering place—he had been told to stop there—the others caught up with him. Hereupon there was a readjustment, and their next going found the Collins rig leading with Blazing Star behind, and Belle with Hartigan in the second buckboard.

That was a drive of much consequence to two of the party. In that second buckboard the fates laid plans, spun yarns, and rearranged many things. Hartigan opened his heart and life. He told of his mother, of his happy childhood; of his losses; of his flat, stale, unprofitable boyhood; of Bill Kenna and his "word as a man"; of his own vow of abstinence, kept unbroken till he was eighteen. He gave it all with the joyous side alone in view, and when a pathetic incident intruded, the pathos was in the things, not in the words of the narrator. The man had a power of expression that would have made a great journalist. His talk was one continuous entertainment, and lasted unbroken to the half-way house, where they were to stay an hour for rest and food.

How sweet it is to tell one's history to a woman who takes in every word as of large importance! How pleasant it is to confess to a keen and sympathetic hearer. The twenty-five miles passed far too soon. It was short, but long enough for large foundations to be laid.

Belle was only twenty-two, but hers was a wise head. Hartigan had spoken freely about himself and thus had conferred in some large sort a right to advise. She had deliberately constructed a new mood for his thoughts, so that the horrors of the Bylow cabin were forgotten. The questions now for him and for her were, how to set him right with the church, and how begin all over again. Hartigan's idea was to go openly before the whole congregation with a humble apology, and publicly promise to abstain from drink forever. Belle vetoed this emphatically.

"Never rub your head in the mud," she said. "You make your peace with God first, then with Dr. Jebb, and the deacons. Pay no attention to any one else. There will be some talk for a while, but it will die away.

"You don't know the Black Hills as I do, Jim. People out here don't take things quite so seriously as eastern folk. Many a western preacher carries a flask of brandy as snakebite antidote or chill cure. Not long ago I heard of a minister up north who was held for horse-stealing. Yes, more than once. And how he explained it, I don't know: but he is preaching yet. I don't mean to make light of these things, Jim, but I want to keep you from a kind of reparation which will be more of a shock to the people than what they now know. We must have some sense of proportion. Since there was no public scandal, you will find that the whole matter will be overlooked."

Belle was right; he knew she was; and later events proved it.

Most men propose when they find "the one woman"; but some don't. Many marriages take place without any formal proposal. The man and the woman come together and discover such sympathy, such need of each other, that they assume much that remains unspoken. Nothing was said of love or marriage on that journey from Deadwood, but James Hartigan and Belle Boyd were conscious of a bond that happily and finally became complete. Thenceforth he made no move without consulting her; thenceforth she had no plans in which he was not more than half.

They were ten miles from Cedar Mountain when the last change was made. Those who noted their arrival some while later saw Belle ride up the Main Street with her aunt, and tie up at her father's door. Twenty minutes later Hartigan rode beside the doctor's rig to his home, at the other side of the town.

CHAPTER XXI

THE ORDEAL

Jim went at once to Dr. Jebb's to report. Mrs. Jebb opened the door, greeted him with a hearty handshake, and was more than usually cordial. Dr. Jebb was kind, but embarrassed. He offered Jim a chair and began nervously:

"There was a rumour—there—that is—we missed you on Sunday."

Jim, with characteristic directness, said: "Doctor, I'll tell you all about it." Just then there was a timid knock and Mrs. Jebb reappeared. "May I be present, Jim?" she said. "I understand that you have something to talk about, and you know, you were always my boy."

Dr. Jebb looked puzzled. Jim said: "If I can't trust you, who is there left to trust?" And then told the story of his fall. He painted himself not quite so black as he might have done the day before, but black enough.

Dr. Jebb looked terribly worried and distressed. "I don't know what to say," he kept repeating. "All my heart is with you, but my judgment condemns you. I don't know what to say."

Then Mrs. Jebb spoke. "Now, Josiah, you know perfectly well that your affections always were a safer guide than your judgment. There was no bad intention on the part of the sinner—for we are all sinners—this was just an unfortunate accident, and Jim shows in every possible way his regret. There has been no public scandal, and so I think you had better drop the whole thing and forget it. I know enough about Jim to know that he has made out the worst possible case against himself."

"That may be," said Dr. Jebb, "but I fear we must bring the matter up before the deacons, at least."

"As long as you don't make it public by bringing it before the church," said Mrs. Jebb, "all right."

Thus it was that Dr. Jebb sent out a notice, to such of the deacons as he could not see personally, that a meeting was to be held at his house that night.

In the same afternoon another interview took place in Cedar Mountain. School-trustee Higginbotham was sitting in his office when the schoolteacher came up the boardwalk and into the insurance office.

"Hello, Jack."

"Hello, John"; and the visitor sat down. Higginbotham glanced at him and noticed that his face was drawn and his eyes "like holes burnt in a blanket." His fingers trembled as he rolled a cigarette.

"Say, John," Lowe began nervously, "in case any rumour gets around that the Preacher and I were a little reckless at Bylow's, you can contradict it. At least there's nothing in it as far as I am concerned. I think the Preacher must have taken some before I arrived. He showed the effects, but not much."

"Hm," said Higginbotham. "You got there late?"

"Yes, you see we—that is, both of us—went there to stop that spree—and we did, in a way, but things got a little mixed."

"How was that?"

"Well, I went there to help him and I did what I could for him, but they had had some already. We spilled the keg on the floor and the fumes were pretty strong and affected him a little. Didn't amount to much. I did what I could. It was strong enough to affect me—unpleasantly, too. I thought I'd just let you know in case there was anything said about it."

As soon as he was gone, Hannah appeared. Apparently, she had overheard the conversation. "Well, did you catch on?"

"Partly; how did it strike you?"

"I think he is trying to save his own skin by dragging in the Preacher."

"I think so, too; but all the same, I won't use his story if it can be dispensed with. The less we dig into this thing the better."

A little later the notice came from Dr. Jebb, inviting Deacon Higginbotham to a meeting at his house that evening, for important business. As he walked across the village Charlie Bylow stepped out from a dark corner near Dr. Jebb's house.

"Say, Deacon," he began, "I've been waiting to see you. I know what is on to-night. I want you to know it was a put-up job. It was the schoolteacher worked it. The stuff was doped all right. The Preacher went there to stop it as he did the other time, but they fooled him and trapped him."

"Yes, I thought so," said the little deacon, "and how was it worked?"

"Well, I don't just exactly know. I haven't been on good terms with my brother since I joined the church, so I don't go to his house any more; but I heard some talk about its being the 'slickest thing ever.' I know the Preacher went there to stop it and that they trapped him and that it was Jack Lowe did it."

"Will you go before the deacons of the church and tell them that—if it is necessary?"

"No," replied Bylow uneasily; "at least I don't want to go before any meeting. I only know that's right; that's the way it happened; and I don't want any one to blame Mr. Hartigan." Here Charlie abruptly ended and went away.

Higginbotham turned back to his house. Hannah listened with the keenest attention and then said: "It's easy to straighten it all out. I'll see Belle and tell her to go to Jim at once and keep him from talking. You know what he is when he gets going. He'll talk too much and spoil it all." Thus these two loyal friends laid plans to screen him.

At Jebb's house, Higginbotham took the earliest occasion to warn Jim.

"Now don't talk. Simply answer one or two questions when asked and as briefly as possible. 'Yes' or 'No' is enough. You know we've got to satisfy the old Deacon Blight crowd somehow." And Jim promised to obey.

Dr. Jebb called the meeting to order and, at once, Higginbotham arose and said: "Mr. Chairman, I think it would be better for Mr. Hartigan to retire to another room." So Jim went out.

Dr. Jebb then gave a brief and rather halting account of a "certain rumour reflecting on the sobriety of his assistant." Before he had more than outlined the facts, Higginbotham jumped up:

"Dr. Jebb, you have alluded to a rumour. I call it a shameful fabrication, with no basis in fact. I have made a thorough investigation and am prepared, with two reliable witnesses, to prove that Mr. Hartigan went to the Bylow cabin to prevent a disgraceful spree, as he did once before. They had prepared by getting a keg of whiskey. This liquid sin, if I may so call it, Mr. Hartigan spilled on the floor; unfortunately, it was in a small, close cabin and the fumes affected his head so that he was temporarily ill. These are the facts; and to prove them I have two reliable witnesses. Call in Charlie Bylow and John Lowe." He looked with a pretense of expectation toward the door; getting no response he said: "Humph, not arrived yet. Well, we won't wait. In the meantime, I must say that to my mind altogether too much has been made of this accident and I am satisfied to dismiss the subject if the rest of the deacons consent."

"No, I don't consent; I don't think we should," said Deacon Blight. "We can't afford to have a scandal about our spiritual leader. Let's prove it or disprove it right now."

And, acting on the majority vote, Dr. Jebb called Jim Hartigan to appear. Dr. Jebb was supposed to be chairman, but Higginbotham was irrepressible.

"I want to ask one or two questions," he called out; and, without waiting for permission, he began: "Now, Mr. Hartigan, I understand that you went to the Bylow Corner last Saturday night to prevent a whiskey spree, as we know you have done before; that in some way the fumes of the liquor entered your head and so overpowered you that you were ill afterward; and that it was a painful surprise to you, as one well known to be a teetotaller. Isn't that so?"

"Well, yes," said Jim, in some perplexity; "but it was this way——"

"Never mind the way of it," said Higginbotham emphatically. Then, turning to the others: "I don't see that we need go any further."

"Hold on, hold on," said Deacon Blight; "I'd like to ask one or two questions. You admit being under the influence of liquor at Bylow's?"

"Yes," was the reply.

"Were you ever under the influence of liquor before?"

"I was."

"Once, or more than once?"

"More than once," said Jim. He would have said "many times" but for a scowl from Higginbotham.

"Oh, ho!" said the deacon. "When was that?"

"Before I was converted."

"Never since?"

"No; except last Saturday."

Here Dr. Jebb interrupted. "It seems to me that we need not follow the subject any further than to inquire into the mental attitude of the brother who fell into the snare. I know it is one of absolute contrition now, especially as the affair was of the nature of an accident during the discharge of his duty. It seems to me, therefore, that we should accept his expression of penitence coupled with a promise to abstain so long as he is here with us."

Jim volunteered to abstain for all time, but Higginbotham's moderate counsels prevailed.

Deacon Blight thought that the transgressor should be suspended from office pending a fuller investigation. Deacon Higginbotham thought that it had already been more than fully investigated. Deacon Whaup had never heard of the affair until this evening, but thought that Mr. Hartigan ought to retire during further discussion.

As soon as Jim was outside, Higginbotham, fully determined to stop all further talk, said: "Dr. Jebb, I move we accept the promise Mr. Hartigan has given and table the whole matter. It is absurd to follow it further in the light of what we know—making a big mountain of a very small mole-hill."

Blight, however, didn't think so. He argued for delay and for stern measures. Dr. Jebb put the motion and it was carried with but one dissenting vote; and so the matter was officially closed. As they dispersed, Dr. Jebb reminded them that the deliberations of the Board of Deacons were to be considered strictly confidential.

And Jim went forth with strange and mixed feelings. He was grateful for Higginbotham's determined protection and yet he would have held the Board in higher respect if it had punished him severely. Such was the nature of the ardent Celt.

CHAPTER XXII

THE THREE RELIGIONS CONFRONT HIM

Jack Shives's blacksmith shop, off the Main Street of Cedar Mountain, was noted for two things: the sound, all-round work it turned out in the smithy line, and the "perchers," an ever-present delegation of village characters that sat chewing straws as they perched on the shop lumber. Most of them came to hear old Shives talk, for Jack was a philosopher and no subject was out of his field. Hartigan liked Shives, enjoyed the shop with its smoke and flying sparks, and took a keen relish in the unfettered debate that filled in the intervals between Shives's ringing blows on the anvil.

Dr. Jebb thought himself a very up-to-date divine. He had tried to have a sort of free discussion in his study Sunday nights after meeting, but the restraint of parsondom was over it all. He was really a painfully orthodox old person; all his up-to-dateness was within the covers of the catechism, and the real thinkers kept away. Dr. Carson had better success, but he was a bitter politician, so that all who differed from him on national or local politics avoided his house. The blacksmith shop, however, was open for all, and the real discussions of the village were there. Shives had a masterful way of assuming the chairmanship, and of doing the job well, often while pounding the anvil; sometimes an effective punctuation of his remarks came in the hiss of hot iron thrust in the tank, and Shives enjoyed the humour of obliterating his opponent for the moment in a cloud of steam.

Jim Hartigan, with his genial, sociable instincts, was found in Shives's shop more often than in the tiny room which, with the bed, table, and books, was all he had in the way of home. Dr. Jebb was afraid to take any large part in these deliberations. They were apt to discuss what he considered the undiscussable foundations of the Church. But Dr. Carson was one of the most strenuous of the debators.

"I tell you, there ain't a bit o' use o' your talking," said Shives. "If I stick my finger in that fire, I'm a-going to get burnt and all the prayers and repentance I can put up ain't a-going to wipe off that burn. I've got to suffer for what I do just the same, whether I belong to church or not."

"Sure, now," said Hartigan, "if I see your point, there is little to it. You are talking about sin being its own punishment, which is true; but suppose a doctor came along and by his work and skill saved you from losing the finger altogether and in the end your finger was little the worse and you were much the wiser—what about your theory then?"

"That is not the point. If it was the same thing, when I hurt my finger I would only have to say, 'I repent; the Lord will take my punishment,' and at once my finger would be restored as it was before."

"Well, that may be your Church's creed, but it isn't mine," said Hartigan; and they wrangled till the blacksmith halted in his raking of the coals, turned to Hartigan, and beating in the air with his coal rake like a band leader with his baton, he said with punctuated emphasis: "My creed tells me I must suffer for my own doings just as surely as if I lay my finger on this anvil and hit it a crack with the hammer, and no man can save me from that, and if you tell me that God is a wild beast and merely wants a victim to punish, no matter who, then I want to know where the justice comes in. There is not any greater wickedness than to let the guilty escape, except it be to punish the innocent; and that's the whole sum and substance of your religion, which was neatly summed up by old Blue Horse down at Pine Ridge. After he had heard the missionary explaining it for about the thousandth time, he said: 'Ho, me see now; your God is my devil.'

"I tell you there's only one sum and substance of all religion that's worth while, and that is to be a kind, decent neighbour, do your work, and help others to do theirs. You will find that set forth, straight as a string, in your own textbook, where it says, 'Love your neighbour as yourself.'" And the blacksmith drew the radiant iron from the forge to pound, pound, pound, amid the laughter that proclaimed the defeat of the Preacher.

Hartigan was never strong on theology. At college he had neglected the chance to learn the cut and parry in that strangest of all games, and the puzzle for which he had no quick answer was that of the burnt finger. In the smithy debates the answer had to be quick, or it was no answer at all. He had lost the chance and was mortified to see the verdict of the crowd against him.

"Jack," he said, "I want you to come to church and see how simple it all is."

"Church. Huh! I think I see myself," said the blacksmith.

"That's not fair," said Hartigan. "You condemn church without going to see what it is."

"Oh, I've been there a-plenty."

"When?"

"Twenty years ago."

"Oh, pshaw! It's all changed since then."

"Is it? That's a good one. I thought God's religion was unchangeable for ever and ever. I tell you, young fellow, if you keep on working and thinking you will wind up with a religion of common sense and kindness which, as near as I can make out, is what the man Jesus did preach."

"Then why don't you come to hear it?" retorted Hartigan.

"Because ye don't preach it."

"That's not a fair way to put it," reiterated Hartigan.

"See here," said Shives, "I will go to church next Sunday and right along, *if* whenever you get off some fool statement that every one knows is nonsense, you let me or some one get up and say, 'Now prove that, or take it back before you go further.'"

Hartigan was worsted. He did not retreat, but he was glad of the interruption furnished by a wild horse brought in to be shod. Here he took the lead and showed such consummate horse sense in the handling of the animal that the blacksmith growled, "If you'd put some of that into your pulpit, I'd go to hear you."

As Jim mounted Blazing Star and rode away at an easy swing, all eyes followed him, and the blacksmith growled: "'Homely in the cradle, handsome on the horse,' they say. He must 'a' been a clock-stopper when he was a kid. Pity to waste all that on a pulpiteer."

Later, the Preacher had a full discussion with Belle. The blacksmith had dented Hartigan's armour in several places. Where was the justice in punishing one being for another's sins? Even if the sufferer was willing, it was still wicked injustice. How could repentance wipe out the self-brought injury? These were among the puzzles. Dr. Jebb was his natural helper, but the Preacher brought them first to Belle. She had gone deeper and further than he had. She dreaded doctrinal discussion, but at length said:

"Did you never hear of the transfusion of blood whereby a man may give of his strength and, by suffering, save a friend from death? Did you never hear of a man tottering and almost down who was found by a friend at the right moment, helped to greater strength by mutual suffering, and so restored to his balance before he went down to ruin?"

And the fervent answer was, "Yes, I have."

New vistas were opened to them by this open-hearted talk—truly communion—and as they rode through the gray-bloomed sage they followed still the thought. Then he waved a hand and raised his face toward Cedar Mountain with its column seeming small against the sky.

"I want you to see it, Belle. I want you to stand there with me and know how much it means when your spirit is just right."

She swung her horse with his and they headed for the trail. He had talked to her about it before, but he had felt a little disappointed that her imagination was not stirred as his had been—that the mystery and charm, the emotional awe, so easy for his Celtic blood, had not been conjured up in her by his words. But he still had hopes that the feeling of the far-up shrine would weave enchantment of its own; and he told her of the second sight that the fay of his mother's land could give if one sang a song of the one right pitch in the glen of the "very stone."

So they rode through the sage to the trailing cedar robe and followed upward till the upper edge of the fragrant woods was reached. There they tied the horses and climbed on foot to the upland. The grass among the rocks was yellow now, and high gentians seized on the rare moment to flaunt their wondrous blue against that perfect background. A flock of autumn birds rose up and flew on, as the climbers, reaching the Spirit Rock, paused and turned to look out over the golden plains to the east, over the blue hills to the north, and into the purple glow that the waning sunlight left on all the west.

Belle rejoiced in it for its material beauty and its wealth of colour; and Jim, shyly watching her, said:

"Sometimes as I stand by this rock pinnacle and look over the plain, I feel as if I were an ocean rover, high up in the lookout, peering over the rough and tumbling sea. It possesses me with more than the power of a dream." Then, after a pause: "See, here is where the Indian boy was sitting as he kept his fast and vigil. I wonder what he saw. Some day, Belle, I want to take that vigil. Do you remember that the prophets of old always did so when they sought light? I am learning that the Indian had some light, and to-day I have done as he would do, I have brought my sacred medicine with me." He produced a little cedar box that his father had made. He opened it and deeply inhaled its fragrance. "That is cedar, Belle; it carries me back to other days when, under the cedar shingles, my mother put her arm about me and prayed that I might find the Eternal Guide."

He took out his mother's Bible, her photograph and the daguerreotype of his father. These were his sacred relics, and with them was a bundle of cedar twigs to keep the fragrance ever there—to keep continually with them the power, through smell, to conjure up those days and thoughts of her love. Belle took them reverently and gazed at the prim old pictures; then she looked him squarely in the eyes, intensely for a moment, like one who looks through a veil for the first time and sees a hidden chamber unguessed before.

"Belle," he said, and his voice was a little husky; "if I had gone on to the Big Cheyenne that time, I would have built a fire as soon as I had the chance and burnt all these to ashes; and then what—God only knows, for these were the vessels of my sanctuary; this was the ark of my covenant, with the rod that budded, the tables of the law, and the precious incense." She laid her hand on his in silent comprehension and he went on. "All my life I have had two natures struggling within me; and the destroyer would have won, and had won, when you turned the rout. If you had not come to me in Deadwood I would surely have burnt these relics. Now you understand. I couldn't speak about it down there; but up here it is easy. Some time I may be missing for a couple of days. Do not worry then; it will only mean I have gone up into my mountain. I am seeking the light that comes from prayer and fasting and vigil in a high place."

"I know those things as words," she said. "Just as we all learned them in Sunday-school; but you make them as real as this mountain, a part of my very life."

He replaced the relics in their cedar box and she realized that for the first time she had had a glimpse of the deep and spiritual quality of his soul.

BOOK III

THE HORSE PREACHER

CHAPTER XXIII

BLAZING STAR

The Angel of Destiny who had special charge of Jim had listed and measured his failings and had numbered them for drastic treatment. The brawling spirit of his early days, the proneness to drink, the bigoted intolerance of any other mode of thought than his own, the strange mistake of thinking physical courage the only courage, a curious disregard for the things of the understanding—each was the cause of bitter suffering. Each in its kind was alloy, dross, and for each the metal had to pass through the fires and, purified, come forth.

Hartigan's love of sport was rooted deep in his nature and Fate gave it a long fling. It took no cruel or destructive form, nor did it possess him as a hate; but certain things held him in passionate allegiance, so deep and so reckless that when their fever was upon him nothing else seemed worth a thought. And the chiefest of these was his love of horses. A noble thing in itself, a necessary vent, perhaps, for the untamed spirit's love of untrammelled motion but it was inwrought with dangers. Most men in the West in Hartigan's day—as now—were by nature horse-lovers; but never, so far as Cedar Mountain knew, had there been a man so horse-crazy as the Rev. James Hartigan. Already, he was known as the "Horse Preacher."

It was seldom that an animal received so much personal care as Blazing Star; it was seldom that a steed so worthy could be found; and the results were for all to behold. The gaunt colt of the immigrant became the runner of Cedar Mountain, and the victory won at Fort Ryan was the first of many ever growing in importance.

You can tell much of a man's relation to his horse when he goes to bring him from pasture. If he tricks and drives him into a corner, and then by sudden violence puts on the bridle, you know that he has no love, no desire for anything but service; in return he will get poor service at best, and no love at all. If he puts a lump of sugar in his pocket and goes to the fence, calling his horse by name, and the horse comes joyously as to meet a friend, and with mobile, velvet lips picks the sugar clean from the offering palm and goes willingly to saddle and bit, then you know that the man is a horse man, probably a horseman; by the bond of love he holds his steed, and will get from him twice the service and for thrice as long as any could extort with spur and whip.

"Whoa, Blazing Star, whoa", and the gold-red meteor of the prairie would shake his mane and tail and come careering, curvetting, not direct, but round in a brief spiral to find a period point at the hand he loved.

"Ten times," said Colonel Waller, of the Fort, "have I seen a man so bound up in the friendship of his dog that all human ties had second place; but never before or since have I seen a man so bonded to his horse, or a horse so nobly answering in his kind, as Hartigan and his Blazing Star."

The ancients had a fable of a horse and a rider so attuned—so wholly one—that the brain of the man and the power of the horse were a single being, a wonderful creature to whom the impossible was easy play. And there is good foundation for the myth. Who that has ridden on the polo field or swung the lasso behind the bounding herd, can forget the many times when he dropped the reins and signalled to the horse only by the gentle touch of knee, of heel, by voice, by body swing, by *wishing* thus and so, and got response? For the horse and he were perfectly attuned and trained—the reins superfluous. Thus, centaur-like, they went, with more than twice the power that either by itself possessed.

Fort Ryan where the Colonel held command, was in the Indian reserve and five miles south of Cedar Mountain. The life of the garrison was very self-contained, but Cedar Mountain had its allurements, and there were some entertainments where civilian and soldier met. The trail between was a favourite drive or ride and to Hartigan it became very familiar.

There was one regular function that had a strong hold on him. It took place every other Saturday afternoon on the parade ground, and was called general riding exercises, but was really a "stunt show" of trick riding. After they began to know him, the coming of Hartigan with his horse was hailed by all with delight. The evenings of these festal days were spent in the gymnasium, when there was an athletic programme with great prominence given to sword play, boxing, and singlestick, in which Hartigan was the king; and here his cup of joy was full.

"Ain't it a shame to waste all that stuff on a preacher?" was the frequent expression of the soldiers. Though what better use they would have made of it, was not clear.

Many a dark night Hartigan rode home from the Fort after the evening's fun was over leaving it entirely to his horse to select the road, after the manner of the wise horseman. In mid-August there had been one of the typical Black Hill storms. After a month of drought, it had rained inches in a few hours. The little Rapid Fork of the Cheyenne was a broad flood which carried off most of its bridges, including that on the trail to the Fort. The rain had ceased the day before, but the flood had subsided very little by

Saturday night as Hartigan mounted Blazing Star and set out for the fortnightly affair at Fort Ryan.

The sky was still blocked with clouds and at eight o'clock it was black dark, so Hartigan left the selection of the trail, as a matter of course, to Blazing Star. From the time of leaving the last light in Cedar Mountain till they drew up under the first lantern at Fort Ryan, Hartigan never saw the horse he was riding, much less the road he was riding on: nor had he touched the reins or given by word or pressure of knee any signal of guidance. The night was too black for his senses, but he knew he was committing his way to senses that were of a keener order than his own, and he rode as a child might—without thought of fear. He could feel it when they were going down into the canyon of the Rapid Fork, and at the bottom of the slight descent he heard the rush of waters, and noted that Blazing Star lowered his head and snorted softly more than once. He heard the tap of the hoofs on the timber of the bridge, and then they ascended and came in a little while to the lantern at the door of the gymnasium in the barracks.

"Hello, Hartigan! Where in the world did you come from?" was the cordial greeting of Colonel Waller.

"Where could I come from but Cedar Mountain?"

"The deuce you did."

"Why not?"

"How did you cross the creek?"

"By the bridge."

"Oh, no, you didn't."

"I surely did," said the Preacher.

"Well, you didn't, because there isn't any bridge. It all went out last night," was the Colonel's astounding answer.

"Be that as it may," said the Preacher, "I have come here direct from Cedar Mountain. I left at eight o'clock and here I am, arrived by the road at eight forty-five; and I crossed the Rapid Fork of the Cheyenne on the bridge. I didn't see it. I didn't see my horse from start to finish. I didn't see one inch of the road; but I heard it and felt it. Anyway, I'm here."

That night the Preacher stayed at the Fort, but he was up at daylight. So were the officers, for they had laid bets on this matter. They came to the little canyon, the river, and the place of the bridge; the bridge was gone; but, yes, surely there was one long stringer left. It had been held by the bolt at one end, and the officer charged with repairing the bridge had swung it back into place that very afternoon, and made it firm to serve as a footbridge, though it was barely twelve inches wide.

There, plainly written in the soft earth, was the story of the crossing. Blazing Star had descended the bank, and had missed the narrow stringer by a yard. He had nosed along till he found it and had crossed over on that with the delicate poise and absolute sense of certainty that would have been destroyed had the rider tried to give a guiding hand. And the end would have been sure death had Hartigan not trusted to his horse so utterly. The best of steed and man had thus begot a creature on a higher plane—in spirit and effect the centaur of the ancient tale.

CHAPTER XXIV

RED ROVER

August was advancing with everything shaping for a great local event. The Corn Dance of the Indians to celebrate the first of the new crop was an old festival and brought hundreds of them together. In addition, the government had selected September fifteenth for the semi-annual issue of the treaty money. This was a coincidence of festivals that insured a great attendance and at all such times horse-racing was the favourite sport.

On the Fourth of July of that year the Indians had produced an extraordinary buckskin cayuse which, in spite of its humble origin and raw exterior, had proved speedy enough to defeat all opposition and capture the big purse. Interest in the opportunity for revenge had grown every day since, and the fact that each Indian family was to get one hundred dollars in cash, enhanced the chances of a fat purse. A winning horse was the first need of the ranchmen and they turned at once to Hartigan and Blazing Star. They were much taken aback to receive from him a flat refusal to enter or to let any one else enter Blazing Star for a race. In vain they held out great inducements, possibilities of a huge fortune, certainly of a big lump sum down in advance, or almost any price he chose to ask for Blazing Star.

Hartigan's reply was an emphatic "No." And that was the end of it.

There was nothing for the whites to do but find another racer. There certainly was no such horse as they needed in all the country; had there been, they would have known it; and those who took the matter to heart were planning a visit to Illinois or Kentucky even, where it was simply a matter of money to get a blooded horse that would settle the issue.

While on a long hard trip for the spiritual help of brethren in the South, Jim was left for a day at Chadron, Nebraska, a distributing point for settlers coming to the Platte. With the instinct born of his Western life, Jim made for the big horse corral, which is always on the outskirts of a prairie town and where he knew he could pass a pleasant hour or more. It was, as usual, crowded with horses of low and middle class degree—some old and worn, some young and raw, many extraordinary pintos, one or two mounts above the average of size or beauty, but nothing to secure more than passing attention.

The scene in and about the corral held a great fascination for Jim. There were cowboys and stable hands; farmers whose horses were in the corral or whose homes were in the prairie schooners anchored on the plain near-by;

men were coming and going, and groups of children rollicked about the camp fire.

As Hartigan looked on, a young fellow—whose soft, slow speech and "r"-less words were certain proof of Southern birth—led from a stable a tall, clean-limbed horse and, flopping into the saddle with easy carelessness, rode away. As he passed, the horse's coat of bronze and gold fairly rippled in the sun as the perfect muscles played beneath, and the delight that Jim got, none but a horseman would understand. As the lad cantered away to a camping group and returned, the Preacher had a fair view. The horse might have been twin brother to his own, and he did not need the rider's assurance that the steed was a "Kaintucky blood all right."

In all the Western towns an interesting custom has grown up in the matter of registering. The chief hotel is accepted as the social centre and clubhouse, so that a man arriving in town, whether he puts up at the hotel or not, goes to the register and enters his name. "Never fail to register; it may be handy to prove an alibi," has become a saying. Jim went to the hotel with an idea. He registered, glanced over the other names and learned that Cattleman Kyle was then in town. It was easy to find him in a place of this size, and after a brief search Jim hailed him boisterously from afar:

"Say, Kyle, I've found what you are looking for."

"What's that?"

"A horse. A real horse. A winner."

"What? Are you willing to sell Blazing Star?"

"No!" was the forceful answer. "Come and see."

And Kyle did see. His eye kindled as he watched the glorious creature in the sun.

"By jinks! He's all right. He's better than Blazing Star."

"Not on your life!" said Jim, with sudden heat, "but he's what you are after."

They walked casually up to the young rider. Kyle began:

"Say, young fellow, is that horse for sale?"

"Yo' the fo'th pah'ty to-day to ask that," was the softly cooed answer. "No, he ain't fo' sale."

"Looks to me like a Kentucky blood," said Kyle. "Are you going to keep him in this country or ride him back?"

"Wall, I'm h'yah to stay, and I guess he stays with me."

"What are you going to feed him on? You can't get timothy or beans or oats out here. He couldn't keep up on prairie hay; and, if you did try it, he'd get the loco weed."

This was a good shot and the rider had no ready answer, so Kyle continued. "How old is he?"

"Fo' last spring and sound as a bell; hasn't a fault," was the reply.

"Why don't you swap him for something that can stand the country?" said Kyle. Then, as the Southerner did not reply, Kyle continued: "I'll give you two steady young saddle horses raised in the country and proof against pinkeye and loco weed."

"If you add about a thousand dollars, I might consider it," was the response.

That was the beginning of bargaining, and the end was that the Kentuckian got two native saddle horses and two hundred and fifty dollars cash. Cattleman Kyle got the beautiful Red Rover and Jim Hartigan experienced just a twinge of jealousy as he saw the new champion and heard his praises sung. Kyle's intention had been to keep Red Rover and rejoice in the beauty and power of the new possession; but the problem of how to win the next race made every other consideration secondary.

It is well known that a skilful trainer can knock twenty-five seconds off a horse's mile time; or even more, if he can be trained on clean oats and timothy hay. There were oats, hay and skilful trainers in the cavalry barracks at Fort Ryan. There were none of these things at Kyle's ranch on the Big Cheyenne; hence, after much debate, Red Rover was transferred, without profit or loss, to Captain Wayne and was thenceforth the central figure and chiefest hope of the Fort Ryan stables.

Naturally, one of the first things to be done was to get a gauge on Red Rover's speed by a race with Blazing Star. It was only a race "for fun," and Jim gave his place to a lighter man; but he watched with an eagerness not easily expressed in words, and his heart swelled with joy—yes, into his very throat—when it was made clear, that, while Red Rover was good, Blazing Star was better.

All these things were events of the first magnitude to the horseman's world that centred at Fort Ryan. The love of horses is common to most men, but it is dominant in the West, and rampant in the mounted soldier. The general interest of officers and men grew into a very keen and personal interest as the training went on, and touched fever heat when it was definitely announced that on Treaty Day, September fifteenth, there was to be a race for a purse of one hundred dollars, as a nominal consideration, and betting to any extent on the side. Meanwhile, word was sent to the Pine Ridge Agency that the whites were not discouraged by their defeat in July, but would come again with their horse in the Corn Feast time for a new race.

Then, one fine morning in early August, a long procession of Indians appeared on the hills, singing their marching songs, trailing their travois and tepee poles. They set up their camp not far from Fort Ryan; and soon, Red Cloud, with a few who were near him, rode in to call on Colonel Waller. The latter received them on the piazza of his quarters, and, after a smoke, learned that they had come to accept the challenge to race their horses. When and where should it be? It was arranged that on the fifteenth of September they should meet at Fort Ryan, and that the race should come off on the two-mile course at the Fort. After smokes, compliments and the exchange of some presents, Red Cloud withdrew to his camp.

The following day, as his trainer was putting Red Rover through his paces around the course, there was a group of Indians on their horses at the racetrack; silent, attentive, watching every move. At dawn, the day after, the sentry reported that a band of mounted Indians were on the racetrack. From his window the Colonel watched them through a telescope. He saw them studying the ground; and then a naked youth, on a spirited buckskin, galloped round. It was easy for the Colonel to note the time by his stop-watch and thus have a rough idea of the pony's flat speed on the two miles. He was not surprised one way or the other. The time was considerably over four minutes, which merely proved it to be an ordinarily good horse. But, of course, he knew nothing of the handling; was this top speed? or was the driver holding the horse in? In ten minutes the Indians were gone.

The next day, a party rode out from Cedar Mountain to see the Indian camp; and, leading the light-hearted procession, were Belle Boyd on her pony and the Preacher on Blazing Star. It was not easy to see Red Cloud. He was much wrapped up in his dignity and declined to receive any one under the rank of "Soldier High Chief" (Colonel). But they found much to interest them in the Sioux camp, and at length, were rewarded by seeing the war chief come forth, mount his horse, and ride, with others, toward the Fort. Turning aside, at the racetrack, Belle and Jim saw Red Rover come forth for his morning spin. The Red men drifted to the starting point, and just as the racer went away an Indian boy on a buckskin broncho dashed alongside and kept there round the track. Whether it was a race or not no one could say, for each rider was jockeying, not willing to win or lose, and it had the appearance of a prearranged dead heat. One of the officers called out: "Say, boys, that's their same old buckskin cayuse. What do you make of it?"

It was the white jockey who replied: "If that's their speeder, it's a cinch. I could have run away at any time."

A senior officer spoke up: "I kept tabs on it, and it's just the same time practically as the Colonel took on his stop watch yesterday. We've got them this time."

What the Indians learned was not revealed. But, next morning, Red Cloud called upon the Colonel. He smoked a long while before he made clear what he was after. "Did the Colonel want a fair race, or not?"

"Why certainly a fair race."

"Then send to Red Cloud a load of the white man's grass that has a tail like a rat; and give him also some of the long white seed, a pile as high as a man's knees, so that the pony might eat and be strong, and make good race."

The Colonel's eyes twinkled. "Ho, ho!" he thought, "the crafty old villain has been learning something."

Now though the Colonel of a frontier post has ample power, it would have been very unwise of him to sell any stores to the Indian; he might, however, without risk of censure, have given him the asked-for supply, had he deemed it advisable. But why should he help the enemy's horse? So he shook his head and said he was "not allowed to sell government stores." And Red Cloud turned away, with an expression of scorn.

The next day, a minor chief tried to buy some oats from the stable man; but, being refused, went off in silence; and, two days later, the Indian Camp was gone.

The news soon spread abroad that the famous buckskin cayuse had been up to go over the track, and that Red Rover had played with him. "It was a cinch," they could win any money they liked; and then the betting became crazy. The Indians have no idea of anything but an even bet, but that was good enough. The day of the race there were to be fifty thousand government dollars distributed among them; and every white man, soldier or civilian, who could raise a little cash, was putting it up on a certainty of doubling.

The days and all they held were a terrible strain on Jim Hartigan. How he itched to be in it! Not once, but many times, he rode to Fort Ryan to see Red Rover training; and more than once he rode around the track to pace the Rover. His face, his very soul, glowed as he watched the noble animal, neck and neck with his own fair steed. "The only horse that ever had made Blazing Star let out."

Then, near the end, in very pride—he could not help it—he put Blazing Star to it and let them see that while Red Rover might be good, he was only second best after all.

"It wasn't racing," he explained to Belle, "it was just speeding up a little. Sure, I want the white man's horse to win over that Indian pony. It would never do to have the broncho win."

There seemed no probability of that; but there was one group of interested white men who were not quite so satisfied. Cattleman Kyle and all the ranchers on the Cheyenne wanted a sure thing; and there was no way to make sure, but by a trial race that was a real race. So they used the old-time trick of the white man who wishes to get ahead of the Indian: they hired another Indian to help them.

There had always been war and hatred between the Crows and the Sioux. The war was over for the present; but the Crows were very ready to help any one against their former enemies. Enlisted by the ranchers the Crow spies reported that the Sioux were training their horse not ten miles away in a secluded secret canyon of the Yellowbank, a tributary of the Cheyenne River. And thither by night, with all possible secrecy, went Kyle with a dozen more. Among them was Hartigan. Why? Partly because they wanted him along, for his knowledge of horses and jockeys, and chiefly because he himself was mad to go, when he heard of it. The whole colour of the adventure, the mere fact of its being an adventure, were overpowering to his untamed twenty-five-year-old spirit.

They hid their horses in a distant valley; then, in the early dawn, they followed their dusky guide to a little butte, where they made themselves as comfortable as possible to await the sunrise.

"Well," said Jim, "considering I'm freezing to death an' mortal hungry, and sitting on a bunch of cactus, and playing pick-pocket with another man's secrets and ashamed of myself, I'm having a divil of a fine time!" And they chattered and their teeth chattered, till a dog barked far below, and they heard the coyotes singing back their long soft call; and in the growing light they discovered an Indian tepee, with smoke issuing from the vent hole. Near by was a rude corral. The smoke increased—then grew less; soon sparks flew out; the light in the sky grew brighter; the music of the coyotes died away; and, in a little while, the glory of the sun was over the world.

Now they saw an old woman go forth to the corral and, following her, a youth. Unfastening the rude gate, they entered; and the boy presently rode forth on a beautiful buckskin pony, well made and spirited. Yes, the very same one they had seen on the race track at Fort Ryan. They saw him ridden to water; then, after a short canter, back to the corral. Here they watched the old woman rub and scrub him down from head to foot, while the boy brought in a truss of very good-looking hay from some hidden supply. The old woman went carefully over the bundle, throwing away portions of it. "She throw away all bad medicine plants," said the Crow. After half an hour, another Indian came forth from the lodge and brought a bag of something for the pony. They could not see what it was, but the Crow Indian said it was "white man's corn, the little sharp kind that makes a horse's legs move very fast."

"Bedad, there's no mistaking that," said Hartigan; "they're training on oats; an' that hay is too green for prairie grass and not green enough for alfalfa. I wonder if they haven't managed to get some timothy for their 'hope of the race!'"

The first important fact was that the cattlemen had discovered the training ground of the Indian racer; the second that the Red men were neglecting nothing that could help them to win. Now to be a complete story of a good scouting, these watchers should have stayed there all day, to see what the Indian methods were; but that would have been a slow job. They were too impatient to wait. It was clear, anyway, that the redskins had adopted all they could learn from the whites, and that the buckskin cayuse was no mean antagonist. The Crow scout assured them that every morning, an hour or so after eating, the pony was raced up to "that butte, round and back here. Then, by and by, sun low, go again."

So, fully informed, the white spies retired; sneaked back to their horses and in less than two hours were at Fort Ryan.

"Well, Colonel, we sure saw the whole thing," said Hartigan. "They are not taking any chances on it. 'Tisn't much of a stable—nary a shingle overhead—but they're surely training that buckskin; and it's hand-picked hay they give him and sandpapered oats, worth gold; and they don't neglect his coat; and by the same token it's out for a race they are."

And now Kyle unfolded his plan to the Colonel. It was nothing less than this: to send a half-breed trader to the Indian training camp with a supply of whiskey, play on the weakness of the Red man till man, woman and boy, and others if there were any, were stupid drunk; then have Red Rover brought secretly, and at dawn, take the buckskin out of the corral, put a jockey on each, develop the best speed of both horses around the Indian training track, and so get an absolute gauge to guide the betting.

At first, the Colonel demurred. "Was it quite honourable?"

"Why not? Didn't they come and run their horse against ours in a trial, right here on the garrison track, without asking our leave? We are not going to hurt the pony in any way."

The temptation was too much for human nature. The Colonel finally agreed; and all that was needed was the working out of details. Hartigan was eager to be one of the jockeys. "Sure it wasn't a real race in the sense that stakes were up." The Colonel shook his head. "If you were about one hundred pounds lighter we'd be glad to have you, but one hundred and eighty pounds is too much for any horse."

It was no easy matter to get the right weight. The cavalrymen were all too heavy; but an odd character had turned up, the second son of an English baronet, a dissipated youth, barely a hundred pounds in weight; an agglomeration of most weak vices, but thin, tough, and a born and trained horseman. He was selected for one, and Little Breeches, a cowboy of diminutive proportions, for the other. All the material was now in sight for the scheme.

CHAPTER XXV

THE SECRET OF YELLOWBANK CANYON

Lou Chamreau was of French and Indian blood, chiefly Crow Indian. For twenty years he had been trading out of Pierre, Dakota, among the western tribes. He spoke French and Crow perfectly, he knew a little Sioux, and he was quite proficient in the universal Sign Language. Lou had lost money on the July horse-race, and was quite ready to play the white man's game.

On a certain afternoon in the latter part of August the trader might have been seen driving a very rickety wagon along the rough trail through the Badlands twenty miles to the eastward of Fort Ryan. Much hard luck had pursued him, if one might judge by the appearance of his outfit and from his story. In his extremity his teamster had left him and he was travelling alone. It was just as he reached the boulder-strewn descent into Yellowbank Creek that the climax came. The wagon upset and, falling some twenty feet, was lodged between the cutbanks in very bad shape. The horses were saved though the giving way of the harness; and having hobbled and turned them out to graze, Lou mounted a butte to seek for sign of help.

The sun was low in the west now; and across the glowing sky he noted a thread of smoke. Within a few minutes it had been his guide to an Indian tepee—a solitary tepee in this lone and little-known canyon of the Yellowbank—and entering, he recognized an old acquaintance. After sitting and smoking, he told of his troubles and asked the Red man to come and help get the wagon out of the gully.

The Indian made the signs: "Yes, at sunrise."

Chamreau smoked for a time, then said: "I'm afraid I'll lose the 'fire water' in that keg. It may be leaking under the wagon." To which the Sioux warrior said:

"Let us go now."

The keg was found intact, and to obviate all risk, was brought to the Indian camp. Chamreau deferred opening it as long as he could, so that it was midnight before the "Cowboy's delight" was handed round, and by three or four in the morning the camp was sunken in a deadly stupor.

According to the plan, Chamreau was to take a brand from the lodge and, in the black night outside, make a vivid zigzag in the air a few times, when his plot was obviously a success. But he became so deeply interested in giving realism to his own share of the spree that he forgot about everything else, and the rest of the scheme was omitted, so far as he was concerned.

But with the dim dawn there arrived in camp a couple of horsemen, one an Indian. The camp was dead. With the exception of a dog at the doorway and a horse in the corral, there was none to note their arrival. The dog growled, barked and sneaked aside. The Crow Indian hurled a stone with such accuracy that the dog accepted the arrivals as lawful, and sat down, afar off, to think it over.

The inmates of the lodge; man, woman, boy and Chamreau, were insensible and would evidently remain so for many hours. The Crow Indian and Kyle took brands from the fire and made vivid lightnings in the air. Within ten minutes, a group of horsemen came trampling down the slope and up the pleasant valley of the Yellowbank.

It was not without some twinges of conscience that Hartigan peeped into the lodge to see the utterly degrading stupefaction of the poison, but he was alone in feeling anything like regret. The rest of the party were given over to wild hilarity. At once, they made for the corral. Yes, there he was, really a fine animal, the buckskin cayuse that had proved so important. And there, carefully protected, was a lot of baled timothy hay and fine oats, brought there at great cost. It is not often that a lot of jockeys and horsemen are so careful of the enemy's mount. They handled that buckskin as if he had been made of glass, they watered him, they groomed him, they gave him a light feed and walked him gently up and down. Then, as the sun rose, he was taken for a short canter.

"He's pretty good," said the jockey as they came in, "but nothing wonderful that I can see."

Meanwhile, Red Rover was also watered, fed, rubbed down, limbered up, and after every loving, horse-wise care was spent on both animals, the jockeys were given their mounts and headed for the starting point on the two-mile course.

First they ambled easily around the track to study the ground. They started together and ran neck and neck for a quarter of a mile, then pulled rein, as this was a mere warm-up. Then they returned to the starting post, and the cowboy jockey on the buckskin said: "Well, boys, he's a good bronk, but I don't seem to feel any blood in him."

At the signal, they went off together, and behind them Captain Wayne, the Preacher, and a dozen more white men who were interested. These onlookers dropped behind as the racers went at high speed, but the view was clear, even when afar. The tall sorrel horse was a little ahead, but the buckskin displayed surprising power and speed. At the turning point he was very little behind. And now, on the home run, was to be the real trial. Would the bottom of the prairie pony overmatch the legs of the blooded horse?

The spectators were assembled at the place half way down, to meet them coming back, and follow close behind. It grew very exciting as both horses developed their best speed, and as they came to the winning post, it was clear to all that the buckskin had no chance in a fair race with Red Rover. It was incidentally clear to Hartigan, and those near by, that Red Rover had no chance against Blazing Star, even though the latter bore a heavy load; but that was not the point of general interest.

The serious business happily done, they tenderly groomed the buckskin and returned him to the corral, gave him a good supply of hay and said good-bye to the drunken Indians, the two-faced Chamreau, and the glorious Yellowbank, with its lonely lodge, its strange corral and its growlsome Indian dog.

CHAPTER XXVI

PREPARING FOR THE DAY

They were a merry lot that galloped back to Fort Ryan that morning, and a still merrier crowd that gathered at Cedar Mountain, when it was whispered about that in a fair and square try-out the buckskin cayuse was badly beaten by Red Rover. The white men had a dead sure thing. "Now is the time, boys, most anything you like, raise money anyhow, you can't go wrong on this. We've got the wily Red men skinned. Now we'll get our money back and more." "Of course it's fair, anything's fair to get ahead on a horse race." And as the tale was whispered round, it grew until it would seem that Red Rover had cantered in, while the buckskin strained himself to keep within a couple of hundred yards of the racer.

So the gossip went and one serious thing resulted: the training slackened. Why bother when the horse was going to have a walk-over? The Colonel was too much engrossed with other matters to do more than give good advice. The trainer's laxity pervaded those about him, and Red Rover was let down with all the rest. When they ran out of baled timothy the shortage was not revealed till it occurred. This meant a week's delay. The trainer, going to Cedar Mountain on a celebration, left an underling in charge who knew no better than to stuff the horse with alfalfa for a change, and a slight cold was the result. What the Colonel said when he heard of it was not couched in departmental phraseology.

Gambling has always been a racial sin of the Indian. He did not drink or horse-race or torture pioneers till the white man taught him; but gamble he always did. And under the stimulus of great excitement and new stakes the habit became a craze. Within a few days, Red Cloud appeared at the Fort with a great retinue, a whole village complete when they camped, and announced that he and his people had some fifty thousand dollars in sight to stake on the race; which, of course, was to be a scratch race for both. The soldiers, being very human, raised all they could—and much that they couldn't, really—to cover this handsome sum. Red Cloud then returned to his camp.

The next day he was back to say that, in case the whites had no more money to bet, the Indians were willing to bet horses and saddles, goods, etc., and thereupon a new craze possessed them. A government plough was wagered against a settler's looking-glass, a hen and her chickens against a buffalo robe, and many another odd combination. The Indians seemed to go wild on the issue. At last the U. S. Indian Agent came to the Colonel to protest.

"Colonel, I can manage these people all right if they are let alone, but this horse race and the betting are upsetting everything. I suppose you have a dead sure thing or you wouldn't be so reckless, but you are making awful trouble for every one else, and I wish you'd put on the brakes."

The Colonel either could not, or would not; for the excitement grew as the day came near. As a last effort the Indian agent, one of the few who were conscientiously doing their best for the Indians, went to Red Cloud to protest and warn him that the whites were laying a trap for him and his people and would clean them out of everything.

Red Cloud's eyes twinkled as he said: "Yes, they always do."

"I mean on the horse race; they will skin you; don't you know they've had your horse out in a trial race with theirs, and that it's no race at all?"

Again the Chief's eyes lighted up. He gave a little grunt and said. "Mebbe so."

Hartigan suffered all the agonies of crucified instincts in this excitement. He longed to be in everything, to bet and forecast and play the game with them all. What would he not have given to be the selected jockey, to smell the hot saddle every day, to hear the sweet squeak of the leather or feel the mighty shoulder play of the noble racing beast beneath him. But such things were not for him. He was shut in, as never monk was held, from earthly joy; not by material bars and walls, but by his duty to the Church, by his word as a man, by the influence of Belle.

She trembled in her thought for him at times, his racing blood was so strong. She often rode by his side to Fort Ryan and watched him as he looked on at the training of the Rover. His every remark was a comment of the connoisseur. "Look at that, look at that, Belle. That's right, he stopped to change his feet. He's a jockey all right. He ought not to do that tap-tapping with the quirt—the horse doesn't understand it, it worries him. I don't like to see a man knee-pinch a horse in that way; it tells on a two-mile run. He's heavy-handed on the reins; some horses need it, but not that one," and so on without pause.

Never once did his conversation turn on the Church or its work; and Belle was puzzled and uneasy. Then, one day when she and Hartigan were to have ridden out, he sent a note to say that he was in trouble. Blazing Star was hurt. Belle went at once to the stable and there she found the Preacher on his knees, in an armless old undershirt, rubbing linament on to some slight bump on Blazing Star's nigh hock. A sculptor would have paused to gaze at the great splendid arms—clean and white and muscled like Theseus—massive, supple, and quick. Hartigan was very serious.

"I don't know just what it is, Belle; it looks like a puff, but it may be only a sting or a bot. Anyway, I'm afraid it's rest for a week it means," and he rubbed and rubbed the embrocation in with force, while Blazing Star looked back with liquid eyes.

This seemed like a misfortune, but it proved a blessing, for it kept Hartigan out of the racing crowd for a week at a time when he was skating on ice that was very, very thin.

As Saturday came, the Rev. Dr. Jebb received an unexpected call from a very regular caller—the Rev. James Hartigan—to ask if Dr. Jebb would kindly take both sermons on Sunday next. Blazing Star had a puff on his nigh hock, inside, a little above the leg-wart; it might not amount to much, but it required a good deal of attention every few hours, both day and night, to prevent the possibility of its becoming serious from neglect.

CHAPTER XXVII

THE START

September came, with all the multiplied glories of the Black Hills—calm, beautiful weather in a calm and beautiful country. For days back, there had been long strings of Indians, with their families and camp outfits, moving down the trail between the hills, bound all for the great raceground at Fort Ryan. Lodges were set up every day. Each of the half-dozen tribes formed its own group. Ranchmen came riding in, followed by prairie schooners or round-up wagons, for their camps; motley nondescripts from Deadwood and places round about. There were even folk from Bismarck and Pierre and, of course, all Cedar Mountain and the soldiers from the Fort.

"Sure, I didn't know there *were* so many people," was Hartigan's remark to Belle, as they rode on the morning of the fifteenth about the camp with its different kinds of life. Then, after a long pause and gaze around, he added, in self-examining tone: "Faith, Belle, it seems to me that, being a Preacher, I ought to get up and denounce the whole thing, preach right now and evermore against it, and do all I can to stop it, but—heaven help me if I am a hypocrite—I don't feel that way at all; I just love it, I love to see all these people here, I love to see the horses, and I wouldn't miss that race if it were the last thing on earth I was to look on. Oh, I haven't been betting, Belle," he hastened to explain as he saw the look of dread on her face. "I've kept clear of it all, but God only knows what it means to me."

"Never fear, Belle," he went on, "I won't ride in a race, I won't bet; I've given my word."

"Oh, Jim, you are a riddle; you are not one, you are two men; and they fight the whole time. But I know the wiser one is winning and I think the best friend you ever had was that big fellow that threatened you with the 'bone-rot' if ever you broke your word. I believe in you more and more," and impulsively she laid her hand on his with a warmth that provoked such instant response that she smote her horse and swung away—fearful of a situation for which she was not ready.

At three o'clock, an officer from the Fort rode over to Red Cloud's lodge and notified him that in one hour the race was to begin. The War-chief grunted.

At four, the crowd was dense around the track, and the country near seemed quite deserted. Near the starting post, which was also the finish, were a huge crowd and a small army of mounted men. Suddenly shots were heard, and a great shout went up from the Indian camp; then forth came Red Cloud, in all his war paint and eagle feathers, followed by other warriors; and carefully led in the middle of the procession was the famous buckskin cayuse, sleek, clean-limbed, but decorated with eagle feathers in mane and tail, with furry danglers on his fetlocks and a large red hand painted on each shoulder and hip. He had no saddle and was led with an ordinary hackima of hair rope around his lower jaw. He walked alertly and proudly, but showed no unusual evidence of pace or fire.

Then a cannon boomed at the Fort, and from the gate there issued another procession, soldiers chiefly, following their Colonel. First among them came a bugler, the officers, then next a trooper, leading the white hope— the precious Red Rover. His groomed and glossy coat was shining in the sun; his life and power were shown in every movement as he pranced at times, in spite of the continual restraint of his trainer, who was leading him. On the other side, rode Peaches, the little English jockey. It was a bitter pill to the Americans that they should have to trust their fortunes to an English rider, but all their men were too heavy, except Little Breeches, and, he, alas, had fallen into the hands of the whiskey mongers. The ladies of the garrison rode close behind; and last, came the regimental band, in full thump and blare. As they neared the starting post, the band was hushed and the bugle blew a fanfare; then, with the Colonel leading, the racer was taken to the starting post.

Red Cloud was there calmly waiting with his counsellors and braves and the buckskin cayuse.

"Are you ready?" shouted Colonel Waller.

"Ho," said Red Cloud, and with an imperious wave of his hand he indicated "Go ahead!"

The light racing pad was put on Red Rover, the jockey mounted and rode him at a canter for a hundred yards and back, amid an outburst of applause as the splendid creature showed his pace. Then the groom approached and tightened the cinch.

The buckskin cayuse was brought to the front. Red Cloud made a gesture. A sixteen-year-old boy, armed with a quirt, appeared; an Indian gave him a leg up, and, naked to the breech clout on the naked horse, he sat like a statue. Jim got a strange thrill as he recognized him for the vigil-keeper of Cedar Mountain.

"Well," grumbled the Colonel, as he noted the jockey, "that's a twenty-five pound handicap on us, but I guess we can stand it." Yet, when they saw the two horses together, there was less disparity in size than they had supposed. But there was something about the buckskin that caught Hartigan's eye and made him remark: "It isn't going to be such a walk-over as our fellows think." And the trainer of Red Rover, as he noted the round barrel, clean limbs, and flaring nostrils of the buckskin, had for a moment just a guilty twinge as he recalled how lax he had been in the training after that run at Yellowbank Canyon.

But all was ready. The white men won the toss for choice and got the inside track; not that it mattered very much, except at the turn. The crowd was sent back to the lines, the riders held the racers to the scratch and, at a pistol crack, they bounded away.

Those that expected to see something spectacular at the start were disappointed. The English jockey leaned forward, touched Red Rover with his whip, and alongside the Indian boy on the buckskin did the very same thing. The Indian boy smiled and the Englishman responded, but in a superior way. He felt it was almost unfair to run against such a child, and in such a race, which wasn't a real race at all, in spite of the heavy stakes.

Thus they rode side by side at a good pace for half a mile, during which the buckskin drifted behind a little, now a length, now a length and a half. Next the copper-coloured jockey touched him up and, before the white man knew it, the bounding buckskin closed again and came right up, but now on the inside track. If the Englishman had not felt so confident, he would have stopped this well-known trick. It might not have been easy, since there were no lines or posts except the turning point, but it could have been prevented by deft man[oe]uvring. However, the Indian was now abreast on the inside and as the Englishman watched him he concluded that this child of nature was not so simple as he looked. He comforted himself with the thought that the other would need all he could get out of jockeying.

CHAPTER XXVIII

THE FINISH

The first mile was covered in good, but not remarkable time. Then they came to the turning point. There was just the chance of changing places here, for the inner horse had the disadvantage of the sharper turn, but the Indian boy made sure by dropping back a half length and the turn was made without a reverse. After them now with shouts of joy went all the mounted men who had been waiting and rode in a thundering charge, yelling and cheering. The white jockey knew now that he was not dealing with a fool. The red boy, though not so well mounted, was just as good a rider as himself, and twenty pounds lighter, besides being without leathers, which raised the handicap to fully twenty-five pounds. In that first half mile on the home stretch the buckskin still was head and neck behind. Then the riders put forth all their skill and each did his best to call forth every ounce of strength and every spurt of speed in his mount.

The Indian boy let off his native yell and cried: "Ho, Huya—Huya—Huya!" and the keen quirt flashed and the buckskin flew.

"Ho, Rover! good boy, git, git!" and the white man smote the shining flank; and both the noble brutes responded as they had not done before. The sense of play was gone. It was now the real and desperate race. The gazing thousands ranged about knew that, and the mingled roar of all their voices rose to a mighty booming sound.

"Ho, Rover! Run, boy, run!"

"Huya, Shunguna, Ho! Ho! Yeh! Yeh! Yeh!" and the redskin rider smote hard those heaving flanks.

Flash, flash, those shadowy hoofs; thud, thud, upon the plain; the buckskin's neck forged slowly on, now lapped the red-gold shoulder of his foe. The redskin shrieked, the riding mob behind gave voice and rode like madmen. The racers plunged and plunged, the riders lay down almost to their necks, plying their quirts and shouting words of urge.

The buckskin still won inches on the race, but the Rover led. The last, the final furlong was at hand. The riders yelled, the rabble yelled, guns were fired in mad excitement, and all restraint was gone. It was win—win— burst—die—but *win*! And never jockeys harder rode and never horses better ran; the test was fair. Red Rover did his best, yet his rival's legs in that last spurt moved as a rabbit's legs, a maze of shadowy pounding limbs, and—sickening sight—the buckskin with the copper rider forged still more ahead—a neck, half a length ahead—and the race was *won*.

Peaches was in tears. "Colonel," he said, in a broken voice, "it was that twenty-five pound handicap did it; it wasn't fair."

The Colonel growled something about "a lot of fools to let up on the training after that Yellowbank trial."

Hartigan was standing near; gloomy, but not so gloomy as the rest; and when there came a chance to be heard, he said: "Colonel, once I see a horse close to, in fair daylight, I can always remember him afterward. I've been looking over their buckskin cayuse, and it's *not the same one* we raced in the Yellowbank."

The Colonel turned quickly around. "Are you sure?"

"Absolutely certain," was the answer.

"My goodness—you are right. I distrusted the whole business from the start. You are right; they fooled us on a stool-pigeon; this whole thing was a put-up job. The simple Red man!"

The "perchers" were gathered at the blacksmith shop next afternoon. "Well," said Shives, "I've done fifteen dollars' worth of work to-day and haven't taken in a cent." The audience grunted and he went on. "Every tap of it was for broken-down bums trying to get out of town—skinned by the simple Red man. Horses shod, tires set, bolts fixed, all kinds of cripplements. All they want is help to get out, get out; at any price get out. Well, it'll do you good, the whole caboodle of ye. Ye started out to do, and got done—everlastingly soaked." The blacksmith chuckled. "Serve you all right. I'm glad ye got it."

As Hartigan appeared, swinging a big stick and singing "The Wearing of the Green," Shives asked: "Well, Jim, how much did you lose?"

"Nothing," sang Hartigan cheerfully; "I don't bet"; and he went on singing, "'Tis the most distressful country this that ever yet was seen."

"Lucky dog! All the sports round this neck o' the woods are ruined. They say no gentleman will bet on a sure thing. H'm, maybe not. Well, fellows, cheer up; no man ever yet was made, until he had been ruined a couple of times; and all I hope is that the Reds will get up another race and soak ye to the limit. Then maybe some o' ye will brace up and be men; but I dunno."

"Guess they've soaked us to the limit now," was the general voice of those assembled.

Poor Higginbotham had gone in rather strong for him, in spite of his wife, and there was no blue sky in his world, or prospect of it.

Then they turned on Hartigan, who was going through the movements of singlestick, on the open floor. "Was he white, or wasn't he? How could he stand by and see the whole settlement skinned alive by Red Injins when he had the game in his own hands? Why didn't he enter Blazing Star? He didn't seem to take much interest in the affair, probably he wanted the Red skins to win." The jibe stung Jim to the quick; he ceased his exuberant exercise; the song died on his lips, and he strode away in silence.

CHAPTER XXIX

THE RIDERS

It is the continual boast of the cowboys that they are the best riders on earth. It is the continual boast also of Cossack, Boer, Australian, Gaucho, and all who live on and by the horse. And when we sift the claim of each of those named we find that it is founded wholly on this, that they can sit on the back of any steed, however wild, and defy all its efforts to dislodge them. All their standards are designed to show the power of the man to overpower the horse. But there is one very large consideration that seems not to enter their consciousness at all, and that is how to get the best out of the horse—to develop and utilize, not crush its power. We undoubtedly find this idea best established in the riding schools of Europe. In these grammar schools violence is forbidden, almost unknown. For a man to fight with his horse would be a disgrace; to abuse or over-ride him—a shame; to lade him with a three-pound bit and a thirty-pound saddle—a confession of inability to control or stay on. In every part of the world where the horse has been developed, it has been in exact ratio with the creed of the riding schools. No one that has seen both classes of riders can have a doubt that the best horsemen in the world are those of Europe, who control the horse with skill—not brute force. The cowboys are mere broncho-busters.

Hartigan had gathered not a little of true horse learning in his early days, and he was disgusted now to see how lightly and cheaply the westerner held his horse. "Break him down and get another" was the method in vogue; and the test of a rider was, "Can he ride a horse to death?" The thirty-pound saddle used was an evidence of the intent and a guarantee of the result. As soon as he could afford it, Jim sent back to Chicago for an English pad, the kind he was used to, and thus he cut his riding weight down by nearly twenty pounds. Then there arrived at Fort Ryan a travelling inspector, who spent a month teaching the men the latest ideas in the care of horses. Among the tricks was the "flat ambush." This is how it is done: With reins in the left hand, and that hand in the mane at the withers, you stand at the nigh shoulder; lift the nigh front foot in your right hand till the hoof is near the horse's elbow; pull the horse toward you with the left hand in the mane; talk gently; pull, and press. If your horse trusts you, he will gradually bend over toward you; lower his body to the ground; and at last lie flat, head and all, with the animal's legs away from you. Behind the horse's body the rifleman may squat, shoot from cover, and have an ample breastwork if the animal is trained to "stand the gun." It is a pretty trick, though of less practical use than was expected. It is, however, a quick measure of the horse's confidence in the rider; and it speaks well for the 99th Cavalry that more than half the horses learned it in a week. This was a new game to Hartigan, and he found a fresh joy in it as an excuse for fussing around the stable and playing with his horse.

October came in with glory on the hills. The plains were golden in their autumn grass, and on a wonderful day in the early part of the month Hartigan and Belle went riding down the canyon.

Belle had a scheme for coördinating their church work with that of the Baptists and Presbyterians, both represented now in their town of fifteen hundred inhabitants. But before she could get it laid before Jim, he was extolling the quick responsiveness of Blazing Star, and must needs demonstrate the latest accomplishment the horse had learned. That over, Belle resurrected her plan; but a gunshot at Fort Ryan switched the current of his thoughts to the eventful race.

Belle changed the subject and unfolded a scheme for getting all the Bylow children into the Cedar Mountain school the coming winter. They had just come to a little twelve-foot cut-bank gully, and Jim exclaimed: "Now, Belle, just watch him take it," and over they sailed, the perfection of grace. "I tell you, Belle," he went on, "it was a great idea to get that eastern pad. I've cut down my riding weight nearly twenty pounds by dropping all that gear. Blazing Star can clear six inches higher and go a foot farther in a jump, and I'll bet it gives him one hundred feet in a mile run."

Again Belle harked back to the school project. "It could be done for half the teacher's salary and every one of the neglected children might get a chance. It all depends on the attitude that School Trustee Higginbotham takes. My idea is to approach him through Hannah. She has a mighty level head, and if you and Dr. Jebb——"

"Oh! look at this coyote!" ejaculated Hartigan. "I must give him a run"; and away he went. For half a mile there was an open flat, and the superior speed of the horse reduced the distance, at a very rapid rate. But the coyote reached a gully and disappeared with the quickness and cleverness of its race. Hartigan came galloping back.

Belle was looking amused and also worried. "Oh, Jim," she said, "I don't know what I am going to do with you. You won't talk Church, you won't talk school, you won't talk shop. All your thoughts are centred on horses, hunting—and coyotes," she added with a laugh.

"Sure, Belle, I never see a coyote run without thinking of a night I spent on the Cheyenne, when that puling little English lord spent the whole night shivering up a tree, to hear me and Little Breeches snoring on the ground and he thought it was wolves eating us up, because a little while before a coyote yelled in the bushes——" and again he was off in a racy account of those thrilling moments.

"Jim," she said, "I am going to say nothing but 'yes' and 'no' for a while, until you exhaust all your horse talk. Then I am going to make one more effort."

"A jack rabbit, by the powers!" Sure enough, a big white jack leaped up and darted away. A jack is speedier than a coyote, so Hartigan could not resist. "Hi, Hi, Hi!" he shouted to Blazing Star; and with flat hand on the croup, he raised the speed to top gear in a few jumps.

It was a fair sight to behold, and to many a cow-man it would have been information. The jack rabbit, next to the antelope, is the speediest quadruped on the plains. The cowboy does not try to follow the jack rabbit, but the blooded racer did. In a quarter of a mile the horse was nearly on him. He dodged like chain lightning—dodged as his life had taught him to dodge before the coyote and the hawk. The horse slowed up; the rabbit crossed a ridge; and when the rider reined upon the top, the jack was no more seen.

But just ahead was a finer sight. A band of antelope sprang forward with their white sterns shining. Of all the quadrupeds on the Plains, the antelope is the speediest. The greyhound can catch the hare; but is left a hopeless laggard by the swift-footed courser. No mounted Indian ever dreamed of overtaking the antelope in open chase. In speed it stands the highest in the West. Jim had often wished to match his steed against these plains-born coursers; but, hitherto, although antelope were often seen, they were protected by rough gullies or boulders or badger holes. A band of antelope on a level, open stretch was a glorious chance.

Bending low over his horse's neck, he shouted: "Now, Blazing Star, go it; ho! boy, go it!" and struck the flank behind for clear interpretation. The horse sprang forth at speed. The bounding wild things, just ahead, laid back their ears and went so fast that not a leg was seen, only a whizzing, blurred maze. And Blazing Star took in the thought and travelled faster and faster. The furlong start they had began to shrink.

"Good boy!" the rider shouted in elation. "Go it! go it, Blazing Star!" The antelope spurted—for a moment held their own; then, weakening at a mile, they lost so fast that Jim yelled and swung his hat, and in a little more the herd was overtaken. Fear seemed to rob them of power as Blazing Star dashed in among them. The bright-eyed pronghorns swerved; and the band split wide, and the horse dashed through. As he wheeled and galloped back, he shouted: "You saw that, Belle? You saw it? It has never been done before. In a fair race, on open stretch, they had two hundred yards' start and I caught them in a mile. Now I know what Blazing Star is. No creature on legs can beat him; no horse in the West can match him."

In a little while the riders turned again to Cedar Mountain. Hartigan led the way—and the talk. It was a stirring ride, but Belle's face wore a worried look when he left her.

CHAPTER XXX

THE FIRE

Every new town in America has the same set routine of experience. It springs up on land selected and laid out by a real estate speculator. The flimsiest and most combustible of buildings are rushed up. When the town has about five thousand inhabitants and these fire-trap buildings are close enough to burn one another, a fire breaks out and sweeps the whole thing away, destroying human lives, valuable stock, and priceless records; after which begins the epoch of brick buildings and fire prevention.

Cedar Mountain had not reached the size or compactness required for the wipe-out when its baptism of fire took place. Hartigan was roused in the night by a noise outside. Going to the window, he saw the sky filled with the glare of fire. As quickly as possible, he dressed and ran forth, becoming deeply agitated when he found that the fire was in the hotel whose stable housed Blazing Star. It was with a dreadful heartsink that he ran there. The stable was smoking, but not yet afire, and, with a thankful heart, he hurried Blazing Star forth, got him away to a safe place, and returned just in time to see the stable and all its immovable contents go up in a ruddy roar as the hay and straw took fire.

There were no human lives lost; nor any dwellings other than the hotel—for there was a clear space around that fire-trap and there had been no wind—but it was a valid baptism of fire. It resulted in the organization of a Volunteer Fire Brigade, and it also resulted in Hartigan's determination to erect a stable of his own, where he could have his horse under his eye, day and night. What he built was not a large stable, only ten by twelve feet, of rough pine lumber, with tar-paper weather-proofing and no floor, but he did it entirely with his own hands at a material cost of twelve dollars; and he put his soul into it. There were two stalls, one for Blazing Star and one for supplies. There was much good-humoured jesting at the "Horse Preacher" while the stable was building and the story went the rounds that he often used the empty stall for a study, in preference to the silent little room in the house. In any case, he hand-picked the hay to guard against the poisonous loco-weed, and washed the oats, to shut out any possibility of smut.

Immediately after the fire Higginbotham began to talk business to Jim. A mutual affection had grown up and the little agent and his wife had early become prominent in the church. As deacon, Higginbotham rendered good service, although it was noted that his judgment was always best after he had talked matters over at home. He was not averse to using his church connection for business purposes. In fact, he had been heard to say that the Church itself was chiefly a huge fire insurance company, taking risks for the next world instead of this. On the morning after the fire, he was up betimes to sail with the wind, to take advantage of the stir-up that the public mind had got; and he secured a lot of new business.

"Now, Mr. Hartigan, why don't you insure that horse of yours? Just think where you would have been if you hadn't got him out in time last night. Why, I knew a man who bought a horse for fifty dollars in the morning, insured him for two hundred and fifty dollars at noon, and next night he was burnt up. The very next day he got his check for two hundred and fifty dollars. That's the way our company does business; all in twenty-four hours."

The idea of a joyful profit out of Blazing Star's incinerated remains was distinctly unpleasant, much like asking a mother to realize on her baby, and Hartigan took out no policy, but it had the effect of making him try to set a market value on the horse.

It was late in the season now, October was nearly gone; but still he and Belle rode forth together.

"What is next Sunday's lesson?" was Belle's very usual question. "Well," said Hartigan, "I came across a text that filled me with joy. 'When Amaziah, King of Judah, was murdered,' it says, 'They brought him upon horses and buried him with his fathers in the city of Judah.'

"Brought him on horses. What a picture, Belle! Just think of that royal stiff strapped square across the backs of four fine horses, all bridled together, and then driven madly across the desert, through the land of the freebooting Arabs, who would be more than apt to seize the corpse and hold it for a ransom. What a race! You bet they had horses then! They were Arab stock all right. I wonder no artist ever put that royal funeral on canvas. How does it strike you, Belle?"

"Wild enough and picturesque enough for the Black Hills; but I don't seem to get the lesson, I might almost add another text to your list: 'A horse is a vain thing for safety.'" Then, suddenly, she said: "Have you seen Colonel Waller lately?"

"No."

"Is it too far to ride there?"

"Not if you can stand it."

"I can; but I wish you'd tighten my cinch."

Jim was well pleased to be her groom; and, hauling on the strap, his hat tipped off and his head touched her knee, she laid her hand on his head and a thrill went through him. Belle knew the game and the risks, in spite of her very old-fashioned parents. All along, she had held him back to a certain line; even though it was clearly understood to both of them and all their world that he was her avowed and accepted lover. She gloried in his physical charm and power. She took a woman's pride in his devotion, and maybe, most of all, in her sovereignty over him; she realized more clearly than any one else, how completely he was her plastic material. A mighty engine, indeed, he had need of a skilful engineer. A splendid steed of rarest power and gift, his power and gift were useless, even worse, without the deft control of the rider, who should become in a sense his soul, as the captain is the soul of a great ship. And Belle had come to know that the best work she could ever hope to do was as the captain of this ship.

And what was to hinder? Belle knew; her soft brown eyes could see much farther through the stone wall than could his piercing eyes of blue. She estimated at its true potency the passion that now threatened to wreck his career. A lover of horses always, an absolute worshipper of Blazing Star, he was barely held in restraint by his promises and fears of Church discipline, and Belle foresaw a time when his wild, impulsive nature would break out. He would surely be swept away by the wild currents of which the horse race is the vortex; and, having once lost hold, he would go the pace, break all rules, and end...? She knew, but dared not say.

Winter would soon be on them and, with that, the end of their happy rides together on the plains. The different life enforced would put them more apart—cut off these saddle *tête-à-têtes*, and with all the happenings, past or future, in her mind Belle was ready for a woman's game; the time had come to play it. That tightening of the cinch was not by chance.

They rode a race for a mile and Jim gallantly held back his mount so that she should keep the lead. They passed a slough along whose edge the gentians still were blue; she wanted some, and when he brought them she patted his hand, and gave the flowers an honoured place. Suddenly a coyote appeared and she raced with him on its trail till it was lost to view. She called forth all her horsemanship to match his, and make him feel their perfect harmony; and as they rode side by side, she laid her hand on his arm to call attention to some creature of the plains when at other times she would merely have spoken. It thrilled and stirred him, so he tried to follow up this willingness for touch. But she swung away each time. Then at a later keep-your-distance hint she gaily held out a hand to him and teased him by eluding his grasp. But not for long; with a great spurt he swept upon her, seized the tantalizing hand now accidentally bared, and the thrill of her touch, the joy of acceptation in that tiny squeeze, went warmly kindling through him. His colour came, his bright blue eyes grew brighter, he glowed in body and in spirit. Never before had she seemed so absolutely fascinating; never before had he felt how much she was to him, how wholly desirable and lovely she was, how much his measure of all good things. But he was such a boy in this side of life that he had never said one open word of love. He was as shy as most youths are at sixteen.

They were half way to the Fort now, the level plain spreading for a mile about them. There was no chance of interruption. Their horses had drawn close together again. She said, "Look at the bruise on my hand from last week's ride through the brush." He seized the hand; there was no bruise to be seen, but he bent his head and fervently kissed the place.

"Jim, do you really care so much?" she asked, with a sidelong glance and a little flush.

"Oh, Belle, you know—you must know——" And he choked.

"I wouldn't like to see you hold any other woman's hand that way." Their horses' shoulders rubbed and she accidentally swayed toward him; she seemed to lose her balance. In a minute his strong arms were about her; a great emotion swept him and all his ardent soul was aflame. With sudden abandon of all restraint, he showered on her lips a lover's passionate kisses, and forced his unwonted tongue and lips to shape the old refrain: "I love you; I love you; I love you better than my life."

She hid her burning face, but he held her tight, and the horses moved as one.

"Will you, Belle? Will you be my wife? I can't do anything without you. You have saved me from ruin. I can't do anything without you."

A jack rabbit sprang from under their feet, and Blazing Star, true to his training, darted away; and so the pair were forced apart. But, in a moment, Jim was back.

"Will you, Belle? Won't you take me?" He seized her hand and would have sought her lips again, but she held him back.

"I will, Jim, on one condition. Will you promise?"

"Anything. I'll promise anything I have or can be. Tell me what it is, Belle?"

"I will not tell you now; but I will before we get back to Cedar Mountain. Now let us ride"; and she touched her pony with the quirt, and led at a gallop which ended only at the house of Colonel Waller in Fort Ryan.

CHAPTER XXXI

LOVE IN THE SADDLE

"Here come Apollo and Psyche," said Mrs. Waller, as she glimpsed them from the window. The Colonel was just leaving for his office and called to them, "Good morning! Go on in; Mrs. Waller is at home. I'll be back in half an hour."

Already there was a fire in the house, for the nights were chilly, and when the Colonel returned, they were sitting around it in the parlour.

"I want to see the stable," said Belle, so forth they went together, Hartigan with Mrs. Waller leading, and Belle with the Colonel. She lingered till the others were out of easy hearing, then led up to the subject of the horse race.

"It's a pretty sore subject yet," answered the Colonel. "Most of my men are pinching their families on half pay to work off their debts to those wily redskins."

"Do they have to pay?" said Belle.

"Well, these are debts of honour, you know, and in the man's code, that puts them ahead of rent, clothing, food, or mortgages."

"I suppose the men have got a lesson that will cure them of gambling for evermore?"

"Oh, no. Not at all. All they are thinking about now is where to get a horse that can turn the tables."

"Seems to me like burning one's hand because one got a finger scorched."

"Well, that's the man of it," said the Colonel. "If we could get Jim to run Blazing Star, the whole garrison would mortgage their lives for cash to stake on it and win back all they had lost or risked."

"Well, he won't; I tell you that. But why don't you buy Blazing Star, Colonel?"

"Because he won't sell. We've tried every way. I never saw a man so daffy over his horse."

"What would you consider a fair price, Colonel?"

"Well, Jim gave five dollars for him, to begin with, and refused two hundred and fifty dollars when he proved what stuff he had got. I should say three hundred dollars would be a fair price, four hundred dollars a good price and five hundred dollars an absolutely outside record price—scaled wholly on the fact that he's the fastest horse on these plains."

"Would *you* give five hundred dollars?"

"Yes, I would. I'll give Hartigan five hundred dollars for Blazing Star right now, in hard cash; but I don't say I'll hold it out very long. Accidents will happen; winter is coming, and a bad wintering often ruins a horse."

"Will you take the first chance to offer that to Hartigan? He'll refuse; but say you'll leave it open for a week, and I think you'll get Blazing Star."

The Colonel laughed a little, and wondered what was up. His wife, when she heard of it, said: "Ho, ho! I know; they want to get married, and that's the easiest way to raise the needful."

And thenceforth she took a motherly interest in the handsome couple.

Within half an hour the Colonel found the chance to make his offer; and got what he expected, a flat refusal.

"Sure, Colonel, it would be like selling the hand off my arm or the soul out of my body."

"Well, well," said the Colonel, "never mind. I won't take your answer now; we'll leave it open for a week."

After the midday meal, Jim and Belle mounted and rode away. Jim thought to take matters up where he had left off, but he found Belle inclined to be shy and rather preoccupied. He made several ineffectual attempts to get her to talk, but she always relapsed into silence. They were, indeed, half-way back, when Hartigan began for the fifth time:

"You said you would tell me on the road back."

"Tell you what?"

"Tell me the condition on which you will have me."

He leaned over and put his arm around her. This time she did not elude him. He clasped her and sought her lips and she allowed her head to sink on his shoulder while he gathered the reins of both horses in his hand, that they might not separate. She seemed content.

"You do care for me, don't you?" she whispered.

"Oh, Belle! I'd do anything for you. I'd give my life for you."

"You would? Anything?"

"Only try me."

"Would you give up the ministry if I asked you?"

"If—if—you thought it was right—I know it would be right. Yes, I'd do it."

"Then I won't ask that. I'll put you to a smaller test. Will you face it?"

"I'll promise now; I give you my word before you name it."

"Then this is what I ask—that you sell Blazing Star to Colonel Waller right now, this very day."

"Oh, oh, Belle!" he said, feebly; "Blazing Star!"

"Yes, Jim, that is the condition. I love you, Jim; but you must choose now between us. Is it Belle or Blazing Star?"

For a moment he seemed stunned but he tightened his arms about her, and tense the answer came. "I can't do without you, Belle, I can't do without you. I've given you my word. I take you on your terms."

"Oh, Jim!" and she broke down, passionately sobbing in his arms. "Oh, Jim! You great, glorious, wonderful, blind Jim Hartigan, don't you know that I love you? Don't you know I have thought it all out? Can't you see where Blazing Star was taking you? It is not caprice; you will know some day."

"I know, I know now. I'll do what you say."

"Then turn right around and go back to Fort Ryan." They turned; she led; and they raced without pulling rein.

"Colonel, I've come to take your offer," said Hartigan.

"You're a wise man," said the Colonel. "Come into the office." He drew up a check for five hundred dollars. Jim put it in his wallet and said feebly, "He's yours. You'll be kind to him?" Then he covered his face with his hands, and the tears splashed through his fingers to the floor.

"Never mind," said the Colonel, deeply touched. "He'll be treated like a king. You'll see him in the race next summer and you'll see him win."

In all the blackness of that hour of loss that thought was the one gleam of comfort in the realm of horse. Now he would see his racer on the track. The Church held him, but held his horse no longer.

Then the Angel of Destiny as he downward gazed, said to the Angel of the Fire—and his voice trembled a little as he spoke—"Rejoice, for the furnace was heated exceeding hot and the metal is shining brighter, far brighter than before."

BOOK IV

THE HORSE PREACHER AFOOT

CHAPTER XXXII

THE ADVENT OF MIDNIGHT

The ride home after that fateful decision was an event to be remembered. Jim was on a cavalry mount, loaned for the occasion. Belle felt that since he had given up so much for her, it was her part now to prove how good a bargain he had made; and she exerted all her powers to double her ample hold on his love and devotion. She had no reason to question her power; she had almost overmuch success. Jim wanted her to name the day, but whatever her wishes might have been, her judgment held her back.

"Jim, dear love, don't you see? We must wait a long time. Your income is barely enough for one. You are only a probationer with one year's leave from college, and, at most, an extension of another year possible. What little I can bring as my share of the 'combine' won't go very far."

"Well," said Jim, "I've got the cash to furnish our house with, anyway," and he slapped his hand on his wallet pocket. "I'll put that in the bank till we need it."

"Good boy!" and Belle smiled happily.

Arrived at Cedar Mountain, Jim took the cavalry mount to the livery stable; and three days later, the little stable he had built for Blazing Star was torn down and carried away.

Jim was looking for a new mount, when one day Cattleman Kyle appeared in the town, and they met for a few minutes at the blacksmith shop.

"Hello, Jim! What are you riding these days?" was his greeting.

"To tell the truth, I'm afoot, hard afoot," was the reply.

"Anything in sight?"

"Not yet."

"Come with me for a minute. I'm cutting down my saddle stock for the winter. I've got a bunch of bronchos in the corral by the river. Have a look at them."

Jim went rather reluctantly; his heart was still sore over Blazing Star, and he was not ready yet to put another into the vacant place. After a silent five minutes' walk, they reached the corral with fifty horses of all colours, sizes, and shapes. Then Kyle said: "Jim, I've been thinking, preachers ain't exactly broken-backed carrying their spondulix. I kind o' think I owe ye something in the way of possibilities for putting Blazing Star in hands which may be a big help to me. So there's my bunch; you can go over them at your own time and pick the best as a free gift."

"Ye mean it?"

"That's what I mean, and there's my hand on it," said Kyle. And it was so. That was the way of the old-time cattleman. If he lived at all, his money came in large chunks. He lived lavishly, and made a fortune, if moderately lucky. So they were a generous lot; they were truly cattle kings.

But the cattle king reducing his horse herd does not select his best stock for the hammer; quite the reverse. Some would have called his bunch the scrubs and tailings of the Circle K ranch. Hartigan knew that; but he also knew that it must contain some unbroken horses and he asked to see them. There were ten, and of these he selected the biggest. A man of his weight must have a better mount than a pony. So the tall, rawboned, black three-year-old was roped and handed over to the Preacher. Kyle did not fail to warn him that "Midnight" had a temper.

"Faith, it's mesilf can see that," said Hartigan, "but he isn't broken yet, and that means his temper isn't spoiled. And it's mesilf will bring him to time, and he never will be broke. If your broncho-busters take him in hand, they'll ride him in a week, but they'll make a divil of him. I'll take him in hand and in three months I'll have him following me round with tears in his eyes, just begging me to get on his back, and go for a run."

Who that knows the horse will doubt it? Hartigan's first aim was to convince the black colt that men were not cruel brutes, and that he, Hartigan, was the gentlest and kindest of them all. And this he did by being much with him, by soft talking, by never being abrupt, and by bringing him favourite food. Not in a stable—it was a month before the wild horse would consent to enter a stable—this first period of training was all in a corral. Then came the handling. Midnight was very apt to turn and kick when first a hand was laid on him, but he learned to tolerate, and then to love the hand of his master; and when this treatment was later reinforced with a currycomb, the sensation pleased him mightily. The bridle next went on by degrees—first as a halter, then as a hackimore, last complete with bit. The saddle was the next slow process—a surcingle, a folded blanket and cinch, a double blanket and cinch, a bag of oats and cinch and, finally, the saddle and rider. It was slow, but it was steadily successful; and whenever the black colt's ears went back or his teeth gave a rebellious snap, Jim knew he was going too fast, and gently avoided a clash. Never once did he fight with that horse; and before three months had passed, he was riding the tall black colt; and the colt was responding to his voice and his touch as a "broken" horse will never do.

"Yes," said Kyle, "I know all about that. It costs about twenty-five dollars to learn a horse that way, and it costs about five dollars to break him cowboy way. An average horse is worth only about twenty-five dollars. The cowboy way is good enough for our job, so I don't see any prospect of change till we get a price that will justify the 'training.'"

Belle was an intensely interested spectator of all this Midnight chapter. She wanted Jim to get a good horse that he would love, but oh, how she prayed and hoped he would not happen on another speeder! She knew quite well that it was about one chance in ten thousand; but she also knew that Jim could make a good horse out of mediocre material; and it was with anxiety just the reverse of his that she watched the black colt when first they rode together. He was strong and hard, but, thank heaven, she thought, showed no sign of racing blood.

"Of course, he'll come up a little later, when I get him well in hand," Jim explained apologetically.

And Belle added, "I hope not."

"Why?" asked Jim in surprise.

"Because, you might ride away from me." And she meant it.

CHAPTER XXXIII

THE SOCIABLE

Christmas time with its free days and its social gatherings was at hand; and the Church folk must needs respond to the spirit of the season with a "sociable." In such a meeting, the young minister is king—that is the tradition—and on this occasion it was easier than usual to crown the heir apparent. At least twenty girls were making love to Jim, and he was quite unconscious of it all, except that he thought them a little free, and at length he recited an appropriate couplet from "The Solitude of Alexander Selkirk": "They are so unaccustomed to man, their tameness is shocking to me." He joked and laughed with all; but ever he drifted over toward Belle, to consult, to whisper, to linger.

For such affairs there is a time-honoured and established programme that was fairly well adhered to at least in the early part. They met at the church parlours and gossiped; had a prayer, then more gossip; next followed tea and cakes in a poisonous abundance, and more gossip. Now the older preacher, as expected, read a chapter out of some safe story book, amid gossip—harmless in the main, but still gossip. Next the musical geniuses of the congregation were unchained. A perfectly well-meaning young lady sang, "Be kind to your brother, he may not last long," to an accompaniment of squeaks on the melodeon—and gossip. A boy orator recited "Chatham's speech on American Independence," and received an outburst of applause which, for a moment, overpowered the gossip.

Lou-Jane Hoomer, conspicuous for her intense hair and noisy laugh, had been active in getting up the sociable, and now she contributed of her talents by singing "Home, Sweet Home." About the middle of the second period, according to custom, the preacher should recite "Barbara Frietchie" to a whispering chorus of gossip. But Jim was brought up in a land not reached by Barbara's fame and he made a new departure by giving a Fenian poem—"Shamus O'Brien"—with such fervour that, for the moment, the whisperers forgot to gossip.

Belle, as the manager of the affair, was needed everywhere and all the time, but made no contribution to the programme. Lou-Jane scored such a success with "Home, Sweet Home" that she was afterward surrounded by a group of admirers, among them Jim Hartigan.

"Sure," he said, she "was liable to break up the meeting making every one so homesick," and she replied that "it would never break up as long as he was there to attract them all together."

John Higginbotham, with his unfailing insurance eye, pointed out that the stove-pipe wire had sagged, bringing the pipe perilously near the woodwork, and then gossiped about the robberies his company had suffered. A game of rhymes was proposed. In this one person gives a word and the next to him must at once match it with an appropriate rhyme. This diversion met with little enthusiasm and the party lagged until some one suggested that Jim recite. He chose a poem from Browning, "How They Brought the Good News from Ghent to Aix." He put his very soul in those galloping horses and wondered why the poet said so much about the men and so little about the steeds. Dr. Jebb could not quite "see the lesson," but the fire and power of the rendering gripped the audience. Dr. Carson said, "Now you're doing real stuff! If you'd cut out all your piffling goody talk and give us life like that, you'd have all the town with you."

Lou-Jane was actually moved, and Belle glowed with pride to see her hero really touching the nobler strings of human emotion—strings that such a community is apt to lose sight of under cobwebs of long disuse but they are there and ready to resound to the strong, true soul that can touch them with music.

But what was it in the trampling horses that stirred some undiscovered depth in his own heart? How came it that those lines drove fogbanks back and showed another height in his soul, a high place never seen before, even by himself? And, as those simple townfolk, stirred they knew not how, all clamoured for another song, he felt the thrill that once was his in the far-off stable yard of Links, when Denny Denard, brandishing a dung-fork, chanted "The Raiding of Aymal." Now it all came back and Hartigan shouted out the rede:

"Haakon is dead! Haakon is dead!Haakon of the bronze-hilt sword is dead.His son's in his stead;Aymal, tall son of Haakon,Swings now the bronze-hilt sword of his father.He is gone to the High-fieldenTo the high pasture to possess the twelve mares of his father;Black and bay and yellow, as the herdsman drave them past him;Black and yellow, their manes on the wind;And galloped a colt by the side of each."

So he sang in a chant the saga-singer's tale of the king killing all the colts save one that it might have the nursing of the twelve. His eye sparkled and glowed; his colour mounted; his soul was so stirred with the story that his spirit could fill the gaps where his memory failed. The sense of power was on him; he told the swinging tale as though it were in verity his own; and the hearers gazed intensely, feeling that he sang of himself. It was no acting, but a king proclaiming himself a king, when he told of the world won by the bronze sword bearer mounted on the twelve-times-nourished stallion colt; and he finished with a royal gesture and injunction:

"Ho! ye, ye seven tall sons of Aymal,Comes there a time when face you many trails;Hear this for wisdom now;Twelve colts had I and all save one I slew.The twelve-times-nourished charger grewAnd round the world he bore meAnd never failed; so all the world was mineAnd all the world I ruled.Ho, children of the bronze-hilt sword,Take this for guiding creed:Pick out your one great steedAnd slay the rest and ride."

And when he smote the table with his fist the folk in that poor, simple hall were hushed with awe. They had no words to clothe the thoughts that came, no experience of their own to match them. There was a pauses—a silence; a slow, uncertain sounding of applause. Carson glared half hypnotized; then said to himself: "This is not Jim Hartigan; this is the royal saga who sang."

What he clearly expressed, the others vaguely but deeply felt. As for Belle, the passion and the power of it possessed her. She was deeply moved—and puzzled, too. It was a side of Jim she had not known before. Later, as they went home together hand on arm, she held on to him very tightly and said softly: "Now I know that you are marked for big things in the world."

CHAPTER XXXIV

SPRINGTIME

Have you seen the springtime dawn on the Black Hills? No? Then you have never seen a real spring.

For long, dark, silent months the land has lain under a broad white robe, the plains are levelled, hidden, and the whiteness of the high spaces sweeps down to meet, on the lower hills, the sudden blackness of the forest pine. And now you know why these are named Black Hills. Full four white moons have waned; the blizzard wind has hissed and stung, till the house-bound wonder if the days of spring will ever come. In March, when the northward-heading crows appear, the sting-wind weakens, halts; the sweet south wind springs up, the snow-robe of the plains turns yellow here and there as the grass comes through, then lo! comes forth a world of crocus bloom. The white robe shrivels fast now, the brown pursues it up the mountain side till at the last there is nothing left but a high-up snow-cap hiding beneath the pines, slowly dissolving in a million crystal rills to swell the rolling Cheyenne far below. The spring birds fill the air, the little ones that twitter as they pass, and the great gold-breasted prairie lark that sings and sings: "The Spring, the Spring, the glory of the Spring!" Then all the world is glad, and stronger than the soft new wind, deeper than the impulse of awakening flower bulbs, broader than the brightening tinge of green—is the thrill of a world-wide, sky-wide joy and power, the exquisite tenderness and yearning which if you know, you know; and if you do not know it none can make you understand.

"O God of the blue and the green and the wind, oh, send me what my spirit craves." That is the prayer, the unspoken prayer, of every sun-wise creature in these days; and the wild things race and seek, and search and race, not knowing what draws them ever on; but they surely know when they find it, and then they are at rest.

And they rode, Belle and Jim, the big square man, and the maid with the age-old light in her eyes, and they rejoiced in the golden plains. They rode with the wild things of the plain, and though they talked of the past and the future there was for them but one thing worth a thought, the golden present in their golden youth.

"Oh, Belle, what fools we are! We talk of the past and of far-off days, of the blessings that are ahead of us, and I know there is no better joy than this, to ride and shout and be alive right now with you!"

Midnight had burgeoned out into a big strong horse; not swift, but staunch and better fitted than the other for a rider of such weight. The wound of losing Blazing Star had healed, and the scar it left was a precious thing to Jim much as the Indian holds his Sun Dance scars as proofs of fortitude unflinching.

Fort Ryan and all the plains were in a rosy light this spring. It was a threefold joy to ride on Midnight, with Belle, and to visit Blazing Star in his stall at the Fort. Hartigan felt a little guilty as the gentle creature would come and nose about for sugar lumps while Midnight would lay back his ears at the approach. Midnight had a temper, as was well known; but it was never let forth, for the master that had so little skill in handling men was adept with the horse.

These were very full days for Jim and Belle, though they took their happiness in very different moods. There never was a grown man more incapable of thought for the morrow than Hartigan; he was alive right now, he would right now enjoy his life and Belle should be the crown. But in her eyes even his imperception discovered a cloud.

"What is it, Belle? Why do you get that far-off troubled look?"

"Oh, Jim, you big, blind, childish giant; do you never think? You are only a probationer with one year's leave. That year is up on the first of May."

"Why, Belle darling, that's five weeks off. A world of things may happen before that."

"Yes, if we make them happen, and I'm going to try."

"Well, Belle, this thing I know; if you set your mind to it I'd bet—if I weren't a preacher—I'd bet there's not a thing could stand against you."

"I like your faith, Jim; but 'faith without works is dead'; and that means we must get up and rustle."

"What do you suggest?"

"Well, I have been rustling this long while back. I've been working Dr. Jebb and Mrs. Jebb and anybody else I could get hold of, to have your probation extended for another year. And the best news we have so far is the possibility of another six months. After that, you must go back to college to complete your course."

COLLEGE! Jim was thunderstruck. How many a man has all his dream of bliss summed up in that one word—college? "Oh, if only I had money enough to go to college!" is the cry of hundreds who hunger for the things that college means; and yet, to Jim, it was like a doom of death. College, with all the horror of the classroom ten times worse since knowing the better things. College in the far-off East—deadly, lifeless, crushing thing; college that meant good-bye to Belle, to life, and red blood on the plains. Yes, he knew it was coming, if ever he gave the horrid thing a thought; but now that it was close at hand the idea was maddening. College was simply another name for hell. The effect of the sudden thought on his wild, impulsive nature was one great surging tide of rebellion.

"*I won't go!*" he thundered. "Belle, do you suppose God brought me out here to meet you, and have you save me from ruin and help me to know the best things on earth, just to chuck it all and go back to a lot of useless rot about the number of wives the kings of Judah used to have, or how some two-faced Hebrew woman laid traps for some wine-soaked Philistine brute, and stuck the rotten loafer in the back with a kitchen knife all for the pleasure and glory of a righteous God! I don't want any more of it, Belle; *I won't go!* You've told me often enough that my instincts are better than my judgment, and my instincts tell me to stay right here," and his face flushed red with passion.

"Dear boy! Don't you know I'm trying to help you? Don't you know I mean to keep you here? You know that we can get anything we want, if we are willing to pay the price, and *will* have it. I mean to keep you here; only I am trying not to pay too high a price."

She laid her hand on his. He reached out and put an arm about her. She said nothing, and did nothing. She knew that he must blow off this fierce steam, and that the reaction would then set in with equal force.

They rode for a mile in silence; she wanted him to speak first.

"You always help me," he said at last, heaving a great sigh. "You are wiser than I am."

She gently patted his cheek. He went on: "What do you think I should do?"

"Nothing for three days; then we'll see."

They galloped for half a mile, and every sign of worry was gone from his face as they reined their horses in at the stable of Fort Ryan.

- 153 -

CHAPTER XXXV

WHEN THE GREASEWOOD IS IN BLOOM

Big things were in the air, as all the horsemen knew. Blazing Star had wintered well and, being a four-and-a-half-year-old, was in his prime. Red Rover in the adjoining stable was watched with equal care. Prairie hay was judged good enough for the country horses; but baled timothy, at shocking prices, was brought from Pierre for the two racers; and, after a brief period of letdown on clover and alfalfa, the regular routine diet of a race horse was begun, as a matter of course. Little Breeches had left, chiefly because of unpleasant remarks that he continued to hear in the stable. He had taken a springtime job among the cattle. So Peaches, having no other string to his bow, allowed the officers "to secure his services as second assistant trainer," as he phrased it, or, as they with brutal simplicity put it, "as stable boy." He accepted this gravely responsible position on the explicit understanding that allusions to the late race were in bad taste.

Why should these two horses be so carefully trained? There was no race on the calendar. No, but every one assumed that there would be a challenge, and nobody dreamed of declining it. So, one day when all the plains were spangle-glint with grass and bloom, the sentry reported horsemen in the south, a band of Indians, probably Sioux. It was an hour before they halted near the Fort, and Red Cloud, on a fine strong pony, came with his counsellors around him to swing his hand in the free grace of the sign talk, to smoke and wait, and wait and smoke, and then speak, as before, on the Colonel's porch.

"Did the Soldier High Chief want a race this year?"

"Sure thing," was all the interpreter had to transmute.

"When?"

"As before."

"When the greasewood blooms, on the white man's big noisy wet Sunday?" For the treaty money was to be paid that day. And Colonel Waller's eyes lit up.

So it was arranged that the Fourth of July they should race as before on the Fort Ryan track; the horses were to be named on the day of the race. And Red Cloud rode away.

Jim Hartigan was present at that interview; he watched their every move, he drank in every word, and he rode at a gallop till he found Belle. "Belle, the race is on for the Fourth of July, they're going to enter Blazing Star. Oh, glory be! I'll see that race; I'll see Blazing Star show all the country how."

"Yes, unless you are sent back to college."

"Oh, Belle, that's a cruel one. Just as everything looks gay, you hand me that," and his face clouded. He knew too well that there was little likelihood of an extension; it was most unusual. Why should an exception be made in his case?

"You know, Jim," she said very seriously, "we have been trying to move the president of the college; and the fact that you are so much of a favourite is additional reason for getting you back. The president has turned us down."

"Well, Belle, I simply won't go."

"You mean you will break with the Church?"

"I'll avoid that as long as possible, but I won't go back—at least, not now."

"Jim," she said, with a twinkle in her eye, "the president turned down Dr. Jebb and John Higginbotham and you; but we were not licked. Mrs. Jebb, Hannah Higginbotham, and myself went after the president's wife, and this morning Dr. Jebb got a new mandate; not all we asked, but your furlough is extended for six months more."

"Hooray! Whoop!" was the response.

"Yes, I thought so," said Belle. "That's why I asked Dr. Jebb to let me break the news. For a serious divinity student, it's wonderful what a good imitation you can give of a man who hates books."

"Well, now, Belle, you know, and I know, and all the world knows, I can preach a better sermon than Dr. Jebb, although he has studied a thousand books to my one and knows more in a minute of time than I can ever know in a month of Sundays. And, if I go to college and learn to talk like him, I'll put people to sleep in church just as he does. Hasn't the attendance doubled since I came?" There was no question of that due in part to the growth of the town, and partly also to Hartigan's winning personality and interesting though not very scholarly sermons.

"All right," said Belle. "You are saved from the terrible fate for six months. Be happy."

And he was. To such a buoyant soul a guarantee of six months' freedom put slavery so very far away that it was easy to forget it.

CHAPTER XXXVI

Shoeing the Buckskin

Hartigan and the blacksmith were at it hard again.

"Look a' here," said Shives, "I want ye to notice all this here Church business was faked up by that man Paul, or Saul, or whatever he called himself; and the real disciples would have nothing to do with him. They threw him down cold whenever he tried to mix in. Now if you chuck him and stick to the simple kindness of the old-timers that really did sit around with the Master—Paul *never even saw* Him!—I'm willing to hear ye. But a man that writes whole screeds about getting or not getting married and what kind of frippery women have to wear on their heads, well, I've got him sized up for a fellow that had a dressing down from some woman and probably deserved all he got—and more."

It was a long speech for Shives and more than once John Higginbotham tried to break in.

But Shives struck the anvil a succession of ringing blows which overpowered all rival voices as effectively as any speaker's gavel could have done. Then, turning suddenly on Higginbotham, he said, "See here, *Deacon*" (and he stressed the "Deacon"), "if you take the trouble to read a publication called the Bible, and in particular the early numbers of the second volume, you'll find that the Big Teacher taught socialism—and the real disciples did, too. It was that little lawyer feller Paul that succeeded in twisting things around to the old basis of 'get all you can; there must always be rich and poor'; and it ain't a bit of use your preaching to a man 'don't steal,' when his babies are crying for bread. I know I'd steal fast enough; so would you, if you were anything of a man. It would be your 'fore-God duty to steal; yes, and murder, too, if there was no other way of feeding them that He gave you to feed. And the law has no right to preach 'no stealing' when it fixes it so you can't help stealing. If this yere government of ours was what it pretends to be and ain't, it would arrange so every man could get enough work at least to feed him and his folks and save himself from starvation when he was sick or old. There wouldn't be any stealing then and mighty little of any other crime.

"That's my opinion; and I tell you it was that way the Big Teacher preached it in the beginning, as you can see plain enough. And the first ring of disciples were honest socialists. It was that letter-writing advance agent of the trusts that you call *Saint* Paul, that managed to get control of the company and then twisted things back into the old ways. And in my opinion the hull bunch of you is crooks hiding behind the name of a good man who threw you down cold when He was alive. And the very words He used happens to be a verse I remember: 'Ye compass sea and land to make one proselyte and when he is made ye make him twofold more a child of hell than yourselves.'"

And the anvil rang, "clang, clang, clang!"

"Now, Shives," bawled Jim in his stentorian voice, "you haven't *begun* to think. And every statement you make is wrong and none of your quotations ever happened before; otherwise, I am quite willing to accept everything you say. For example——"

"Hello! who's this?"

Up to the door of the blacksmith shop came riding a band of mounted Indians. First of these was a middle-sized man with large square features, a single eagle feather in his hair. Hartigan recognized at once the famous War Chief, Red Cloud, the leader of all the Sioux. Riding beside him was an interpreter, and behind him was a small boy, mounted on a tall pony— buckskin, so far as one could tell, but so shrouded in a big blanket that little of his body was seen; his head was bedizened with a fancy and expensive bridle gear.

The whole shop turned to see. The interpreter got down and approaching Shives, said, "You can shoe pony, when he ain't never been shod?"

"Sure thing," said Shives, "we do it every day."

"How much?"

"Five dollars."

"Do him now?"

"Yes, I guess so."

The interpreter spoke to Red Cloud; the Chief motioned to the boy, who dropped from the blanketed pony and led it forward.

"Bring him in here," and Shives indicated the shop. But that was not so easy. The pony had never before been under a roof, and now he positively declined to break his record. Some men would have persisted and felt it their duty to show the horse "who is boss." Shives was inclined to be masterful; it was Hartigan who sized up the situation.

"He's never been under a roof, Jack. I wouldn't force him; it'll only make trouble."

"All right; tie him out there." So the pony was tied on the shady side of the shop.

Hartigan turned to the half-breed interpreter to ask, "What do you want him shod for?" It was well known that the Indians did not shoe their horses.

The half-breed spoke to Red Cloud, who was standing near with his men, talking among themselves.

The Chief said something; then the interpreter replied, "By and by, we race him, maybe on the Big Wet Sunday; prairie wet, so he go slow."

There was a general chuckle at this. Sure enough, the Fourth of July, presumably the race day in mind, it nearly always rained; and for the wet track they wanted their racer shod.

There are few short operations that take more horse management that the first shoeing of a full-grown horse, especially a wild Indian pony. Nearly everything depends on the handling and on the courage of the pony. In nine cases out of ten, the pony must be thrown. On rare occasions a very brave horse, of good temper, can be shod by a clever farrier without throwing. But it takes a skilful shoer, with a strong and skilful helper, for the assistant must keep one front foot of the horse off the ground all the time the hind shoe is being put on, or the shoer is liable to get his brains kicked out. As they were discussing the need of throwing the pony, the interpreter said:

"Red Cloud no want him thrown. Chaska hold him." The bright-eyed boy from the mountain top—yes, the same—came forward and, holding the pony's head, began crooning a little song. The pony rubbed his nose against him, recovered his calm, and thanks to Hartigan's help—for he had volunteered eagerly to lend a hand—the operation progressed without mishap. There were, however, one or two little tussles, in which the great blanket slipped off the pony's back and showed a rounded, beautiful barrel of a chest, hocks like a deer, and smooth, clean limbs; a very unusually fine build for an Indian pony.

"By George! He's a good one," said Jim, and his heart warmed to the brave pony. The falling of the blanket also showed some white spots, left by ancient saddle galls. Hartigan, after a discriminating glance, said:

"Say, boys, this is their racer all right. This is the famous Buckskin Cayuse. He's a good one. Now you see why they want him shod."

What a temptation it was to the white men; how easy it would have been for Shives to put one nail in a trifle deep, to send that pony forth shod—well shod—but shod so that within the next ten miles he would go lame, and in the race, a month ahead, fall far behind—if, indeed, he raced at all. Yet, to his credit be it said that Shives handled that pony as though it were his own; he gave him every care, and Red Cloud paid the five dollars and rode away content.

Jim gazed after the little band as they loped gently down the street and round the curve till a bank cut off the view. "Say, boys, this is great," he said, "I wouldn't have missed it for anything. There's going to be a real race this year."

There could be no question of that. The securing of Blazing Star was a guarantee of a wonderful event if widespread interest and fine horseflesh could make it so.

CHAPTER XXXVII

THE BOOM

With the definite assurance of Blazing Star being entered, every man in Fort Ryan focussed his thoughts on how he might best turn the race to account, wipe out the damage of the last defeat, and recoup his loss with a double profit. They were very sorry for themselves, most of these losers; especially sorry that they, who could really enjoy money and who had actual need of so much, should lose their all to a lot of Indians who neither sought nor cared for cash and whose only pleasure in the race was the gambling spirit, the excitement of the game. This time the whites were going to leave no stone unturned to make a "killing." Every plan was discussed, and there were not lacking those who called Shives by ugly names—behind his back—for not seizing on the chance, when it was so easily in his hands, to put the Indian racer under shadow of a sure defeat. But they made no such speeches when the Colonel was in hearing.

Yet, after all, what did it matter? They had the ace in their hands now. There was no horse on the plains could run with Blazing Star; and, training with him, in the best of care, was the Red Rover, only a little less swift than the Star, now that careful methods had brought him his full-grown strength and speed. Microscopic studies were made of every fact that seemed to furnish a gauge of the horses' powers, and this was clear: Blazing Star was easily first; Red Rover would make a good second; and the buckskin cayuse could not possibly do so well as the Red Rover under the new training and lighter leather gear. Of course, the horse was not to be named until the day and hour of the race, but it was quite certain that the Indians would enter the Buckskin. Vague reports there were of a wonderful pinto that the Red men had somewhere in training; but the Crow spies could furnish no corroboration of the report; and, in any case, the shoeing of the Buckskin was a guarantee that the Indians meant to enter him.

From all of which there was but one logical conclusion. So the message went forth through the length and breadth of Dakota, "Come on, we've got a dead-sure thing. Come on, and bring all you can raise or borrow." It is wonderful, the faith of the racetrack gamblers in a tip! Their belief in the "hunch" is blind and absolute; hope never dies on the racetrack, even though, once in a while, it goes into a very deathlike swoon.

Not merely Dakota responded to the chances of the coming race, but Wyoming, Minnesota, Iowa, Nebraska, yes, even Illinois. And Cedar Mountain post office began to have hopes of stepping up to a higher round on the official scale, as the mail matter, registered and special, poured in. Letters postmarked "Deadwood" came by the score; others from Minneapolis and St. Paul were abundant; while, of course, there was the usual grist from Custer City, Bismarck, Pierre, Sidney, Cheyenne, and Denver. John and Hannah Higginbotham could not, owing to John's position as Church deacon, take an active part in the gambling; but they invented a scheme of insurance on a 50 per cent. premium basis which was within the Church law, though, when translated into terms of the track, it was merely a two-to-one bet on the field.

The autumn race had played havoc with so many savings funds and so much actual cash in business that a great number of those badly hit had vowed that they would never again go in; and they clung to their new resolve through May and most of June. But, as the training went on and the talk went around, and other men went in—all the wise ones, horse-wise, talk-wise, and otherwise—the subtle fascination grew and, a month before the race, the same old madness glamoured every mind; the same old guiding star—so often proved a spook-fire, but this time surely a star—was leading, hypnotizing, shining just ahead. The racing men once obsessed, the world of half-way interest followed even faster, till near the end of June, except for a few immune from principle or poverty, the whole community of South and West Dakota had but one talk—the race, and what they risked or hoped to make on it.

One must remember that the West has always been the land of boom. It is filled with the energetic and enterprising who, by a natural process, are selected from the peoples of the East; and the stuff such booms feed on, grow on, and grow mighty on as they feed, is Hope. Every Westerner knows that the land is full of possibility, opportunity—free, equal opportunity multiplied; and he hopes that his name will be the next one called by fortune. To respond to the call at whatever cost—to be ready to respond—that is the condition of life worth while. A dozen bad defeats are passing trifles if the glad call only comes and one fail not to rise to it. So it is ever easy in a land of such undaunted souls to start a boom. Hope never dies in the West.

Reader, I have ridden the Plains and seen many a settler living with his family in one small, dirty room, constructed out of sods with a black dirt roof, and dirt and dust on everything, on every side. I have seen them with little food, pinched and sick and struggling with poverty and famine. I have seen them in every dreadful circumstance of want and wasting pain that could be named in the sum of horrors of the vilest Eastern slum: and yet they made no bid for sympathy or help, or for a moment lost their pride; for one great fundamental difference there was between them and the slummers of the East: the prairie pioneer is *filled with hope*! Hope gleams in his eye; he lives in a land of hope; he was lured to the West by the blazing star of bright new Hope; just on a little way it shines for him; and every sod upturned and every posthole sunk, or seed put in, is turned or sunk or sown in the light of strong, unfading hope. Just a little while, a few short months, maybe, and he believes, he *knows* his name will be the next one called.

O land of hope, land of the shining four-rayed star, long, long may you remain the world's great vale of youth, where none grow old at heart or pray for death, for none can ever wholly lose their glimpse of that beckoning hope. The fountain of eternal youth springs up and gushes 'neath no other light.

O star of Hope! O blessed Lodestar of the soul! Long, long, yes, ages long may you be there, swung in the sky for all the world to see and know that while they live and *will*, there gleams a God-lit beacon in the West, the light of the land of hope.

CHAPTER XXXVIII

WHEN THE CRAZE STRUCK

"Brethren and sisters," said Dr. Jebb, in the Wednesday meeting established for general discussion, "I consider it my duty to speak openly and officially in condemnation of this outbreak of the fearful, soul-destroying vice of gambling that is sweeping over the land, over the country, over the town, I might almost say over this congregation. Never, in all my experience, has this inclination run so riotously insane. Not men of the world merely, but members of the Church; and the women and little children who can barely lisp the shameful word, are betting on the race."

The reverend doctor had much more to say in fierce denunciation, but Hartigan, while regretting the sinfulness of the habit, pointed out that this was a land of few pleasures and a land of horses; and if, as was natural, they sought to get their pleasure out of their horses, then surely Dr. Jebb would not consign them all to hell for it, but take a view more in line with the Christian charity of the Church.

Deacon Higginbotham rose to expound his theory of risk. Every man who took a risk of profit or loss was gambling; and everybody did it, so all were gambling, every one. "Now, see, we have a fire insurance risk on the this church, which means the church is gambling against Providence. So, clearly, the gambling itself is not a sin, it is the accessories of gambling that make for evil. For example, if we gamble with cards, sitting up all night in a stuffy room, drinking bad drinks, smoking bad smokes, speaking bad words, neglecting our business, neglecting our morals, hurting our health—then these things are bad. But, if we gamble out in the sunlight, on a beautiful prairie, on beautiful horses—now please don't mistake me; I'm not betting on the race——"

Here Hannah pulled his coat tail and he sat down. The fact of the matter was, he had issued a number of insurance policies on the race, and was quite ready to issue any number more.

It was well known that Dr. Jebb had invested his little savings in Deadwood town plots; and when Dr. Carson rose and asked if any one present had ever risked money on a probable rise in town plots—gambled, in fact, on the chances of a boom—Dr. Jebb turned scarlet and Dr. Carson laughed outright. Whereupon the Rev. James Hartigan whispered to the Rev. Dr. Jebb, who nodded; and the Reverend James, standing up, said: "Let us close the meeting with prayer."

If the Church—with all its immunities, safeguards, antitoxins, influences, warnings, prophylactics, creeds, vows, exposures, denunciations, traditions, and holy leaders—should become infected with aggressive interest in the speed contest to the extent of outward and visible material risk, what was likely to be the condition of the ungodly? It is said that the real estate boom of Minneapolis and the gold craze of Deadwood were psychological trivialities compared with the sudden great boom in betting that set in during the last week of June at the Black Hills; and the only reason why the wagering cataclysm was less disastrous than it threatened to be was because it ended quickly.

Fifty thousand dollars of treaty money was in the hands of Red Cloud and his people; fifty thousand more went to the Cheyennes under Howling Bull. The ranchmen were ready with an equal sum, and Fort Ryan was not far behind. By noon the fifty thousand dollars had been distributed to the Indians; by one o'clock every cent of it was put up on the race in equal bets. Who was to be stake holder? How much was each stake to be held or awarded? These were problems of some intricacy in view of the fact that the Indians could not read a word or trust any white man except the Indian Agent and Father Cyprian, the Jesuit missionary, both of whom declined to have any hand or part in the matter.

The plan devised by Red Cloud and accepted by the whites was as follows: every pair of stakes was tied together and marked with two names, the white man's and the Indian's—the latter's mark or totem being used. They then were piled up in a lone tepee, half way between the Fort and the Indian camp, and the tepee put under guard of an Indian and a white soldier. The understanding was that as soon as the race was over the winners should take possession of the lodge and distribute the contents among themselves, as indicated by the marks.

There was nearly one hundred thousand dollars in cash piled up in that Indian lodge in twin bunches. Of course, it was easy to arrange the money that way, and possible to make bundles of robes, bridles, beadwork, buckskin, pemmican, and weapons. It was even practical to pair off ploughs and bureaux; but the difficulties became huge and complex when horse was wagered against horse, or cow against cow, and even more so when cow was put up against horse; for, obviously, they could not be laid away in pairs, pending the decision; so that an elaborate sort of tally stick was instituted with some success, but even so a number of disputes ensued.

There was not a trooper who did not wager all the cash he had or could by any means get. There was not an officer who was not dragged in by the growing power of the craze. And daily, parties of Indians came to the Fort to put up cash, or peer around to get a glimpse of the horses. The whites made no attempt this time to spy on the Indians—their last experience had not been very encouraging. Anyway, why should they? They had all the cards in their hands. The shoeing of the Buckskin, the known importation of oats and timothy, the absence of reliable proof that the Indians had any other horse, were conclusive on that side; and on their own, the Rover could beat the Buckskin, even as Blazing Star could beat Rover; so, allowing for an accident, they had two winning horses to choose from.

John Higginbotham, who represented the bankers of the little wooden Bank of Cedar Mountain, had to send to Deadwood for a fresh supply of mortgage blanks, an assistant inspector of risks, and all the cash they could spare for the present need. Colonel Waller began to take alarm. The men were mortgaging their pay for months ahead, although many were still in debt from the autumn before. One young officer whose pay was pledged for a year in advance did not hesitate to pledge for the following year, so sure was he.

As early as the middle of June, the long lines of mounted men with prairie schooners were seen crawling over the plain to northward and eastward, while down the mountain roads came Indian bands in ever-growing numbers. The authorities might well have taken alarm but for the fact that the gathering was to be at Fort Ryan where there were ample troops to deal with any possible situation. Then over the hills from the south came Red Cloud with all his clan, and many more besides. Mounted men in hundreds, with travois and different kinds of carts, carrying tepees, provisions, household goods, and with them—straggling off or driven by the mounted boys—were herds of prairie ponies, in scores or even hundreds, the Red men's real wealth, brought now to stake, they fondly hoped, against the horses of the regiment at Fort Ryan. On the old camp ground by the river below the Fort, the Indians pitched their village, and every day came others of their race to set up lodges, and add to the lively scene. On the other side was a growing canvas town of whites with every kind of sharper and blackleg that the surrounding settlements could contribute from their abundant shady population.

Prominent among the visitors at Fort Ryan was the Indian Commissioner, with the local agent as his assistant. He opened a temporary office in the barracks, and the morning of his arrival many a lively scene took place as gorgeously dressed bucks, with wives and interpreter, gathered there to receive their treaty money. Although the Colonel was careful to exclude all liquor dealers and known sharpers from the Fort during the issue of the cash, he could not exclude them from the Dakota prairie, and they were hanging about everywhere with their unholy wares and methods. Firewater was, of course, the most dangerous snare; but a great deal of trick robbery was carried on with gaudy knick-knacks for which unbelievable prices were asked and got. The Indians might have parted with all their cash on that morning but for the need they felt of having it to cover their bets on the race.

Red Cloud and his counsellors had been many times to Colonel Waller's house. They had come with money bets, they had come with promises, and now they came with horses, eager to bet horse against horse for the mounts of all the regiment. The Indian chief did not understand the Colonel's refusal until he was told that a mythical Great High Chief named Unca-Sam was the owner of the cavalry mounts—that though Unca-Sam was over a hundred years old, he was a young man yet and knew all that was done in the West. Then it slowly dawned on Red Cloud that these men were riding horses that did not belong to them; he despised them for it, but his Indian honesty made him see how impossible it was to bet the horses that they did not own. However, he managed to stake a throng of ponies against the cattle of the ranchers, and thus the wealth of one side was staked against that of the other.

Next morning saw many wagons come to the Fort, with squaws beside their Indian drivers. They stopped at the Colonel's house, the covers were removed, and great piles of beadwork, coats, leggings, moccasins, baskets, war-clubs, and other characteristic things of Indian work were revealed. It was made clear that these were offered as stakes; would the whites match up the goods? In a spirit of fun, at first, the women of the Fort, as well as the men, began offering household goods or personal gear; a frying pan against a baby-bag, a pair of corsets against a medicine flute, a bureau against a war bonnet. Then, bitten by the craze, they kept on till everything was matched and all the goods tied up in bundles, according to the established custom, to lie in the big, special tepee under guard.

Another band of Red men followed with some tepees that they offered against government tents and, on being refused, finally wagered them against provender and hay. Each day there were new offers as groups of Indians came to the Fort, so that as soon as an Indian outfit on wheels came slowly up, it was quite understood that it was bringing new material to put up on the race. It was toward the end of the time that Red Cloud and his retinue came again, riding in much solemnity. Ignoring all others, he went to Colonel Waller's house and, in his usual deliberate way, after smoking, he began:

"Maybe so, you bet big?"

"Yes, indeed," was Waller's answer.

"Good. We bet all Dakota. You bet United States. Maybe so—yes?"

"No, no," laughed the Colonel.

"You win, we go away out west. We win, you all go back east. Maybe so—yes?"

"No," said the Colonel. "I am only a little chief. The Great High Chief, Unca-Sam, would not allow it."

Red Cloud smoked a while, then resumed:

"Heap afraid, maybe so?" Then, after a pause, "We bet Pine Ridge, you bet Fort Ryan—yes?"

Again the Colonel had to protest that only the Great Father Unca-Sam could deal in such matters; and Red Cloud grunted, "Heap scared," made a gesture of impatience, and rode away.

CHAPTER XXXIX

JIM'S BET

Jim Hartigan had as little interest in money as any Indian. All the things he loved and the pleasures he sought were the things that money could not buy. He wanted to ride and race, be alive, to love and be loved, to get the noblest animal joys, and soar a little—just a little—in the realm of higher things. Money as a power had not been listed in his mind, till a chance remark from Belle gave a wholly different trend to his thoughts.

"Jim, if I had about a thousand dollars, I think I'd be tempted to risk it. I'd go to Deadwood and start a produce commission business there."

That was all she said, and it was spoken lightly, but her words sank deep in Hartigan's mind.

"A thousand dollars might, after all, spell heaven"; and he pondered it long and hard. As mere business, it would not have held his thought an hour; but as a way to bring the happy time more near, it filled his mind for days, but he told her nothing of it. It was in the blacksmith shop that the next step was suggested. John Higginbotham had the floor; as he entered, Jim heard him say to some one in the crowd:

"I'm no betting man. As a deacon of the Church, I cannot countenance betting. As an insurance agent, however, I am quite ready, in all fairness, to negotiate your risk. You simply take out a policy on the—ah—event, reflecting your judgment of the probabilities You pay your premium—100 per cent, or whatever it is—and I, as your agent, place this risk with some established company, or responsible person sufficiently furnished with capital, to assume the liability. Then, as in the case of fire, or marine, or other insurance, the event decides the issue, and the insured draws his insurance in accordance with the terms, less the modest 5 per cent, that I receive for my perfectly legitimate trouble and expense."

Jim had never seen it in that light before; he rather liked the idea. After all, he was heart and soul in the race His joy in Blazing Star was hardly less than it had been; and why not manifest it in a way which held in it the possibilities of the wealth he needed? Why not take out an insurance policy on Blazing Star's winning? He thought of it more and more, and a few days later when he was depressed for once, Belle out of town, and the gloomy prospect of college before him, he drew his precious five hundred dollars from the bank and took it to John Higginbotham to deposit as his premium on insurance that the white men's horse would win the race. He had a feeling that Belle would not approve. But he did not tell her about it, for he wanted to surprise her when he should walk proudly up and put in her hand the one thousand dollars that would surely be his. He felt sure, but not happy; his judgment said "go ahead"; his instincts called a halt; but he went ahead.

Next day he went to Higginbotham. Hannah was there and a look from the deacon kept the Preacher quiet on the matter. When a chance came, the former said: "'Tain't so easy now, Jim. Every one knows the white men's horse is going to win, and there are no more even takers. I'm afraid the best I can do is offer you a two hundred and fifty dollar insurance with a five hundred dollar premium down, and your premium back, of course, if you collect the insurance, less my regular commission."

"All right," said Jim, a little disappointed "let it go at that," and away he went.

Hannah did not usually take a daily part in the office unless John was away; but something about Hartigan's visit prompted her to look more keenly through the books. It was her first knowledge of the new kind of "insurance" and she and John talked it out.

"All the companies are doing it now. It's no risk for us. We'll get over two thousand dollars in commissions anyhow." But Hannah was not content. She went over every item and presently she came on Hartigan's five hundred, offered two to one.

"Humph!" she said, "does Belle know about this insurance business?"

"I don't know," said John uneasily.

"She ought to know."

"If she makes him withdraw, we lose our 5 per cent.," said John, knowing quite well that that would hit Hannah very hard.

"I don't care," said Hannah, "I'm going to tell her."

It gave Belle a decided shock. It also explained to her Jim's peculiar behaviour during the last two days. Here was where his horse mania was leading him. She was not deceived by the glib terms of "insurance," nor as to the certainty of scandal, but she did not know what to do. Her first impulse was to go direct to him; and yet, that would put her in the position of a spy with a charge of treachery. No, that would be stupid. It was such an assumption of mastery, and such an exposure of Hannah's business impropriety as well that she hesitated; then, in a flash, she said:

"Hannah, I have two hundred and fifty dollars of my chicken money in the bank; I was saving it for something very different. I'll take that 'insurance.'

But not a word at present of who it was that took it. If you must give a name, say his insurance was taken up by 'Two Strikes.'" And in her heart she thought: "It is not my road; it is not a good road; but it is his road, and I'll take it till I bring him back."

CHAPTER XL

The Crow Band

Even far Montana heard the news, and, winding through the hills, there came one day a band of Crows from their reservation on the Big Horn. They came with only their light travelling tepees; and the intense dislike in which they are held by the Sioux and Cheyennes was shown in the fact that they camped far away in a group by themselves.

The Crows are noted for their beautiful lodges and their inveterate habit of horse stealing. They also have this unique fact on their record—that they have never been at war with the whites. They will steal a white man's horses fast enough, but they have never tried to take a white scalp. Their party consisted chiefly of men and a few surplus horses. But for the lodges and a few women, it might have passed for a war party.

The Crows are among the numerous claimants of the title "best horsemen in the world." If reckless riding in dangerous places without being thrown is good ground for the claim, then is the claim good; and it becomes yet stronger in view of the fact that most of their riding is barebacked. When they came to the Fort that day it was as though they were riding for their lives. They were but a score and were admitted without question. They paid their respects to Colonel Waller and then, after smoking, announced that they had money and goods to bet on the race. They were disappointed to find how much too late they were; everything was already up. So they rode away.

They did not go near the Sioux and Cheyenne camp; not that there was much danger of their suffering bodily harm, but they had been unmistakably informed that they were not welcome, though the action went no further than ignoring them. Next morning, when Blazing Star and Red Rover were doing their turn, there were no keener onlookers than the Crows. By look and grunted word they showed their appreciation of the noble brutes.

The Chief came to the Fort to find out if the Colonel would sell Blazing Star after the race.

"We give twenty horses," and he held up both hands twice.

"No."

"Three hands ponies," and they held up both hands spread three times.

"No, he is not for sale."

Late that day Red Cloud and Howling Bull came to Colonel Waller and, after preliminaries, conveyed the information and warning: "All Crows heap big thief. You watch him; he steal horse every time, heap no good."

The third of July came, and the plain looked like a city of tents. Many traders were there to open temporary stores; and it is doubtful if any single race in the Western world has attracted more people or created intenser interest. The Cheyennes gave a great dance in honour of the Sun. They invited all the Sioux to come, and the whites invited themselves. Belle and Jim were there and saw much to please and much to disgust them. The general impression was one of barbaric splendour, weird chanting, noisy tom-toms, and hypnotic pulsation. It was mostly repellent, but sometimes the rhythm stirred them, and provoked a response which showed that the wild musicians were playing on instincts and impulses that are as wide as humanity.

Most horsemen like to keep their training ground in some sort private; but the garrison had given up all attempts at that, so far as Blazing Star and Red Rover were concerned. Every one knew, every one was interested, and each day there was an eager crowd waiting to feast their eyes on the two splendid racers. And they were well worth it. Even Jim had to acknowledge that Blazing Star was looking better now than ever before.

"Look at that neck, Belle, see how it arches, see the clean limbs; isn't he trained to perfection? If I only—if——" then he stopped himself.

As he fondly watched the horse with glowing eyes, he said: "Of course, we don't know anything at all about where or how he was bred, but I should say that that is a blood Kentucky, nearly pure—Kentucky gold dust."

Among the spectators were the two Indian Chiefs in their warpaint—Red Cloud of the Sioux, and Howling Bull of the Cheyennes. They spoke little to each other, for neither knew the other's tongue; but they made little gestures of the sign language, and any keen observer knowing it could catch the ideo-signs: "Good, good; by and by; we see good race; brave, swift," and so on. Later: "Yes, after one sleep. Rain heap, yes."

Jim watched them closely. "See that, Belle? he says: 'To-morrow it rain heap,' I wonder how he knows. They call the Fourth of July the Big Wet Sunday, because it usually rains then. I wonder how it will affect the race."

"Jim, you said they had shod the buckskin cayuse in expectation of a wet track."

"Yes; that's a mystery; how can they tell? The air is full of rumours, anyway. Chamreau says that Red Cloud has been seeking everywhere for fast horses. He had a man go as far as Omaha and another to Denver. Some say he did pick up a racer, a half-blooded Kentucky—some that he had got a wonderful pinto cayuse from Cheyenne; this latter is the more persistent rumour, though Chamreau says he can't find any one who has actually seen one or the other. Anyhow, no one knows what their entry will be. We have a pretty good idea of ours"; and Hartigan smiled proudly.

The two chiefs, with their followers, conversed earnestly, and with much gesture. They looked and pointed at the Crow camp and the rain sign came in many times, and emphatically. The old feud between the Sioux and the Crows had broken out afresh in a trader's store. Two young men from the opposing camps had quarrelled. They had drawn their knives, and each had been wounded. These things were common talk, and Belle and Jim watched the two chiefs ride toward the Crow camp with an eager curiosity to know more about it. When the Red men were a mile away and within half a mile of the Crow village, they followed at a good pace and reached the tepees in the secluded corner in time to see the two visiting chiefs making an address mainly by signs, as they sat on their horses. Chamreau was there, and in answer to Jim's question translated Red Cloud's address to the Crows thus:

"You make bad medicine so we lose race, we kill you." Then, indicating Howling Bull, "He say, 'you make bad medicine, bring rain, I kill you.'"

Having delivered their ultimatum, the visiting chiefs turned haughtily and rode to their own camp.

"I don't know just what they really did say," said Hartigan, "but if I'm any judge of looks, there'll be trouble here if those Crows don't get out."

It was four o'clock in the morning of the Fourth of July when the thunderbolt struck Fort Ryan. It was not very loud; it damaged no building; but it struck the very souls of men. A thousand thunder claps, a year's tornadoes in an hour, could not have been more staggering; and yet it was only four words of one poor, wheezing Irish hostler at the Colonel's window:

"Colonel! Colonel! For the love of God—come—come—come at once—*Blazing Star is gone!*"

"*What?*" and the Colonel sprang up.

The reveille had sounded, the men were just rising; but one group there was already about the stable talking with an air of intense excitement. The Colonel went without waiting to dress—the officer of the day with him. In terrible silence they hurried to the stable; there was Rover in his box, whinnying softly for his morning oats; but the next—the box of Blazing Star—was empty; and the far end, the outer wall, showed a great new doorway cut. Beyond, out in the growing light, troopers rode to every near-by lookout; but never a sign of horse did they see, or, indeed, expect to see. The case was very clear; the horse was stolen, gone clean away—their hope for the race was gone.

These were terrible moments for the hapless grooms and guards. Human nature, in dire defeat, always demands a victim; and the grooms were glad to be locked up in the guard house, where at least they were out of the storm of the Colonel's wrath. As the light grew brighter a careful study laid bare the plan of robbery. The stables formed, in part, the outer wall of the quadrangle. They were roofed with pine boards, covered with tar-paper on cedar corner posts; the walls, however, were of sods piled squarely on each other in a well-known Western style, making a good warm stable. It was a simple matter to take down quickly and silently this outer wall from the outside, beginning at the top, and so make another exit. This had been done in the dead of night. And the track of the racer told the tale like a printed page.

A general alarm had gone forth; all the Fort was astir; and the army scouts were by the case forced into unusual prominence. It was Al Rennie spoke first:

"Colonel, it's a-going to rain, sure; it's liable to rain heavy. I suggest we take that trail right away and follow before it's all washed out."

"The quicker the better," said the Colonel.

Riding ahead on the trail like a hound went the old trapper-hunter-scout with a band of troopers following. They had not gone a quarter of a mile before the rain began to spit. But the line of the trail was clear and it was easy for the practised eye to follow. It headed east for half a mile, then, on a hard open stretch of gravel, it turned and went direct for the Crow camp. Rennie could follow at a gallop; they rounded the butte, cleared the cottonwoods, crossed the little willow-edged stream, and reached the Crow camp to find it absolutely deserted!

The rain was now falling faster; in a few minutes it set in—a true Dakota flood. The trail of Blazing Star—clear till then—was now wholly wiped out. There was nothing but the unmarked prairie around them; and the guide, with the troopers, soaked to the skin, rode back with the forlorn tidings.

CHAPTER XLI

THE PINTO

Under such a cloud of disaster men cared little what the weather was; the deluge of rain seemed rather appropriate. There was even a hope that it might rain hard enough to postpone the race. But at ten it stopped, and by eleven it had cleared off wholly. The race was to be at noon.

Word had been sent to Red Cloud, asking for two days' postponement, which was curtly refused. "White man heap scared maybe," was his scornful reply.

The Colonel held a hasty council of war with his officers. Their course was clear. In Red Rover they still had a winner and the race would come off as announced; such a horse as Blazing Star could not long be concealed; they would follow up the Crows and recover him in a few days. So, after all, the outlook was not so very dark.

Already the plain was surging with life. Gaily-clad Indians were riding at speed for the pleasure of speeding. Thousands of gaudy blankets—put out to air in the sun—seemed to double the density, colour, and importance of the camp. New wagons came with their loads, new life developed; now came a procession of Indians singing their racing songs, for the Indian has a song for every event in life; bodies of United States troops were paraded here and there as a precautionary and impressive measure; the number of Indians assembled, and their excitability, began to cause the authorities some apprehension.

The Boyds were there in their democrat and had brought picnic food for all day; but Hartigan was a special favourite at the Fort, and he, with Belle, was invited to join its hospitable garrison mess, where social life was in gala mood. It was an experience for Belle, for she had not realized before how absolutely overwhelming a subject the horse race could be among folk whose interests lay that way, and whose lives, otherwise, were very monotonous. She was a little shocked to note that every one of the wives at the table was betting on the race—in some cases, for considerable money. The one restraining force in the case was the absence of takers, since all were backing Red Rover.

An amusing incident occurred when, during the meal, a bead-eyed young squaw entered the mess room and stood a little inside the door.

"What does she want?" asked the Colonel.

Then the interpreter: "She wants to bet on the race. She wants to bet her baby against yours."

A pretty good proof of a sure thing, for no race loves its children more than the red folk. An Indian has no compunction whatever in staking his treaty money, which comes so easily and may as lightly go; he does not hesitate to risk all his wealth, for after all wealth is a burden; he will even wager his wife, if the game possesses him; but he is very shy of staking his children. He does it on occasion, but only when he considers it a foregone result—a certainty of winning.

The Indian Agent had many close conferences with the Colonel. He strongly disapproved the whole racing excitement and plainly indicated that he held the Colonel responsible. What would happen when these excited fifteen hundred Sioux and Cheyenne warriors—not to speak of some five thousand women and children—met defeat, was a serious problem. Had the situation been sooner realized, the whites could have organized into some sort of home defense. Red Cloud and Howling Bull, so far as could be discerned, contemplated the scene, and the coming event, with absolute composure.

Huge pools of water had blue-patched the racetrack after the downpour; but these had drained off to a great extent, leaving the track a little greasy perhaps, but quite usable; and Jim recalled with interest the shoeing of the Buckskin. "This was what it was for; how did the heathens know it was coming?" By mutual agreement, at length, the race was postponed for two hours, which, under such a sun, would bring the track back nearly to normal; and since the Indians had had the Buckskin shod, it was the same for both. It was decided that the start should be made when the sun was over Inyan Kara, the tallest of the hills in sight to the west; this meant, as nearly as possible, at four o'clock.

At two o'clock all the world seemed there. There were mounted Indians—men and women—by thousands, and at least a thousand mounted whites besides the soldiers. The plain was dotted with life and colour from far beyond the Indian camp to Fort Ryan; but the centre of all was the racetrack; and camped alongside, or riding or sitting near, was the thickest group of folk of both races, bound to lose no glimpse of the stirring contest.

The delay made for new excitement; the nerve strain became greater as each hour passed. The white soldiers did what they could to hold the crowd, and the Indians called on their own "Dog Soldiers" or camp police to do the same. Fortunately, it was a good-natured crowd; and the absconding of the Crows had removed the largest element of risk, so far as violence was concerned. Jim was ablaze with the wildest of them all. He rode away and back at a gallop to work it off. Belle was too tired to join these boisterous runs, so he rode alone at first. But another woman rider was there; from the crowd Lou-Jane Hoomer spurred her bay, and raced beside him. She was an excellent horsewoman, had a fine mount, and challenged Jim to a ride. Handsome, her colour up, her eyes sparkling, Lou-Jane could have ridden away, for she had the better mount, but she didn't; she rode beside him, and, when a little gully called for a jump, they jumped together, and found abundant cause for laughter. Twice they went careering, then back to Belle, and when next Jim's itch for speed and life sent him circling, Belle was rested enough to follow everywhere.

At a quarter to two the bugle of the Fort was blown, and there issued forth the proud procession with Red Rover in the middle, led beside his jockey, who rode a sober pony. It was Little Breeches this time. There is one thing that cannot be explained away, that is defeat. Peaches had been defeated; his chance came no more.

Red Rover was magnificent, trained to a hair, full of life and fire. Of all the beautiful things on earth, there is nothing of nobler beauty than a noble horse; and Rover, in his clean-limbed gloss and tensity, was a sight to thrill the crowds that were privileged to see him spurn the earth, and arch his graceful neck, and curvet a little for the subtle joy that comes of spending power when power is there in a very plethora. Every white man's eye grew proudly bright as he gazed and gloried in his champion and fear left all their hearts. At the starting post, they swung about, Little Breeches mounted, and a mighty cheer went up. "Ho, Red Cloud! Where's your horse? Bring on your famous Buckskin now"; and the rumbling of the crowd was rising, falling, like the sound of water in a changing wind.

Far down the valley, near the Ogallala Camp, a new commotion arose and a wilder noise was sounding. There was the shrill chant of the "Racing Ponies" with the tom-toms beating, and then Red Cloud's men came trotting in a mass. As they neared the starting point, the rabble of the painted warriors parted, and out of the opening came their horse, and from the whites went up a loud and growing burst of laughter. Such a horse as this they had never seen before; not the famous Buckskin, but *the mysterious pinto pony*, wonderful, if weird trappings could make him so. On his head he wore an eagle-feather war-bonnet; his mane was plaited with red flannel strips and fluttering plumes; his tail was even gaudier; around each eye was a great circle of white and another of black; his nose was crossbarred with black and red; his legs were painted in zebra stripes of yellow and black; the patches of white that were native to his coat were outlined with black and profusely decorated with red hands and horseshoes painted in vermilion; on his neck was a band of beadwork, carrying a little bundle of sacred medicine; and, last, he had on each ankle a string of sleigh-bells that jingled at each prancing step. A very goblin of a horse! His jockey was, as before, Chaska, the Indian boy, stripped to the breechclout, with an eagle feather in his hair and a quirt hung on his wrist.

Never, perhaps, was a more grotesque race entry in all the West; and the difference between the burnished form of Red Rover in his perfect trim, and this demon-painted Pinto gave rise to an ever-growing chorus of shouting, laughter, rough jibes, and hoots of joy.

Jim took in the Indian horse with the keenest of eyes. "Well, boys, he may be only a pinto cayuse, but he's way ahead of their Buckskin. Look at that action. Bedad, they've got him shod!"

The Pinto seemed as tall as Red Rover and, so far as trappings allowed one to see, he was nearly as fine in build. Diverse feelings now surged in the crowd. Many of the whites said, "Well, it was true after all, Red Cloud, the old fox, he sent to Omaha, or maybe Illinois and bought a racer. The shoeing of the Buckskin was a blind. Or maybe, at that time, their racer had not been secured."

Old Red Cloud slowly rode by with his square jaw set, his eyes a little tight, observing all; but he gave no sign of special interest.

With two such keen and nervous racers it was no easy matter to get a fair start; but at length they were man[oe]uvred into line, side by side. The pistol cracked and away they went, while all the crowd held still, so very still for a moment that you could have heard for a hundred yards the medicine song of the Indian boy:

"Huya! Huya! Shungdeshka, Shungdeshka! (Fly! Fly! my Eagle! Fly! my Pinto Eagle!)" And that wild-eyed Indian pony sprang away as fast as the blooded horse beside him. So far as any one could tell it was an even match.

The white man had won the inside track again; and remembering how the Indian boy had got that advantage in the last race, he was on the watch. But nothing happened; the horses led off side by side, shoulder to shoulder. At the turning post was a waiting throng that received them with a cheer, to follow again in their wake, like madmen let loose on hoofs. The horses seemed to thrill to the sound and bent to it faster.

Around the post they had swung, perforce in a large circle, and the Pinto lost a good half length. Now Little Breeches saw his chance and, leaning forward well, he smote with the quirt and pricked those bronzy flanks, while Rover bounded—bounded to his limit.

But the Indian boy's magic song rang out again: "Huya Huya, Huya deshka! Huya, Huya, Huya deshka! (Oh, Eagle, fly, fly Eagle, my Pinto fly!)" And the Pinto seemed to unchain himself, as a hawk when he sails no more, but flaps for higher speed. With thunderous hoofs the wild horse splashed through a pool, came crawling, crawling up, till once again he was neck and neck with the wonderful flying steed in the coat of gold.

Little Breeches shouted, "Hi! Hi! Hi!" and spurred and smote. Chaska glanced at him and smiled, such a soft little smile. The eagle feather in his hair was fluttering, and the smile was still on his lips as they reached the last half mile. Then, in weird and mouthing tone, Chaska sang of wind and wings:

"Ho, Huya, Huya deshka,Huya, Huya, Huya deshka,Woo hiya, Woo hiya, Woo hiya,Unkitawa, Unkitawa, Ho!"

Strong medicine it must have been, for the Pinto thrilled, and bounded double strong. The white man yelled and spared not lash nor spur. Red Rover flinched, then sprang as he had never sprung before. But the demon pony in the motley coat swung faster, faster, faster yet; his nostrils flared; his breath was rushing—snorting—his mighty heart was pounding, the song of the wind and the flying wings seemed to enter into his soul. He double-timed his hoofbeats and, slowly forging on, was half a length ahead. The white man screamed and madly spurred. Red Rover was at topmost notch. The demon pony forged—yes, now a length ahead, and in the rising, rumbling roar, passed on, a double length, and *in. The race was won, lost, won lost*—the Pinto pony crowned; and the awful blow had struck!

CHAPTER XLII

THE AFTERTIME

The crack of doom will never hit Fort Ryan harder. When the thousand painted Sioux came riding, yelling, wild with joy, shooting their rifles in the air, racing in a vast, appalling hoof tornado down the long track and then to the lodge of all the stakes, they went as men who are rushing to save their own from some swift flood that threatens. But they got an unexpected shock. The red sentry and the white sentry were standing—sullen, for they were forced to miss the race. Still, the result was clear.

The Sioux were each for claiming the bundle with his name. But the soldier on guard, with fixed bayonet, ordered all the frenzied rabble back.

"I don't know anything about your darned race, and here I stand till I get orders from my officer."

It was the very impudence of his courage that saved him from what they thought righteous vengeance. The Colonel came at once. The guard saluted and withdrew and the Red men seized their spoils. And, strange to say, among themselves they had not one dispute; none tried to overreach; each knew his mark and claimed his own.

The whites were like men under a gallows doom.

"Stung, stung!" was all the Colonel had to say.

The Adjutant, an erratic officer, had lost half a year's pay. The magnitude of the disaster was almost national, he felt, and sadly, shyly, he said: "Will you have the flag at half-mast, Colonel?"

"No!" thundered the Colonel. "I'll be darned if the flag shall hang at half-mast for anything less than the death of an American."

And the Rev. James Hartigan! He stared stonily before him as the race was won.

Belle was at hand and she watched him closely. He turned deathly pale.

"What is it, Jim?" she said quietly, and laid her hand on his.

"Oh, Belle, this is awful."

"Why, Jim? Why should you care? It isn't as if it were Blazing Star. We're sorry for all those men, of course; but maybe it's the best thing for them. I think now they'll realize the curse and folly of racetrack gambling."

"Oh, Belle, if you only knew," groaned Jim.

"Knew what, Jim dear? It seems to me those men are getting their deserts. I know you and Dr. Jebb did all you could to hold them back, and denounced all racing as it properly should be."

Jim turned his head away and pressing his forehead with his great powerful hand, he groaned.

"Jim, dear boy, why do you take it so hard? Why should you worry? I'm sorry for the women and children that will suffer for this, but I have little pity for the men; the fools, *they* knew what they were doing."

"Let's ride away," he said; and as he turned, he saw Red Cloud, calm and dignified, on his horse watching wagon after wagon go by filled with plunder, on its way to the Indian camp.

Jim and Belle rode away from the painful scene. She was leading for the Fort; but he said, "I must see Higginbotham." She followed as he went to the tent with the sign, "John & Hannah Higginbotham—Insurance." A number of Indians were in and about, laughing merrily and talking in their own tongue. Jim waited till the tent was clear, then dismounted. Belle was for following, but Jim said, "Would you mind holding the horses? I won't be a minute." His face was so drawn and sad that she was deeply touched. She had meant to prick and lash him for a while yet, but now in pity she forbore.

He entered. The Deacon was sitting at a little desk. Beside him was a small safe; it was open, but nearly empty now.

"Well," said Jim gruffly, almost savagely, "what's to do?"

"Nothing," said the Deacon calmly. "You've lost. The Indians have been here and got most of their plunder. Your five hundred is now the property of a person named 'Two Strikes' who will, doubtless, call presently and secure the indemnity, less my reasonable 5 per cent. commission."

Jim turned in silence. As he joined Belle, she said, "Here, Jim, help me down; I want a word with the Deacon."

Jim stammered, "I—well—ah——"

She paid no attention, but said, "Now lead the horses over there." When he was safely away, she entered. The Deacon's eyes twinkled. "Good afternoon, Two Strikes, you people have made a great killing."

"Yes," she said calmly; "I've come for my share."

He opened the safe, took out the last of the packets tied up in a particular shape, and said in businesslike tone, "Two hundred and fifty dollars premium, five hundred dollars insurance, 5 per cent, on indemnity collected is twenty-five dollars; shall I hold it out?"

"No," she said; "I'll keep that bunch untouched. Here it is." She handed him his twenty-five dollars, put the seven hundred and fifty dollars in her side bag, and went forth. Jim stared at her in a frightened way as she came.

"Belle," he said huskily, "what did he say?"

"Oh, nothing special. Judging from his looks, I don't think he's lost any money."

"Did—did he tell you anything?"

"About what?"

"About me?"

"No. Why? Why do you look so terribly upset, Jim?" and mounting, she rode off beside him.

"Oh, Belle, I can't lie to you. I'll tell you all about it. Belle, I put up all I had, the money I got for Blazing Star. All we were to furnish with. I wanted to hand you the money *you* wanted. Calling it insurance blinded me; the temptation was too much. I should have known better. Oh, Belle, will you ever forgive me? I'm nothing but a gambler," and, crushed with shame, he repeated, "I'm nothing but a criminal racetrack gambler."

An overwhelming compassion swamped her. She leaned toward him and said softly, "So am I, Jim, I'm just as bad as you are."

"What—what do you mean?"

"Jim, do you know the name of the Indian that got your stake?"

"Yes. He said it was 'Two Strikes.'"

"Jim, dear, I am 'Two Strikes.' Here is your money back; only it's our money now, Jim darling. Now never a word of this to any human soul"; and screened by the cottonwood trees, they fell sobbing in each other's arms.

CHAPTER XLIII

FINDING THE LOST ONE

Colonel Waller had been telegraphing from Cedar Mountain to all reachable parts of the North where the Crows were likely to be, without getting one word of comfort. Then up to the door of his house the morning after the devastating race came Red Cloud of the calm, square face, and behind him riding, a dozen braves.

At precisely the right moment prescribed by etiquette, he opened: "Me savvy now why you no run heap good horse."

"Humph!" said Waller.

"Didn't I tole you watch when Crow come?"

"Humph!" was the answer.

"You no got him back yet—no?"

"No," said the Colonel, with some asperity.

"Why? White scout no follow trail?"

"The rain wiped out all trail," was the answer.

"Your scout heap no good," said Red Cloud. Then, after a dozen slow puffs at his pipe, during which he gazed blankly and far away, the Indian said: "Ogallala very good scouts. Maybe so they find trail. What you give for follow Crow? Maybe find, bring back your pony."

Without a doubt, this was the easiest way. The Ogallala scouts would gladly pursue their ancient enemies and force them to give up the stolen horse. These men knew which line the Crows would most likely take, and could probably pick up the trail in a day. Prompt action was necessary. The Indian bands were breaking up and going home laden with plunder, their fresh trails would render it impossible to follow the trail of the horse thieves. The Colonel's mind was quickly made up.

"Red Cloud," he said emphatically, "I'll give you two hundred and fifty dollars cash if you find Blazing Star and bring him back here in good condition within one week."

The Indian Chief smoked for a few puffs and said: "Seven suns, no good. Crow country far away; one moon maybe."

Reckless riders like the Crows might easily ruin a horse in one month; so, at length, a compromise was reached, whereby Red Cloud was to receive two hundred and fifty dollars if within two-weeks; and one hundred if a month passed before the return. Then the Sioux Chief rose "to find his young men," and his party rode away.

It was nine the next morning when the sentry discovered a considerable body of mounted Indians in the northeast, riding rapidly toward the Fort. Had it been from the south, he would scarcely have made a report. Before ten o'clock they had arrived. They numbered about fifty warriors in full war paint. They were singing their war songs, and fastened to their coup sticks were one or two terribly fresh-looking scalps. At their head was Red Cloud. A hundred troopers were under arms, so they did not hesitate to admit the Indians. The warriors passed through the gate; then spreading out before the Colonel's house, their opening ranks revealed the noble form of Blazing Star. Bestriding him was the boy Chaska, his bright eyes and clear white teeth gleaming in a smile.

A mighty shout went up among the white men as the blooded racer was led to the Colonel's office. One or two formalities, and the two hundred and fifty dollars was paid over to Red Cloud. Blazing Star was hastily examined, found in perfect trim, then handed over to the Irish hostler.

"You take him to the stable," was all the Colonel said, but he said it in large capital letters and it was full of grim threats and reminder, hostler Mike led the lost darling back to the stable where a crowd of men were waiting.

Red Cloud crammed the new wealth into his tobacco pouch and rode away at the head of his men.

Al Rennie felt sick with disgust that he should fail when the trail was fresh, while the Sioux, on a washed-out trail, made such a showing in so short a time. He was puzzled, too, by the scalps. The two he managed to examine were not fresh. But he had to swallow his disgust.

All that day the Indian bands had been going off. Their camps were breaking up; they were dispersing to their homes. The Plain was nearly deserted that afternoon when hostler Mike took Blazing Star out into the heat of the sun to give him the thorough washing and cleaning that he surely needed. A minute later, Mike came rushing across the square to the Colonel's office.

"Colonel, Colonel," he gasped, "come here, sir."

"What's the matter with you?" said the Colonel in a voice of wrath which boded ill for a new blunder.

"Colonel, come at once. Come, it's Blazing Star."

There was a total lack of soldier decorum in the hostler's address. He was so intensely excited that the Colonel overlooked the informality and went quickly to where Blazing Star was standing tied to the washing post.

"There, sir; look there—and there!" ejaculated Mike with growing excitement, as he pointed to Blazing Star's legs. "And look at that!" and he swept his bony finger round the big liquid eye of the racer. The Colonel looked, looked closer, parted the hair, looked down to the roots and saw *paint—red paint, white paint, black paint*—traces of horseshoes, red hands, white patches and stripes; not much, but enough to tell the tale.

Without a question, *Blazing Star was the Pinto that had won the race!*

The simple Red men knew that the Buckskin was overmatched, so they secured the only horse on the plains that *could* win. They drove the Crows away at the right moment to leave a red herring trail. Then, having captured the stakes, they calmly collected two hundred and fifty dollars for restoring him to his owner. The simple Red men!

And when Jim Hartigan heard of it he yelled with joy. He laughed; he almost cried. After all, his horse had won; his Blazing Star was the steed of all the plains. He was tossed with different moods—regret and joy, grim humour, sadness and madness; he was stirred to the depths; all his primitive nature was set free. He did not sleep for hours, and when the dawn was near, his boyhood memories filled his brain and he was back in the livery stable garret once again, and repossessed of all his boyhood's ways and words he softly swore himself to sleep.

CHAPTER XLIV

A Fair Rider

Life at Cedar Mountain had dropped to normal. Charles Bylow and his wife were regular church members now, and no warmer, truer friends on earth had Hartigan. Pat Bylow had gone to Deadwood seeking work on the railway and it was said that his wife was still importing an occasional flask; but no more sprees took place. Jack Lowe had left Cedar Mountain abruptly after the Bylow affair. Higginbotham had spread the truth about Lowe's part in the drugged liquor and the schoolteacher had received pointed advice to leave the town. He lost no time. Dr. Carson and Jack Shives were alternately confronting each other with abstruse problems; John and Hannah Higginbotham were building an addition to their house and getting a hired girl; and old man Boyd was worrying over a possible extension of the road to Deadwood, which might seriously hurt his business.

Jim found life very sweet as he grew into the hearts of the townsfolk and came to know their perfectible qualities; he was acquiring a fine reputation for pulpit oratory. Every Thursday and every Sunday afternoon and evening were spent at the Boyds' as their accepted son-in-law to be. On these occasions it was his keenest pleasure to lay his sermons and plans before Belle for her criticism and approval. When they were not together indoors, they were in the saddle together; all the world knew, understood, and wished them joy.

The Hoomers had come to be prominent in the church now—at least, Ma Hoomer and Lou-Jane had. It was Lou-Jane's doing. And Hartigan, after long delay, felt bound to pay them a pastoral visit. Lou-Jane was heartiness and propriety combined. She chatted gaily on every subject he opened; showed no forwardness; was even shy when, after dinner, he sat down near her. Her riding at the racetrack was vividly in his mind and she blushed quite prettily when he referred to it in admiration.

"You should see my pony take a fence," she said.

"Well, sure; that's what I'd like to see," was the response.

"Some day soon, maybe."

"Why not now?" he inquired.

"I must help mother with the dishes."

And he thought: "Isn't she fine? I like a girl to consider her mother." But he lingered and chatted till the dishes were washed; then he suggested: "If I go out and saddle your pony, will you show me that jump?"

"Certainly," she answered, with a merry laugh.

He went to the stable, saddled and brought the bay horse. Lou-Jane put her foot in the stirrup and swung into the saddle before he could offer his help.

"Drop all the bars but the middle one." Hartigan did so, leaving only the three-foot bar of the pasture. Lou-Jane circled off and cleared it without an effort.

"Raise it one," she shouted.

He did so, and over she went.

"Again."

Now, at four feet, the pony rose and went over.

"Another," and he raised to four and a half feet. As before, she and her pony sailed over like one creature.

"Again," and he raised it to five feet. The pony rose with just a hint of effort. One front hoof touched, but he made the jump in triumph. Lou-Jane laughed for joy and circled back, but, warned by that toe tap, jumped no more. She leaped from the saddle before Jim could come near to help and in his frank, beaming admiration she found what once she had hungered for in vain.

As he rode away that day, his unvoiced thought was: "Isn't she fine—and me misjudging her all the time! I'm ashamed of myself."

Lou-Jane watched him out of sight, waving a hand to him as he topped the hill. The visit and Hartigan's open delight in her riding had stirred her very much. Was it loyalty to Belle that led her to throw up a barrier between herself and the Preacher? or was it knowledge that the flowers are ever fairest in the fenced-in field? This much was sure, the interest of passing attraction was giving place to a deeper feeling. A feeling stronger every month. Lou-Jane was in the game to win; and was playing well.

August, bright and fruit-giving, was passing; September was near with its dryness, its payments on the springtime promises; and Belle, as she gazed at the radiant sky or the skurrying prairie dogs that tumbled, yapping, down their little craters, was tormented with the flight of the glowing months. In October the young Preacher and she must say good-bye for a long, long time, with little chance of any break till his course was completed, and he emerged a graduate of Coulter. That was a gloomy thought. But others of equal dread had come of late.

Hartigan was paying repeated pastoral calls at Hoomers' and last week Jim and Lou-Jane had ridden to Fort Ryan together. It was a sort of challenge race—on a dare—and Jim had told Belle all about it before and after; but just the same, they had ridden there and back and, evidently, had a joyful time.

Jim was a child. He always thought of himself as a coarse, cruel, rough brute; but really he was as soft-hearted as a woman; and, outside of his fighting mood, nothing pained him more than the idea of making any one unhappy. His fighting moods were big and often; but they had existence only in the world of men. He believed himself very wise in the ways of life, but he had not really begun to see, and he was quite sublimely unconscious of all the forces he was setting in motion by his evident pleasure in the horsemanship of Lou-Jane Hoomer and in their frequent rides together.

Lou-Jane had a voice of some acceptability and she was easily persuaded to join the choir. A class in Sunday-school was added to her activities, and those who believed the religious instinct to be followed closely by another on a lower plane, began to screw up their eyes and smile when Lou-Jane appeared with Jim.

The glorious September of the hills was waning when a landslide was started by a single sentence from Lou-Jane. She had ridden again with Jim to Fort Ryan. Her horse had cleared a jump that his had shied at. Mrs. Waller had said to her across the table, half in fun and meaning it every word:

"See here, I won't have you trifling with Mr. Hartigan's affections; remember, he's preëmpted."

Lou-Jane laughed with delight. And, looking very handsome all the while, she said with mock humility: "No one would consider me a rival."

Jim told Belle every word of it; he was simplicity itself in such things; he didn't seem to have any idea of the game. He was wholly oblivious of the little cloud which his anecdote left on her. It was a little cloud, but many little clouds can make a canopy of gloom and beget a storm. Then came the words. It was at one of the church evenings in the parsonage—a regular affair, but not soaring to the glorious heights of a sociable—that the words were uttered which wrought a mighty change. Jim had alluded to the inevitable journey East in October, not half a month ahead now, when Lou-Jane Hoomer announced "I'm going East, too. My dad is giving me a trip back to Rochester to see grandma," she said.

"Why, Rochester is just a little run across the lake from Coulter College," exclaimed Jim.

"Maybe I'll see you when I am there," said Lou-Jane. "What fun!"

Every one applauded and Jim said: "Well, that would make a pleasant change in the dreary grind."

Belle's only comment was, "How nice!" and she gave no sign of special interest; but a close observer might have seen a tightening of her lips, a sudden tensity of look. The merry chatter of the parlour ceased not and she seemed still a factor in all its life, but the iron had entered her very soul. She played her part as leader, she gave no outward sign of the agony of fear that filled her heart, but she took the earliest reasonable time to signal Jim and steal away.

CHAPTER XLV

THE LIFE GAME

Trump cards you must have to win in the life game; and you must know how to play them, or a much poorer hand may beat you. You must know the exact time to play your highest trump, and there is no general rule that is safe, but Belle had a woman's instinctive knowledge of the game.

In two weeks Jim was to leave Cedar Mountain. Belle had reasoned with him, coaxed him, cajoled him into seeing that that was the right trail for him. He must complete his college course, then they could marry with the sanction of the Church and be assured of a modest living. But the rules were strict; no ungraduated student might marry. The inadequacy of the stipend, the necessity for singleness of aim and thought, the imperative need of college atmosphere—these were absolute. Viewed from any standpoint, celibacy was the one wise condition for the untrained student.

It had taken all of Belle's power to make Jim face the horror of those classrooms in the far East; and from time to time his deep repulsion broke into expression. Then she would let him rage for a while, chew the bit, froth and rail till his mood was somewhat spent. And when the inevitable reaction set in she would put her arm about him and would show him that the hard way was surely the best way, and then paint a bright picture of their future together when his rare gifts as an orator should bring him fame, and secure a position in the highest ranks of the Church. Thus she had persuaded him, holding out the promise that every vacation should be spent with her; curbing her own affections, even as she had curbed his, she walked the path of wisdom—determined, resigned—in the knowledge that this was the way to win. And Jim had come to face it calmly now, even as she had done. The minute details of the plan were being filled in. Then came those little words from Lou-Jane.

Had Jim been a worldly-wise person with many girl friends and a mouth full of flattery for them all, Belle would have paid no attention to the proposed visit of Lou-Jane to Rochester. Knowing Jim as she did, and having a very shrewd idea of Lou-Jane's intentions, Belle realized that this was a crisis, the climax of her life and hopes, that everything that made her life worth while was staked on the very next move.

She said little as they walked home from the parsonage, but her hand, locked in his arm, clung just a little more than usual, and he was moved by the tenderness of her "Good-night."

Little she slept that night; but tossed and softly moaned, "That woman, that coarse, common woman! How *can* he see anything in her? She is nothing but an animal. And yet, what may happen if he is East and she is playing around, with me far away? It cannot be. I know what men are. Now he is mine; but, if I let him go far away and she follows——

"It cannot be! It must not be—at any price, I must stop it. I must hold him."

And she tossed and moaned, "At any price! At any price! I'd do anything——"

The simple, obvious plan was to put him under promise never to see or hear from Lou-Jane; but her pride and her instincts rebelled at the thought. "What? Admit that there was danger from that creature? No, no—why, that would have just the wrong effect on him; she would become doubly interesting; no, that would not do. She would ignore that—that—that snake. And then what?

"At any price, this must be stopped"; and out of the whirling maelstrom of her thoughts came this: "If I cannot keep her from going, I'll go, too!" How? In what capacity? Belle knew enough of his mind to be sure that however the plan was carried out, it would shock his ideas of propriety and be a losing game.

Lou-Jane was playing better than she was, and it maddened her ever more as she realized that the present plans could end only in one way—the way that she, at any price, must stop. And in the hours of tumult, of reasoning every course out to its bitter end, this at length came clear: There was but one way—that was *marry him now*. It was that or wreck the happiness upon which both their lives had been built. And yet that meant ruin to his whole career. She, herself, had told him so a hundred times. "He must go back to college. He must not marry till his three years were completed." These were her very words.

It seemed that ruin of his hopes was in one scale; ruin of hers in the other. And she tried to pray for light and guidance; but there do seem to be times when the Lord is not interested in our problems; at least, no light or guidance of the kind she sought for came.

And she wrought herself up into a state of desperation. "At any price, this must stop," she kept saying over and over. Every expedient was turned in her mind and its outcome followed as far as she could; and ever it came back to this—her hopes or his were to be sacrificed.

"*I will not let him go*," she said aloud, with all the force of a strong will become reckless. "It would certainly be my grave; but it need not be his.

There are other colleges and other ways. I'm not afraid of that. At any price, I must keep him. I'll marry him now. We'll be married at once. That will settle it."

The storm was over. The one plan was clear. That she would take—take and win; but, oh, how selfish she felt in taking it! She was sacrificing his career.

Yet ever she crushed the rising self-accusation with the "There are other colleges and other ways. I'll open the way for that." That was the sop to her inner judge, but the motive power was this: "At any price I must hold him." And convinced that the time had come to play her highest trump she fell asleep.

The following morning found Belle fully prepared for energetic action. She cleared the table and washed the dishes, putting them in their accustomed places, and stopped suddenly with the last of the china in her hand, wondering how long it would be before she held it again. Upstairs, she quickly packed her hand-bag for "a one-night camp" and, keeping ears and eyes alert, noted when at length her father had gone to his office and her mother had settled to her knitting. Then she went to her room and set about a careful toilet. The rebellious forelock was curled on a hot slate pencil and tucked back among its kind. Over each ear, she selected another lock for like elaboration. She put on her most becoming dress and studied the effect of her two brooches to make sure which one would help the most. She dashed a drop of "Violetta" on her handkerchief and pinched her cheeks to heighten their colour and remove the traces of the previous night's vigil. The beauty-parlour methods were not yet known in Cedar Mountain.

Jim always dropped in for a chat in the morning and it was not long before his cheery whistle sounded as down the street he came to the tune of "Merry Bandon Town." In his right hand he twirled a stout stick in a way that suggested a very practical knowledge of the shillelah. The flush of health and of youth suffused his cheeks and mounted to his forehead. All signs of worry over his impending fate were gone; indeed, no worry could live long in his buoyant mind; its tense electric chargement was sure death to all such microbes. Arrived at the Boyds', he did not stop to open the five-foot gate. Laying his fingers on the post, he vaulted over the pickets.

Belle met him on the porch. From somewhere back, Ma Boyd called out a thin-voiced "good morning," as they went into the front room.

"My little girl looks pale to-day," he said, as he held her at arm's length.

"Yes, I didn't sleep well. I wish I could get out for a few hours. Can't you take me?"

"Sure, that's what I came for," he answered gaily.

"I don't feel much like riding, Jim. Can you get a good buckboard?"

"Why, yes, of course I can. Carson says I can have his double-harness buckboard any time, ponies and all."

"Good! Just the thing. I want to go out to Bylow's Corner to make a call, and maybe farther, if we can manage. I'll be ready by the time you are here with the rig."

She went to her desk and wrote a note to her father. Somehow, mother didn't seem to count.

DEAR DAD: If I am not home to-night, I shall be with Aunt Collins.

Lovingly, BELLE.

Then she put it in his tobacco jar, where he would be certain to see it on coming home for dinner, and where Ma Boyd would never dream of looking.

When Jim returned she carried a hand-bag: "Some things I need," and she laughed happily as he lifted her into the rig and inquired if she wasn't taking a trunk. Then away they went, as they had so many times before.

Youth and health, love and beauty; October and the Dakota Hills—what a wonderful conjunction! The world can do no better to multiply the joy of being alive. If either had a care, it was quickly buried out of sight. Jim was in rollicking mood. Not a prairie dog sat up and shook its tail in time to its voice, but Jim's humour suggested resemblances to some one that they knew; this one looked like Baxter, the fat parson of the Congregationalists; "that little one's name is likely Higginbotham; see how Hannah makes him skip around. And there goes Lawyer Scrimmons," he chuckled, as a blotched, bloated rattlesnake oozed along and out of sight at the hint of danger. Two owls that gazed and blinked in silence were named for a pair of fat twin sisters of their church; perfectly well-meaning, but without a word of conversation or any expression but their soulful eyes. And a solitary owl that gazed from the top of a post straight up in the sky was compared to an old-time Methodist woman with her eyes uplifted in prayer while the collection plate was shoved under her nose.

Bylow's Corner was reached all too soon. As Jim was about to draw up Belle said: "Let's go on farther; we can take them in on the road back. Let's go as far as Lookout Mountain." And Jim was happy to go.

They were six miles from Cedar Mountain now, with no more houses by the road for miles. Belle had fallen silent. It was all as she had planned, but somehow the firm resolve of the night before seemed open to question now. She gazed absently away over the level, toward a distant hillside, and the smile faded from her lips. To his next light speech she barely made response. He threatened to charge a "thank you ma'am" at high speed if she didn't laugh. Then, getting no response, he burst out:

"What the divil is the matter with my little girl to-day? Have ye anything on your mind, Belle?"

This was the fork in their trail: either she must tell him or give him up. For a fraction of an instant she lived through the agony of doubt. Then, with a certainty she had not thought possible, she said: "Yes, Jim, I surely have."

"Well, shake it off, Belle. Let some other mind have it. Use mine, if you'll allow that I have one."

"I haven't slept all night for thinking of it, Jim," she began.

"Thinking of what?"

"Your going away."

His face clouded; he became suddenly silent and she continued:

"Jim, dear, I've tried to keep my feelings out of it altogether; I've argued it out, using nothing but my judgment, and it seemed the wise thing for you to go back East to college. All my judgment says: 'send him back'; but, oh, all my instincts say 'keep him here.'" She covered both his hands with hers and put her cheek on them for a moment.

"I'm always trying to be wise, Jim, but I suppose I'm really very stupid and very weak like most humans; and there come times when I feel like kicking everything over and saying 'what's the use?' This time I'm going to let my feelings hold the reins."

"Why, Belle darling! That sounds more like me than you."

"Jim, as I lay awake last night, a voice seemed to be sounding in my heart: 'Don't let him go. If he goes, you'll lose him, you'll lose each other.' Jim, do you suppose God brought you and me together in this way, to be so much to each other, to be exactly fitted to round out each other's life, to let us separate now?"

"Belle, I believe He sent me out here to meet you, and any one coming between us is going against God."

"I know, Jim. And yet I have the feeling, which I can't shake off, that as sure as you go back to college, I shall lose you."

"Then, by Heaven! I won't go; and that settles it, Belle. I'll chuck the whole thing." And his forehead flushed with passion.

She dropped her face on her knees and shook in a paroxysm of weeping. All the emotional side of her nature—so carefully repressed throughout these weeks and months of struggle—swept away their barriers. Now that she had spoken the fear that was in her heart, the reality of the danger that threatened their happiness crushed her down. Jim threw his arm around her. "Belle, Belle, I can't see you cry that way. Belle, don't! We are not going to part."

It was long before she found her voice. In broken sounds she sobbed: "I can't give you up now," and she leaned toward him though still she hid her face.

"Belle, why do you talk of such a thing? You won't give me up, because I won't let you. I won't go, Belle, that's settled."

Her only answer was to cling to him passionately. After a long silence, during which the ponies dropped to a walk, she said half questioningly:

"Jim, we can't—give up all and—and—separate now."

"Belle darling," and Jim suddenly became calm and clear in thought, and a strange new sense of power came on him as he gripped himself, "there are times when a man must just take the bit in his teeth and break through everything, and I'm going to do that now. There's just one way out of this; we're half-way to Deadwood. Let's go right on and get married. The college and everything else can go to the divil so long as I can be with you.

"Will you agree to that?" he asked, lifting her head from his shoulder and looking into her eyes.

"Jim," she said, pushing him gently away from her and leaning back so that they occupied the sides of the wide seat, "let's be fair with each other. For a long time you've had your fling at the hardship of going back to Coulter while I have urged you to go. This is my fling at it"—she smiled at him through her tears—"my rebellion, so perhaps we're quits. But the problem still remains. I thought about it all last night and I decided I could not let you go—that it meant the end of our hopes. When you first asked me, up the road, I doubted my right to tell you the fears I had. But, oh, Jim, it is *our* happiness, *ours*, not yours or mine alone. If we have that we can *make* the rest come right. If we lose that——"

"But we're not going to lose it," he cried, "if you'll only answer my question, Will you marry me to-day if we go on to Deadwood?" He put out his arms to her and she yielded with a happy sob to his ardour. Holding her and pressing his lips to hers, he said simply: "I am very happy."

After a little while she took his head between her palms and looking into his face with eyes that sought his spirit, as though she would pledge her faith to his, she said: "You will never be sorry for this, darling."

At Lookout Mountain was the half-way house. They fed their horses, rested an hour, and then sped on. At four o'clock they reached Deadwood. Jim put up the horses at the little inn, whose parlour he remembered; together they went to the jeweller's shop, purchased a ring, and then to the mayor's office.

The great man was busy with affairs of State, but the world has a kindly heart for lovers and the experienced official can recognize them afar. He glanced over a crowd of many men advancing various claims, and said, with a knowing smile, "Hello!"

"License," was all Jim said, and a subdued "Ha, Ha!" was the amused response.

The mayor pulled out a drawer, produced a form, and rattled off the usual questions: Name? Age? Married before? etc., filling it in; then did the same for Belle. "Now stand up. You swear to the truth of each and all of the statements?" Each of them raised a hand and swore.

"Want to finish it up now?" said the mayor.

"Yes."

"Put on the ring and hold her hand." Jim did so. The mayor stood up, holding their clasped hands in his left. He raised his right and said: "James and Belle, in accordance with the laws of the United States and of the State of Dakota, I pronounce you man and wife." He signed the paper, gave each in turn the pen to sign, and said, "Now I want another witness."

"Sure, I'd like to be in on that there dokiment," said a rough voice.

"Can you write?"

"Bet your life I can."

A big heavy man came forward; the mayor handed him the pen; and, after the word "Witness" he wrote, "Pat Bylow, of Cedar Mountain"; and then with a friendly grin he offered his hand to the Preacher, and they gripped hands for the first time.

"Two dollars, please," said the mayor.

Jim paid it, and he and Belle stepped forth as man and wife.

CHAPTER XLVI

WHAT NEXT?

According to an ancient custom, the newly wed should cease from their calling in life and disappear for a time, and the practice has long been well honoured by observance. But Mr. and Mrs. Hartigan had large and immediate problems to face. They breakfasted at Aunt Collins's and set out at once for Cedar Mountain. Belle was quite aware, reasonably and instinctively, that she must expect a reaction in Jim after the emotional outburst that had led him so far from their sober plan of a week before; and she exerted herself to fill every minute with the interests of this new life they had begun. But she was not prepared for something which did begin. From that hour of the great decision Jim seemed bigger and stronger. She had been thinking of him as a promising child. Now he was her equal in the world of affairs. He was growing faster than she. They were near the edge of the town when she saw a cottage with the sign up, "To let." It was very attractive in its fresh paint and obviously it had just been finished.

"Jim, maybe that was made for us. Let's see it." They tied up the horses and entered. It was indeed small. The Preacher had to stoop at the front doorway and turn side-wise to enter the cellarway, but it was clean and prettily placed with a view to the south, and had four rooms and cellar.

Belle gazed from the window through the gap between the hills and said, "I wish I knew some things that I will know within a week"; then, after a pause, "but I don't; let's go."

As they were getting into the buckboard Jim remembered having left behind a package which Aunt Collins wished to send to her sister, Mrs. Boyd. As they drove hastily back they met a new, strange sight in Deadwood. A man in a sort of military uniform was marching along carrying a big drum which he pounded rhythmically; behind him were a dozen men and women in poke bonnets and blue skirts. Above them was a flag inscribed "Salvation Army." They stopped to sing a hymn, and were soon surrounded by a crowd of people who made scoffing remarks. The leader prayed, and all joined in a warlike hymn punctuated by the thunderous drum.

There can be no question of the power of the drum on simple and primitive natures. Something in Jim responded to it at once. The commonplace words of the commonplace leader were without power to move, and the droning hymn was soporific rather than inspiring; but the rhythmic thump, thump, thump, seemed to strike the chords of his being; and a hypnotic tensity began. He gazed at the sad face of the fanatic, and forgot everything else, till Belle roused him with a businesslike, "Let's go, Jim."

Arrived at Cedar Mountain, they knew at once from the smiles and greetings of a few friends whom they met that the town had heard the news. They went to the Boyd home where Ma Boyd wept and feebly scolded, then wept some more. Pa Boyd said "Humph!" Loading his pipe he smoked in silence for five minutes and then began to laugh quietly. At length, clapping Hartigan good-naturedly on the back, he observed: "Well, boys will be boys. But I did think Belle was too level-headed and businesslike to go off on a panicky proposition like this. Howsomever, it's done; now the question is, what next? I can forgive; folks can forgive, but the Church won't. Now what's next?"

Seeing that the home folks were well enough disposed, Jim didn't wait to discuss details but set out alone to call on the Rev. Dr. Jebb. Mrs. Jebb opened the door herself and looking up at the handsome face she laid her hand on his arm with a pleased laugh and said: "Good for you!"

Dr. Jebb was very grave. "My dear boy, don't you see how serious it is?"

"Just as serious as it can be, doctor; I know that," and Jim laughed.

"But do you realize you have broken with the Church? You cannot go to college now. You are out of a living. You must think about some other means of livelihood."

"All of which I know, and knew when I took this step."

"As your pastor, I must chide you severely," said Jebb; "as your superior officer, I must pay you the twenty-five dollars that is your full and quit payment of salary up to October thirty-first; as the head of this body in Cedar Mountain, I must notify you that your connection with the congregation as assistant pastor is ended; as your brother in Christ, I invoke God's blessing on your somewhat hasty action; and, as your friend and Belle's, I offer you my poor help in whatsoever way I can serve you." And as Jim took his leave, much touched by the old doctor's gentleness, the pastor followed him to the door with his wife. With one of his sudden happy impulses Jim stooped and kissed Mrs. Jebb and the two old people were still in the doorway watching him as he turned for a final wave at the gate.

The blacksmith shop was the next place of call. Not that Jim sought it, but he couldn't well avoid it, and he was hailed by all as he came near. Shives came forward in his characteristic way, holding out his hand. "Wall, wall!

Now I know you are human in spite of your job! You've gone up about ten pegs in my scale."

Carson was there and met him with a broad grin. "So that's what you borrowed my team for? Ho, ho! Well, I'll forgive you, if you bring them back and promise not to get the habit."

After much well-wishing Jim started down the street. He had only gone a short distance when the sound of some one running and calling his name made him halt. It was Higginbotham who had hastened on the first news of his arrival to make a business proposition. "Of course, I know, Jim, that you are a capitalist, and Hannah and me have been thinking it would be a good idea to establish a branch in Deadwood. Hannah is 'round calling on Belle, to fix it up."

As indeed she was at that very moment. Jim got the whole project from Belle on his return, but there were serious difficulties in the way of Hannah's scheme. Jim had no taste or capacity for business. All Belle's time would be needed for the household. Furthermore, Jim still felt that the ministry was his calling. They pondered it long and discussed it freely. Belle knew she could make the business a success, but it would be by sacrificing many things that they had dreamed of and planned for their first home. That night they knelt down together and prayed for the guidance of the Great Guide. Jim opened the Bible three times, with his eyes closed, and laid his finger at hazard on a text, and these were the three that decided his fate: Kings, XIX:20—And he said unto him Go back again. 2 Thess. II:13—God hath from the beginning chosen you to salvation. Daniel IV:35—According to his will in the army of heaven.

"There, Belle, could anything be plainer? We are ordered back to Deadwood. I must join the Salvation Army."

Belle was torn between her business instincts, her religious training, and her absolute devotion to her hero. But whatever the sum total, thus much all things agreed on: they must get away from Cedar Mountain. Whither? There seemed no answer but Deadwood.

The next day Mrs. Jebb gave a reception for the young people and Cedar Mountain turned out strong. Three was the hour named, and at four the parsonage was full. Belle was dressed in the simple gray that intensified her colour, her brown eyes and gold-brown hair were shining; standing at the end of the parlour she looked very lovely, and all Cedar Mountain glowed with pride in her.

Jim was in his glory. He frolicked with everybody and was in the midst of a gallant speech to Shives's daughter when some one tapped his arm and dragged him off. It was John Higginbotham, anxious to get his scheme more clearly into Jim's mind. "Not only was the main line of insurance good, but everything pointed to a land boom soon in Deadwood. Once the boom struck, the insurance could be temporarily sidetracked. Then, allowing seven hundred and fifty dollars capital, of which five hundred dollars could be invested in lots on 10 per cent. margin, this would secure five thousand dollars' worth of lots, or fifty small lots at present prices; in the ordinary course of the boom, this would speedily reach fifty thousand dollars, when, of course, he would sell and——"

"Hartigan!" cried a voice. "Who, in Heaven's name, is concealing you? Oh, here you are." It was Dr. Carson. "I've been thinking of you a lot ever since this news broke and I've decided that you are more like a man than a preacher. Why don't you cut out all this piffling holy talk and go in for something you can do? Now, my theory is that each man can do some one thing better than any one else; and, if he has the luck to have that one thing for his life calling, he's going to make a success. You know horses better than any man I know. You knew enough to steal my team, for example, when you meant to elope."

"Now, see here," Hartigan objected.

"Don't interrupt me," said Carson. "Jim, this is my honest advice: get out of this rotten little town. Go to Deadwood, or any other big, rotten town, and start in on the horse business and something will happen worth while."

Jim's eyes glowed. It was curious how the word "horse" fascinated him. "I'll surely take the first two moves you advise: I'll get out of this town and I'll go to Deadwood. But——" He stopped. He didn't say it, but he had given his "wurd as a mahn" long ago that his life should be devoted to the Church.

Little Peaches was there in a very high collar and sang, "Jerusalem the Golden," till tears came to the eyes of the audience. As he began the third score, Colonel Waller and his staff arrived. The old soldier's eyes gleamed as he measured the tall, straight form of the Preacher. "Well, Jim, can't I persuade you to enlist? We need a few like you."

"Sure, I'm enlisted now," was the reply, "and going to the front; and when I am gone, don't forget my horse."

"Ha, ha! We are not likely to," said the Colonel. "The wisest thing you ever did for yourself was when you sold him."

As the party began to break up Hannah Higginbotham plucked Jim's sleeve and whispered: "If John comes chasing you with a scheme, don't pay any attention to him. He'd try to talk business if you were both swimming for your lives; but a week from now, we'll come to see you at Deadwood. I've fixed it up with Belle."

As Jim waited for Belle, who was having a few last words with Mrs. Jebb, Charlie Bylow came rather shyly forward with his wife. "Mr. Hartigan, I've got a good team now; in case there is any moving to do, I'd like to do it for you." And then as if he thought Jim might not understand he said: "We owe a lot to you and we'd like a chance to pay it back."

There was one old acquaintance that did not turn up. That was Lou-Jane Hoomer. Probably she was busy packing her trunk for the visit to Rochester; at any rate, upon her return from the East, she joined the Congregationalists, where she sang regularly in the choir and soon made such an impression on the baritone that they found increasing comfort in each other's company.

CHAPTER XLVII

BACK TO DEADWOOD

Two days later Jim and Belle were again on the Deadwood trail. It seemed that each new chapter of their lives must begin on that trail. They were in a new buckboard, the gift of Pa Boyd, driving Midnight in harness. That same morning Charlie Bylow had left for Deadwood with his team and wagon. The latter was loaded with gifts from Cedar Mountain friends, some of them sufficiently absurd—for example, framed chromos, a parrot cage, a home instructor in Spanish, and a self-rocking cradle—but there was also a simple sufficiency of household furniture.

The buckboard overtook the wagon in the morning and arrived at Deadwood by one o'clock. Jim was for going to the hotel and dining, but Belle thought it better to see the estate agent first, and within half an hour they had deposited the first month's rent for the white cottage. Strange to tell, though the cottage had stood empty and uncalled for during the previous six months, there were two other applications on the afternoon that the Hartigans secured their lease.

Their furniture arrived late in the day, and those who have watched newly-mated birds carry the sticks and straw of their first nest, will understand the joy experienced by Belle and Jim in planning, arranging, and rearranging this first home. Whether it is larger bliss to carry sticks or to bill and coo cannot be guessed, and perhaps it does not matter, for every stone in the perfect arch is bearing all the arch. The first night in their own—their very own—home, with no one but themselves, was a sweet contentment for the time and a precious memory afterward. As they sat hand in hand looking from the little window down the valley, where the golden west was blocked by the high, dark hill, they knew calm for the first time after many days of tempest, and Jim's fervent soul found words in the ancient text: "Truly the light is sweet; and a pleasant thing it is for the eyes to behold the sun."

A very blessed thing is the sunrise on Deadwood. It means far more than in most towns, for the shut-in-ness of the gulch makes night so very night-like, and the gloom is king till the radiant one mounts to flood the place with a sudden sunrise—a little late, perhaps, but a special sunrise for the town.

It was their first real breakfast together. Jim rose and lighted the fire in the stove. Belle made the coffee and fried the eggs. It was all their own and there is something about such a breakfast that gives it the nature of a sacrament, with youth and health, beauty and love, assembled to assist, and a special angel of happiness to bless it with his shining eyes.

As their talk turned to future plans, Jim's idea was to settle down, find quarters for Midnight, then visit the Salvation Army barracks and wait in the crowd till an opportunity to speak should occur. After that he had no doubt his pulpit eloquence would open a way to secure an appointment.

Belle's idea was totally different. "No, Jim, that won't do. If we enter the town by the back door we'll always be back-door folk. I propose to come in by the front way, and have a red carpet and a triumphal arch for our entry. Don't do anything until I have tried a plan of mine. Meanwhile, you look after Midnight."

Jim's curiosity was very large, but he smiled and asked no questions, and Belle set out for a visit to Uncle Collins. "It has to be done just right," she explained to that gentleman after an elaboration of her idea. Belle knew instinctively that all their fate in Deadwood would turn on the colour of their coming. Uncle Collins entered wholeheartedly into the plan and that week, much to Jim's amazement, the local press came out with a column article:

DISTINGUISHED ARRIVALS IN DEADWOOD

Our townsfolk are to be congratulated on the latest increase to our population. The Rev. James Hartigan and his beautiful bride, formerly Miss Boyd, of Cedar Mountain, have yielded to the call of Deadwood and decided to make their home in the mining capital of Dakota. They have taken the White Cottage on Southview Avenue (Muggins & Mawlins Real Estate Company) and will be at home Friday afternoon.

Dr. Hartigan was educated at Coulter College, Ontario, and won his spurs long ago as a pulpit orator. While devoting his life to the ministry, he is also a man of means and is likely to make important investments in Deadwood as favourable opportunities present themselves. In fact, it was largely the need of such opportunity that led to the selection of Deadwood as his future home.

We are proud of the tribute to our promise as a town, and the distinguished couple will find us ready to greet them with a hearty welcome.

Jim laughed joyously as he read it in the paper next day. "Sure, Belle, every word of it is true and everything it leaves you believing is a lie. I never knew how far astray you could put folk by telling the simple truth."

One or two meetings in the street and a few observations from Aunt Collins, led Belle to expect some callers on Friday afternoon, but she never dreamed of the reception that did take place. Fortunately she had notice, an hour before, to treble the amount of tea provided; then, in a flash, a great idea entered her head.

"Jim," she said, "this is going to be a very important event in our lives, we are going to meet some people to-day who will shape all our future. There will be men of business here and men high in the churches; they will be sure to make you some sort of an offer, many offers of different kinds. Encourage them, don't turn any of them down; but don't definitely accept any of them. Now promise, Jim, you won't accept any of them."

"I wouldn't dare," said Jim, "after this"—and he held up the local paper with a grin. "I'm in the hands of my manager."

It was well for him that he agreed. Mrs. Collins was there to assist—beaming with pride. Uncle Collins came late and looked bored and uncomfortable. Belle was in her glory. She was of that delicate type which changes much with varying circumstance, and now she seemed radiantly beautiful. All the guests that day agreed that they were far and away the handsomest couple that had ever come to Deadwood, and surely they should have known, for all Deadwood came. The mayor came because he felt a fatherly interest in the couple he had married; and besides, they were an important accession to the population. "Hartigan," he began, "If I had your money I'd make a deal with the Northern Pacific. I tell you their new president is a live wire. He's ready to close on any good idea," etc., etc. The ministers came because they had heard of Dr. Hartigan's accomplishments and wished to pay their respects; and Dr. Hooper, of the Congregationalists, said he would be glad if Dr. Hartigan would occupy his pulpit the coming Sunday. The Rev. Dr. Mackenzie, of the Presbyterian Church, offered his pulpit; and so did the Rev. Dr. Jowley, of the Evangelicals. To all of these Jim made gracious and happy replies, deferring definite answer until he should be able to consult his date book and complete certain other arrangements.

The Presbyterian also took the opportunity of privately whispering to Dr. Hartigan that he, Dr. Mackenzie, had "just discovered a rare business opportunity—a whole block of staked and patented gold claims on the same lead as the 'Homestake'; the owner was compelled to sell out owing to family troubles, and would take ten thousand dollars cash for 49 per cent. of the stock—an absolute certainty of a million within a year! Dr. Mackenzie would turn over this unique and dazzling opportunity to Dr. Hartigan for the modest sum of one thousand dollars, which was less than 10 per cent., if expenses were included...." and so on, at much length.

The head of the Bar-Bell Ranch called because he had heard of the famous racer, Blazing Star, that was bred in the Hartigan stables, and he would like Dr. Hartigan to visit him and see his horses.

The insurance companies also were represented, and Bob Davidson—he declined at all times the "Mr."—managed to get in a word privately to the effect that he hoped that the Reverend Hartigan would make no business alliance until he had been to the Davidson office and seen the possibilities of one or two little schemes that needed "only a very little capital to pay——"

The reception lasted three hours and the account of it in the paper next day covered several columns. The impression it left on Jim was pleasing, but confusing. The single immediate and pleasant result was when the local lumberman, learning that Hartigan wished to erect a stable for his own team, volunteered to send round one thousand feet of the special siding, of which he was exclusive agent, together with the necessary amount of tar paper, on condition that the stable should bear the signboard:

SQUELCHE'S SPECIAL MATCHED SIDING
JOHN JOHNSON, SOLE AGENT

So the siding came and Jim built the stable with his own hands and gloried in every nail as he drove it. Midnight was thereupon withdrawn from a livery stable and installed with due pride and pomp.

CHAPTER XLVIII

THE FORK IN THE TRAIL

The reception was over. Jim and Belle had supped at Aunt Collins's and were back again in the cottage, sitting by the kitchen stove, in which Jim had just kindled a blazing fire, for the evenings were cold. They were glad to be together again by themselves, and to talk things over.

Jim put a new block in the stove; then, sitting down, remarked: "For a capitalist who contemplates buying up part of the town, securing a new railroad, and cornering a township of gold ore, this is quite a modest layout."

"Now while it's fresh," she replied, "let's have the whole thing; especially the invitations." She took paper and wrote them down as he recited them. Then, with a good deal of shrewdness, she proceeded to appraise one by one.

The gold mine, the railroad, and the livery barn she treated with a joyous laugh; she liked them as symptoms. The town lot matter was worth looking into.

As for the invitations to preach, compared with the Presbyterians, the Evangelicals were a larger body; but the Congregationalists, much smaller, were more solid. The last had a fine church with a strong membership of well-to-do men, but they also had an able preacher of their own particular doctrines, so that Belle gave preference to the Evangelicals.

"We must concentrate our big guns on them, Jim; get out your best sermon, the one on 'Show thyself a man' (1 Kings II:2). Keep that for the big crowd in the evening. Next Sunday, at the Congregational Church you can give them the same thing, for it will be a different crowd; but at night, why not give them your sermon on 'Kindness' that made such a hit in Cedar Mountain."

"Well, where does the Salvation Army come in, Belle?"

"It doesn't come in just now"; and inwardly she hoped she might be able to keep it out altogether. Play for time and hope for luck was her plan. But she was secretly worried by the superstitious importance which he attached to the three texts, picked at random from the Scripture that day in Cedar Mountain, and by the interpretation he gave them. But she thought it best to avoid the subject. First she sorted the invitations, adjusted a desirable programme, and then sent a courteous reply to each, accepting or declining.

And it was done in such a way that none were hurt and most were pleased. Then happened two of the accidents she had prayed for. As Jim strode home about noon one day, he heard a rabble of small boys jeering and shouting, "Holy Billy! Holy Billy! Salvation! Salvation!" He turned to see them pursued by a fat, middle-aged man, who after several attempts to drive them away, at length seized a pitch fork from those exhibited outside a hardware store and, intent on revenging himself, ran after the children. The youngsters fled, save one, who fell; and the furious fat man made a vicious prod with the fork. It might easily have proved fatal, but Jim was near enough to seize the man's arm and wrest the fork from him. The fat man was white with rage. He blustered a good deal and finally went off sputtering comically although he used no cuss-words.

That evening Jim and Belle went to the Salvation Army barracks, with the fixed intention of taking part in the worship as fully as might be permitted. On their arrival Jim was utterly surprised to find that the uniformed Captain in command was the fat little fury of the street episode; and still more astonished when that rotund person peremptorily ordered him out of the building. As the rest of the Salvationists dutifully supported their Captain, Jim had no choice, and with a feeling of sadness that was not shared by Belle, he turned out into the street.

There are many drives about Deadwood, but not many good roads. The scenery, not the pavement, is the allurement; and in the morning, the young couple took a short drive to learn the trails. They had not gone a mile when they were brought to a standstill by a lumber wagon stuck in the middle of the narrow road and quite immovable. It was not the weight of the load or the fault of the road, but because one of the horses was on strike—he baulked and refused absolutely to pull. Held up by the blockade, on the other side, were two buggies with men and women.

The teamster was just a plain, every-day bungler. He began by urging the obstinate horse with voice and whip; but at each fresh application the creature merely laid back his ears, shook his head, and set his feet more resolutely against all progress. At last the driver worked himself into a rage. He lashed the horse with all his strength, the only effect being to leave long lines on the animal's coat and cause him to kick out frantically with his hind feet.

"Man alive!" said Jim, leaving Belle's side and walking forward, "that's no way to handle a horse. Let me——"

A volume of abuse interrupted him. "You go on and mind your d—n business," said the teamster. "I'm taking care of this." In uncontrollable fury he beat the horse over the head with the butt end of his whip till it broke in two.

"See here, if you don't stop that I'll take a hand in it!" shouted Jim, thoroughly aroused.

The answer yelled back was not printable. It reflected not only on the Rev. James Hartigan, but on all his ancestors. Then, in an instant, the insane brute took a wooden hand-spike from his load and dealt the horse a terrific blow on the head. The beast staggered, almost fell, but recovered just as the driver, shouting, "I'll larn you!" landed another blow and hauled back for a third that would have felled if not killed the horse. But Jim got there first. He jerked the club out of the man's hand and as the attack turned on himself, he laid the driver out with a deft tap of the kind he knew so well. The other man with the load now rushed at Jim to avenge his fallen leader. But it is easy to meet that sort of onset when you know the game and have the muscle. The second went down on top of the first teamster amid loud cheers from the men in the buggies.

Five years before, in this country, Jim would certainly have been shot within the first five minutes, but the law and order society had been doing good work, and now men did not carry revolvers as of old, so nature's weapons counted as firearms once had done.

"Jim!" called Belle feebly. "Let's go." He turned; she was ghastly pale, as she held on to Midnight. She had never before seen men fight. She was appalled and terrified.

"Dear child," he laughed, almost gleefully, "you're not used to it. Don't take it so seriously. Sure it's fun and it's missionary work. Don't be worried at seeing men tumbled over. As soon as those two fools come to and stand on end, I'll show them how to drive a horse." He straightened out the two men he had stunned, and then went to the trembling horse.

As he laid his hand on its shoulder it shrank. He talked softly and began to examine the harness. Sure enough, there was a mass of cockle burrs caught in the long mane and wedged under the collar, so that every pull of the harness drove the sharp spines into the animal's shoulder. Jim loosened the collar, cut off the mass of burrs, sacrificed his handkerchief to make a soft pad, and replaced the collar. Meanwhile, the two teamsters were sitting up and looking on with little joy in their faces.

"Now you two ignorant babes, I'll show you how to drive a horse that you've made baulky; and I want you to know that there are not any baulky horses; it's baulky drivers that make the trouble." He went to the creature's head, talked to it, stroked its nose, blew in its nostrils, and continued to talk till the ears no longer lay back at his touch. Presently the eyes ceased rolling and the legs were not bracing nervously.

"Now," said Jim softly, "will you be after pulling a little? Yes? Come now," he coaxed wheedlingly, "come now," and he tightened the lines. But the horse shook his head, showed temper as before, and held back.

"Oh, that's what ye want, is it?" said Jim. "All right, back up it is," and gently man[oe]uvring, he shouted: "Back!" Both horses backed. He kept them backing, and by deft steering, held the wagon in the road. Back they went steadily. Now the baulky horse indicated his willingness to go on; but Jim wasn't ready. It was back, back, and back some more. For a hundred yards he kept it up. At last, when he changed about and gave the order to "Get up!" the one-time baulky horse was only too glad to change his gear and pull his very best. Jim took the load up the little hill, and on a quarter mile, where he waited for the original teamsters to come up.

"There, now," said Jim as he handed over the lines to the sullen driver, "you should have found that bunch of cockle burrs. It was all your fault, not the horse's. And if he hadn't responded to the backing, I'd have tied a pebble in his ear and left him for a few minutes to think it over. Then he'd have gone all right; it never fails. I tell you there aren't any baulky horses if they are rightly handled."

A cheer came from the buggies as the load of timber rolled away around the hill. As Hartigan got in beside Belle the two rigs came by. The men shouted, "Good for you! That was a fine job."

Jim blushed with pleasure; it was all so simple and familiar to him; but when he turned to look at Belle, she was white and ill. "Let's go home, Jim," she whispered. He looked at her in some surprise; then slowly it dawned on him—she had never before seen the roughness of men fighting. To him it was no more than the heavy sport of the football field. To her it was brutality unloosed; it was shocking, disgusting, next to murder. With mingled feelings of regret, amusement, and surprise he said, "Dear heart, you take it all too seriously." Then he put his arm about her, tender as a woman, and a few minutes later placed her gently in the rocking chair in the white cottage.

CHAPTER XLIX

THE POWER OF PERSONALITY

"Who is that?" said an elderly man in one of the buggies that passed Hartigan after the adventure with the baulky horse.

"I think it's the new preacher," said the driver. "Anyhow, we can easily see." They watched the buckboard with the black horse and saw it turn in at the white cottage.

"My guess was right, Mr. Hopkins," said the driver. "I haven't been in church for two years, but I'm going to hear that fellow preach next Sunday, all right."

"Why don't you go to church?" said the older man, who by his dress and manner was apparently some one of social importance.

"Oh, I dunno. I got out of the habit when I came out West," said the driver.

"Why do you want to hear this man?"

"Well, he kind o' makes one think he's 'some punkins.' He's a real man. He ain't just a sickly dough-lump as the bunch mostly is."

John Hopkins, President of the Dakota Flour and Milling Company, Regent of Madison University, man of affairs, philosopher and patron of a great many things, was silent for some time. He was pondering the question of the day and the light just thrown on it. Why don't men go to church? This Black Hills driver had answered: "Because the preachers are a bunch of dough-lumps." Whatever this might mean, it was, at best, a backhanded compliment to Hartigan. Yet, the driver was anxious to hear the new preacher. Why? Because he was impressed with his personality. It all resolved itself into that; the all-ruling law of personality. How wise, thought Hopkins, was the Church that set aside rules, dogmas, and scholastic attainments to make room for a teacher of real personality; such was the Founder's power.

Along with the livery driver and a hundred more than the church could hold, Hopkins went that night to the Evangelical Church to hear Hartigan. The Preacher's choice of hymns was martial; he loved the trumpets of the Lord. His prayers were tender and sincere; and his sermon on kindness— human kindness, spontaneous, for its own sake, not dictated by a creed— was a masterpiece of genuine eloquence. His face and figure were glorified in his effort. The story of his active sympathy with the injured horse had got about, and won the hearts of all. They came ready to love him, and—responding to the warm, magnetic influence—he blazed forth into the compelling eloquence that was native to his Celtic blood. He was gentle and impassioned; he spoke as never before. They heard him breathlessly; they loved his simple, Irish common sense. He held them in the hollow of his hands. The half hour allotted had been reached, and his story was told, and yet, not fully told. For a moment he paused, while his eyes sought a happy face in the nearest pew. Belle gently drew her watch. Mindful of their careful plan, he stopped at the signal, raised his hands, and said, "Let us pray." With one great sigh, the congregation kneeled before him, and with him, in body and spirit, and prayed as they never before had prayed in Deadwood.

After the service the young preacher came forward to meet the people. He was uplifted and radiant with a sense of power, with all the magic influence of the place and thought; and they crowded round him, many with tears in their eyes.

An elderly man of polished manner pushed through the circle and shook him by the hand. "I'm a stranger in town," he said; "here's my card. May I call on you to-morrow?"

"Certainly," said the Preacher. And the stranger disappeared.

There was a holy joy enveloping the little white cottage that night as they sat together reviewing the events of the day. "Don't you see, Jim, how much better it was to stop then? It's a thousand times better to have them go away saying: 'Why did he stop so soon?' rather than: 'Yes, wonderful, inspiring; but too long.' They will now be keener than ever to hear you. You never spoke so well before. Oh, my dear, I was never so proud of you! Now I know, without a doubt, that you are a chosen vessel of the Lord."

He held her in his mighty arms and kissed the gold-brown hair. "It's all your doing, Belle. I'm a rudderless ship without you." Then, after a long pause: "I'm thinking of my first visit to Deadwood."

She spoke no word, but pressed her frail face against the knotted muscles of his great throat and gently stroked his cheek.

CHAPTER L

THE CALL TO CHICAGO

"Get up, you lazy giant; the breakfast is ready," she called from the dining room. In truth, he had been up to light the fire and chop some wood, but was now reading in bed.

"Jim, I want you to be prepared for something very important to-day. I have a presentiment that this means something." She held up the card that had been presented after the service the evening before, and read:

MR. JOHN HOPKINS, ENGLEWOOD, CHICAGO

"If he comes with a proposition, don't accept it off-hand. Ask for a little while to consider."

Belle put on her smartest frock that morning and pressed Jim's trousers and tied his necktie repeatedly till its form was right. With a very critical eye she studied his appearance and her own, and that of the house, from every angle. Why? Would any business man make note of such things? Detailed note, no; perhaps not. But the sum total of such trifles—expressing decorum, experience, worldly wisdom of the kind that makes itself felt as tact, and judgment that is better than genius as guarantee of success—would unquestionably produce its effect.

Promptly at ten thirty A.M., Mr. John Hopkins called. He apologized for the unseemly hour, but said he was leaving town at noon. His first impression of Belle was a very delightful one. He found her refined and cultured and he recalled the advice of a certain old bishop: "Never give a call to a clergyman unless you are satisfied to call his wife as well." There was no use denying it, the wife was as important as the preacher; she could build up or disrupt the congregation, and so she made a double problem; that is why Rome ruled the wives out altogether.

Mr. Hopkins was a citizen of the world; he approached the object of the visit gracefully, but without loss of time. The Evangelical Alliance needed a man of personality and power to carry on its work in the slums of South Chicago among the iron-workers. The church cared nothing about creeds or methods—applied no gauge but results; the best result was a diffusion of human kindness. The salary was twenty-five hundred a year, with one week vacation at Christmas and one month at midsummer. He, John Hopkins, as President of the Board of Deacons, was empowered to select a man, and now made formal offer of the post to the Rev. James Hartigan. Mr.

Hartigan might have a week to decide; but Mr. Hopkins would greatly prefer it if Mr. Hartigan could decide before noon that day when Mr. Hopkins was leaving town. Until stage time he could be found at the Temperance House.

He rose quickly to go. Belle asked if he would, at his convenience, put the offer in writing, so that they might be clear as to details, indicating whether it was understood to be by the year and permanent, or for a time on approbation.

"I'll do that now," he replied. Taking the writing materials that she brought, he wrote and signed the formal call, with the intimation that it was for one year, subject to renewal.

As soon as their caller was safely gone, Jim picked up Belle in his arms and, marching up and down with her as if she had been a baby, he fairly gasped: "You are a wonder! You are a wonder! If I had gone my way, where should I be now? A drunkard or a cowboy; maybe in jail; or, at best, a doorkeeper in the Salvation Army. Oh, Belle, I swear I'll never pick a trail or open my mouth—never do a thing—without first consulting you." And the elation of the moment exploded into a burst of Irish humour. "*Now*, please ma'am, what am I to do?"

"What are *we* to do, you mean," retorted Belle. "Well, in view of the fact that we haven't got the cash the folks here think we have, we must do something. Twenty-five hundred dollars a year is an improvement on three hundred a year, and as there is no other positive offer in sight, I vote for accepting."

"That settles it. What right has a worm like me to vote?"

"That's a poor metaphor, Jim; try again."

"All right! The mighty Captain of this warship accepts the advice of the insignificant pilot—who happens to know the channel. How is that?"

"It can't be done, Jim. I may help the guiding, but without you I'd have nothing to guide. Each of us gives his best to the combine—each is a half of the arch; not simply are we twice as strong together, but twenty times as strong as we should be singly."

"Now for the call. Do you realize, Jim, that it means good-bye to the prairies, good-bye to the hills, and good-bye to Midnight?"

Jim nodded and looked grave. Belle went on: "But it also means living the life that you long ago elected to live—being a chosen instrument of good to bring blessings to those whose lives are black with sorrow and despair. It means giving up all the physical pleasures you love so deeply and rightly; but it also means following the Master. Which is it to be?"

"I know," he responded, "I know. But Belle, dear, I never had a moment of doubt when I had to decide between Belle and Blazing Star; why should I hesitate now when it's Midnight or Christ?"

So the letter was written and delivered forthwith at the Temperance Hotel. One week later Belle and Jim were driving again toward Cedar Mountain, headed for the railway which was to take them to Chicago. As they swung down the trail Belle looked out on the familiar objects and said:

"Here we are again at the beginning of a new chapter; and again it starts on the old Deadwood trail."

CHAPTER LI

THESE LITTLE ONES

It was a long but easy journey down south to the Union Pacific, and finally east to Chicago. And when the young couple, whom the passengers watched with much interest, arrived at the great city, they found half a dozen men and women of importance awaiting them at the Union Station, with more servants to assist them than they had pieces of luggage. Mr. and Mrs. Hopkins, with their own carriage, were in attendance to offer the hospitality of their house to the Rev. James Hartigan and his bride. It was a long drive to Englewood; but everything that kind friends, clear skies, and human forethought could do to make it pleasant was fully done. For the time being, they were installed in the Hopkins mansion—a veritable palace—and for the first time Jim had the chance to learn how the rich folk really live. While it was intensely interesting, he was eager to see the field of his future work. Belle, however, agreed with their host and hostess that it would be worth while to see a little of Chicago first.

The stockyards are either fascinating or intensely disgusting. The Hartigans had their fill of them in five minutes. The Art Institute had not yet been built, but there were museums and galleries and good music in many places. Lincoln Park and the great rolling, gusty lake were pleasant to behold; but to Jim, the biggest thing of all—the thing of which the buildings and the crowds were mere manifestations—was the vast concentration of human life, strife, and emotion—the throb and compulsion of this, the one great heart of the West.

There was dirt in the street everywhere; there were hideous buildings and disgusting vulgarities on every side, and crime in view on nearly every corner; but still one had to feel that this was the vital spot, this the great blood centre of a nation, young, but boiling with energy, boundless in promise—a city with a vital fire in its heart that would one day burn the filth and dross away and show the world the dream of the noblest dreamers all come true—established, gigantic, magnificent. There is thrill and inspiration—simple, natural, and earthy—in the Canyon where the Cheyenne cut the hills; but this was a different thrill that slowly grew to a rumble in Jim's heart as he felt the current floods of mind, of life, of sin, of hope that flowed from a million springs in that deep Wabash Canyon that carved in twain the coming city of ten million hopes that are sprung from the drifted ashes of a hundred million black and burnt despairs.

Hartigan had ever been a man of the saddle and the open field; but gazing from the top of that tall tower above the station, sensing the teeming life, the sullen roar, far below, he glimpsed another world—a better thing, for it was bigger—which, in its folded mantle, held the unborn parent, the gentler-born parent, of the mighty change—the blessed cleanup that every wise man prays for and works to bring about.

What place were they to occupy in this maelstrom? Two ways were open— one, to dwell in the dungeons and the horrors as poor among the poor; the other, to come as different beings—as frequent visitors—from another world. Jim, with his whole-souled abandon, was for the former; but Belle thought that all he would gain in that way would be more than offset by loss of touch with the other world. At that time those two worlds were at war and she contended that his place was to stand between the world of power and the world of need.

Their compromise was a little flat on the second floor of a house in Englewood, near enough to the rolling Lake to afford a glimpse of it and convenient to the open stretch that is now the famous Jackson Park. Here, with pretty rugs and curtains and pictures of horses and hills, they lined the home nest and gathered the best thoughts of the lives they had lived. Here at all times they could come assured of peace and rest.

Then came the meeting with the Board of Deacons, the preliminary visits to the field of work, where the streets were full of misery and the slum life rampant. A few short blocks away was another world—a world of palaces. Jim had never before seen massed misery; he had never before seen profligate luxury, and the shock of contrast brought to him the sudden, overwhelming thought: "These people don't want preaching, they want fair play. This is not a religious question, it is an economic question." And in a flash: "The religious questions *are* economic questions," and all the seemingly wild utterances of old Jack Shives came back, like a sudden overwhelming flood at the breaking of a dam. In an instant he was staggering among the ruins of all in religious thought that he had held holy.

When he reached their apartment that evening he was in a distraught condition. For some time he paced up and down. At last he said: "I must go out, Belle. I must walk alone." He spoke with intense emotion. He longed for his mountain; there was but one thing like it near—the mighty, moving lake. He put on his hat and strode away. Belle wanted to go with him, but he had not asked her; her instinct also said "no"; besides, there was the physical impossibility of walking with him when he went so striding. She sat down in the dusk to wonder—to wait.

He went to the lake shore. A heavy gale was blowing from the north and the lake was a wild waste. It touched him as the sage plains did; and the rough wind helped him by driving away all other folk afoot. Northward he went, feeling, but seeing nothing, of the rolling waters. Jack Shives with his caustic words came back to mind: "It's their 'fore-God duty to steal if their babies are hungry and they can't feed them any other way." Jim had never seen these things before; now they were the whole world; he had seen nothing else these slumming days. His spiritual ferment was such that, one by one, all the texts he had read came back as commentaries on this new world of terror. He recalled the words of the Master: "Your Heavenly Father knoweth ye have need of these things"; the fearful doom of those that "offend these little ones"; the strict injunction to divide with the needy and care for the helpless; and again, the words, "The Kingdom of heaven is within you"—not in a vague, unplaced world after death, but here, now— and those who thought that, by placating the custodians of costly edifices, they were laying up "treasure in heaven" were blindly going to destruction.

He strode in the night with his brain awhirl. The old texts held for him some new power: "Seek ye first the kingdom of God and His righteousness, and all these things shall be added into you"; and again, "The kingdom of heaven is within you"; "Sell all that thou hast and give to the poor." In vain he sought for inspired words that would reestablish the happy land beyond the grave that his teachers had ever pictured in set phrase. Yet every word of the Master pointed the other way. "*Here*"; "*now*"; and "*first within*" was the kingdom. And the hollowness of all the rich man's preachment—that the poor must suffer patiently in hope of a reward beyond the grave—was more and more a hideous stratagem as in his mind arose together two portrait types: the pinched, sullen, suffering face of the slums and the bloated, evil face to be found on the boulevard.

The mockery of it horrified as the immensity of it all swamped him. He had no mind, no equipment, for the subtleties of theology, and his head was a whirl of maddening contradictions, till the memory of his mother's simple devotion came like a cooling drink in his fever: "Never mind trying to reason it all out; you can't do it; no one can. Only ask what would the Master have done?" Yes, that was easy. "Feed the hungry, clothe the naked, visit the sick"; and turning, he wheeled homeward. The upheaval of all foundations seemed less dreadful. He could not expect to reason it all out. It was enough to do as the Master would have done; and, whether it was the feeding of the multitude, the healing of the lepers, the gentleness to the woman taken in adultery, or the helping of the man who fell among thieves, there was no doctrine, no preaching—only kindness shown as sympathy and physical help in their troubles, here and now. The words of another childhood friend came back to him—those of Fighting Bill Kenna. He used to say, "I don't care a dom what he is, if he's a good neighbour." Yet the neighbour in question was a papist and they were kind and friendly every day of the year, except on those two set apart by the devil to breed hate. Kenna was right where his heart led him and wrong where his creed was guide.

Hartigan could not have told why he went alone on that walk. He only knew that in this crisis something cried out in him to be alone with the simple big things. Why should the worldly-wise companion he had chosen be left out? He didn't know; he only felt that he wanted no worldly wisdom now. He wished to face the judgment day in his soul all alone. He would not have done so a year before; but the Angel of Destiny had led on an upward trail and now he was brought aside to the edge so that he might look over, and down, and know that he was climbing.

Belle met him at the door. Her face was anxious. But his look reassured her. He took her on his knees as one might lift a child and, sitting with his arm around her and gazing far away, he said: "I had a landslide, Belle. All my church thought and training were swept away in a moment. I was floundering, overwhelmed in the ruin, when I found a big, solid, immovable rock on which I could build again. It was not the Church, it was my mother gave it to me. She used to say: 'Don't try to reason it all out; no one can. Only try to do as the Master would do'; what that is we are not always sure; but one who followed Him has told us, 'Keep cool and kind and you won't go far astray.'"

She looked into his face and saw something that she had never seen there before. The thought that flashed through her mind was of Moses and how his countenance showed that a little while before he had talked with God. She was awed by this new something he had taken on; and her instinct hushed the query that arose within her. She only gripped his hand a little and looking far away, said slowly: "There are times when He comes to talk with His own. I think he wanted to walk with you alone by the lake and talk, as He one time walked with His men on the shore of Galilee."

"My mind is clear now, Belle," he continued, "if these people want me to begin here merely as orthodox pulpit preacher, I must give up the post. That is what I want to be, but this is not the time or place for it. If, on the other hand, they will let me try to help those who need help, and in the form in which they need it—well and good; I will do my best to understand and meet the problems. But we must at once have a clear understanding."

She put her arms about him and after a little silence said: "I am with you to the finish, Jim. I know you have received a message and have guidance as to how it should be delivered."

It was in the little flat, with sagebrush in the vases, that they thought it out, and reached a solution that was the middle of the road. The first presentation of his new understanding Jim made to the Board of Deacons two days later. He said:

"When a man is swimming for his life, he does not want to discuss politics. When a man's children are hungry, he can't be expected to respect the law that prevents him from feeding them. When a man has no property, you needn't look to him for a fine understanding of the laws of property. When a man has no chance for lawful pleasures in life, he cannot be blamed much for taking any kind that comes within reach. When a man's body is starved, cold, and tormented, he is not going to bother about creeds that are supposed to guide his soul."

"All of which we freely admit," said Mr. Hopkins, with characteristic gravity. "The problems that you name are very real and grave, but they are the problems of the nation. Rest assured that every man of force in America to-day is aware of these things, and is doing all he can to meet them squarely. Moreover, they are being met with success—slow, but continued success.

"Are you prepared to outline the plan by which you would contribute to the local solution of these national problems?"

Yes, Hartigan had it there on paper. "I must approach these people through the things which they know they need. They don't feel any need of a church, but they do feel the need of a comfortable meeting place where the wholesome love of human society may be gratified. Their lives are devoid of pleasure, except of the worst kinds. This is not choice, but is forced on them; there is not a man, woman or child among them that does not— sometimes, at least—hunger for better things—that would not enjoy the things that you enjoy, if they had the chance. I want harmless pleasures in abundance put within their reach.

"Man is an animal before he is a soul; so I would begin by providing the things needful for a body. All men glory in physical prowess; therefore I want a gymnasium, and with it, the natural accompaniments of bath house and swimming tank. In short, I don't want a church; I want an up-to-date People's Club, with a place for all and a welcome for all."

The deacons sat back and gazed at one another. "Well," said Deacon Starbuck, president of the Stock Bank, "you surely have a clear-thinking business head among your gifts."

There was a distinct split in the views of the Board. The older men objected that this was an organization for propagating the Gospel of Christ, not for solving economic problems, and proved with many Scripture texts that we must "first of all seek the Kingdom of God and His righteousness," after having secured which, the rest would follow.

But the younger men took Hartigan's view that it was no time to talk politics to a man when he was swimming for his life. Fortunately, Hopkins was able to stave off action, pending a fuller discussion, and brought that on at once.

"Let us understand. Is the club to be a charity, a benevolence, or a business proposition—that is, a free gift, a partly supported institution, or a dollar-for-dollar bargain?"

The older men believed in charity. Jim opposed it as wrong in principle. As a business proposition it was hopeless, at present; so he definitely labelled it a "benevolence."

"All right," said Hopkins, "now how much money do you want, and how long to make good?"

Again Jim referred to the paper in his hand.

"I want twenty-five thousand dollars cash to provide and equip a temporary building; I want five thousand a year to run it, and I want one thousand dollars a year salary paid to my wife, who is with me in all things, and will give all her time to it. I want three years to make good, that is to make a noticeable reduction in drink and crime, which is the same thing, and this we shall gauge by the police records. By that time I shall have fifteen hundred families in touch with the club, paying dues to it. I shall stand or fall by the result. If I satisfy you, I shall ask for a hundred-thousand-dollar building at the end of that time."

"You say nothing about street sermons," said a plaintive old gentleman with a long white beard and the liquid eyes of an exhorter.

"No, not one. I don't want them. I can work better indoors."

The president said, "Well, Mr. Hartigan, perhaps it would be well for you to retire, in order that we may freely discuss your plan. As you seem to have it on paper, would you mind leaving the document?" Jim hesitated, glanced at it, then handed it to Mr. Hopkins. It was all in a woman's hand.

In fifteen minutes, Jim was summoned to learn the decision. They accepted, not unanimously, but they accepted his entire proposition, with the exception of one item; they would not pay salary to or officially recognize his wife. It was a bitter pill, and Jim's eyes were brimming with tears and his face flushed at the injustice when he went home to tell her. Poor little woman! Her lips tightened a trifle, but she said: "Never mind, I'll work for it just the same. I'm afraid they are still in the Dark Ages; but the light will come."

CHAPTER LII

THE BOSS

It had been a private dwelling, far out on the prairie once, but the hot, steady lava flow of the great city had reached and split and swept around the little elevated patch of grimy green with its eleven despairing trees. A wooden house it was, and in the very nature of it a temporary shift; but the committee—Hopkins, Hartigan, and Belle—felt it worth looking into.

With the agent, these three went over it and discussed its possibilities and the cost. Ten times in that brief talk did Hopkins find himself consulting Belle when, in the ordinary process, he should have consulted Hartigan. Why? No man raises himself to the power and pitch that Hopkins had attained, without a keen, discriminating knowledge of human nature. And he felt the fact long before he admitted it even to himself: "Yes, he's a pair of giant wings, but she's the tail, all right." And he was not displeased to find this original estimate justified by events.

The three years' lease was signed; and a bulletin board appeared on the bravest of all the battered old trees at the front—the very battle front. A gnarled and twisted cedar it was, and when a richer name than "Club" was sought for the venture, it was this old tree that linked up memory with itself and the house was named, not "The People's Club," as at first intended, but "Cedar Mountain House"—the word "mountain" being justified in the fact that the house was on a prairie knoll at least a foot above the surrounding level.

The bulletin board displayed this to all passers-by:

CEDAR MOUNTAIN HOUSE

Notice

A Meeting to organize this Club will be held here on these premises Sunday afternoon next. Men and women who are interested are cordially invited.

REFRESHMENTS

The Board of Deacons would have had a wrangle over each and every word of that notice. That was why they never saw it till long afterward.

"Now what's going to happen?" said Hopkins.

"A few will come and act very shyly; but I've a notion the refreshments will bring them," was Belle's guess.

"I am afraid we have omitted something of importance," said Jim. "We are invading a foreign savage country without taking any count of the native chiefs."

"What's your idea?" said Hopkins, sharply.

"I mean, we have arranged matters with the real estate man, and the Church workers and the police; but we haven't taken the trouble to look up the ward boss."

"We ignored the boss because we thought he was an enemy," said Hopkins.

"I'm not so sure about that," said Jim. "I've been talking with the police sergeant, who knows him well. He says he's a queer mixture of prizefighter and politician. He can protect anything he likes, and pretty nearly drive out anything he doesn't like. Isn't it worth while making a bid for his support? It may please him to be asked."

"Who is he?"

"Oh, a saloon-keeper, Irish, ex-pugilist. His name is Michael Shay. He's easy to find," said Jim.

"Let's go now," said Hopkins. "But I'm afraid that this is where you drop out, Mrs. Hartigan."

So they went down to the headquarters of the boss. It was an ordinary Chicago saloon of less than ordinary pretensions. The plate-glass and polished-mahogany era had not yet set in. The barkeeper was packing the ice chest and a couple of "types" were getting their "reg'lar" as the two strangers from another world entered. The build of Hartigan at once suggested plain-clothes policeman, and the barkeeper eyed him suspiciously. Hopkins spoke first:

"Is the boss in?"

The barkeeper made a gesture, pointing to the back room.

"May we see him?"

"I s'pose so." And again, with a jerk of the thumb, the back room was indicated.

The two walked in. It was a small room, meanly furnished, with a square table in the centre. Sitting by it were three men. Two were drinking beer— one a small, thin man; the other a red-faced specimen with rotund outline. The third and biggest was smoking a briarwood pipe. He was a heavily built man with immense shoulders square jaw, and low, wrinkled forehead; deep under his bushy eyebrows were two close-set, twinkling gray eyes, which were turned on the visitors with a hostile stare.

"Is Mr. Michael Shay here?" asked Hopkins.

"I'm Mike Shay," said the smoker, without rising or removing his pipe; "what do ye want?" There was a sullen defiance in the tone that showed resentment at the different dress and manner of the strangers.

"We have come to ask for your support for the club we are going to open in the old house down the street."

"Support nuthin'," was the gracious reply.

Hopkins began to explain that this was not to be a rival show—no drinks would be sold; the idea was merely to found a place of amusement for the people. The only effect on the boss was to evoke a contemptuous "E-r-r-r!" and an injunction, in Chicago vernacular, to get out of that as soon as they liked—or sooner. And, by way of punctuation, he turned to expectorate copiously, but with imperfect precision at a box of sawdust which was littered with cigar stumps. The interview was over—he wished them to understand that. He turned to his companions.

Hartigan felt that it was his chance now. He began: "See here, now, Michael Shay; you're an Irishman and I'm an Irishman——"

"Oh, g'wan!" and Shay rose to walk out the back way. As he did so, Jim noticed fully, for the first time, the huge shoulders, the strong, bowed legs, the gorilla-like arms; and the changing memory of another day grew clear and definitely placed. There could be no doubt about it now; this was bow-legged Mike, the teamster of seven years before.

At once, a different colour was given to Jim's thought and manner; no longer cautious, respectful, doubtful, he began in his own more boisterous way, "Say, Mike. I have a different matter to talk about now."

Mike stopped and stared.

Jim proceeded. "Were you ever at Links, Ontario?"

"Maybe I was, an' maybe I wasn't. What's that to you?"

"Well, do you remember licking a young fellow there for jerking the roof log out of the hotel with your masting team of oxen?"

"Bejabers, I do that"; and Mike's eyes twinkled for the first time with a pleasant look.

"Well, Mike, I am that fellow; an' that's what ye gave me." Jim raised his chin and showed an irregular scar.

"Well sure, that's the Gospel truth"; and Michael grinned. "By gosh, that's the time I had to skip out of Chicago. A little election fuss ye understand,"

and he chuckled. "Set down. What'll ye drink?" and the huge hand swung two chairs within reach.

"No," said Jim. "I'm not drinking to-day; but I want to tell you that I was only a kid when you licked me. I swore that some day I'd meet you and have another try. Well, I've filled out some in the last seven years, an' some day, when ye feel like it, we might put on the gloves together."

Mike chuckled, "Now you're talking! What's the matter with right now?" and he pointed to a room farther back. "But, say, ye ain't in training, are ye?"

"No; are you?"

"No."

"Then come on."

Mike opened the next door and led the way into a larger room, with the fixings of a regular boxing academy, followed by his friends and one or two additional customers from the bar room.

Hopkins followed Hartigan, and was filled, apparently, with strange and mixed emotions. "Really, Mr. Hartigan, as President of the Board of Deacons, I must protest against this whole shocking procedure." Then, in a different tone: "But, as a man, by jinks! I'm going to see it through."

"Why not?" said Jim. "Sure it's simple and easy. In about three rounds, I'll get him or he'll get me; then we'll shake hands and all be good friends ever after. It couldn't have happened better."

Both men stripped to the waist, and the contrast was as great as the resemblance. Broad, equally broad, and superbly muscled, the saloon-keeper was, if anything, heavier, but there was just a suspicion of bloat over all his frame. Jim was clean built, statuesque—a Jason rather than a Hermes. He was by six inches taller, but the other had just as long a reach. And, as the officious patrons of the "pub" strapped on the gloves and made the usual preparation of wet sponge and towel, it seemed in all respects an even match—in all respects but one; Jim was twenty-odd, Mike was forty-odd.

The small man with a squeaky voice installed himself as timekeeper. He struck the gong, and the boxers met. Jim always smiled and bared his teeth while boxing. Mike was one of the bull-dog jaw; he kept his lips tight shut, and his small eyes twinkled with every appearance of rage.

On the first round, the great experience of the pugilist enabled him to land one or two heavy jolts, and when the gong sounded the time-limit, Jim had got rather the worst of it.

The second round opened much like the first. Jim landed on Mike's under jaw more than once; and Mike got in a body blow that was something to think about.

It was the third round that told the tale. What chance in a fight has forty-five against twenty-five? The extra weight of the prize fighter was mere softness. His wind was gone; and half the time had not passed before Jim landed under his left jaw the classic punch that Mike had one time given him, and Mike went down like a sack of meal.

In five minutes, he was up and game, but the bout was over. The men shook hands, and Michael, rapidly recovering his spirits, rumbled out of his deep chest: "Bejabers, it's the first time in five years I've been knocked out—and it was done scientific. Say, Hartigan, ye can put me down for a member of your club; or yer church or whatever the dom thing is an' I'll see ye get whatever ye need in the way of protection; an' if ye want to sell any liquor on the sly, that'll be all right. You count on Mike."

Then, with a singular clearing of hate and an access of good feeling—psychological reactions which so often follow in the wake of a finish fight—the men all shook hands and parted in excellent humour.

"By George!" said President Hopkins of the Board of Deacons, "I wouldn't have missed that for a thousand dollars. It was perfectly bully—just what we wanted! I've heard of things like this, but never really believed they happened. It's a new side of human nature for me. I wouldn't have missed it for—no, not for five thousand dollars."

CHAPTER LIII

THE FIRST MEETING

The notice on the old tree had been up a week. By Thursday there had been no sign of response; on Friday Jim had had it out with the boss; and Saturday morning the community seemed, in some subtle way, to be greatly stirred by the coming event. Sunday afternoon there was a fairly good assemblage of men and women in the large room of the rearranged old house. Bow-legged Mike was not present; but the little man with the squeaky voice—commonly known as "Squeaks"—was there to represent him, as he did in divers ways and on different occasions in the ward.

Hartigan and Hopkins were on the platform. Belle sat at a small table to act as recording secretary. Hopkins opened the meeting by introducing Hartigan, who spoke as follows:

"My friends; we are assembled to discuss the formation of a club to provide for the residents of this district such things as they need in the way of a convenient social meeting place and whatever else is desirable in a club. We have not fully worked out our plan, but this is the main idea: the club will be called Cedar Mountain House; it will be managed by five governors— two of them appointed by the men who own the building lease; two of them elected by the people who join; these four to elect a fifth as chairman of the board.

"The club is open to men and women twenty-one years of age; their families come in free on their tickets. The dues are to be ten cents a week, or five dollars a year. This covers the gymnasium, the lecture hall, the library, and the baths. Now we are ready for any questions."

A very fat woman, with a well-developed moustache, rose to claim the floor, and began: "I want to know——"

Hopkins interrupted: "As the Chair is not acquainted with all present, will the speakers kindly announce their names?"

The woman made a gesture of impatience—evidently every one should know *her* name: "I am Dr. Mary Mudd, M. D., of Rush College, unmarried, Resident Physician of the Mudd Maternity Home and the winner of the Mudd medal for an essay on misapplied medicine. There! Now I want to know are women eligible for office in this club?"

To which Hopkins replied: "Since women are admitted to membership and pay dues, they are eligible for all offices."

"Well, now, I'm with you," said Dr. Mudd; and she sat down.

Now arose a thin, dark man with a wild shock of hair, a black beard, a red tie and a general appearance of having -*ski* at the end of his name. "I vant to know do you hev to be religious your vay in dis cloob?"

"Kindly give your name," said the Chair.

"Veil, I'm Isaac Skystein; I'm a renovator of chentlemen's deteriorated vearing apparel, and I vant to know of dis is a missionary trick, or do it be a cloob vere von can talk de freedom of speech?"

"You do not have to belong to any Church," announced the Chairman.

"Vell; is it to be de religious talk?"

"Once a week, or maybe once a month, there will be a debate in this hall, at which entire freedom of speech will be allowed."

"Dat mean I can get up an' say I doan take no stock in your dern religion? I vant de freedom of de speeches, Ya!"

"It means that, at the proper time, each will have a chance to get up and say exactly what he thinks within the decencies of debate."

"Vell, I tink I'll join for a vhile, anyvay."

Then a red-faced man introduced himself. "I'm Jack Hinks, teamster, and I want to know if any drinks will be sold on the premises."

"No, sir; nothing intoxicating."

"I mean on the sly."

"No, sir: nothing, absolutely nothing."

"Well, Mike Shay tipped me off that it was to be 'wet' on the quiet."

"He made a mistake; this is to be a strictly teetotal club."

"That settles it. What's the good of a club where you can't have no fun? Good night!" and out he went.

A lanky youth with unhealthy rings around his eyes and brown stains on his thumb asked if there were to be boxing lessons and would Mr. Hartigan tell them about the scrap between himself and Mike Shay. Mothers asked if a baby corral would be instituted, to set the mothers free for a few hours each day. A tall, pale young man with a Southern coo, asked "whether Negroes were to be admitted." The Chair dodged by saying: "That will be decided by the vote of the majority."

A male person, with a beard and a tremulous voice, asked what the club's attitude would be toward the Salvation Army. Before the Chair could reply, little Skystein jumped up and shouted: "Mr. Chairman, ve don't vant 'em; dey's all feelin's an' no brains. You don't see no Chews in de Salvation Army—it's too many emotions; de Chews got too much intellects, ve don't vant——"

"I rule you out of order!" shouted the Chair. "Sit down! Now for your question: The club will welcome the Salvationists as individual members. It does not recognize them as a body."

A fat, unsuccessful-looking man, asked if it held out any chance for a job; and a red-headed masculine person of foreign design rose to inquire whether the bathing would be compulsory. A preliminary vote was overwhelmingly in favour of the five-dollar dues, though a small minority thought it should be free; a group of four persons believed they should draw compensation for coming.

The meeting answered every expectation; it fully introduced the club and its leaders; it demonstrated the views of the possible members, and gave the Board of Deacons a new light on human nature. All the business of definite organization was deferred to the next meeting, to take place one week later.

CHAPTER LIV

THE FORMATION OF THE CLUB

Foundation Sunday came, and with it a respectable crowd at the House. There were some who had brought babies—which was unfortunate, but unavoidable—and there were one or two men too hilarious for good manners; but the crowd was, on the whole, good-natured and desirable.

Mike Shay was not there, although Jim had tried to get him; but Mike had a curious diffidence about appearing in public. All his power was underground, and all his methods behind the scenes. Squeaks was there to keep an eye on things, and his little bleary, ferret eyes watched each person and detail with cunning, if not with discernment.

It was made perfectly clear that only members in good standing had votes.

"Vell, vot dot mean, dot good at stannin'? Don't ve vote settin' down?" demanded Skystein.

"It means members whose dues are fully paid, and who are not under indictment for serious breach of rules."

"I want to pay one year's dues for myself and Mr. Michael Shay," said Squeaks; and he walked to the secretary and paid ten dollars. This indorsement by the boss produced immediate results.

"I'll take a year's membership," said a big, coarse, red-faced man. And he rolled up the aisle to deposit his five dollars, giving his name as Bud Towler. Jim remembered him as the third person in the back room the day he met Michael Shay. He had not seen him since.

So many more came up now, mostly to pay a month's dues, which was the minimum, that Belle was worked hard and other business was stopped.

Then, when all who wished to pay and register had done so, the voice of Squeaks was heard: "I have here a list of names that I want to propose for charter membership," and he read off a list of twenty-five men, none of them present. Bud Towler got up and seconded the lot; the Chair was asked to put the names to immediate vote, as it was a charter meeting; all were carried, and Squeaks came forward and paid twenty-five dollars dues for the lot to cover the next ten weeks, that is, to the end of a year.

Belle whispered to Hopkins as Squeaks retired. The Chair nodded, rose and explained. "In drawing up our constitution, we deemed it best, in the interests of democracy, to do all voting by ballot and to exclude all proxies."

"Dot's right, dot's all right!" shouted Skystein.

"Mr. Chairman, I protest," came the wire-like voice of Squeaks; this measure, would, naturally, mean the disfranchisement of every man whose business happened to keep him away at election time. How much more reasonable it would be for him to empower some trusted friend to represent him and his views, etc., etc.

On the matter of the ballot he was not so strong, but he did think "that the manly, straightforward way was for a voter to announce his vote and not be ashamed of his principles. Of course, he was aware that there was much to be said on the other side, but he was in favour of proxies and open voting."

"So am I," shouted Towler. "We ain't got no right to rob a man of his vote because he happens to be a night watchman."

"Ah, vat's de matter mit ye?" said Skystein. "Effery-body knows you an' Squeaks is in cahoots to run de hull push cart."

There was a good chance of a row; but Hopkins explained that voting by mail was a different thing from voting by proxy, and every member in good standing would get the chance to vote by mail on important matters, when he could not be present.

No one could long have been in that meeting without realizing that it was a veritable microcosm—a little world in which were all the struggling, rival elements, the good and evil forces of the big world. Not a problem that was tormenting the country but was represented in vital strength in that club group. It was full of lessons and grave responsibilities.

They were now ready for the elections. Squeaks rose and said: "Since the owners of the lease are to nominate two of the four governors, it would clear things up if their nominations were made first and the club elections afterward."

This at once confronted Hopkins with a problem. He had a free hand, but he was puzzled, because while it was understood that he was to be president and Hartigan the active governor on the spot, they had not secured a third man who, as governor, could be counted on for a continued whole-souled support. It was Dr. Mary Mudd that let the daylight into this problem by rising to say:

"Mr. Chairman, I understand we are free to elect a woman to the board of governors as well as to any other office."

Hopkins had not thought of that, but the broad principle had been established and he replied "Yes."

"Very good," said Dr. Mudd, "now there's a chance for common sense as well as decency."

In a flash, Hopkins got the answer to his own problem. Belle Hartigan had steadily been winning his appreciation. His admiration for her clear-headedness and business training was increased at each meeting. He knew now pretty well how often her brain was behind Jim's actions. In any event, the trial would be for only two and one-half months, when elections were to take place for the new year. He bent toward her: "Will you be one of the appointed governors for the rest of the year?"

"Yes."

Hopkins rose and announced that the owners of the lease appointed Mr. and Mrs. Hartigan as the two governors to represent them.

This was warmly applauded, especially by the women—led by Dr. Mudd. There followed some sharp electioneering and the members elected Squeaks and Skystein to represent them. Dr. Mudd, who had been nominated, demanded a recount of the votes, but the election was sustained. The four governors then met and within five minutes agreed on Hopkins for president. So the board was formed and for good or ill, the club was launched—in the slum, of the slum, and for the slum—but with a long, strong arm from the other world; an outside thing, but meant in kindly help.

BOOK V

THE CALL OF THE MOUNTAIN

CHAPTER LV

IN THE ABSENCE OF BELLE

Every citizen of South Chicago remembers the work of the Cedar Mountain House; how it grew and prospered, and how the old building became too small and an annex across the street was called for. How its greatest strength lay in the monthly free discussion of *any subject* approved in advance by the governors. How the rival parties of Skystein and Squeaks alternately pulled and pushed each other about. How musical genius was discovered in abundance and an orchestra formed as well as a monthly minstrel show. How pool tables were introduced and a restaurant started. How the movement to introduce beer was defeated by a small majority. How, after due discussion, they adopted some seemingly hard policies, such as the exclusion of all Negroes and Chinamen. How Squeaks led an abortive attempt to disqualify all Jews. How the gymnasium became the focal centre of all the boys in the neighbourhood. How they organized a strong-arm squad of a dozen club members who acted as police, and without offense, because they were of themselves. At the end of the first six months, the House had more than justified its existence. It had nearly four hundred members and was doing work that in a higher state of civilization would be the proper care of the government.

It would have been hard to say who was the chief. Belle had been the planner and executor and now was not only a governor, but secretary and head of the women's department, on a fair business basis. But the growth of power in Jim was obvious. It had all been very new to his ways of thinking and, after all, Links and Chicago have little in common. Belle had a business training that was essential, and her quick judgment helped at every turn for it is a fact that second-class judgment right now is better than first-class judgment to-morrow. The full measure of her helpfulness in bearing the burdens was made transparently clear by a sudden crisis in their affairs. A telegram from Cedar Mountain arrived for Belle.

Mother very ill. Come at once—FATHER.

It was impossible for both to go, so Belle set off alone for Cedar Mountain, leaving Jim in charge of the flock at the Mountain House. Alone—he didn't think it possible to feel alone in such a crowd. His work was doubled in the absence of Belle, although Dr. Mary Mudd gave not a little help in the mothers' department. It was a good thing for Jim to find out just how much he owed to his wife. There was a continuous stream of callers at the office with requests or complaints. These had all been met by Belle. She had an even poise, a gentle consideration for all, and certain helpful rules that reduced the strain, such as exact hours for work, one call at a time, and written complaints only. Jim's anxiety to placate and smooth out led him to undertake too much, and the result was a deluge of small matters of which he had previously known nothing. The exasperating accumulation of annoyances and attacks, in spite of all his best and kindest endeavours, invoked a new light.

"Oh, if Belle were only here!" was his repeated thought. "I don't know how she manages, but she does. It's mighty strange how few of these annoyances came up when she was in the office." He began to realize more and more her ability. "She has more judgment, more tact than any of us; she has been meeting these things all along, and saving me from them by settling them without me. Yes, she's wiser than I am in such matters."

So he wrote her of his troubles. He detailed many cases in point and added: "We miss you awfully; every one in the House complains. I haven't got your cleverness and tact. It seems as if I made enemies every time I tried to make friends. Come back as soon as you can." And if the truth must be told there was a little flush of pleasure and triumph in her soul. "Now he knows what I have known so long." And who shall blame her for gloating a little over the deacons who, in the beginning, were unwilling to recognize her? But she had to send a discouraging reply. For the angel of destiny said: "No, it is now time for him to walk alone" and the telegram ran:

Cannot come; Mother is very low.

After the first shock of disappointment he braced up, and, like a man who has been retreating and who knows in his heart that he never meant to make a stand as long as some one else could be depended on, he upbraided himself and turned to face the fight. "There is a way of doing it all, and I can do it." And in the resolve to win he found new strength. In many small, but puzzling matters, he got guidance in the practical sayings of men like Lincoln and Grant: "Be sure you are right, then go ahead"; "Every one has some rights"; "In case of doubt, go the gentle way"; "Never hunt for trouble." These were samples of the homely wisdom that helped him and proved that the old proverbs are old wisdom in shape for new use.

One man came to complain that a member had been drunk and disorderly at a certain other place the night before. A year ago, Jim would have said that it was a disgrace and that he would make a thorough investigation, which would have meant assuming a special guardianship of each and every member all the time. Wiser now, he said, "Since it was not on our premises, we have no knowledge of the matter." On the other hand, it was a serious affair when a member brought in a bottle of strong drink and treated a number of weak friends until there was a wild orgy going on in one of the rooms, in spite of official protests from those in charge. This was clearly high treason; and repressing a disposition to gloss it over, Hartigan expelled the principal and suspended the seconds for long periods.

During a boyish contest in the gymnasium, a man somewhat in liquor, shouted out a string of oaths at the youngsters. Jim rebuked him quietly for using such language there, whereupon the man turned upon him with a coarse insult and, misunderstanding the Preacher's gentleness, struck him a vicious blow, which Jim only partly warded off. "If you do that again, we may have to put you out," said Jim, inwardly boiling under the double insult. Fortunately, the man's friends interfered now and got the fellow away. For this Jim was most thankful. Afterward, he rejoiced still more that he had restrained himself; and he knew Belle would flush with pride at this victory over self, this proof of a growing self-control.

Another week went by and again came word that Belle could not return for perhaps ten days at the earliest. A dozen broils that Jim had been postponing for Belle to arbitrate had now to be considered. Dr. Mary Mudd was the leader of an indignant party of women to complain that though the men were not more in numbers than the women they had appropriated sixty out of the one hundred coat hangers.

Rippe, the tailor, was there to complain that Dr. Mary Mudd always walked up the middle of the stairs, unlawfully delaying the traffic, instead of keeping the proper right side. With his outstretched arms, he illustrated the formidable nature of the barrier. Dr. Mudd retorted that said Rippe had repeatedly smoked in the ladies' room, etc., etc. But these were small matters easily adjusted. Two, much more serious, came on him in one day.

First, he yielded to the temptation of having a beautiful banner hung on the wall, because it was contributed and very decorative. It bore a legend, "No popery." This was much in line with his private views, but it made a great stir and cost them a score of members, as well as incurring the dislike of Father O'Hara, hitherto friendly. His second blunder was to allow the cook in the restaurant to put scraps of pork in the soup, thereby raising a veritable storm among the many keen debaters of the kosher kind, and causing the resignation of Skystein from the board—temporarily at least.

It would have been much to Jim's taste to have an open war with Father O'Hara and his flock. His Ulster blood was ready for just such a row. And in his heart he believed pork and beans quite the best of foods. But his opinions were not law; he had been learning many things. Others had rights; and he won the disaffected back, one by one, by recognizing the justice of their claims and by making kindly personal calls on each of them.

Thus Jim Hartigan got a new knowledge of his own endowment and discovered unsuspected powers. He had held his peace and triumphed in a number of trying situations that two or three years before would have ended in an unprofitable brawl. He had controlled his temper, that was a step forward and he was learning to control those about him as well as manage an organization. He had begun to realize his *prejudices* and to learn to respect the beliefs of others even when he thought them wrong. The memory of Father Cyprian and the Sioux boy had helped him to deal kindly and respectfully with Skystein and Father O'Hara.

Strange to say, it was a travelling Hindu who supplied him with the biggest, broadest thought of all. This swarthy scholar was deeply imbued with the New Buddhism of Rammohan Roy and, when asked for his opinion of some Romanist practices, he remarked softly, but evasively, "My religion teaches me that if any man do anything sincerely, believing that thereby he is worshipping God, he *is* worshipping God and his action must be treated with respect, so long as he is not infringing the rights of others."

Jim took a long walk by the lake that day and turned over and over that saying of the Hindu in the library. The thing had surprised him—first, because of the perfect English in the mouth of a foreigner, and secondly, because of the breadth and tolerance of the thought. He wondered how he could ever have believed himself open-minded or fair when he had been so miserably narrow in all his ideas. Where was he headed? All his early days he had been taught to waste effort on scorning the ceremonials great and small of Jews, Catholics, yes, of Baptists even; and now the heathen—to whom he had once thought of going as a missionary—had come to Chicago and shown him the true faith.

Striding at top speed, he passed a great pile of lumber and sawdust. The fresh smell of the wet wood brought back Links—and his mother, and a sense of happiness, for he had given up "trying to reason it all out." He was no longer sure, as he once was, that he had omniscience for his guide. Indeed he was sure only of this, that the kindest way is the only way that is safe.

There was daylight dawning in his heart, and yet, across that dawn there was a cloud which grew momentarily more black, more threatening. Paradoxical as it seemed, Jim was intensely unhappy over the abandonment of the ministerial career. The enduring force of his word as a man was only another evidence of the authentic character of that deep emotional outburst which had pledged him openly to the service of Christ. The work at the Cedar Mountain House for a while satisfied the evangelical hunger of his ardent soul. It was good, it was successful, it was increasing in scope; but of its nature it could never be more than secular; it was social work in its best form—that was all. The work of which he dreamed, and to which he had consecrated his life was the preaching of the Gospel, and, as the months passed, an unrest—the like of which he had hardly known—took possession of him. These last weeks of Belle's absence had brought on one of his periodic soul-searchings and the gloom of it was as thick as a fog when the mail brought word of Belle's return. As he sat with her letter in his hand his mind went back to the hills and the free days and he longed to go back—to get away from the ponderous stolidity of this pavement world.

He met her at the station and her joyousness was as a shock to him. And yet, how hungry he was for every least word of that lost life.

"Oh, Jim, it was glorious to ride again, to smell the leather and the sagebrush. I just loved the alkali and the very ticks on the sagebrush. I didn't know how they could stir one's heart."

His eye glowed, his breath came fast, his nostrils dilated and, as Belle looked, it seemed to her that her simple words had struck far deeper than she meant.

"And the horses, which did you ride?" he queried. "How is Blazing Star? Are they going to race at Fort Ryan this year? And the Bylow boys, and the Mountain? Thank God, men may come and go, but Cedar Mountain will stand forever." He talked as one who has long kept still—as one whose thoughts long pent have dared at length to break forth.

And Belle, as she listened, saw a light. "He is far from forgetting the life of the Hills," she said to herself as she watched him. "He is keener than ever. All this steadfast devotion to club work is the devotion of duty. Now I know the meaning of those long vigils, those walks by the lake in the rain— of his preoccupation. His heart is in Cedar Mountain." And she honoured him all the more for that he had never spoken a word of the secret longing.

CHAPTER LVI

THE DEFECTION OF SQUEAKS

Michael Shay had come to the club in person once or twice, but did not desire to be conspicuous. It was clear now that the club was not to be the political weapon at first suspected. The boss had another organization through which to hold and make felt his power; but the fact that it pleased a number of his voters was enough to insure his support.

Squeaks, however, was quite conspicuous and present on all important occasions; it was generally supposed that he was there in the interests of Shay, but that was not clearly proven. It was obvious that the club was not in any way lined up for or against Shay. It was, however, believed by Belle that Squeaks was there in the interests of Squeaks and none other.

This strange, small person had a small, strange history—so far as it was known. A lawyer, he had been disbarred for disreputable practice, and was now a hanger-on of the boss, a shrewd person, quite purchasable. He was convinced that he was destined to be a great boss, and satisfied that Cedar Mountain House would help his plans—which lay in the direction of the legislature—hence he sought to identify himself with it. For the present, also, he stuck to Shay.

The approved boss system of the time rested on a regiment of absolutely obedient voters, who voted not once, but many times in as many different wards as needed. They were thoroughly organized, and part of their purpose was to terrorize independent voters, or even "remove" men who developed power or courage enough to oppose them; so the "reliable squad" was important. As their ranks contained many convicts or men qualified for life terms, they were a dangerous and desperate lot. They responded at once and cheerfully to any duty call, and one "removal" per night would have probably been less than average for a boss-ruled city in those days. For this they received protection; that is, the police and the Courts were so completely in the scheme that it was sufficient, on the arrest of a "reliable," if the boss sent word to the judge or State's attorney "to be keerful" as this was "one of our boys." Promptly a flaw would be discovered in the indictment and the case dropped.

The boss who derives power from such a machine must ever look out for the appearance of a rival, hence Shay's early watchfulness of the club; but that gave place to a friendly indifference. He was a man superior to his class, in some respects; for, though brutal and masterful on occasion, it was said that he never "removed" a rival. At most, he had applied pressure that resulted in their discreetly withdrawing. And he cared little for money. Most bosses are after either money or power or both. Shay loved power. The revenues he might have made out of tribute from those protected were not well developed, and most of what he received he disbursed in generous gifts to those in his ward who needed help. It was said that no man ever went hungry from Mike Shay's door, which was perfectly true; and the reward that he loved above all things was to be pointed out on the street or in the car as "Mike Shay." To overhear some one say, "That's Michael Shay, the big Boss of the South Ward," meant more to him a thousand fold than any decoration in the gift of the greatest of Old-World potentates.

Hartigan learned that he could go to Shay at any time for a reasonable contribution, after having made it clear that it was for some one in distress—not for a church. The only return Shay ever asked was that Jim come sometimes and put on the gloves with him in a friendly round. Most of Shay's legal finesse was done through Squeaks. That small, but active person was on the boards of at least twenty-five popular organizations, and it was understood that he was there to represent the boss. Extraordinary evidence of *some one's* pull was shown when one day Squeaks was elevated to the Bench. It was only as a police magistrate, but he was now Judge Squeaks, with larger powers than were by law provided, and he began to "dig himself in," entrench himself, make his position good with other powers, in anticipation of the inevitable conflict with Boss Shay. It became largely a line-up of political parties; Squeaks had made a deal with the party in power at Springfield, and gave excellent guarantees of substantial support—both electoral and financial—before the keen-eyed myrmidons of Shay brought to the boss the news that Squeaks had turned traitor.

Then the war was on; not openly, for Squeaks had scores of documents that would, before any impartial jury, have convicted Shay of manipulating election returns, intimidating voters, and receiving blackmail. It was important to get possession of these documents before they could be used. While the present party held power in State politics, there would be no chance for Shay to escape. There were two possibilities, however; one, that the election close at hand might reverse the sympathies of those in power; the other, that Squeaks might find it unwise to use the weapon in his hands.

Now was the Cedar Mountain House in peril, for Shay's support was essential. At a word from him, the police might call the club a disorderly house, and order it shut up. The fact that Squeaks was a governor strengthened the probability of drastic action. On the other hand, Squeaks as police magistrate, could restrain the police for a time or discover flaws in as many indictments as were brought up. The District Court could, of course, issue a warrant over the head of the police magistrate; but the Court of Appeals was friendly to Squeaks and would certainly quash the warrant; so that, for the time being the many unpleasant possibilities simply balanced each other, and the club went on in a sort of sulphurous calm like that before a storm.

Then came an exciting day at the club. By an unusual chance both Shay and Squeaks met there and the inevitable clash came. Angry words passed and Shay shouted: "Ye dirty little sneak, I'll fix ye yet!" Squeaks, cool and sarcastic, said: "Why don't ye do it now?" Shay rushed at him with a vigorous threat, and would have done him grievous bodily injury but for the interference of Hartigan and others. Shay waited at the gate for Squeaks, but the Judge slipped out the back way and disappeared.

It was Bud Towler who called on the Judge with a letter from Boss Shay, demanding the return of certain personal papers and authorizing said Bud to receive them. To which Judge Squeaks replied: "He better come for them himself. He knows where I live. I'll be home every night this week."

And thither that night with two friends went Shay. It was a very simple lodging. These men habitually avoid display. The janitor knew all too well who Shay was.

"Is Squeaks at home?"

"Yes, I believe so."

"I'm going up to see him, and if I lay him over my knee and spank him till he squeals, ye needn't worry; it's nothing." Then up went Shay, while his friends stayed below, one at the front of the house and the other in the lane that commanded the back.

The trembling janitor heard the heavy foot go up the wooden stairs; he heard a voice, then a crash as of a door forced open, then heavy steps and a pistol shot. A window was opened behind the house, and *something* was thumped down into the back yard. A little later, the boss came hurriedly down the stairs. The timid janitor and his trembling wife saw the big man step out with a bundle under his arm. Then all was still.

After twenty minutes of stupefaction, they began to realize that they should go up to the Judge's room. They mounted the stairs together, carrying a lamp. The door had, evidently, been forced. The room was in some disorder; the drawers of the desk were open, and papers scattered about. On one or two of the papers was fresh blood. The window was closed, but not fastened; the end of the curtain under it seemed to give proof that it had recently been opened. On the sill was more fresh blood.

There was no sign of the Judge.

As they gazed about in horror, they heard a noise in the back yard and looking out saw, very dimly, two men carrying off a heavy object, they lifted it over the back fence and then followed, to disappear.

Schmidt, the janitor, was terror-stricken. Evidently, the Judge had been murdered and his body was now being made away with. What was to be done? If he interfered, the murderers would wreak their vengeance on him; if he refrained, he would be blamed for the murder or at least for complicity.

"I tink, Johann, dere's only one ting, and dat is go straight an' tell de police," said his wife. As they stood, they heard a light foot on the stairs. Their hearts stood still, but they peered out to see a woman in a gray cloak step into the street, and they breathed more freely. Now they rushed to the station house and told their tale in tears and trembling.

The Police Captain was scornful and indifferent. Had there been but one witness, he might have ordered him away; but two witnesses, intensely in earnest, made some impression. He sent an inspector around to see. That official came back to report the truth of the statement made by the Schmidts, that the Judge's room was empty, upset, and had some blood stains; but he attached little importance to the matter. He had, however, locked up and sealed the door, pending examination.

Next morning, there was an attempt to hush the matter up, but a reporter appeared in the interests of a big paper, and by a clever combination of veiled threats and promises of support, got permission to see the room. The reporterial instinct and the detective instinct are close kin, and the newspaper published some most promising clues: The Judge was visited at midnight by a man whom he had robbed and who had threatened to kill him; a broken door, papers stolen, a scuffle, traces of human blood (the microscope said so) in several places, blood on the window sill, a heavy something thrown out of the window and carried off by two men, blood on the back fence, and no trace of the Judge.

It was a strong case, and any attempt to gloss it over was rendered impossible by the illustrated broadside with which the newspaper startled the public.

CHAPTER LVII

THE TRIAL

All Chicago remembers the trial of Michael Shay. It filled the papers for a month; it filled folk's minds and mouths for two. Many a worse murder had been quietly buried and forgotten, but this was too conspicuous. The boss, facing a decline of his power, had undoubtedly murdered the man he had begun to fear, and the parties in control of all the machinery of justice were against the accused.

The case was thoroughly threshed out. Shay had openly threatened the life of Squeaks; he had tried before to do him hurt; had gone with two men to Squeaks's lodgings; had warned Schmidt that there was going to be "a little fuss"; had broken open the door and got certain papers—his own property, undoubtedly, but now splashed with blood; a shot had been heard—a heavy something thrown from the back window and then carried off by two men; blood on the floor, the sill and the back fence; and the Judge had disappeared from the face of the earth. The case was clear, the jury retired, but quickly brought in a verdict of guilty, although at every point there was nothing but circumstantial evidence.

Jim Hartigan was one of the first friends to call on Shay after his arrest, and Belle came soon after. They heard his story, which was simple and straight: Squeaks was holding the papers which would be, at least, damaging to Shay's property and reputation; he got them in confidence and then defied Shay to come and take them. Shay decided it would be well to take two witnesses and went, as planned, to Squeaks's apartments. Finding the door locked and believing that Squeaks was inside, he forced it open; the room was dark and no one was there. He lighted the gas and rummaged through the desk for the papers that belonged to him, paying no attention to any others. He saw blood on some of the papers, but didn't know where it came from. As he was coming away, he heard a pistol shot, either upstairs or outside, he didn't know which. He knew nothing about anything thrown from the window. He got his own property and came away.

Although every particle of evidence adduced by the prosecuting attorney was circumstantial, it was very complete. Some juries would have felt reasonable doubt, but no one could get over the facts that Shay had threatened Squeaks's life and that Squeaks had disappeared after a visit from Shay which left traces of blood in Squeaks's apartment. The trial over, the verdict of guilty rendered, Shay was asked if he could offer any reason why he should not be condemned. He rose and said: "Only that I didn't do it. I never saw him from that time in the club a week before."

Then the judge pronounced the awful words: "...Hanged by the neck till you are dead." Shay sat stunned for a minute, then, when the jailor tapped his shoulder, rose and walked silently forth to the cell of the doomed.

It is the hour of trial that sifts out your friends. There were two at least who followed every move in that crowded court room—Hartigan and his wife. They had learned that the crude, brutal exterior of the prizefighter held a heart that was warm and true. They had learned that they could go to him with certainty of success when they wanted help for some struggling man or woman in their ward. They knew that he would not drive a bargain for his help, nor plaster his gift with religious conditions. It was enough for him to know that a fellow-being was in need and that he had the power to help him. Shay was a product of submergence and evil system; he was wrong in his theories, wrong in his methods, wrong in his life; but his was a big, strong spirit—ever kind. And out of the strange beginnings there had grown a silent but real friendship between the Hartigans and himself.

On the black day of the verdict and the sentence, Belle and Jim were sadly sitting at home. "Jim," she said, "I know he didn't do it; his story is so simple and sound. It's easy to get human blood if you have a friend in the hospital; he is innocent. We know that Squeaks could easily have access to a room upstairs; that bundle may have been thrown out from the window merely as a part of a plot. Everything is against Shay now because he is in wrong with the party; but, surely, there is something we can do."

"His attorney asked for an appeal, but I am afraid it won't be entertained; there is no new evidence—no reason for delay that they can see or wish to see."

"That attorney has behaved very suspiciously, I think. Don't you think the governor might intervene with at least a commutation?" she suggested.

"The governor! His worst enemy," said Jim. "The governor's been after him for years."

Hope seemed gone. They sat in silence; then she said: "Pray, Jim; maybe light will come." And together they prayed that the God of justice and mercy would send his light down among them and guide them in this awful time. It was a short and simple prayer, followed by a long silence.

Belle spoke: "There is only one thing that can be done; that is find Squeaks. I know he is living somewhere yet, gloating probably over the success of his plan to get rid of Shay. I know he is alive, and we must find him. We have one month to do it, Jim. We must find him."

Jim shook his head. "We've tried hard enough already. We've examined every corpse taken out of the river or exposed at the morgue."

"Well; doesn't that help to prove that he is alive?"

"We've advertised and notified every police station in the country," Jim continued.

"They don't want to find him, Jim; they're on the other side."

"I don't know what else to do."

"Jim, I've read enough and seen enough of human nature to know that, if Squeaks is alive, he's not hiding in California or Florida or London; he's right here in South Ward where he can watch things. It's my belief, Jim, that he's been in the court room watching the trial."

Jim shook his head; but she went on. "This much I'm sure; he would hang around his former haunts, and we should leave nothing undone to find him."

They went first to Shay's attorney, but he dismissed the idea as chimerical, so they dropped him from their plans. Together they set to work, with little hope indeed, but it was at least better to be up and doing. Judge Squeaks's office was small, easily entered and productive of nothing. The police would give no information and seemed little interested in the new theory. Squeaks's lodgings yielded nothing new, but they found that Belle's theory was right; he had also had a room on the floor above. The woman in the gray cloak had called on him once or twice in the previous month and had come once since. She was a sort of janitress, as she had a key and straightened up his room. There was no hint of help in this. There was only one of his haunts that they had not thoroughly examined, that was the club. There was no need for that, as they knew every one that came and went, at least by sight.

Mrs. Hartigan was sitting in the club office at the back of the building next day when Skystein came in, and sat down to go over some club letters, officially addressed to him. As he read he made a note on each and sorted them into three neat piles. Belle watched him with interest that was a little tinged with shame. It is so human to consider a man inferior if he does not speak your language fluently, and the early impression they had gotten of Skystein gave them a sense of lofty pity. But it did not last. At every board meeting they had found reason to respect the judgment and worldly knowledge of the little Hebrew; those keen black eyes stood for more than cunning, they were the lights of intellect. Belle turned to him now. If any one knew the underworld of the South Ward it was he, and what he didn't know he had means to find out.

She openly, frankly, told him all she knew and suspected. He heard her at first doubtingly, then with growing interest, then with a glare of intense attention and conviction at last. His eyes twinkled knowingly as she expressed her opinion of the attorney. Skystein uttered the single word "fixed." Then he tapped his white teeth with his slender forefinger and rose to get the membership roll. He looked over it, but got no help; there was no one entered within the last few months that they could not fully account for.

They sat gazing in silence through the window into the adjoining reading room when an elderly woman came in and sat down. She wore a gray cloak and large goggles.

"Who is she?" said Belle. "I've seen her often enough, but I don't remember her name."

"Dat's Mrs. Davis: she's been coming only about five months. She was one of Squeaks's members."

A ray of hope shot into Belle's brain. "This fits the description of Squeaks's cleaning woman. She knows where he is hidden; she takes him food and keeps him posted. She is here now for the news." The woman at the desk raised her face; through the goggles and through that inner window she saw the two gazing at her. She rose quickly, but without hurry, and left the building. Skystein turned after her, without actually running, but she had disappeared.

"That woman knows where Squeaks is hiding," said Belle. But what became of her was a puzzle. They were confronted now by a stone wall, for there was no trace of her. The old janitor at Squeaks's lodging had not seen her for two weeks and she did not again appear at the club.

Michael Shay's religion so far as he had any, was of the Ulster type, and Jim Hartigan was accepted as his spiritual adviser and allowed to see him often. Jim and Belle agreed that it was well to tell him everything in their minds, to keep alive the light of hope, or maybe get from him some clue. Two weeks passed thus without a hint. Then, one evening as Skystein came late to the club, he saw a woman go out. He went to the desk and asked who it was. The register showed a strange name, but the clerk thought it was the gray woman till she looked at the name. Skystein rushed out as fast as possible, just in time to see a gray-cloaked figure board the car. There was no hack in sight so he leaped on the next car and followed. He was able to watch the car most of the time, but saw only one woman leave it. She was in black. At length, he got a chance to run forward and mount the first car. He stayed on the platform and peered in. There was no gray-cloaked woman. He asked the conductor, and learned that a woman had got on and taken off her cloak till she went out again three blocks back. At once his Hebrew wit seized these two ideas: she had deliberately turned her cloak; she was eluding pursuit.

Skystein went back at once to the street where the black-cloaked woman had descended. Of course, he saw nothing of her, but there was a peanut vender of his own race, at the corner. Skystein stopped, bought a bag of peanuts and began to eat them. Casually he asked the merchant if that woman in gray bought peanuts there. The vender didn't seem to comprehend, so Skystein addressed him in Yiddish; told him the woman was a detective, and promised to give ten dollars for information as to where she lived or what she was after. The expression on the peanut man's face showed an eagerness to find out the facts with all possible speed. But a week went by and he had nothing to report.

Meanwhile, Jim was at Joliet in daily conference with Shay, reporting to him the success or ill success of the search; reporting, alas, how little help they got from those who were supposed to forward the ends of justice. Money was not lacking, but it would help little; if an open campaign were conducted to find the man they believed to be in hiding, it might put an insuperable obstacle in the way. The governor was approached, but he was little disposed to listen or order a stay, least of all when they had nothing but a vague theory to offer.

Four days more went by, and Skystein found the peanut man in high excitement. He had seen the gray woman; she passed down his street and, before he could follow, turned into a side street; he left his peanuts and ran to follow, but got no second glimpse. She must have gone into one of the near-by tenements. "Didn't Mr. Skystein orter pay for de peanuts stole by de boys, as well as de reward."

Two days of life remained to Shay. Hope had died out of their hearts. Hartigan was preparing him for the great change that is always a bitter change when so approached. Belle still clung to hope. She posted herself where she could view the street, and made judicious inquiries, but got no help. The gray mantle was not a complete identification; the woman might have a dozen mantles. She went to the police station to enlist their cooperation. The Precinct Captain took no stock in the story and refused to order a house-to-house search. Finally—for even police are human—he promised to search any particular house when it was indicated, and to give reasonable support to any move that was obviously in the cause of justice.

The morning of the execution came and nothing had developed to revive their hopes. Belle was on watch at the street corner when on the main avenue an excitement occurred. A Savoyard with a dancing bear was holding a public show and gathering in a few coins. An idea came to her;

she made her way through the crowd and said: "Here, is a dollar, if you make him dance before every house on this street." The Savoyard smiled blandly, bowed, pocketed the dollar and, leading the bear into the side street that Belle had watched so long, began the droning song that caused the animal to rear up and sway his huge, heavy body round and round as he walked. All the world came forth to see, or peered from upper windows; all the world was watching the strange antics of the bear—all but one. Belle's keen brown eyes were watching the crowd, watching the doorways, and watching, at length, the windows with desperate eagerness for sign of the gray woman. There seemed to be no gray woman; but, of a sudden, she saw a thing that stopped her heart. Flat against the window of a second-floor room, and intently watching the bear, was the pale, wizened, evil face of Squeaks!

Belle's hand trembled as she noted the house, the number and the very room; then, passing quickly around the corner, she hailed a cab and drove for life to the telegraph office, where she telegraphed Jim:

"Hold up the execution for two hours; we have found Squeaks."

(Signed) "BELLE"

Then away to the police station. "Captain, Captain, I've found Squeaks! Come, come at once and get him."

"I have to know about it first," said he, calmly.

"Oh, Captain, there is no time to lose. It is ten o'clock now; the execution is fixed for noon."

The Captain shook his head.

"Then telegraph the Governor," she begged.

"He wouldn't pay any attention to your say-so."

"Then come at once and see; I have a cab here."

The Captain and two men went with Belle. They entered the cab. "I'll give you double fare to go your fastest," Belle said through her white, compressed lips; and the kindly cabman, sensing something out of common, 'Said, "I'll do my best, miss."

In ten minutes, they were in the side street. The bear was gone, the crowd was gone. The police entered without knocking, went to the second floor, to the very door and then knocked. There was no answer. The Captain put his shoulder to the door and forced it in. There, sure enough, standing in an attitude of fear in a far corner was the thin woman of the gray cloak.

"Where is Judge Squeaks? He was seen in this room half an hour ago."

"I don't know what you mean," and she covered her face with her skinny hands and began to cry.

"You must come to the station at once," said the Captain. Then to Belle: "Will you testify that this is the woman?"

Belle was white and trembling, but she walked up and said: "I will testify that this is—" She reached forward, peering at the woman's hidden face. Then seizing the loose hair, Belle gave one jerk, the wig came off, and they were facing Judge Squeaks!

"My God!" was all the Captain had to say. "The telephone as quick as possible! You hold him." He dashed down the stairs and made for the nearest long distance wire. It was half an hour before they could connect with Springfield, only to learn that the Governor had left for Chicago and was expected to arrive there about noon.

CHAPTER LVIII

In the Death House

Shay sat calmly waiting as the big clock ticked his life away that morning in the house of death at Joliet. At eleven o'clock, Hartigan received Belle's telegram: "We have found Squeaks." He rushed to the Sheriff with it. That officer was very sorry, but "no one except the Governor had any right to order a stay."

"Why, sir," said Jim, "you are not going to hang an innocent man, when here is proof of his innocence."

"There is no proof in that telegram. I don't know who "Belle" is. I get my orders from the Courts. No one but the Governor can order a reprieve."

Jim sent a telegram to Springfield only to learn, as Belle had done, that the Governor had left for Chicago. He sent telegrams to every one who had the power to help. He telegraphed Belle; he rushed to the Sheriff to beg for God's sake but one hour's reprieve. He hurried to the penitentiary to find another telegram from Belle:

Pray without ceasing for an hour's delay. We have Squeaks now.

But the clock ticked on. He literally ran to Michael's cell; the jailer opened the way. "Michael," he gasped, "we have found Squeaks; we know you are innocent."

Michael was the calmest of all. "Whatever is God's will I'll take without a grumble," he said, and sat smoking.

At a quarter to twelve the Sheriff appeared.

"Why, Sheriff, you are not going to—when you know the reprieve is on the way. You are not going to let a technicality lead you into murder?"

"I have no change in my instructions," said the Sheriff, "and no proof that any change is on the way."

"Why; this is monstrous," gasped Jim. "An hour's delay is all we ask, so the Governor can be reached."

The Sheriff motioned the guard to move on, and Shay walked firmly between the two officers. They came into the prison yard. There assembled were a score of officials and newspaper men.

"Have you any final statement to make?" asked the State officials.

"Nothing, only that I am innocent and Squeaks is alive at this moment."

That was an old story—an old trick to win time. The officers were preparing to act, when Hartigan pale and exultant, swinging the last telegram before the Sheriff, re-read it and for the first time truly got its meaning. He said: "Let us pray."

They kneeled down, all of them, in accordance with the ancient custom, and Jim began to pray. His voice was broken and husky, but it grew steadier as he appealed to the God of Justice and Mercy. He prayed and prayed; the clock struck twelve, but still he prayed. "Pray without ceasing," Belle's message had said. His gift of speech stood by him now; a quarter of an hour passed and still he was pouring out petitions to the throne of grace; another quarter of an hour and his voice was a little weary, but he prayed on. Still another, and another, and the clock struck one. All those men still kneeled, dead silent, except for a low, sobbing sound from the little group farther off. The Sheriff waited uneasily; he coughed a little and waited for a gap—but there was no gap; Jim bared his heart to God that day. He prayed as he never did before and all his bodily strength went into his prayer. At a quarter past one, when he was still calling on the God of Life for help, the Sheriff knew not what to do, for by the unwritten law the man of God had a right to finish his prayer. At half past one, the Sheriff moved uneasily and at length uttered a faint "Amen," as though to give the signal to stop. As it had no effect he realized for the first time just what Hartigan's desperation and iron will were leading him to do, he took cover under the technicality and played the game with him. Shay would have a chance as long as the Preacher's voice lasted. The party all stood, hats off, except those around the condemned one. They still kneeled, some of them, while others in bodily weariness, were frankly sitting on the scaffold. And the Preacher prayed on. His voice was thick and husky now; he could scarcely enunciate the words. The big clock ticked and two was struck. Still Jim prayed, as one who hopes and clings to any hope.

There were uneasy movements among the witnesses. The Sheriff said "Amen" twice again, quite loudly so that no one else should interrupt, but he was under a terrible strain. It was ten minutes after two when a shout was heard from the outer office and a warden with a paper came running, shrieking, "*Reprieve! Reprieve!*"

Jim turned to look and closed his prayer: "...and this we ask for Jesus's sake"; then he fell flat upon the scaffold.

"I knew she would, I knew she would; Belle never failed me yet," were the first words he uttered when he revived.

The Sheriff read the Governor's telegram to the crowd:

"Reprieve Michael Shay for three days."

As they led him back to the house of death, which was to him a house of resurrection, there was the whistle of a special train followed by the clatter of a carriage approaching the gate. Whoever it was had the right of entry. Hurried footsteps were heard, and short, low words. Then the doors swung wide for—the Governor himself, John Hopkins, and Belle. White fear was on their faces till they met a warder who knew.

"All right, sir; we got it in time."

"Thank God!"

"Yes, sir; two hours after the time fixed. But the minister was in the middle of his prayer and he didn't seem to finish till it came."

The party entered the death house, and at once were ushered into the room where Shay and Jim were sitting. Jim was weak and worn looking. The warden announced, "The Governor." Jim rose, and in a moment, Belle was in his arms. "I knew you would. I knew you would. I got your message. I prayed without ceasing. I would have been at it yet."

Mike Shay, calm until now, broke down. Tears ran from his small gray eyes, and clutching the soft hand of his deliverer, he murmured: "There ain't anything I got too good for the Hartigans. Ye—ye—ye—oh, God damn it! I can't talk about it!" and he sobbed convulsively.

The Governor shook his hand and said: "Michael Shay, I think the danger is over so far as you are concerned; all will be well now that Squeaks is found." Shay mumbled a "thank you." "Don't thank me," replied the man of power. "You may thank the loyal friends who found the trap and found the answer and found the Governor, when almost any other man or woman would have given up."

CHAPTER LIX

THE HEART HUNGER

When the flood rushes over the meadow and tears the surface smoothness, it exposes the unmoved rock foundation; when the fire burns down the flimsy woodwork, it shows in double force the unchanged girders of steel. Storm and fire in double power and heat had been Jim's lot for weeks and, in less degree, for months. Now there was a breathing spell, a time to stop and look at the things beneath.

It was a little thing that gave Belle the real key to a puzzle. It occurred one afternoon in the apartment and Belle saw it from the inner room. Jim thought he was alone; he did not know she had returned. He stood before the picture of Blazing Star, and lifting down the bunch of sage he smelt it a long time, then sighed a little and put it back. Belle saw and understood. The rock foundation was unchanged; he loved and longed for the things he had always loved, and the experiences of these months had but exposed the granite beneath. The thought that had been in her heart since the day he put the ring on her finger, rose up with appalling strength. "He gave up everything for me. I taught him that his duty lay through college and then made him give that up for me." She had been quick enough to mark the little turnings of his spirit toward the West when there were times of relaxation or unguardedness. But she had hitherto set them down to a general wish to visit former scenes rather than to a deep, persistent, fundamental craving.

Many little things which she had noted in him came up before her now, not as accidental fragments, but as surface outcroppings of the deep, continuous, everlasting granite rock, the real longing of his nature; and the strength of its fixity appalled her. As she watched from the outer room on that epochal afternoon, she saw him kneel with his face to the western sky and pray that the way might be opened, that he yet might fulfil the vow he made to devote his life to bearing the message of the Gospel. "Nevertheless, not my will, but Thine be done."

He sat long facing the glowing West which filled his window and then rose and walked into the inner room. He was greatly astonished to find Belle there, lying on the bed, apparently asleep. He sat down beside her and took her hand. She opened her eyes slowly as though awakening—gentle hypocrite.

"I didn't know you were back," he said. She closed her eyes again as though they were heavy with sleep. It was a small fraud, but it set his mind at ease, as she meant it should.

After a time, she roused herself and began with enthusiasm: "Oh, Jim, I have had such a clear and lovely dream. I thought we were back at Cedar Mountain, riding again in the sagebrush, with the prairie wind blowing through our very souls."

She watched his face eagerly and saw the response she expected. It came in larger measure than she had looked for. "I felt as though I could do anything," she went on, "go anywhere or take any jump; and just as I was riding full tilt at the Yellowbank Canyon, you took me by the hand and held me back; then I awoke and you *did* have my hand. Isn't it queer the way dreams melt into reality?" She laughed happily and went on as if he were opposing the project: "Why not, Jim? You need a holiday; why shouldn't we go and drink a long deep draught of life in the hills and sage? I know we'll get a clearer vision of life from the top of Cedar Mountain than we can anywhere else."

"It seems too good to be true," he slowly answered, and his voice trembled. Less than half an hour ago he had prayed for this and suddenly the way seemed plain, if not yet open.

The winter and spring had gone, and the summer was dying. In all this time the Hartigans had carried their daily, hourly burden, without halt or change. Whatever of hardship there was, came in the form of thwarted plans, heart-cravings for things they felt they must give up. Jim made no mention of his disappointments and, so far as he could, he admitted his hunger neither to himself nor to Belle. It was merely a matter of form, applying for a month's leave; this had been agreed on from the beginning. The largest difficulty was in the fact that they must go together—the head and the second head both away at once. But there were two good understudies ready trained—Skystein and Dr. Mary Mudd—with Mr. Hopkins as chairman to balance their powers. Michael Shay too, came to offer gruffly and huskily his help: "If I can do anything, like puttin' up cash, or fixin' anybody that's workin' agin you, count on Mike." Then after a pause he added, a little wistfully: "I ain't got many real friends, but I want to have them know I'm real, and I know the real thing when I find it."

A conference was finally held and the management of the Club was turned over to the chairman and his aides for a month. Jim and Belle were like children on leave from boarding school. They packed in wild hilarity and took the first train the schedule afforded for Cedar Mountain.

CHAPTER LX

THE GATEWAY AND THE MOUNTAIN

August with its deadening heat was over; September, bright, sunny and tonic, was come to revive the world. Rank foliage was shaking off the summer dust, and a myriad noisy insects were strumming, chirping, fiddling, buzzing, screeping in the dense undergrowth. It was evening when they boarded the train for the West and took the trail that both had taken before, but never with such a background of events or such an eagerness for what was in the future. As the train roared through the fertile fields of Illinois, with their cornfields, their blackbirds and their myriads of cattle, red and white, the sun went down—a red beacon blaze, a bonfire welcome on their pathway just before the engine—a promise and a symbol.

It was near noon the next day when they reached the junction and took, the branch line for the north. The first prairie-dog town had set Jim ablaze with schoolboy eagerness; and when a coyote stood and gazed at the train, he rushed out on to the platform to give him the hunter's yell.

"My, how sleek he looked! I wonder how those prairie dogs feel as they see him stalk around their town, like a policeman among the South Chicago kids!"

When a flock of prairie chickens flew before the train he called, "Look, look, Belle! See how they sail, just as they used to do!" As though the familiar sights of ten months before were forty years in the past.

They were in the hills now, and the winding train went more slowly. Animal life was scarcer here, but the pine trees and the sombre peaks were all about. At five o'clock the train swung down the gorge with Cedar Mountain before it, and Jim cried in joy: "There's our mountain; there's our mountain!"

There was a crowd assembled at the station and as soon as Jim appeared a familiar voice shouted, "Here he is!" and, led by Shives, they gave a hearty cheer. All the world of Cedar Mountain seemed there. Pa Boyd and Ma Boyd came first to claim their own. Dr. Jebb and Dr. Carson forgot their religious differences in the good fellowship of the time, and when the inner circle had kissed Belle and manhandled Jim to the limit of custom, a quiet voice said: "Welcome back, Mr. Hartigan," and Charlie Bylow grasped the Preacher's hand. "I brought my team so I could take care of your trunks." There was only one small trunk, but he took the check and would have resented any other man having hand or say in the matter.

That evening the meal was a "welcome home," for a dozen of the nearer friends were there to hear the chapters of their hero's life. Jim was in fine feather and he told of their Chicago life as none other could have done, with jest and sly digs at himself and happy tributes to the one who had held his hand when comradeship meant the most.

A month of freedom, with youth, sounds like years. Many plans were offered to fill the time. An invitation came from Colonel and Mrs. Waller to spend three days at Fort Ryan. In a delicately worded postscript was the sentence: "Blazing Star is well and will be glad to feel your weight again."

"Blazing Star and Cedar Mountain!" shouted Jim as Belle read the letter the next morning at breakfast. And then, much to Pa Boyd's amusement he broke out in his lusty baritone:

"'Tis my ain countree,'Tis my ain countree!'The fairest brightest landThat the sun did ever see."

Midnight and the horse that had been Belle's were waiting in the stable.

"Now, where shall we go? Up Cedar Mountain, to Fort Ryan, or where?" asked Belle as they saddled their mounts. His answer was not what she expected. Cedar Mountain had ever been in his thought. "If only I could stand on Cedar Mountain!" had been his words so many times. And now, with Cedar Mountain close at hand, in sight, he said: "Let's ride nowhere in particular—just through the sage."

They set off and veered away from Fort Ryan and any other place where men might cross their path. The prairie larks sang about them their lovely autumn song—the short, sweet call that sounds like: "*Hear me, hear me! I am the herald announcing the King.*" Fluttering in the air and floating for a moment above the riders they carolled a wild and glorious serenade that has no possible rendition into human notation. After a hard gallop they rode in silence side by side, hand in hand, while Jim gazed across the plain or watched the fat, fumbling prairie dogs. But ever he turned his face and heart away from Cedar Mountain.

At first it had been to him but a mighty pile of rocks; then it had grown to be a spot beloved for its sacred memories. It had become a symbol of his highest hopes—the blessed things he held too good for words. He was riding now in the lust of youthful force; he was dwelling not in the past; or the hopeful far-ahead; he was in the living *now*, and, high or low, his instinct bade him drink the cup that came.

As the sun went down, he drew rein and paused with Belle to gaze at the golden fringe that the cedars made on the mountain's edge in the glow. He knew it and loved it in every light—best of all, perhaps, in its morning mist, when the plains were yet gray and the rosy dawn was touching its gleaming sides. He was content as yet to look on it from afar. He would seek its pinnacle as he had done before, but something within him said: "No; not yet."

And the wise young person at his side kept silence; a little puzzled but content, and waiting, wisely waiting.

CHAPTER LXI

CLEAR VISION ON THE MOUNTAIN

Kind friends and hearty greetings awaited the Hartigans at the Fort. Colonel Waller, Mrs. Waller, and the staff received them as long-lost son and daughter; and with the least delay by decency allowed they went to the stable to see Blazing Star, still Fort Ryan's pride. The whinnied welcome and the soft-lipped fumbling after sugar were the outward tokens of his gladness at the meeting.

"He's the same as ever, Jim," said the Colonel, "but we didn't race last summer. Red Cloud came as usual, but asked for a handicap of six hundred yards, which meant that they had not got a speeder they could trust. We had trouble, too, with the Indian Bureau over the whole thing, so the affair was called off. As far as we know now, Blazing Star is the racer of the Plains, with Red Rover making a good second. He's in his prime yet; he could still walk a stringer on a black night, and while you are here at the Fort he's yours as much as you want to use him."

Jim's cup was filled to overflowing.

Their midday meal over, a ride was in order; first around the Fort among the men—Captain Wayne, Osier Mike, Scout Al Rennie—then out over the sagebrush flat. "Here's the old battle ground of the horses; here's where you chased the coyote, and here's where Blazing Star took you over the single stringer bridge on that black night." It was less than a year he had been away, and yet Jim felt like one who was coming back to the scenes of his boyhood, long gone by. His real boyhood in far-away Links was of another world. Fightin' Bill Kenna, Whiskey Mason, the Rev. Obadiah Champ, the stable and the sawmills, his mother—they were dreams; even Chicago was less real than this; and he rode like a schoolboy and yelled whenever a jack rabbit jumped ahead of his horse and jerked its white tail in quick zigzags, exactly as its kind had done in the days when he lived in the saddle.

After dinner, by the log fire in the Colonel's dining room, Mrs. Waller raised the question of their plans. "Now, children" (she loved to be maternal), "what do you want to do to-morrow?"

There was a time when Belle would have spoken first, but there had been a subtle, yet very real, change in their relationship. Jim was a child three years before, dependent almost entirely on her; now she was less his leader than she had been. She waited.

Gazing at the fire, his long legs straight out and crossed at the ankles, his hands clasped behind his head, he lounged luxuriously in a great arm chair. Without turning his gaze from the burning logs he began:

"If I could do exactly what I wished——"

"Which you may," interjected Mrs. Waller.

"I'd saddle Blazing Star and Red Rover at seven o'clock in the morning and ride with Belle and not come back till noon."

"Ha, ha!" laughed Mrs. Waller and the Colonel. "You children! You two little, little ones! Well, we must remember that Belle is still a bride and will be for another month, so we'll bid you Godspeed on the new wedding trip and have your breakfast ready at half past six."

Early hours are the rule in a fort at the front, so the young folk were not alone at breakfast. And when they rode away on their two splendid horses, many eyes followed with delight the noble beauty of the pair—so fitly mounted, so gladly young and strong.

"Now, where, Jim?" said Belle, as they left the gate and thundered over the bridge at a mettlesome lope. And as she asked, she remembered that that was the very question he used always to put to her.

"Belle" (he reined in Blazing Star), "I have been waiting till it seemed just right—waiting for the very time, so we could stand again at our shrine. Sometimes I think I know my way and the trail I ought to seek, and sometimes I am filled with doubt; but I know I shall have the clear vision if we stand again as we used to stand, above our world, beside the Spirit Rock, on the high peak of our mountain."

And then, in the soft sign language of the rein let loose, the ribs knee-nudged, they bade their horses go. Side by side they rode and swung like newly mated honkers in the spring—like two centaurs, feeling in themselves the power, the blood rush of their every bound. In less than half an hour they passed the little town and were at the foot of Cedar Mountain. The horses would have gone up at speed, but the riders held them in, and the winding trail was slowly followed up.

The mountain jays flew round the pines before them as they climbed; an eagle swung in circles, watching keenly; while, close at hand, the squirrels dropped their cones to spring behind the trunks and chatter challenge.

At the half-way ledge they halted for a breathing. Belle looked keenly, gently into Jim's eyes. She was not sure what she saw. She wondered what his thoughts were. The brightness of the morning, the joy of riding and being, the fullness of freedom—these were in glowing reflex on his face, but she had seen these before; yet never before had she seen his face so tense and radiant. Only once, perhaps, that time when he came home walking in the storm.

He smiled back at her, but said nothing. They rode again and in ten minutes came to the end of the horse trail. He leaped from the saddle, lifted her down, and tied the horses. With his strong hand under her arm, he made it easy for her to climb the last steep path. A hundred feet above, they reached the top, above the final trees, above the nearer peaks, above all other things about them except the tall, gray Spirit Rock. Below spread a great golden world; behind them a world of green. The little wooden town seemed at the mountain's foot—Fort Ryan almost in shouting hail, though it was six miles off; beyond, was the open sea of sage, with heaving hills for billows and greasewood streaks for foam.

Jim gazed in utter silence so long that she looked a little shyly at him. His face was radiant, his eye was glistening, but he spoke no words. The seat they had used a year before was there and he gently drew her toward it. Seated there as of old, he put his arm about her and held her to him. She whispered, "Make a fire." She had indeed interpreted his thought. He rose, lighted a little fire on the altar at the foot of the Spirit Rock, and the smoke rose up straight in the still air. It ascended from the earth mystery of the fire to be lost in the mystery of the above. How truly has it been the symbol of prayer since first man kindled fire and prayed.

Jim took his Bible from his pocket and read from the metrical Psalm CXXI:

I to the hills will lift mine eyes,From whence doth come mine aid;My safety cometh from the LordWho heaven and earth hath made.

"They always went up into the hills to pray, Belle, didn't they? The fathers of the faith never went down into the valley when they sought God's guidance. I don't know why, but I know that I don't feel the same, away down there on the plains as I do up here. I see things more clearly, I have more belief in Him and know He is near me.

"The clouds have been gathering in my mind pretty thick and dark; yes, darker the last half year, Belle. I began to doubt myself as I never did. Even when we were winning in our Chicago fight, I wondered whether I was doing right. I couldn't see clearly, Belle, and then my doubt grew stronger and even you could not understand; there was something within that told me to go back to Cedar Mountain. Ever since we got here I have been waiting for the moment when I could come to the mountain. From here, a mile above the sea, I know that I shall see the way of wisdom. I wonder if you know what that Rock means to me with that little thread of smoke going up?

"Belle, men called Bill Kenna a ruffian and a brute. I guess he was, too, but he had a brave, warm heart. His whole religion was to feed the hungry and honour his word as a man. That was about all he taught me; and he loved my mother—that's enough; it bit in deep. When I gave my word as a man on that wild night four years ago when I heard the call, I vowed that I would, from that time on, devote my strength to telling others what I had found and try to make them find it, too. That was my vow, Belle; I've tried to keep it. I gave up things out here because they seemed to come between. I may be doing right in the city slum work, but it is not what I set out to do; I am not keeping to the trail."

Poor Belle! The periods of vague unrest she had noted; that time of fervent prayer; the reasons she had urged upon him for returning to college, and the crisis in which she had forced him to give it up—all now came back to her in quick succession. She remembered the weakness that had so nearly ended all and how he had overmastered it—that craving for drink, so strong from inheritance and from the evil habits of his earliest manhood. Amid daily temptations of the Chicago life, it had not seemed to touch him even as temptation. The horses that he loved he had given up for principle. The surface plasticity he still showed was merely the velvet that concealed the rod of steel and why he seemed so weak she knew now, was that he was so young, so very immature, a man in stature, a little happy child at heart. And the sting of sudden iron hurt her soul.

To say that she was shamed by remorse would not be fair; but the sum of her feelings was that he had given up all for her; she owed him something to atone.

There is clear vision from the hilltop—the far-sight is in the high place. The prophets have ever gone up into the high places for their message. The uplift of Cedar Mountain was on his spirit and on hers. She spoke softly, gravely, and slowly: "Jim, God surely brought me into your life for a purpose and, if I am no help, then I have failed. As surely as He sent us to Chicago to fight that fight and overcome the things about as well as the things inside, He also sent us here to-day to show our inmost souls, to get light on ourselves, to learn the way we must go. I have learned, for my spirit's eyes are clearer now and here than they ever were in my life before, and some things have come to me so vividly that I take them as commands from Him who set this rock up here and brought us in this frame of mind to see it. Jim, you must go back to college; you must finish your course; you must carry out your vow and consecrate yourself to spreading the gospel of His love."

Jim stared with glowing eyes as Belle went on: "I've thought it all out, Jim. I know it is mine to open the way now, as once I closed it."

He clutched her in his arms and shook with a sudden storm of long pent-up feeling, now bursting all restraint. He had no words; he framed no speech; he was overwhelmed.

Why put it into words? They understood each other now. He had gone to the city because that seemed the open way. He had taken up the purely secular work of the club while his inmost soul cried out: "This is not what you vowed; this is not the way to which you consecrated all your life." It was for her sake he had turned aside, and now that she announced the way of return, they came together as they never had; now was she truly his in spirit as in law.

It was long before they spoke, and their words now were of other things. The noon train was sounding at the bend; from the ledge below them Blazing Star sent up a querulous whinny. Jim was calm again and Belle was gently smiling, though her eyes still brimmed.

"We shall be late for the noon meal," he said, rising. For a moment they stood before the Spirit Rock, and he said in words of the old, old Book:

"He carried me away in the spirit to a great and high mountain.""It is good for us to be here.""I will lift up mine eyes unto the hills, from whence cometh my help."

They walked hand in hand and silently down the crooked trail to the horses. He lifted her to the saddle and kissed her hand only; but their eyes met in a burning look and their souls met face to face. Then they turned and rode the downward trail, and on the level plain gave free rein to the horses so that they went like hounds unleashed and skimmed the plain and leaped the gulch nor stayed till they reached the Fort and the friendly door where the soldier grooms were waiting.

They rode again the next day, circling the plain where the Indian race had been run and pointing out familiar objects. Jim led the way to the cottonwoods near where Higginbotham's "Insurance Office" had stood.

He stopped at the very spot and said: "Little girl, do you know what happened here about a year ago?"

"What?" she answered, as though in doubt.

"Guess."

"I can't," she replied. She would not say it. If he wanted it said, he must say it himself.

"It was here that I met 'Two Strikes.' Oh, what a blind fool I have been! If God had only given me a little less body and a little more brain! But it's all right. He knows best. He gave me you and I am thankful for that."

"We understand each other better now, Jim, don't we? I know you were only a child when I first saw you. You are a boy yet, but you will soon be a man. Listen, Jim; I have not ceased to think it over since we stood by the Spirit Rock. Do you remember what I said—you must go back to college? I must open the way. And I will, Jim; I have it all planned out. You must go back, not to Coulter, there are better colleges. They do not all bar married men. There is one in Chicago; Chicago is our gateway still. The Western Theological College is there. They will accept your year at Coulter for entrance and one year's work. I think I can get Mr. Hopkins to let me keep on with the Mountain House. My salary and what we have saved will make us comfortable. I can help in all your studies. In two years you will be through; then the Methodist Church, or any other, will be glad to have you and the way will be open wide. I will not fail you. You shall not fail to keep your word. And when we know, as we cannot know now, you will see that God was guiding me. Maybe He took you from Coulter because you were too young; surely He planned for us and has led us at every turn in the trail. It seems crooked now, but every rider in the hills knows that the crooks in the trail up Cedar Mountain were made to elude some precipice or to win some height not otherwise attainable; no other trail could end at the Spirit Rock, the highest point, the calm and blessed outlook, the top of Cedar Mountain."

"Now, Belle, I understand. My heart told me to wait, then to go up the mountain and find the thing I needed. I knew you would not fail; I knew my mountain meant vision for you and me."

CHAPTER LXII

WHEN HE WALKED WITH THE KING

He must have been a huge, unwieldy egotistical brute who said, "Big men have ever big frames." He might have had Samuel Johnson, Walter Scott, Lincoln or Washington in mind; but, standing ready there to hurl the glib lie in his teeth, were Napoleon, Hamilton, St. Paul, Tamerlane, and the Rev. Dr. Jo. Belloc, President of the Western Theological College in Chicago. He was five feet high in his stockinged feet, thin and wiry, with a large gray head, a short gray beard and keen gray eyes of piercing intensity. When you saw him on the street, you hardly saw him at all; when you met him in a crowded room, you felt that the spirit behind those eyes was a strong one; and when you heard him speak, he grew tall and taller in your eyes—you instinctively removed your hat, for now you knew that a great man and teacher was here.

Why should such a one devote his power to mere denominationalism? Ah, you do not understand. He answered thus to a hostile critic: "My friend, the harvest is huge, the labourers are few; we need more, and many more than we have. If they be of simple sort and not too strong, we teach them the sweep and cut of the scythe, the width of the swathe, the height of the stubble, the knot of the sheaf-band, all that is safe, neither to waste the crop, nor their time, nor cut their fellow harvesters in the legs. But, if we find a giant with his own mode, who cuts a double swath, leaves ragged stubble, smashes oft his scythe, but saves a wondrous lot of grain, we say: 'Praise God! You're doing well; the rules are for the helpless as the fence is for the sheep; but you we judge by your results; keep on.'"

Dr. Belloc was in his office when there came for an interview a man who towered above him as they shook hands. The president motioned him to a seat; then as he turned those piercing eyes on the comely countenance of his caller, the prophet's description of the youthful David came to his mind, "Now, he was ruddy and withal of a beautiful countenance and goodly to look to."

"What can I do for you?" asked the big little man who filled the room, but did not fill the chair.

Jim modestly stated that he believed he had a call to preach the Gospel and he wished to enter college. Then, in answer to questions, he told his story with simple sincerity and fervour. The keen gray eyes were glowing like coals, and although no word was spoken by the man whose soul looked through them, Jim felt his earnest, kindly spirit. He felt, as never before, that "here is one who understands. Here is one in whom I have absolute confidence. Here is one whom I should love to obey."

This leader stirred Jim to the depths. His best, his inmost soul came forth to speak in response to the master mind; and the older man smiled when he heard how the Preacher had hated the books at Coulter. "Coulter," he said, "is a good old college, we accept their entrance; but it is quite likely that our curriculum may more quickly win your interest than theirs did."

As the president pondered the question that had brought them together, the second part of the lines of Samuel's description of David rose in his mind: "Arise and anoint him, for this is he." But the college had its own way of saying these big things; documents, questions, boards, had each a bearing on the matter, or a drop of ink to spend, and each offered a delay to the decisive action that the President had then and there resolved on. But they slowly ran their course and in the early autumn Jim was back, a college boy, and Belle had taken up the ruler's post at the Club.

It was easier every month for Jim to fight the battle with the books, where before he had been badly beaten. No doubt he was helped by his determination to win the fight and by Belle; but the two great reasons were that he, himself, was more developed—had outgrown the childish restlessness of the first attempt; and last but strongest of all, was the compelling personality of the president. With what consummate tact had he first offered to Jim's wild spirit the concrete, the simple, the history of to-day, the things that clearly were of immediate use; and later—much later, and in lesser degree—the abstruse, the doctrinal. And when the younger mind of the student came to a place that seemed too hard, or met a teacher who was deadening in his dullness, it needed but a little heart-to-heart talk with the strong soul in the robe to brace him up, to spur him on.

The president soon discovered Jim's love for heroic verse and at once, by wise selection, made it possible to tie that up with books. When Jim betrayed his impatience of fine-split doctrines, the president bade him forget them and read the lives of Luther, Calvin, and Wesley—take in the facts; the principles, so far as they had value, would take care of themselves. Such methods were unknown to his former teachers. Such presentation— vivid, concrete, human—was what he could understand, and accept with joy.

Two years went by. The first six months seemed slow; The last eighteen all too rapid. Jim had won his fight, he had more than won, for he was valedictorian of his class. The graduation class was much like any other, as the world could see it, yet it differed, too. When the tall form of the student speaker was left standing alone on the platform, there were not lacking those who said: "Never before has one gone from these halls so laden with good gifts; all, all seems showered on him."

In the audience, bound by closer ties than kinship, was one whose heart was too full for any human utterance. For her it was the crowning of their lives; had she not helped to make it possible?

After the set programme was over, Dr. Belloc handed to Jim an official letter. It was a call to be the pastor of the church in Cedar Mountain. Jim could not see the typed words for his tears and the president took it from him to read aloud. As he listened to the words Jim's thought turned to his mother, and in his heart he prayed: "O, God, grant this: that she may see me now."

Reader of this tale, do you recall the history of Cedar Mountain—how the church grew strong in the newly given strength? Those of many diverse churches came, for they said: "We care not what the vessel's shape that draws the blessed water from the well, so long as it be always there and the water pure and plentiful." Then came the great gold strike in the near hills; and the Preacher was troubled till he learned that it had not touched his mountain. Another railway came, and the town grew big and bigger yet. There were those that feared that their Preacher might leave them, for the needs and calls of the great cities are ever loud and forceful. They said: "Our town is not big enough for such a man; he will surely go to the city." But it was not so; for the city came to the man and mightily grew about him.

Two years after the return to Cedar Mountain, late in the day, designedly late, two horses might have been seen ascending the crooked trail through the cedars that mantled the mountain. Familiar forms were these that rode. They had often taken this path before. The first was the Preacher; the second, the woman that had held his hand. But in her arms was another— the baby form of their first-born. This was their first long ride together since he came, this was the elected trail; and, as the big, red sun went down in the purple and gold of his curtains, Jim took the baby and led the way up the last rough trail, to the little upland, right to the Spirit Rock. The red symbols of the Indians had been recently renewed; in a crevice was a shred of tobacco wrapped in red-dyed grass. It was still a holy place, accounted so by those who knew it.

From the bundle that he carried on his back, Jim took a handful of firewood, a canteen of water, and a church baptismal bowl. He filled the bowl and set it on the lowest ledge of the Spirit Rock. Before the rock he lighted a little fire and, when it blazed, he dropped into the flames the tobacco from the crevice. "That is what they wished done with it," he said in reverence. When the thread of smoke went up nearly straight into the sky—an emblem of true prayer that has ever been—he kneeled, and Belle beside him with the little one kneeled, and he prayed to the God of the Mountain for continued help and guidance and returned thanks for the little one whom they had brought that day to consecrate to Him.

Jim wished it. Belle willed it. His mother, he knew, would have had it so. There seemed no better place than this, the holiest place his heart had ever known. There was no better time than this, the evening calm, with all the symbols of His Presence in their glory.

Belle handed the infant to Jim, who sprinkled water on its face, baptizing it in the form of the Church, and then added: "I consecrate thee to God's service, and I name thee William in memory of the friend of my childhood, a man of wayward life, but one who helped to build whatever there is in me of strength, for he never was afraid, and he ever held his simple word as a bond that might not be broken."

THE END